'To your knowledge, is there anything that would preclude you from serving on this jury?'

Murder wasn't the hard part.
It was just the start of the game.

Joshua Kane has been preparing for this moment his whole life. He's done it before. But this is the big one.

This is the murder trial of the century.

And Kane has killed to get the best seat in the house.

But there's someone on his tail. Someone who suspects that the killer isn't the man on trial.

Kane knows time is running out —
but will he get to the conviction without being discovered?

Steve Cavanagh was born and raised in Belfast before leaving for Dublin at the age of eighteen to study Law. He currently practices civil rights law and has been involved in several high profile cases; in 2010 he represented a factory worker who suffered racial abuse in the workplace and won the largest award of damages for race discrimination in Northern Ireland legal history. He holds a certificate in Advanced Advocacy and lectures on various legal subjects (but really he just likes to tell jokes). He is married with two young children.

To find out more, visit Steve's website or follow him on Twitter.

www.stevecavanaghbooks.com
🐦 @SSCav

Also by Steve Cavanagh

The Defence
The Cross (*novella*)
The Plea
The Liar

To Pamela

TH1RT3EN

Steve Cavanagh

ORION

To Pamela

First published in Great Britain in 2018 by Orion books,
an imprint of The Orion Publishing Group Ltd
Carmelite House, 50 Victoria Embankment
London EC4Y 0DZ

An Hachette UK Company

14

A CIP catalogue record for this book is
available from the British Library.

ISBN 978 1 4091 7067 9

Typeset by Born Group

Printed and bound in Great Britain by CPI Group (UK) Ltd, Croydon CR0 4YY

MIX
Paper from
responsible sources
FSC® C104740

www.orionbooks.co.uk

For Noah

The following quotation originally comes from Baudelaire, but the quotation has been stolen many times since. With thanks to Chris McQuarrie for permitting me to steal his version.

"The greatest trick the devil ever pulled was convincing the world he didn't exist."

from the motion picture screenplay *The Usual Suspects*, script by Christopher McQuarrie.

PROLOGUE

At ten after five on a raw December afternoon, Joshua Kane lay on a cardboard bed outside the Criminal Courts Building in Manhattan and thought about killing a man. Not just *any* man. He was thinking about someone in particular. It was true that Kane had, at times, while on the subway or watching passers-by, occasionally thought about killing a nameless, random New Yorker who happened to fall into his line of vision. It could be the blond secretary reading a romance novel on the K train, a Wall Street banker swinging an umbrella as they ignored his pleas for change or even a child holding their mother's hand on a cross-walk.

How would it *feel* to kill them? What would they say with their final breath? Would their eyes change in that moment of passing from this world? Kane felt a ripple of pleasure feed heat into his body as he explored those thoughts.

He checked his watch.

Eleven after five.

The sharp, towering shadows flooded the street as the day melted into twilight. He looked at the sky and welcomed that dimming of the light, as though someone had placed a veil over a lamp. The half-light suited his purpose. The darkening sky returned his thoughts to the kill.

While he'd lain in the street, for the past six weeks, he'd thought of little else. For hours on end he silently debated whether this man should die. Apart from this man's life or death, everything else had been carefully planned.

Kane took little risk. That was the smart way. If you are to remain undetected, you must be cautious. He had learned this long ago. To leave the man alive carried risks. What if their paths crossed sometime in the future? Would he recognize Kane? Would he be able to put it all together?

And what if Kane killed him? There are always a multitude of risks in such a task.

But these were risks that Kane knew: risks that he had successfully avoided many times before.

A mail van pulled up at the curb and parked opposite Kane. The driver, a heavy-set man in his late forties wearing a post-office uniform, got out of it. Regular as clockwork. As the mailman walked past him, and went inside the service entrance to the court building, he ignored Kane lying on the street. No loose change for the homeless. Not today. Not for the past six weeks either. Not ever. And, regular as clockwork, as the mailman walked past him, Kane wondered if he should kill him.

He had twelve minutes to decide.

The mailman's name was Elton. He was married with two teenage kids. Elton ate from an overpriced artisan deli once a week when his wife thought he was out running, he read paperback novels that he picked up for a buck apiece from a little store in Tribeca and wore furry slippers when he took out the trash on Thursdays. What would it *feel* like to watch him die?

Joshua Kane enjoyed watching other people go through different emotions. To him, sensations of loss, grief, and fear were as intoxicating and as joyous as the best drugs on the planet.

Joshua Kane was not like other people. There was no one like him.

He checked his watch. Five twenty.

Time to move.

He scratched at his beard, which was almost full now. Wondering if the dirt and sweat added to its coloring, he slowly got up from the cardboard and stretched his back. Moving brought his own scent to his nose. No change of pants or socks for six weeks, no shower either. The odor made him gag.

Something to take his mind from his own filth was required. At his feet, a moldy upturned ball cap held a couple of bucks in change.

There was satisfaction in seeing a mission through to its conclusion. To see your vision fulfilled exactly as you'd imagined it. And yet, Kane thought it would be exciting to introduce the element of chance. Elton would never know that his fate would be decided in that moment, not by Kane, but by the toss of a coin. Selecting a quarter, Kane flicked the coin, called it in the air, caught it, and laid it flat on the back of his hand. While the coin had spun in the cold mist of his breath, he'd decided that heads meant Elton would die.

He looked at the quarter, shiny and new against the dirt ingrained on his skin, and smiled.

Ten feet from the parked mail van sat a hot dog stand. The vendor served a tall man with no coat. Probably just got out on bail and was celebrating with some real food. The vendor took the man's two dollars and pointed him toward the sign on the bottom of the stand. Beside the pictures of grilled kielbasa sausage was an ad for an attorney and a phone number below it.

HAVE YOU BEEN ARRESTED?
CHARGED WITH A CRIME?
CALL EDDIE FLYNN.

The tall man bit into his dog, nodded and walked away just as Elton came out of the court building hauling three sacks of mail in gray hessian bags.

Three bags. That confirmed it.

Today was the day.

Normally, Elton emerged with two bags or even a single bag of mail. But every six weeks Elton came out with three bags. That extra mailbag was what Kane had been waiting for.

Elton unlocked the rear panel doors on the mail van and tossed the first bag into the back. Kane approached slowly, his right hand outstretched.

The second bag followed the first into the van.

As he took hold of the third bag, Kane rushed toward Elton.

"Hey buddy, you got some spare change?"

"No," said Elton, and hurled the last bag into the van. He closed the right side of the van doors, then took hold of the left-hand door and slammed it shut like a man who didn't own it. Timing was key. Kane stretched out his hand, fast, begging for a

3

few dollars to be placed into his palm. The path of the van door took Kane's hand and the momentum slammed the door shut on Kane's arm.

Kane had timed it well. He listened to the sound of metal hinges as they scissored against flesh, crushing the limb. Grabbing that arm, Kane let out a cry and fell to his knees, watching Elton put both hands on top of his head, his eyes large and mouth distended in shock. Given the speed at which Elton slammed the door, and the sheer weight of the thing, there was little doubt that Kane's arm should've been broken. And a messy break at that. Multiple fractures. Massive trauma.

But Kane was special. That's what his mamma always told him. He cried out again. Kane felt it was important to put on a good show: the least he could do was pretend to be hurt.

"Jesus, watch your hands. I didn't know your arm was there . . . You . . . I'm sorry," said Elton, spluttering.

He knelt beside Kane, and apologized again.

"I think it's broken," said Kane, knowing that it wasn't. Ten years ago, most of the bone had been replaced with steel plates, bars and screws. What little bone that remained was now heavily reinforced.

"Shit, shit, shit . . ." said Elton, looking around the street, not knowing exactly what to do.

"It wasn't my fault," said Elton, "but I can call a paramedic."

"No. They won't treat me. They'll take me to the ER and I'll be left on a gurney all night then sent away. I don't have insurance. There's a med center. Ten blocks away at most. They treat homeless. Take me there," said Kane.

"I can't take you," said Elton.

"What?" said Kane.

"I'm not allowed to take passengers in the van. If somebody sees you up front I could lose my job."

Kane breathed a sigh of relief at Elton's efforts to stick to the Postal Service worker's rules. He had counted on it.

"Put me in the back. That way no one can see me," said Kane.

Elton stared at the rear of the van, and the open side door.

"I don't know . . ."

"I'm not going to steal nothin', I can't move my arm for crying out loud," said Kane, and followed it with a moan as he nursed his arm.

After a moments' hesitation, Elton said, "Okay. But don't go near the mailsacks. Deal?"

"Deal," said Kane.

He groaned as Elton lifted him off the road, and cried out when he thought Elton's hands got too close to his injured arm, but a short while later, Kane sat on the steel floor in the rear of the mail van and made all the right noises to accompany the rocking of the suspension as the van drove east. The rear of the van was separate from the cab, so Elton couldn't see him, and probably couldn't hear him, but Kane figured he may as well make the noise just in case. The only light came from a two-by-two bubbled glass hatch in the roof.

They had barely cleared the vicinity of the courthouse when Kane produced a box cutter from his coat and cut the ties at the top of the three mailbags from the courthouse.

First bag was a bust. Regular envelopes. Second bag too.

The third bag was the charm.

The envelopes in this bag were different, and identical. Each envelope bore a printed red band on the bottom with white lettering that read, "OPEN THIS CORRESPONDENCE NOW. IMPORTANT COURT SUMMONS INSIDE."

Kane didn't open any of these. Instead, he spread each envelope out on the floor. As he did so, he filtered out those addressed to women, and placed them back inside the bag. Half a minute later he had sixty, maybe seventy envelopes spread out in front of him. He took pictures of five envelopes at a time, using a digital camera which he then tucked back into his clothing. He could blow up the images later to focus on the names and addresses written on each one.

His task complete, Kane returned all the letters to the bag, and retied them all with fresh ziplock tags that he'd brought with him. The tags weren't that hard to come by, and they were the same brand used by the court office and the post office.

With time to spare, Kane spread his legs out on the floor and looked at the photos of the envelopes on his camera screen.

Somewhere in there he would find the perfect person. He knew it. He could *feel* it. The excitement sent his heart fluttering. It was like an electric current that rose from his feet and plowed straight through his chest.

After the constant stop and start of Manhattan traffic, it took Kane a few moments to realize the van had in fact parked. He put the camera away. The rear doors opened. Kane clutched the arm with the fake injury. Elton leaned into the van, offering a hand. Cradling one arm, Kane reached out with the other hand, grabbed Elton's outstretched arm. Kane got up. It would be so easy, so quick. All he needed to do was plant his feet, and pull. Just a little more pressure and the guard would be hauled into the van. The box cutter could go through the back of Elton's neck in one smooth motion, and then follow the jawline to the carotid artery.

Elton helped Kane out of the van as if he was made out of glass and walked him into the med center.

The coin had come up tails: Elton wouldn't be touched.

Kane thanked his savior, and watched him leave. After a few minutes, Kane left the center and walked out into the street to check the van hadn't doubled back to make sure he was okay.

It was nowhere to be seen.

Much later that same evening, Elton, dressed in his running gear, left his favorite Deli with a half-eaten Ruben sandwich under one arm, and a brown paper bag of groceries under the other. A tall, clean-shaven, well-dressed man suddenly stood right in front of Elton, blocking his way, causing him to halt in the dark, beneath a broken street light.

Joshua Kane was enjoying the crisp evening, the feel of a good suit and a clean neck.

"I tossed the coin again," he said.

Kane shot Elton in the face, walked briskly into a dark alley and disappeared. Such a quick, easy execution gave Kane no pleasure. Ideally he would've liked a few days with Elton, but he couldn't spare the time.

He had a lot of work to do.

Six Weeks Later

MONDAY

CHAPTER ONE

No reporters sat in the courtroom benches behind me. No onlookers in the public gallery. No concerned family members. Just me, my client, the prosecutor, the judge, a stenographer and a clerk. Oh, and a court security officer sitting in the corner, surreptitiously watching a Yankees game on his smartphone.

I was in 100 Center Street, Manhattan's Criminal Court building, in a small courtroom on the eighth floor.

Nobody else was there because no one else gave a shit. In fact, the prosecutor didn't much care for the case and the judge had lost interest as soon as he read the charge sheet: Possession of narcotics and drug paraphernalia. The prosecutor was a lifer in the DA's office by the name of Norman Folkes. Norm had six months before he collected his pension and it showed. The top button of his shirt was undone, his suit looked as though he'd bought it during Reagan's Presidency, and the two-day stubble on his cheeks was the only thing that he wore which looked clean.

The Honorable Cleveland Parks, presiding judge, had a face that looked like a deflated balloon. He rested his head on his hand and leaned over the judge's bench.

"How much longer do we have to wait, Mr. Folkes?" said Judge Parks.

Norm looked at his watch, shrugged, and said, "Apologies, Your Honor, he should be here any second."

The female clerk rattled papers in front of her. Silence invaded the room again.

"Let me say, for the record, Mr. Folkes, you are a highly experienced prosecutor and I assume you know that nothing irritates me more than lateness," said the judge.

Norm nodded. Apologized, again and pulled some more on his shirt collar as Judge Parks' jowls began to change color. The longer Parks had to sit there, the more his face turned red. That was about as animated as Parks got. He never raised his voice, or wagged an accusing finger – he just sat there fuming. His hatred of tardiness was well known.

My client, a fifty-five-year-old ex-hooker named Jean Marie, leaned toward me and whispered, "What happens if the cop doesn't show, Eddie?"

"He'll show," I said.

I knew the cop would show. But I also knew he would be late. I'd made sure of it.

It could only work with Norm as the prosecutor. I'd filed the motion to dismiss the charges two days ago, just before five when the listing officer had already gone home. Years of practice had given me a good idea of how quickly the office processed paper and set a hearing. With the backlog in court filing at the office, we probably wouldn't get a hearing before today, and the court office would scramble around to find a free courtroom. Motions are normally in the afternoon, around two o'clock, but neither the prosecution nor the defense would know which courtroom we would appear in until a few hours before. Didn't matter. Norm would have cases to do in the morning, in arraignment court, and so did I. The custom would be to ask the court clerk in whichever courtroom we were in, to check on the computer and tell us in which courtroom our motion would be heard later that day. When we got word through from the court clerk with confirmation of our motion venue, any other prosecutor would pick up their cell phone and call their witness, letting them know where they were supposed to be. Not Norm. He didn't carry a cell. Didn't believe in them. He thought they gave out all kinds of bad radio waves. I'd made sure to find Norm earlier that morning, in arraignment court, and let him know the venue for this afternoon's hearing. Norm would rely on his witness doing exactly what he would have to do if I hadn't already told him the courtroom number. His witness would have to check out the court venue from the board.

The board is located in room 1000 in the court building – the clerk's office. Inside that office, along with the lines of people waiting to pay fines, a whiteboard stood up with a list of the trials and motions going for hearing that day. The board is there to tell witnesses, cops, DAs, law students, tourists and lawyers exactly where the trial action is in the building at any given time. An hour before the motion was due, I went up to room 1000, made sure my back was to the clerk, found my motion on the board, rubbed out the courtroom number and scrawled in a new one. A small trick. Not like the long, risky operations I'd run when I was a con artist for ten years. Since I'd become a lawyer I allowed myself the occasional lapse back into my old ways.

Given how long you have to wait for an elevator in this place, I figured my diversion was good enough to set Norm's witness back by ten minutes or so.

Detective Mike Granger walked into the courtroom twenty minutes late. At first, I didn't turn when I heard the doors opening behind me. I just listened to Granger's feet on the tiled floor, walking almost as fast as Judge Parks' fingers rapping on his desk. But then I heard more footsteps. That made me turn.

Behind Granger, a middle-aged man wearing an expensive suit walked into the court and sat at the back. Instantly recognizable, he had a flop of fair hair, a row of TV-white teeth, and a pale, office-bound complexion. Rudy Carp was one of those lawyers who battled out cases for months on the nightly news, appeared on Court TV, got his face on the cover of magazines and had all the courtroom skills to back it up. An official litigator to the stars.

I'd never met the guy. We didn't hunt in the same social circle. Rudy had dinner at the White House twice a year. Judge Harry Ford and I drank cheap Scotch once a month. At one time I'd let the booze get the better of me. Not now. Once a month. No more than two drinks. I had it under control.

Rudy waved in my direction. I turned and saw the judge staring at Detective Granger. When I swung back Rudy waved again. Only then did I realize he was waving to me. I waved back, turned around and tried to refocus. For the life of me, I couldn't figure out what the hell he was doing in my court.

"Good of you to join us, Detective," said Judge Parks.

Mike Granger looked every inch the veteran New York cop. He walked with a swagger – he took off his sidearm, spat out his gum and slapped it onto the pancake holster before leaving it under the prosecution table. No guns were to be taken into court. Law enforcement were supposed to check their sidearms at security. The court officers usually let veteran cops slide, but even the vets knew not to wear a gun on the witness stand.

Granger tried to explain why he was late. Judge Parks cut him off with a shake of the head. Save it for the stand.

I heard Jean Marie sigh. Her black roots were showing through her bleached dye job and her fingers trembled as she brought them to her mouth.

"Don't worry. I told you already, you're not going back to jail," I said.

She'd worn a new black pantsuit for court. It looked good on her – gave her a little more confidence.

While I tried to reassure Jean, Norm got the show on the road by calling Granger to the stand. He was sworn in, and Norm took him through the basics of Jean's arrest.

He was passing 37th Street and Lexington that night, saw Jean standing outside a massage parlor with a bag in her hand. Granger knew she had a rap sheet for turning tricks, back in the day. He stopped, approached her. Introduced himself and showed her his badge. At that point he says he saw *drug paraphernalia* protruding from the top of Jean's brown paper sack.

"What was this drug paraphernalia?" asked Norm.

"A straw. It's routinely used by addicts to snort narcotics. I saw it, clear as day, sticking out of the top of her bag," said Granger.

Judge Parks wasn't surprised, but he rolled his eyes nonetheless. Believe it or not, in the last six months a half a dozen young African American men had been arrested and held by the NYPD for possession of drug paraphernalia because they had soda straws in their possession, usually stuck into the top of a soda cup.

"And what did you do then?" said Norm.

"For me, seeing drug paraphernalia on a person – that's probable cause. Ms. Marie has a record for drugs offenses, so I searched her bag and found the drugs inside. Five small baggies of marijuana in the bottom of the sack. So I arrested her."

It sounded like Jean was going to jail. Second drug offense in twelve months. No probation this time. She was going down for probably two to three years. In fact, I was reminded that she'd already done a little time for this offense. After her arrest she spent three weeks inside before I could get a bail bondsman to write me a bond for her.

I'd asked Jean about the bust. She told me the truth. Jean always told me the truth. Detective Granger had rolled up on her looking for a little free action in the back of his car. Jean told him she was done turning tricks. So Granger got out of the car, grabbed her bag and when he saw the weed inside, he changed his tune; told her he wanted fifteen per cent of her takings from now on or he would bust her right then and there.

Jean told him she already paid two patrol officers in the 17th Precinct ten per cent and from the looks of it they weren't doing their job. Those cops knew Jean and had an easy time looking the other way. Despite her background, Jean was a patriot. Her product was one hundred per cent home-grown US marijuana straight from the state-licensed farms in Washington. Most of Jean's customers were elderly – smoking away their arthritis pains, or getting relief from glaucoma. They were regular customers and no trouble. Jean told Granger to get lost so he busted her and cooked up a story.

Of course, I couldn't prove any of that in court. I wasn't going to even try.

As Norm sat down, I stood up, cleared my throat and adjusted my tie. I placed my feet shoulder-width apart, took a sip of water, and steadied myself. It looked like I was getting comfortable – ready to go at it with Granger for at least a couple of hours. I picked up a page from the file on my desk, and asked Granger my first question.

"Detective, in your statement you said the defendant was holding the carrier bag in her right hand. We know this is a large brown paper sack. Hard to hold in one hand. I take it she was holding the sack by the handles at the top of the bag?"

Granger looked at me like I was the man stripping away his precious time on banal, stupid questions. He nodded and a smile appeared at the corner of his mouth.

"Yeah, she was holding the bag by the handles," he said. He then looked over at the prosecution table confidently, letting them know he had this down: I could tell Norm and Granger had discussed the lawful use of straws at some length in preparation for today. Granger was more than ready for that. He'd expected to have a big argument with me about the straw, and whether it was just being used for a soda – yada, yada, yada.

Without another word, I sat down. My first question was also my last.

I could see Granger eyeing me suspiciously, like he might've just had his pocket picked but couldn't be sure. Norm confirmed he had no desire to re-examine the witness. Detective Granger left the witness stand and I asked Norm to give me three exhibits.

"Your Honor, Exhibit one in this case is the bag. This bag," I said, holding up a sealed, clear evidence bag which contained a brown paper sack with the McDonald's logo on the front. I bent down and picked up my own McDonald's bag. Held it up for comparison.

"These bags are the same size, precisely. This bag is twenty inches deep. I got this one this morning with my breakfast," I said.

I put both bags down, picked up the next exhibit.

"This is the contents of the defendant's bag, taken from my client the night of her arrest. Exhibit two."

Inside this sealed exhibit bag were five small wraps of marijuana. Altogether, they wouldn't have been enough to fill a cereal bowl.

"Exhibit three is a standard soda straw from McDonald's. This straw is eight inches long," I said, holding it up. "This is an identical straw I picked up this morning." I held up my straw then put it on the desk.

I placed the weed inside my McDonald's bag, held it up for the judge. I then took the straw, held it vertically, and dropped it inside the bag with one hand while I held the handles with the other.

The straw disappeared from view.

I handed the bag to the judge. He looked at it, took the straw out and dropped it back inside. He repeated this a few times and even stood the straw upright inside the bag on top of the baggies of marijuana. The straw remained a good five inches from the top of the bag. I knew this because I'd practiced the same thing myself.

"Your Honor, I'm subject to the court stenographer, but my note of Detective Granger's testimony with reference to the straw is, *I saw it, clear as day, sticking out of the top of her bag.* The defense concedes it's possible for the straw to be exposed if the top of the bag is curled up and held lower down. However, Detective Granger confirmed in his testimony that my client held the bag by the handles. Your Honor, this is the last straw – so to speak."

Judge Parks put a hand up. He'd heard enough from me. He turned in his seat and directed his attention to Norm.

"Mr. Folkes, I've examined this bag, and the straw with the actual items located in the bottom of the sack. I am not satisfied that Detective Granger could have seen a straw protruding from the top of this bag. On that basis, there is no probable cause for his search, and all evidence gathered as a result is inadmissible. Including the straw. I am concerned, to say the least, at the recent trend among some officers in classifying soda straws and other innocuous items as drug paraphernalia. Be that as it may, you have no evidence to support an arrest and I am dismissing all charges. I'm sure you had a lot to say to me, Mr. Folkes, but there's no point – I'm afraid, you're too damn *late*."

Jean hugged my neck, partially strangling me in the process. I patted her arm, gently, and she let go. She may not want to hug me when she gets my bill. The judge and his staff got up and left the courtroom.

Granger stormed out, shooting me with his index finger as he left. It didn't bother me, I was used to it.

"So when can I expect you to file an appeal," I said to Norm.

"Not in this life," he replied, "Granger doesn't bust low-level operators like your client. There's probably something else behind this arrest that you and I will never know about."

Norm packed his gear and followed my client out of the courtroom. Just me and Rudy Carp left in the room now. He was applauding, with what looked like a genuine smile on his face.

Rudy stood up and said, "Congratulations, that was . . . impressive. I need five minutes of your time."

"What for?"

"I want to know if you'd like to take second chair in the biggest murder trial this city has ever seen."

CHAPTER TWO

Kane watched the man in the plaid shirt open the front door to his apartment and stand there, stunned into a dead silence. He saw confusion take hold and Kane wondered what the man was thinking. He was sure that at first, the man in the plaid shirt thought he was looking at his reflection; as if some joker had rung his doorbell, then fitted a full-length mirror right across the door frame. And then, when the man realized there was no mirror, he rubbed his forehead and took a step back from the door as he tried to make sense of what he was seeing. It was the closest Kane had come to the man. He'd been watching him, photographing him, mimicking him. Kane looked the man up and down and felt pleased with his work. Kane wore exactly the same shirt as the man at the door. He'd dyed his hair the same color, and with some trimming, shaving, and make-up he'd managed to copy the receding hairline in exactly the same pattern around the temples. The black-rimmed glasses were identical. Even the gray pants carried a precise bleach stain on the lower left leg, five inches from the bottom and two inches from the inside seam. Same boots too.

Turning his attention to the man's face, Kane counted three seconds before the man realized this was not a practical joke and he was not staring at a reflection. Even so, the man looked at his hands, to make sure they were empty. Kane's right hand held a silenced pistol down by his side.

Kane took advantage of his victim's confusion. He pushed the man hard in the chest, forcing him back. Kane stepped inside the apartment, kicked the door shut behind him and heard the door slam against the frame.

"Bathroom, now, you're in danger," said Kane.

The man held up his hands, his lips moved soundlessly as they struggled to find the words. Any words. None came. The man simply reversed down the hall and into his bathroom until the back of his thighs touched the porcelain tub. His hands shook as he held them high, his eyes tracing every inch of Kane, confusion fighting his panic.

Likewise, Kane couldn't help but study the man in the bathroom, and notice the subtle differences in appearance. Up close, he was thinner than the man by a good fifteen to twenty pounds. The hair color was close, but not quite right. And the scar – a small one just above the man's top lip, on his left cheek. Kane hadn't seen the scar from the photos he'd taken five weeks ago, nor did he see it on the picture held by the DMV that appeared on the man's driver's license. Maybe the scar had formed after the license picture had been taken. In any event, Kane knew he could replicate it. He had studied Hollywood make-up techniques; a thin, quick-drying latex solution could replicate almost any scar. Kane nodded. One thing he had got right was the eye color; that at least was an identical match to the contacts. He thought he might need to add darker patches around the eyes, maybe lighten his skin just a little. The nose was a problem.

But one he could fix.

Not perfect, but not bad, thought Kane.

"What the hell is going on?" said the man.

Kane took a folded piece of paper from his pocket and threw it at the man's feet.

"Pick it up, and read it out loud," said Kane.

The man bent low on shaky legs, picked up the paper, unfolded it and read it. When the man looked back, Kane held a small digital voice recorder.

"Out loud," said Kane.

"T-t-take whatever you w-w-want just don't hurt me," said the man, hiding his face from Kane.

"Hey, listen to me. Your life is in danger. There's not much time. Someone is coming here to kill you. Relax, I'm a cop. I'm here to take your place and protect you. Why do you think I'm dressed exactly like you?" said Kane.

Peeking between his fingers, the man looked at Kane again, narrowed his eyes and started shaking his head.

"Who would want to kill me?"

"I don't have time to explain, but this man has to believe that I am you. We're going to get you out of here – get you safe. But I need you to do something first. See, I look like you but I don't sound like you. Read the note aloud so I can hear your voice. I need to learn your speech rhythm, figure out how you sound."

The note shook in the man's grip as he began to read aloud, hesitantly at first, skipping and stumbling over the first words.

"Stop. Relax. You're safe. It's all going to work out fine. Now try again, take it from the top," said Kane.

The man took a breath, and tried again.

"The hungry purple dinosaur ate the kind, zingy fox, the jabbering crab, and the mad whale and started vending and quacking," he said, with a confused look on his face.

"What's that all about?" he said.

Kane hit stop on the digital recorder, raised the gun and pointed it at the man's head.

"The sentence is a phonetic pangram. It gives me a base for your phonetic range. I'm sorry. I lied. *I'm* the man who is here to kill you. Believe me, I wish we had more time together. It would have made things easier," said Kane.

A single round from the silenced pistol cut a hole through the roof of the man's mouth. The gun was a silenced .22 caliber. No exit wound. No blood and brains to clean up, no bullet that needed digging out of the wall. Nice and clean. The man's body fell into the tub.

Kane dropped the pistol in the sink, left the bathroom and opened the front door. Kane checked the hallway. Waited. No one in sight. No one had heard a thing.

Across the hall from the front door was a small storeroom. Kane opened the door, picked up the gym bag and the bucket of lye he'd left there, went back to the apartment, and returned to the bathroom. If he'd been able to kill the man and move the body, he would have completed his work elsewhere, and much more efficiently. Circumstances dictated otherwise. He could not risk moving the body, even in pieces. In the five weeks of surveillance that Kane had undertaken, he'd seen the man leave his apartment on no more than a dozen occasions. The man knew no one in the building, he had no friends, no family, no job, and importantly no visitors. Kane was sure of that. But the man was known in the building, and the local area. He said "hi" to neighbors in the lobby, passed the time of day with store clerks, that sort of thing. Passing acquaintances, but contact nonetheless. So Kane needed to sound like him, look like him, and keep to the man's routine as closely as possible.

With the obvious exception. The man's routine was about to change in the most extraordinary way.

Before he worked on the man's body, he needed to work on his own. Kane took a moment to study the face again, up close.

The nose.

The man's nose bent over to the left side and it was thicker than Kane's. He must've broken it some years before and either didn't have the insurance, the money or the inclination to get it reset properly.

Quickly, Kane stripped off his clothes, folded them neatly, and placed them in the living room. He took a towel from the bathroom, soaked it under the hot faucet in the sink, then wrung it out. He did the same with a facecloth.

He rolled up the wet bath towel until it was a tight roll about three inches thick. He draped the facecloth over the right side of his face, but made sure it covered his nose. The rolled-up towel was long enough for Kane to tie around his head.

Kane stood in the bathroom and took hold of the door handle with his right hand and drew the door toward his face until the edge of the door touched the bridge of his nose. The facecloth would absorb the impact from the sharp edge of the door, so it wouldn't break his skin. Kane angled his head slightly to the left, and placed his left hand on the left side of his face. He felt his neck muscles engage, pushing against his left hand, while pushing back against his own neck. It meant his head wouldn't snap to the left with the impact.

Kane counted to three, swung the door away from him, then reversed it, and slammed the edge of the door into the bridge of his nose. His head held firm. His nose didn't. He could tell by the crunch of bone. The sound was all he had to go by, because he hadn't felt a thing.

The towel around his head prevented the door from hitting his head, and giving him an orbital fracture. An injury like that would lead to a bleed in the eye which would need surgery to repair.

Kane took the towel off his head, lifted the facecloth clear and threw them both in the bathtub on top of the man's legs. He looked in the mirror. Looked at the man's nose.

Not quite.

Gripping both sides of his nose, Kane twisted to the left. He heard the crepitus; the sound that bone makes when it's shattered. It sounded like breakfast cereal, wrapped tightly in a napkin and squeezed. He looked in the mirror again.

Pretty good. The swelling would help too. He could cover up the bruising that would inevitably appear around his nose and eyes with make-up.

He then put on a chemical retardant suit which he'd packed in the gym bag with other items. He stripped the man naked in the bathtub. A puff of white powder escaped into the air as Kane popped the lid on the bucket of lye; the concentrated, powder form. The hot water faucet in the bath was running fast and the water soon reached an unbearable temperature. The man's skin was turning red from the heat. Wisps of blood floated and danced like red smoke in the hot water. Kane measured out three scoops of lye and tossed them in.

When the tub was three-quarters full, he turned off the water. From his bag, he produced a large rubber sheet, unfolded it and draped it over the tub. Tearing open a roll of duct tape, he proceeded to seal the rubber sheet to the tub with long lengths of tape.

Kane knew all kinds of ways to get rid of a body without leaving any trace of himself behind. And this method of disposal he found to be particularly effective. The process was based on alkaline hydrolysis. Bio-cremation broke down skin, muscle, tissue, and even teeth on a cellular level. The lye powder, mixed in the right quantities with water, dissolved a human being in under sixteen hours. Then Kane would have a bath of green and brown liquid, which he would get rid of by draining the bathtub.

The teeth and bones left behind would appear bleached, brittle and could easily be pounded into dust with the heel of a shoe. Kane knew the perfect place to get rid of the bone dust was in a large box of soap powder. Easy to mix up the bone and soap and no one would ever think to look there.

Only thing left in the tub that would need further work would be the bullet, and Kane could toss that in the river.

Nice and clean, just the way he liked it.

Satisfied with his work so far, Kane nodded to himself, and went out into the short hallway of the apartment. A small table sat beside the closed front door. A stack of opened mail lay on the table. At the top of the pile, its red band proud and loud against the white paper, was the envelope Kane had photographed weeks ago. The summons for jury duty.

CHAPTER THREE

On Center Street, parked right outside the courthouse, I saw a black limo with the driver standing on the sidewalk, holding open the rear door. Rudy Carp had asked me to lunch. I was hungry.

The limo driver had parked within ten feet of a hot dog stand that boasted a big picture of my face on an ad board taped on the lower panel of the cart. Like I needed the cosmos to remind me of the difference between me and Rudy. Soon as we got into the limo, Rudy took a call on his cell. The driver took us to a restaurant on Park Avenue South. I couldn't even pronounce the name of it. It looked French. Rudy disconnected his call soon as he left the car and said, "I love this place. Best ramp soup in the city."

I didn't even know what a *ramp* was. I was pretty sure it wasn't an animal, but I played along and followed Rudy inside.

The waiter made a fuss of his guest, and gave us a table in the back away from the busy lunch service. Rudy sat opposite me. It was a napkin and tablecloth joint, with somebody playing a piano, softly, in the background.

"I like the lighting in here. It's . . . atmospheric," said Rudy.

The lighting was so atmospheric I had to use the glare from my cell phone screen just to read the menu. It was in French. I decided to order whatever Rudy was having and be done with it. The place made me uncomfortable. I didn't like ordering from a menu that refused to display prices beside the food. Not my kind of place. The waiter took our order, poured two glasses of water and left.

"So let's get down to it, Eddie. I like you. I've had my eye on you for a while. You've had a couple of great cases in the past few years. The David Child affair?"

I nodded. I didn't like talking about my old cases. I liked to keep it between me and the client.

"And you've had some success in lawsuits against the NYPD. We've done our homework. You're the real deal."

The way he said homework made me think he probably knew I had a reputation before I took the bar exam. All that existed about my former life as a con artist was rumor. Nobody could prove a damn thing, and I liked it that way.

"I take it you know what case I'm currently working on," said Rudy.

I did. It would be hard to ignore it. I'd seen his face on the news every week for almost a year. 'You're representing Robert Solomon, the movie star. Trial starts next week, if I'm not mistaken."

"Trial starts in three days. It's jury selection tomorrow. We'd like you on the team. You can handle a few witnesses with some prep time. I think your style would be highly effective. That's why I'm here. You get second chair, do a couple of weeks' work, and for that you get more free advertising than you could possibly imagine and we could offer you a two-hundred-thousand-dollar flat fee."

Rudy smiled at me with his perfect, bleached-white teeth. He looked like a candy-store owner offering a street kid all the free chocolate he could eat. It was a benevolent look. The longer I stayed quiet, the harder it became for Rudy to hold that smile.

"When you say *we*, who exactly are you talking about? I thought you ran your own ship at Carp Law."

He nodded, said, "I do, but when it comes to Hollywood stars on trial for murder, there's always another player. The studio is my client. They asked me to represent Bobby and they're footing the bill. What do you say, kid? You want to be a famous lawyer?"

"I like to keep a low profile," I said.

His face dropped.

"Come on, it's the murder trial of the century. What do you say?" said Rudy.

"No, thanks," I said.

Rudy hadn't expected this. Leaning back in his chair, he folded his arms and said, "Eddie, every lawyer in this town would kill for a spot at the defense table in this case. You know that. Is it the money? What's the problem?"

The waiter arrived with bowls of soup that Rudy waved away. He pulled his chair close to the table, and came forward, leaning on his elbows as he waited for my answer.

"I don't mean to be an asshole, Rudy. You're right. Most lawyers would kill to get that chair, but I'm not like most lawyers. From what I've read in the papers, and from what I've seen on TV, I think Robert Solomon murdered those people. And I'm not gonna help a murderer walk, no matter how famous he is, or how much money he's got. Sorry, my answer's no."

Rudy still wore that five-thousand-dollar smile but he was looking at me sideways, and nodding slightly.

"I get it, Eddie," said Rudy. "Why don't we call it an even quarter million?"

"It's not about the money. I don't roll for the guilty. I've been down that road a long time ago. It costs a lot more than money can buy," I said.

A realization spread over Rudy's face, and he put the smile away for a while. "Oh, well, in that case we don't have a problem. See, Bobby Solomon is innocent. The NYPD framed him for the murders," said Rudy.

"Really? Can you prove that?" I said.

Rudy paused, "No,' he said, 'But I think you can."

CHAPTER FOUR

Kane stared at the full-length bedroom mirror in front of him. Tucked around the edges of the mirror, between the glass and the frame, were dozens of photographs of the man who was now slowly dissolving in his own bathtub. Kane had brought the photos with him. He needed a little more time to study his mark. One photograph, the only one Kane had managed to take of the man in a seated position, was drawing his attention more than the others. In the photo, the man was seated on a bench in Central Park, flicking crumbs to the birds. His legs were crossed in front of him.

The armchair that Kane had brought in from the living room was around five inches lower than the park bench in the photo, and Kane was struggling to get the angle of his legs just right. He never crossed his legs. It had never felt comfortable, or natural, but Kane was a perfectionist when it came to becoming someone else. It was vital to success.

Mimicry was a gift he'd discovered in school. During recess, Kane would impersonate the teachers for the rest of the class, and his fellow students would roll around on the floor, laughing. Kane never laughed, but he enjoyed the attention. He liked the sound of his classmate's laughter, but couldn't understand why they laughed, nor the relationship between their laughter and his impersonation. Still, he did it every now and again. It helped him fit in. He'd moved around a lot as a kid: a new school, in a new town, almost every year. Inevitably, his mother would lose her job, through sickness or booze. Then the posters would go up around their neighborhood: pictures of family pets that had gone missing.

That was usually when it was time to move on.

Kane had developed the ability to get to know people quickly. He was good at making new friends and it wasn't like he'd had a lack of practice. The impressions broke the ice. The girls in his class would stop giving him strange looks for a few days, and the boys would include him in conversations about baseball. Soon Kane was impersonating celebrities as well as members of the faculty.

He sat up straight and tried again to flick one leg over the other so that it mirrored the photograph. Right calf over the left knee, right foot extended. His right leg slipped off his knee, and he cursed himself. Kane took a moment and repeated the pangram he'd recorded the man uttering just before he'd put a bullet in his head. He recited the words, whispering them softly, then gradually letting the volume rise. Kane replayed the recording, over and over again. Eyes closed, he listened intently. The voice on the recorder could've been better. He could still detect the fear in that voice. Tremors from the back of the man's throat sent ripples over some of the words. Kane tried to isolate them, and repeated them confidently, testing out how they would sound without the fear. The voice on the recorder was fairly deep. He dropped an octave, drank some milk mixed with full fat cream just to clog up his vocal cords. It worked. After some practice, and being able to hear that tone in his own head – Kane felt confident that he could repeat it, or at least get extremely close to it even without the dairy swelling his throat.

After another fifteen minutes the sounds on the recorder, and Kane's speech, were identical. This time, when he swept his leg up over his other knee it stayed there.

Satisfied, he got up, went to the kitchen and returned to the fridge. When he'd poured the milk he'd seen some ingredients in the refrigerator that took his fancy. Bacon, eggs, some cheese in an aerosol can, a pack of butter, some mushy-looking tomatoes and a lemon. He decided that bacon and eggs, maybe with some fried bread, would help his calorie intake. Kane needed a few more pounds to match his victim's weight. All things considered, he could prob-ably get away with weighing less, and he could pad his stomach, but Kane approached these things methodically. If he could get a pound closer to his target tonight by eating a huge, fatty meal, then that was what he would do.

He found a frying pan under the sink and prepared a meal. He read some of the *American Angler* fishing magazines that lay on the kitchen table while he ate. Satisfied, Kane pushed the plate away. Depending on how things went that evening, he knew he might not get another chance to eat until after midnight.

Tonight, he thought, could be very busy indeed.

CHAPTER FIVE

I thought the ramp soup was worth waiting for. It tasted of spring onions, garlic and olive oil. Not bad. Not bad at all. The conversation had stopped as soon as Rudy allowed the waiter to bring over the soup. We ate in silence. After I made sure he'd finished, I put down my spoon, wiped my lips with a napkin and gave Rudy my full attention.

"I think you're tempted by this case. Maybe you want a few more details before you make up your mind. Am I right?" said Rudy.

"Right."

"Wrong," said Rudy. "This is the hottest case to ever hit the East Coast. In a couple of days I have to deliver my opening speech to a jury. I've been on this thing from the beginning and I've gone to great lengths to keep the defense a secret. The element of surprise is crucial in trial. You know that. At the moment, you're not an attorney of record. Anything I say to you right now has no attorney-client protection."

"What if I sign a confidentiality agreement?" I said.

"Not worth the paper it's printed on," said Rudy. "I could wallpaper my house in confidentiality agreements and you know how many have held up? Probably not enough to wipe my ass with. That's Hollywood."

"So you're not going to tell me any more about the case?" I said.

"I can't. All I can tell you is this. I believe the kid is innocent," said Rudy. Sincerity can be faked. Rudy's client was a gifted young actor. He knew how to play for the camera. But Rudy, for all of his bravado, and highly persuasive courtroom skills, couldn't hide the truth from me. I'd only been in his company for a half-hour, maybe more. But that statement felt natural, it felt like he meant

28

it. There were no physical or verbal tics, conscious or unconscious, as he spoke. It was clean. The words flowed. If I had to bet on it, I'd have said Rudy was telling the truth – he believed Robert Solomon was innocent.

But that wasn't good enough. Not for me. What if Rudy had been suckered-in by a manipulative client? An actor.

"Look, I really appreciate the offer, but I'm going to have to—"

"Wait," said Rudy, cutting me off. "Don't say no just yet. Take some time. Sleep on it and let me know in the morning. You might change your mind."

Rudy paid the check, included a celebrity-worthy tip and we left the dark restaurant for the street. The limo driver got out of the front cab and opened the rear door.

"Can I drop you somewhere?" said Rudy.

"My car's parked on Baxter, behind the court," I said.

"No problem. Mind if we swing by 42nd on the way? Something I'd like to show you," he said.

"Fine by me," I said.

Rudy stared out the window, his elbow on an armrest and his fingers delicately stroking his lips. I thought about everything I'd heard. Didn't take me long to figure out why Rudy really wanted me on the case. I couldn't be sure, but I had a question that would clear it up once and for all.

"I know you can't give me details, but answer me one thing. I take it that an important piece of evidence, tending to show that Robert Solomon was set up by law enforcement, didn't magically appear in the last two weeks?"

For a second, Rudy said nothing. Then he smiled. He knew what I was thinking.

"You're right. There's no new evidence. Nothing new in the last three months. So I guess you've got it all figured out. Don't take it personally."

If I got hired to go after the NYPD, then I would be the only lawyer on the defense team handling the police witnesses. I would be the one throwing the shit at the cops. If it worked – great. If it wasn't going down well with the jury – I would be fired. Rudy would get time to explain to the jury that I just got hired a week ago – and that any accusations I made against the cops did not come from the client. I'd gone rogue. Gone way off script. In those circumstances, Rudy could keep on good terms with the jury no matter what happened. I was an expendable member of the team – either a hero or a patsy.

Smart. Very smart.

I glanced up and saw Rudy pointing out the side window of the limo. I leaned forward and followed his line of vision until I saw a billboard for a new movie called *The Vortex*. Billboards on 42nd street weren't cheap. The movie didn't look cheap either. It was an expensive-looking sci-fi piece. The credits below the poster revealed the movie starred Robert Solomon and Ariella Bloom. I'd heard about the movie. Everyone in the country who'd switched on a TV in the past year knew about it too. It was a three-hundred-million-dollar gamble – starring Robert Solomon and his wife, Ariella Bloom. The arrest of a fairly nascent Hollywood bad boy for murder guaranteed mass, frenzied press coverage. In this case there were two murder victims: Bobby's chief of security – Carl Tozer, and Bobby's wife – Ariella Bloom. At the time of the murders, Bobby and Ariella had been married for two months. They'd just shot the first season of their reality show. Most pundits were claiming this trial would be bigger than OJ and Michael Jackson combined.

"That billboard went up last week. PR for Bobby, but the movie has been held in a can for almost a year now. If Robert is convicted it'll stay there. If he gets off after a lengthy trial, it'll stay there. Only way that movie gets released, and the studio makes its money back, is if we demonstrate to the whole world that Robert is innocent. Bobby has signed a lucrative contract for three more movies from the studio. This is their tent-pole franchise. We have to make sure he's able to fulfill that contract. If he doesn't, the studio stands to lose a significant amount of money. Millions, in fact. There's a lot riding on this, Eddie. We need a definitive result in our favor and fast."

I nodded, turned away from the poster. Maybe Rudy cared about Robert Solomon, but not as much as the studio's money. Who could blame him? He was a lawyer, after all.

All the newsstand boards on 42nd carried news of the trial's imminent commencement.

The more I thought about it, the more I thought this case was a nightmare. From the sounds of it, there might be a conflict between the studio and Bobby. What if the kid wanted to plead guilty, or cut a deal with the DA, and the studio wouldn't let him? And what if he was innocent?

We left 42nd and turned south, toward Center Street, and I thought about what I'd heard about the case on the news. Apparently, two police officers responded to a 911 call from Solomon telling police he'd found his wife and chief of security dead.

Solomon let the cops into the house and they made their way upstairs.

On the second-floor landing a table had been overturned. A broken vase beside it. The table sat in front of a window overlooking the back of the house, a small walled-in garden below. There were three bedrooms on that floor. Two lay dark and empty. The master bedroom at the end of the hall was also in darkness. Inside that room they found Ariella and her chief of security, Carl. Or what was left of them. Both lay dead and naked on the bed.

Solomon had his wife's blood on him. Apparently, there was more forensic evidence which the DA's office would only describe as irrefutable proof of Solomon's guilt.

Case closed.

Or so I'd thought.

"If Robert didn't kill those people, who did?" I said.

The car turned onto Center Street, and slowed down outside the courts. Rudy shuffled forward in his seat and said, "We're focusing on who didn't do it. This is a police frame-up. It's textbook. Look, I know this is a big decision. And I appreciate your moral standpoint. Take tonight to think about it. If you decide you want in, call me. No matter what happens, it was a pleasure," said Rudy, handing me his card.

The car stopped, I shook hands with Rudy, the driver got out and opened my door. I stepped to the sidewalk and watched the limo take off. Without seeing the files, I could guess that the cops figured Robert was the killer and maybe set about making sure he got convicted. Most cops just wanted to put bad people away. The more horrific the crime, the more likely the cops were to bend the evidence against the perp. And that wasn't legal. It might be morally defensible, but the cops weren't supposed to interfere with the evidence – because next time they might do the same to an innocent person.

I knew some cops. Good ones. And any cop who manipulated evidence to suit their case was hated more by good cops than defense attorneys.

Rounding the corner to Baxter Street I looked for my car. A blue Mustang. I couldn't see it. I looked around. Then I saw it being hauled onto a flatbed trailer by a city parking official.

"Hey, that's my car," I said, running across the street to the trailer.

"You should've paid for the parking then, pal," said the plump official in a bright blue uniform.

"I did pay for parking," I said.

The parking guy shook his head, handed me a ticket, and pointed at my car as it was lowered by the crane onto the truck. At first I couldn't tell what the guy was pointing at, but then I saw it. Tucked underneath the wiper on my windshield was a McDonald's bag. Thirty or forty straws protruded from the top of the bag. There was something written on the brown paper in black magic marker. My tires hit the flatbed, I levered myself up onto the truck and grabbed the bag. The message read:

"You're LATE."

I threw the bag in the nearby trash can, took out my cell and dialed the number on the card Rudy had given to me.

"Rudy, it's Eddie. I've thought about it. You want me to go after the NYPD? To hell with it. I want to read the files as Robert's lawyer – but on one condition. After I look at the case, if I still believe he's guilty I walk away."

CHAPTER SIX

Any other time of year and I could've walked to the offices of Carp and Associates inside of ten minutes. My own office which, unbeknownst to my landlord, doubled as my apartment, sat on West 46th Street close to 9th Avenue. I pulled my scarf around my neck, huddled into my overcoat and set off from my office close to five thirty. Enough time to grab a slice of pepperoni and a soda on the way, and take my time about it. The sun had already gone down, and the sidewalks were beginning to ice up. I would have to take it slow if I wanted to get there in one piece. My destination – 4 Times Square. What was once called the Condé Nast Building. A legendary, eco-friendly skyscraper of forty-eight floors that ran on solar power. The people inside the building ran on Fairtrade, organic coffee and Kombucha. The magazine publisher, Condé Nast, had moved out in recent years and headed over to One World Trade Center. When they moved out the lawyers moved in.

At five after six I entered the lobby. A hundred feet of polished tiles between the entrance and the reception desk which was shrouded in white marble. The ceiling was maybe eighty to ninety feet high and was made up of row upon row of burnished steel panels, folded to look like the armor of some great beast.

If God had a lobby I guessed it wouldn't look too different from this one.

My heels cracked out a steady beat as I made my way to the reception area. Looking around, I didn't see any couches or chairs anywhere. If you were waiting, then you were standing. The whole place seemed as though it was designed to make you feel small. After what seemed like a long time, I got to the reception and gave my name to a thin, pink-skinned guy in a suit that looked as though it was crushing his bird-like chest.

"Is sir expected?" he asked, in a British accent.

"I have an appointment if that's what you mean," I said.

His lips curled into something that was supposed to look friendly. It didn't. It looked as though he'd just tasted something unpleasant but was trying desperately not to show it.

"Someone will be with you shortly," he said.

I nodded my thanks and took a slow, meandering stroll across the tiles. My phone buzzed in my jacket pocket. The display read, "Christine". My wife. For the past eighteen months she'd been living in Riverhead and working in a medium-sized law firm. Our twelve-year-old, Amy, had settled in well in her new school. Our break-up had taken place over a few years. It had started with my drinking, but the final straw had been a series of cases that had put my family in jeopardy. A year ago Christine and I had thought about getting back together, but I couldn't take that risk. Not until I'd finished with the law. I'd thought about quitting many times, but something always held me back. Before I'd hit the bottle big time, I'd made the mistake of trusting a client and getting him off. Turned out he'd been guilty all along and on some level I'd known it. He went on to hurt somebody real bad. I dealt with that knowledge every day. Every day I tried to make up for it. If I quit, and I stopped helping people I knew that I could probably get through six months, but then I would start feeling it again. Guilt was a tattoo that weighed two hundred pounds. As long as I fought for those clients I believed in, I was slowly shedding that weight. It would take time. I hoped and prayed that Christine would be waiting for me at the end.

"Eddie, are you busy tomorrow night? I'm cooking meatballs and Amy would love to see you," said Christine.

This was unusual. I drove up on weekends and saw Amy. I'd never been invited on a weekday.

"Actually, I might be taking on a new case. Something big, but I can always spare a few hours. What's the occasion?" I said.

"Oh, nothing special. See you at seven thirty?" she said.

"I'll be there."

"Be here at seven thirty, not eight or eight thirty, okay?"

"I promise."

I hadn't had an invite for dinner in a long time. It made me nervous. I wanted us to be a family again, but the work I did brought all kinds of trouble to my front door. For the past few years I'd been racking my brains as to how I could make a move into a more sedate practice. The cases I took led to trouble. And my family didn't deserve that. Lately, I'd felt as though I needed to make the break more than ever. My daughter was growing up. And I wasn't there every day to see that.

Things had to change.

The echo of footsteps drew my attention to a small, hard-faced woman in a black suit. Her blond hair, cut into a fierce bob, swayed and bounced as her heels announced her presence.

"Mr. Flynn, follow me please," she said in an accent with a hint of German beneath it.

I followed her to a waiting elevator. Seconds later we were on a different floor. More white tiles led to a set of glass doors that read, "Carp Law".

Beyond the doors was a war room.

The office was massive, and entirely open-plan apart from two large glass-walled conference rooms to the right. Laptop screens burned into the faces of Rudy's army of lawyers on every desk. Not a shred of paper anywhere. In one of the conference rooms I saw a bunch of suits pointing at twelve people dressed in ordinary street clothes. A mock jury. Some of the big law firms liked to test out their trial strategies in mock trials with a jury mainly made up of out-of-work actors who'd signed thick, scary, confidentiality agreements in exchange for a handsome day's pay. Unlike lawyers, actors tended to scare easy when it came to confidentiality agreements.

In the other conference room I saw Rudy Carp, sitting alone at the head of a long table. I was led inside.

"Take a seat, Eddie," said Rudy, gesturing to a chair beside him. I pulled off my coat, threw it over a chair and sat down at a conference table. It wasn't as big as the main conference room. The table had nine chairs. Four on either side with one at the head of the table for Rudy. Glancing across the room I saw a cabinet filled with awards. I saw statues, figurines and crystals from various venerable institutions such as the American Bar Association. My guess was Rudy put his clients on this side of the desk so they would have a direct view of the trophies sitting atop the cabinet opposite their seat. Part of it was advertising, but I was sure a lot of it was ego.

"I have the case ready for you to take away, and you can read what you need to overnight," said Rudy. The blonde approached, picked up a slim, metallic laptop from the far end of the table and put it in front of Rudy. He swiveled the laptop around and pushed it in front of me.

"Everything you need is on the hard drive. We don't let any paper leave this office, I'm afraid. There are reporters circling our staff. We have to be extra careful. Everyone on the case has a secure Mac. These machines have had their internet disabled so they only connect through a password-protected Bluetooth server in this office. You can take this with you," he said.

"I prefer to read on paper," I said.

"I know you do. I prefer it myself, but we can't take the risk of a single page of this case getting into the papers before the trial. You understand," he said.

Nodding, I opened the lid of the laptop and saw a prompt for a password.

"Forget about that for the moment. There's someone I want you to meet. Ms. Kannard, if you would be so good?" said Rudy.

The lady who'd shown me up turned and left without a word.

My fingers tapped on the polished, oak veneer of the conference table. I wanted to get down to business.

"What makes you think the cops framed Robert Solomon?" I said.

"This is going to annoy the hell out of you, but I don't want to say. If I tell you then you'll focus on that line of evidence. I want you to figure it out on your own. That way, if we both come to the same conclusions I'll feel better about putting that point to a jury," he said, and as he spoke the word jury he flung his gaze, momentarily, at the mock trial going on in the conference room beside us.

"Fair enough. So, how are the mock trials progressing?" I said.

"Not well. We've completed four trials. Three guilty verdicts and one hung jury."

"What was the split?"

"Three not-guiltys. During post-trial interviews those three jurors said they weren't convinced by the cops but they didn't think the officers were corrupt, either. It's a fine line we have to walk. That's why you're walking it. If you fall, you fall. We carry on without you and repair the damage. You understand, right?"

"I thought as much. Doesn't matter to me. Only thing is I haven't decided if I'm all-in yet. I need to read the case. Then I'll decide."

Before I finished the sentence, Rudy stood up. His gaze fixed on the door. Two huge men in black, wool overcoats approached the office. Short haircuts. Big hands. Thick necks. Two more of them approached the office. Same size. Same hair. Same necks. They were following a small man in dark glasses and a leather jacket. One of the big men opened the glass door to Rudy's office, stepped inside and held it open for the little guy. The man in their care entered the office, and the security man left and closed the door.

From my memories of watching him on the big screen, I'd thought Robert Solomon was roughly my height and size. Six feet two inches tall. About a hundred and seventy-five pounds. The man in front of me was five-five, and probably weighed the same as one of his security guard's arms. The leather jacket hung on slim, narrow shoulders and his skinny jeans made his legs look like toothpicks. Dark hair spilled over his face, and large sunglasses covered his eyes. He approached the conference table and I stood up as he held out a pale, bony hand.

I took it, gently. Didn't want to hurt the kid.

"Is this the guy, Rudy?" he said, and instantly I felt like I recognized him. The voice was powerful and melodic. There was no doubting it – this was Robert Solomon.

"This is the guy," said Rudy.

"It's good to meet you, Mr. Flynn," he said.

"Call me Eddie."

"Eddie," he said, trying it on for size. I couldn't help feeling a cheap thrill when he said my name. This was the kid touted to be the next Leonardo DiCaprio. "Call me Bobby."

The handshake, at least, was firm. Sincere, even. He took a chair beside me and we all sat down. Rudy put a document on the table in front of me, asked me to read and sign it. I skimmed through it. A pretty tight retainer agreement, binding me to client confidentiality. While I flicked through the pages I was aware of Bobby, sitting on my right, taking off his glasses and running his fingers through his hair. He was handsome. High cheekbones. Fierce, blue eyes.

I signed the retainer. Gave it back to Rudy.

"Thank you. Bobby, just so you know, Eddie hasn't agreed to take on the case yet. He's going to read the files and then make a decision. See, Eddie's not like most defense attorneys. He follows a . . . well, I think code is too strong a word. Let's put it this way – when Eddie finishes reading the file, if he thinks you're guilty he'll walk away. If he thinks you're innocent he might help us. Helluva way to run a law practice, don't you think?" said Rudy.

"I love it," said Bobby. He put a hand on my shoulder, and for just a few seconds we stared at each other. Neither of us spoke. Just stared. There was an element of searching on both sides. He wanted to know if I doubted him. I was looking for his tells, but also examining his eyes. The fact that he was a gifted actor never once left the front of my mind.

"I appreciate you have your way of working. You want to read the case. I'm cool with that. When it's all said and done, the prosecution evidence doesn't matter. Not to me. I didn't kill Ari. I didn't kill Carl. Someone else *did*. I . . . I found them, you know? Lying naked in my bed. I still see them. Every time I close my eyes. I can't get that picture out of my head. What they did to Ari? It's . . . just . . . Jesus. No one should die like that. I want to see the real killer in court. That's what I want. If I could, I'd watch them burn for what they did."

It's a sad fact that innocent people get accused of crime. Our justice system is built on it. Happens every Goddamn day. I'd seen enough innocent people accused of hurting their loved ones to know when someone is telling the truth and when someone is lying. The liars don't have the look. It's hard to describe. There's loss and pain. But something else is there too. Anger and fear, certainly. And the last thing – a burning sense of injustice. I'd done so many cases like this that I could almost see it dancing in the corner of an eye like a naked flame. Someone murders your family, lover, or friend and you are the one standing trial while the murderer goes free. There's nothing else like it on earth. And it's the same look, all over the world. An innocent man, falsely accused, looks the same in Nigeria, Ireland, Iceland, you name it. If you've seen that look before, you never forget it. It's rare to see that look. When it's there – the person may as well have their innocence tattooed on their forehead. I guessed Rudy had seen it himself. That's why he wanted me to meet Bobby. He knew I would see that innocence, and this would influence my decision more than reading the case file.

Bobby Solomon wore that look.

And I knew I had to help him.

CHAPTER SEVEN

An easy half-hour passed by in Bobby's company. A pot of coffee helped him talk and I drank two cups while I listened. He was a farmer's kid from Virginia. No brothers or sisters. His mom left when he was six. Took off with a guitar player she'd met in a bar. Then it was just Bobby and his father and the farm. He fell into that life pretty easily as a kid, and fell out with it about the same time he figured there might be the possibility of a different life. This realization hit Bobby on a Saturday afternoon when he was fifteen. His girlfriend took a drama class and Bobby got the times mixed up and arrived at the church hall around an hour before the class finished. Instead of waiting outside, Bobby decided to go in and watch.

That day changed everything.

Bobby was simply blown away. He'd never seen theatre before. Didn't understand it, the power of it. This was strange to Bobby because he'd always loved movies, but never really thought about how they were made or the actors involved. When he picked up his girl he fired question after question at her, desperate to find out about acting. He signed up the next week, and six weeks later Bobby got his first taste of community theatre. There was no going back to the farm after that.

"My daddy, he did something very special for me. Day I turned seventeen he sold some cattle, gave me a thousand bucks in my hand. Man, at that time I thought it was all the money in the world. I'd never seen so much money. The bills were mostly tens and five-spots, pitted with soil and whatnot. Real cattle-trader's cash, you know?"

I guessed Bobby was a millionaire, easy. Probably many times over. Still, his eyes sparkled when he talked about that wad of cash his father gave him.

"I folded up that money real good, stuffed half into my wallet and half in my pocket. Then he told me he'd bought me a bus ticket to New York. Jeez, it was like the best day ever. And it was the worst. I knew he was gettin' on in years. He couldn't handle the farm himself. But none of that mattered to him. He just wanted to make sure I got my shot, you know?"

I nodded.

"I took my shot because of my daddy. Seven years as a busboy, waiter, and audition veteran. I did okay. Got less than half of the jobs I went up for. Then one day, the right place and the right time and I'm straight onto Broadway. Those first two years were rough. My dad got sick and I was running back and forth. He got to see my opening night. Saw me play the lead in a Broadway play. He didn't get to stick around for long after that. He didn't get to hear about me getting the call from Hollywood. He would've liked that," said Bobby.

"Did he get to meet Ariella?" I said.

Bobby shook his head, "No, he didn't. He would've really loved her."

He bowed his head. Swallowed. Told me the story.

They'd met on the set of a movie. An independent picture called *Ham*. A coming of age story. They didn't have any scenes together in the movie, but they met on set by chance and after that they spent all their free time together. At that stage Ariella had already played some minor character roles in half a dozen mainstream movies. She had a career going for her that looked to be getting stronger and stronger. The part in the independent movie was her first lead – and she was banking on it being a sleeper hit and her calling card. And it turned out exactly like that. Her rising star meant Bobby's star got pulled alongside hers for a while. Didn't take long for them to become a young power couple. They landed the leads in the sci-fi epic, and signed a deal for a reality series.

"Things couldn't have been any sweeter for us," said Bobby. "That's why none of this makes any sense. I was happy with Ari, things were great. We'd just gotten married. If I get the chance during my testimony I'm going to ask the prosecutor why the hell they think I would kill the woman I loved? It just doesn't make any sense," he said.

41

He slumped in his chair and began rubbing his forehead, gazing off into the distance. I didn't need to go too far to come up with a dozen reasons why someone in his position would kill their new spouse.

"Since I might be working the case, Bobby, you should know I take every meeting as a practice for trial. If I hear you say something inappropriate I have to point it out so you don't do it at trial, understand?" I said.

"Sure, sure. What did I do?" he said, straightening up in his seat.

"You said you were going to ask the prosecutor a question. You're there to *answer* questions. That's what testimony is all about. The worst possible thing that can happen if you ask a question like that is the prosecutor actually gives you an answer. The prosecutor might say you killed Ariella Bloom because you'd gotten everything out of her that you needed, that you didn't love her, that you'd fallen in love with someone else and didn't want a messy divorce, that you'd discovered that she'd fallen in love with someone else and you didn't want a messy divorce, that you were high, that you were drunk, that a sudden jealous rage came over you, or she discovered your darkest secret . . ."

I paused. As soon as I said the word *secret*, Bobby's eyes came to life, shuffled around the room before settling on my face.

It unsettled me. I liked the kid. Now, I wasn't so sure.

"I don't want any secrets between us. Same goes for you, Rudy," said Bobby.

Both Rudy and I were about to warn him not to tell us something that might compromise his defense, but it was too late. Before we could stop him, Bobby told us everything.

CHAPTER EIGHT

A month ago it had taken Kane a full day to get this parking space. On that day he'd managed to get a space close to it, and he'd sat there until the space he wanted became free. Then he'd moved in, and left the car in place. Now, he sat in the driver's seat of his station wagon, drinking hot coffee from a flask. He knew it was all worth it. The parking garage on Times Square was across the street from the Condé Nast building. If you parked on the eighth floor and took one of the ten spaces on the left you could get a pretty good view across the street. High enough to see what was happening on the street, and at eye-level with the offices of Carp Law, which seemed to be lit around the clock. With a pair of small, digital binoculars Kane had watched the defense team prepare for trial. He'd watched the associates give critique as Rudy Carp practiced his opening speech, he'd even watched two of the mock trials.

More importantly, Kane had watched Carp and the jury consultant as they placed eight-by-ten laminated photographs on a large board at the back of the conference room. The photos were of men and women from the jury pool. Some of the photos had changed, from week to week, as they made adjustments and tried to find their preferred jury selection for the trial. That evening, the final twelve had been revealed.

Kane had also listened in on strategy meetings in Rudy Carp's generous, private office. A quick scan of the Carp Law interior with his binoculars had given him an idea of how to get a listening device in there after only a few days' surveillance. It had some risk, but not much. He'd watched Rudy take the package from his secretary, open the box, and examine the trophy. A contortion of twisted metal, affixed to a hollow wooden plinth. A small brass plaque bore the legend, "Rudy Carp, World Lawyer Of The Year. EYLA."

EYLA stood for the European Young Lawyers Association, according to the accompanying note. There was a return address. One of the first things Kane heard over the mic embedded in the fake trophy was Carp dictating a thank you note to be sent to the Post Office box in Brussels that Kane had set up.

From his vantage point in the parking lot across the street, Kane had watched Carp's secretary place the award next to the others.

That was three weeks ago. Two days from trial now and Kane felt confident. The mock trials had resulted in convictions. The defense team were squabbling. Bobby Solomon looked increasingly like a man on the edge of a total nervous breakdown. And to top it all off the studio weren't happy. They were putting Rudy under intense pressure. Hollywood wanted a 'not guilty' for Solomon and so far their money had failed to secure it. The studio executives just didn't understand what was going wrong.

Kane couldn't have been happier.

Then he'd seen the final twelve jurors selected by the defense. There was no guarantee that any of them would make the final list, and he'd seen the picture of the man he now resembled on the list quite a few times, but not tonight.

Kane would need to make some adjustments of his own to the jury list.

As he thought about this, he saw the young lawyer sitting in Carp's office. He'd been given a laptop. Signed a retainer. Now here he was talking to Bobby Solomon. A new lawyer. Solomon was giving this lawyer his life story. Trying to finesse him. Make him care.

Kane pressed the earphones tight and listened.

Flynn. That was the lawyer's name.

A new player. He resolved to look further into Flynn that night. He didn't have time just at the moment. Kane took out his cell phone, a cheap burner, and hit dial on the only number in the phone's memory.

That familiar voice answered the call.

"I'm working. It'll have to wait."

The man who'd answered the call had a deep, resonant tone. There was authority in that voice.

"This can't wait. I'm working too. I'll need you to monitor the police traffic tonight. I'm paying a visit to a friend and I don't wish to be disturbed," said Kane.

Kane listened closely for any hint of resistance, or reluctance. Both men knew the reality of this relationship. It was not a partnership, or collective. The power lay with Kane. It always had, and it always would.

The man said nothing for a moment. Even that small, silent delay began to irritate Kane.

"Do we need to have a conversation?" asked Kane.

"No, we do not. I'll listen in. Where are you planning on visiting?" said the voice.

"Here and there, I'll send a text with a location later," said Kane, and disconnected the call.

Kane was careful. He weighed the risks for every move. Even so, sometimes life threw Kane some curveballs. Roadblocks along the road to his destination. Most he could deal with himself, but occasionally Kane needed help from someone who could access databases or gather information that would be unavailable to most ordinary citizens. Such men were always useful, and this man had proven himself.

They were not friends. Kane and the man were beyond such relationships. When they talked, the man pretended to share Kane's beliefs, and professed his devotion to Kane's mission. Kane knew this to be a lie. The man did not care for Kane's ideology, he only cared about his methods: the simple act of killing, and all the pleasures that came with it.

"I don't want any secrets between us. Same goes for you, Rudy . . ." said Solomon. Kane heard it clear as day, over the mic. He put aside his phone and focused on the conference room. Carp sat with his back to the window. He couldn't see the lawyer's face. Flynn sat to the right of Carp, but was facing away from the window too, looking toward Bobby Solomon. Kane leaned forward and listened.

CHAPTER NINE

There's no such thing as a bad case. Only a bad client. Judge Harry Ford, my mentor, had taught me that a long time ago. He'd been proven right. Time and time again. Sitting in a leather chair beside Bobby Solomon, I was reminded of Harry's advice.

"Ariella and I had a fight the night she was killed. That's why I left the house that night and went on a bender. I . . . I . . . just wanted you to know this. In case it comes up. We fought, but Jesus H. Christ I didn't kill her. I loved her," said Bobby.

"What was the fight about?" I said.

"Ari wanted me to sign the contract for Season Two of *The Solomons*, our reality show. I'd hated having the cameras follow us around, it was just . . . too much. You know? I couldn't do it. We had an argument. Not physical, it was *never* physical. I wouldn't have laid a hand on her. But it was loud, and she was upset. I told her I wouldn't do it. Then I left," said Bobby.

He sat back in his chair, blew out his cheeks and put both hands on top of his head. He looked like a man relieved to get something off his chest. Then the tears came. I studied him closely. The look on his face spoke one word – guilt. Whether it was guilt that his last words with his wife were harsh, or guilt for something else – I couldn't exactly tell.

Rudy got up, held open his arms and gestured for Bobby to give him a hug.

Both men embraced. I could hear Rudy whispering, "I understand, I understand. Okay? Don't worry. I'm glad you told me. It's going to be alright."

When the two men finally let go, I saw Bobby's eyes glistening. He sniffed, wiped his face.

46

"Okay, I think that's all I got. For tonight," said Bobby. He looked down at me, held out a hand and said, "Thank you, for listening. I'm sorry I got emotional. Look, I'm in a tight spot. I'm glad you're gonna help me."

I stood for the handshake. It was surprisingly firm this time. I held on and took a moment to study Bobby up close. His head was still tilted toward the ground. I felt the nerves sending tremors into his hands. Despite the bodyguards, the fancy clothes, the manicures and the money, Bobby Solomon was a scared kid with the prospect of life in jail hanging over his head. I liked him. I believed him. And yet a thread of doubt still dangled there. Maybe this was all an act. A convincer, for me. The kid had a talent. Of that there was no doubt. Did he have enough acting talent to fool me?

"I promise I'll do my best," I said.

He placed his left hand on the top of my wrist and gripped my hand tightly with his right.

"Thank you. That's all I can ask for," he said.

"Thanks, Bobby. That'll be enough for tonight. I'll see you at court in the morning for jury selection. Car will be outside your hotel at eight fifteen. Go get some sleep," said Rudy.

And with that, Bobby waved at us, and left the office. He was immediately enveloped in a cocoon of bodyguards – they were taking no chances. They marched him out of the office in a phalanx of long, cashmere overcoats.

I turned to Rudy. We took our seats.

"So how long had you known Bobby and Ariella were arguing about their reality show?" I asked.

"Since day one," said Rudy. "I figured the client would open up sometime. Seems you have quite the effect on Bobby. He opened up to you straight away."

I nodded, said, "It was good of you to act the part. Let him feel like he'd gotten something off his chest. That'll boost his confidence."

Rudy's face darkened, he gazed at the desk, clasped his fingers together. After a moment, he raised his head, took the laptop from the desk and handed it to me.

"The evidence against Bobby is overwhelming. There's a chance. A slim chance. And I'll do whatever is necessary to make those odds more favorable. Look at the evidence tonight. You'll see what we're up against."

I took the laptop from him, opened it up.

"It would take something extraordinary to kill two people in cold blood. Especially your wife and a man you knew well. It's rare for someone with no history of violence to go off the deep end like that. Any history of psychological problems with Bobby? If there's nothing violent in his medical history it might be worthwhile showing those records to the prosecution," I said.

"We're not using his records," said Rudy, flatly. He pushed a button on the telephone and said, "I need secure transport."

I detected something in Rudy's voice. Either he didn't welcome my views on that part of the case, or he was hiding something. Whatever it was, I guessed it wasn't too important or the prosecution would've found it and used it. I let it go, for now.

The home screen on the laptop asked for a password. Rudy wrote something on a Post-it note, handed it to me.

"This is the password. We're going to make sure you return to your office safely with this. So I'm going to ask a member of our security team to accompany you, if you don't mind."

I thought of the freezing temperature outside and the walk back to my office.

"Does the security guy come with a car?" I said.

"Sure does."

I looked at the note. The password read, "NotGuilty1"

Closing the lid of the computer, I stood up, shook hands with Rudy.

"I'm glad you're officially on board," he said.

"I said I'd look at the case files before I decided," I said.

Rudy shook his head, "No. You told Bobby you'd help him. You promised to do your best. You're in. You believe him, don't you?"

There didn't seem much point in hiding it. "Yeah, I guess I do."

But I've been wrong before, I thought.

"You're just like me. You can tell when you've got an innocent client on your hands. You just feel it. Never met anyone else who could do that. Until tonight," said Rudy.

48

"I'm not Bobby Solomon, Rudy. You don't need to kiss my ass. I know you brought him in here because you wanted me to meet him. You wanted me to look him in the eye. Test him. Make that call. You knew I would believe him. You played me. And while I don't think he's a murderer, I can't be sure he's not playing us both."

He held up his hands, "Guilty as charged. Doesn't change the fact that we have the nightmare scenario, here: an innocent man. Yeah, he can act. But you can't act your way out of a double murder."

The office doors opened. The man who entered the room needed both doors ajar and still he had to shuffle in sideways. He looked around my height. Bald. Broad as the frickin' conference table. Black pants and black jacket buttoned to the neck. He crossed his arms in front, clasped his hands together. I figured he was older than me by five or six years, and he'd been a fighter. His knuckles stood out like gumballs.

"This is Holten. He'll be making sure the laptop, and you, are safe," said Rudy. He bent low, retrieved an aluminum briefcase from below the desk and placed it on top. Holten approached, we exchanged a polite greeting and he went straight to the case. He opened the catches, flipped up the lid and placed the laptop inside a molded recess. I watched Holten close the case, lock it, and take a pair of handcuffs from his coat pocket. He secured his wrist to the handle of the briefcase, picked it up and said, "Let's go."

I thanked Rudy, and was on my way out the door with Holten when Rudy gave me one last piece of advice. "When you read the files, remember what happened in here tonight. Remember how you felt. Remember that you know this young man is innocent. We need to make sure he stays that way."

CHAPTER TEN

Kane had killed the connection on the listening device just after he heard Robert Solomon make his confession. He locked up the station wagon, and transferred to the gray Ford sedan. He sat in the driver's seat, facing the exit ramp to the parking garage. From this vantage point, he could see enough of the street below to spot the big, black SUVs that Carp Law used to move their people.

The Ford's engine ticked over.

Without taking his eyes from the road ahead, Kane leaned over the passenger seat and opened the glove box. He lifted the Colt .45 from its resting place and slid the magazine clear. His fingers found the rounds clipped into the mag. A soft slap echoed in the car as Kane returned the mag to the receiver. Followed by a metallic click from the mechanism as he chambered the first round.

A red Corvette rolled by on the street ahead.

The Colt found a new home in the inside breast pocket of Kane's coat. The clock read seven fifteen.

Any minute now, thought Kane.

He put on a pair of tight-fitting leather gloves. Kane loved the smell of leather. It reminded him of a woman he'd once known. She had regularly worn a black leather biker jacket, white tee and blue jeans. Kane remembered the tight curls in her black hair; her pale skin; the way she snorted when she laughed; the taste of her lips. Most of all, he remembered the biker jacket. That overpowering smell. And the way blood seemed to sit on top of the leather before being gradually absorbed, as if the jacket had been taking a long, slow drink.

Kane gripped the steering wheel.

He listened to the rub of leather on leather – glove on steering wheel. He thought about the sound that had come from the girl's biker jacket

50

as she'd flailed her arms, trying, pathetically, to fight him off. She didn't scream. Not once. Her mouth had opened, but no sound came from her throat. It was only the zip on the biker jacket, jingling, and the sound of leather whipping leather as she had flung her arms at him. It had occurred to Kane that this sound could almost have been a whisper.

The noise of tires squeaking on painted, poured concrete. The sweep of headlights. Kane looked toward the sound and the lights and saw a pick-up truck descending the ramp from the floor above. He didn't want the truck obstructing his line of vision. Kane pulled out and moved to the exit ramp. Stopped. The camera read his license plate. The barrier began to lift. Kane eased the Ford forward.

As he approached the street a black SUV passed him, pulled up outside the Condé Nast building. Kane looked to his right. Looked left. Traffic was clear. He pulled out as slow as he could without drawing attention. There was enough space to drive by the parked SUV, but Kane didn't want that. He rolled up behind it and saw, to his relief, Flynn and the Carp Law security goon exiting the building and heading toward the vehicle. Studying the pair, Kane got the feeling the lawyer was just as much of a physical threat as the guard. It was too dark to make out their faces, but he watched the way they moved. There were that many security men protecting Bobby, it was hard to tell which one it was – they all looked pretty similar. While the guard was squat, broad and muscular – he moved stiffly. It was difficult to tell the guards apart – they were all built like this and moved in the same way. Flynn, on the other hand, moved like a dancer. Or a boxer. Always in good balance. Confident. He was tall, fit. A man who used to work out when he was younger. Flynn carried himself like a fighter.

The guard had one of those briefcases. A laptop case. The firm were tight-assed about their laptop security. No way to hack it remotely, no way to get access to it without using one of their lawyer's individual passwords which changed daily. If he had time with the laptop he could hack it, but he needed to get one first. Without the firm knowing it. Kane had methods, contacts and ways in to the Carp Law building. None could get him the time he needed with the laptop without raising suspicion. And it was impossible to get one of the laptops out of the office with every inch of desk space covered by security cameras. He wanted one of those computers. They contained the Solomon case.

The thought of possessing the files sent prickles of electricity over Kane's skin. The hairs on his neck stood up. Kane let out a tremulous breath. The lawyer and the guard got into the vehicle, and pulled out into the lane.

Kane let out the clutch, and followed.

In this part of Manhattan, at this time, traffic was reduced to a slow crawl. The pace suited Kane. He wanted that briefcase.

A smartphone, unregistered of course, sat in a dock to the right of the steering wheel. Kane accessed Google, and searched for "Eddie Flynn, attorney." To his surprise, the first pages were news articles. Past cases of Flynn's. Scanning each article, Kane decided that Flynn was a considerable threat in the courtroom. This man was dangerous. He flicked past a number of screens which seemed to carry the same stories as before, only reposted on different blogs and media sites. There was no website for Eddie Flynn's firm. Only thing Kane found was an address and a phone number in the Yellow Pages website.

Sure enough, twenty minutes later the SUV pulled up on the right, outside an address on West 46th Street. The same address Kane had found on the internet. Kane pulled in to a space on the left, killed the engine. Grabbing his phone from the port, he put it in his jacket, got out of the car and popped the trunk. He looked around first, making sure there was no one else behind him on the street. It was clear. Beneath a blanket in the trunk, Kane found a set of kitchen knives which he'd had specially made. He selected a filleting knife and a cleaver. Both were in leather protective covers. A backpack sat open and ready beside the blanket. Kane placed both knives in the pack, zipped it up and threw it on his back. When the men were dead, Kane still needed the briefcase. He'd learned, many years ago, that the easiest and quickest way to sever a limb had more to do with skilled butchery than brute force. If he hammered on the dead guard's wrist with the cleaver, it would likely take between five and ten blows to sever the hand. Most of the impact would be absorbed by the muscles and sinew within the wrist. This method would likely take thirty seconds. Instead, Kane planned to take five seconds to run the filleting knife through the muscles and flesh of the wrist, exposing the bone. A single blow from the three-pound cleaver would then complete the job. Estimated time would be fifteen to seventeen seconds.

Kane pulled down his ball cap over his face, closed the trunk and crossed the street.

The security guard with the briefcase chained to his wrist had already exited the vehicle. He stood with his back to Kane, on the street, his hand outstretched to open the rear passenger door. The nearest streetlight didn't penetrate far enough for Kane to get a good look at the guard. Fifty feet between Kane and his target. The door of the SUV opened and Flynn stepped out. He recognized him by the way he moved. Kane reached into his jacket, put his right hand around the pistol grip and placed a light pressure on the trigger.

Forty feet. And Flynn was buttoning his coat, ready to take the steps to his office.

Kane heard a car door slam just ahead of him. He tensed. An older black man in a navy suit walked around the hood of a low, dark green convertible and stepped onto the sidewalk just a few feet in front of Kane and into the glow from a street lamp. He was walking in the same direction, headed toward Flynn's office. Kane couldn't see his face. Just the gray hair on the back of his head.

Kane was about to pull the weapon, and push the man out of the way, when that same man held up his hand and called out.

"Hey, Eddie!"

Flynn turned in Kane's direction. So did the security guard. Both men were on the steps, in an elevated position. Kane dipped his head. He could see their torsos beneath the brim of this cap, but he couldn't see their faces. He didn't want to risk eye contact. Last thing he needed was to be recognized. As the guard turned he whipped aside his coat and gripped a sidearm. The guard and Flynn were both facing in Kane's direction.

He'd lost the element of surprise. If Kane pulled the weapon, he would be seen doing it. In that instance, given average reaction times, it was likely the security guard would get at least a couple of shots off. The guard would have to be the first target.

Kane's boots beat on paving flags. His heart thrashed out a faster rhythm. Blood pounded in his ears. He could almost taste the acrid residue left in the air from gunfire. A delicious chill swept up his spine. This is it. This is what Kane lived for. The glorious anticipation. In one fluid movement, he let out a breath, raised his elbow, and swiftly pulled his right hand from his jacket.

CHAPTER ELEVEN

I'd taken the third step at the entrance to my building when I heard someone call my name on the street. Instantly, I felt Holten tense. He hadn't spoken at all on the drive over, other than to ask me if I was comfortable. He'd given polite, but monosyllabic answers to my small talk. Was Rudy Carp a good boss? Yes, Holten was a private contractor but Carp was easy to work with. Had he worked with the firm for long? Yep. Was he a baseball fan? Nope. Football? Nope. I gave up, figured he was watching the road and I shouldn't distract him. Standing on the steps leading to my front door, I was surprised when he reacted protectively. He didn't do anything, not really. But he just became ready. Ready for anything. I pivoted in the direction I'd heard the call and saw Judge Harry Ford waving at me from the sidewalk. His old, classic convertible was parked up on the street.

I was about to give Harry a wave back when I saw the guy behind him. He wore a ball cap, low over his brow. In the glare from the streetlights, I couldn't see his face. The brim of the cap covered his features. Right then, his face didn't seem that important. I was more interested in his right hand. It was jammed into his inside coat pocket, like he was ready to pull a gun.

In the corner of my eye, I became aware that Holten had clocked the same guy and had placed his palm on his sidearm, slung on his waist. My mouth felt dry and I found that I couldn't take a deep breath. My body had frozen. Whatever basic, primal instincts that survived within me were focusing everything on the approaching man with his hand in his jacket. My body didn't need any distractions, like breathing or thinking. Every muscle and nerve ending suddenly went on high alert. All of the energy my body used was now re-routed to full survival mode. I was glued to the spot. If that hand came out of the jacket with a gun, I was ready to dive for the floor.

The temperature was dropping. I could see fresh ice forming on the sidewalk, glistening in the sodium streetlamps like crushed crystal.

The man drew level with Harry, and whipped his right hand from this pocket. The man's right arm extended, pointed in our direction. There was something shiny and black in his hand. I heard the hollow, sucking pop of Holten's gun clearing its leather holster. As if some kind of internal switch had been activated, I took a massive lungful of air and dropped to my knees. My hands covered my head.

Silence. No gunshot. No muzzle flash. No bullets hitting the bricks over my head. I felt a big hand pat me on the shoulder.

"It's alright," said Holten.

I looked up. Harry was standing beside the man in the ball cap. Both of them were staring at the cell phone in the man's hand. Harry pointed at the cell phone, then pointed west, along 46th Street. The man nodded, said something to Harry and held up the phone. Even from this distance, I could see what looked like a map on the big screen of the smartphone. The man walked past my building, headed west.

"Jesus, Holten. You're gonna give me a heart attack," I said.

"Sorry," he said. "It pays to be careful."

"Eddie, what the hell are you doing?" said Harry.

I stood up, brushed down my coat and leaned over the railing.

"I'm being careful, apparently. What did that guy want?"

"Just a tourist. He wanted directions," said Harry.

I looked over my shoulder. The man had continued on his way, holding his smartphone up in front of him. He had his back to me. I watched him get further away, then swung back to Harry.

"We thought that guy had a gun. The way he was walking up. Kind of *determined*. You ever saw that guy before?" I said.

"Don't know. Didn't really see his face 'cause of the cap. Even if I did see his face, I wouldn't be able to tell you much – I don't have my glasses on," said Harry.

"So how did you drive over here?" I said.

"Carefully," said Harry.

Holten picked up one of my wooden chairs, walked out of my office and put it down beside the front door that led to the landing. He came back in, and gave my office another look over. From the couch, Harry stared up at Holten with the indifference of a man holding a glass of fine Scotch, and knowing exactly how fine it really was.

"There's no real security here, Mr. Flynn. I'll be outside for tonight. In the morning I'll arrange for a safe to be delivered to your office. The laptop is to be kept in this safe when you're not in. That okay with you?" said Holten.

"You mean you're gonna sit outside my office all night?"

"That's the plan."

"Well, you may have noticed the bed in back. I don't have an apartment. I sleep here. I'll probably work all night, so don't worry about it. Go home and get some sleep. I'll be fine."

"If it's all the same to you, I'll stay outside."

"There's a couch. If you're staying then you may as well be comfortable."

He took one look at the couch. Harry had fallen into the middle of it a few years ago and busted some of the springs. It sagged in the middle. As a constant reminder of that night, whenever Harry came over he sat on the far end of the couch, but the springs made him lean toward the middle and made it look as if he could fall into the center valley at any time. I got the impression Holten thought he might be more comfortable on a hard, wooden chair.

"I'm not much good as a security detail if I'm asleep on the couch when someone busts down your door for that laptop. I'll be outside. That okay?"

I looked at the briefcase on my desk, the handcuffs still attached to the handle.

"That's fine with me," I said.

"I'll leave you gentlemen to it," said Holten, as he closed the office door behind him.

"He's a little intense," said Harry.

"There's nothing little about that guy. All the same, I kind of like him. You can tell he's a professional," I said.

"So what's on the laptop that requires this kind of security?" said Harry.

"I could tell you, but you're going to get too drunk tonight to remember so it might be better if we had that conversation tomorrow."

"I'll drink to that," said Harry.

I poured myself two fingers of bourbon, and took a seat behind my desk. Just one drink. To take the edge off. I needed my head clear to read the case files. For now, I could at least relax a little. The lamp in the corner, and my desk lamp with the green, glass shade gave a warm glow to my little office. Leaning back in the chair, I threw a leg on my desk and put the glass to my lips. I could enjoy the odd drink with Harry now. I'd developed that discipline, but it had taken me long enough to do it. Harry had helped.

If it wasn't for Harry, I wouldn't be a lawyer. I got sued for causing a car accident years ago, and defended myself. An insurance scam gone wrong. Harry was the judge. I argued with the other guy's lawyer, won the case and Harry met me afterwards. Told me I should think about a career in the law. Sure enough, a law degree later and I was clerking for Harry while I sat the bar exam. He gave me a new life, away from the cons and hustles on the street. Now I did my shakedowns in the courtroom.

"How's the family?" said Harry.

"Amy is growing up fast. I miss her. Maybe things are looking better though? Christine called me, invited me to dinner," I said.

"That's good," said Harry, excitedly. "You think maybe you can patch things up?"

"I don't know. Christine and Amy are settled in Riverhead. Feels like their lives are moving on, without me. I need a job that won't put my head on the block. Something stable, something boring that won't get me or anyone else into trouble. That's what Christine wants. A normal life."

Even as I said it, I wasn't sure if it was still true. A stable, safe home was what we always wanted. My job prevented that, but now I doubted if Christine still wanted me in her life at all. There was a distance. I hoped the invite to dinner was my chance to get closer to her, again.

Harry sipped at his Scotch, rubbed his head.

"What's on your mind?" I said.

"That briefcase. The Butterbean lookalike sitting in your hallway. That's on my mind. If you're looking for more sedate work, this sure doesn't look like it. Tell me you're not in trouble."

"I'm not in trouble."

"Why do I think that's not the whole story," said Harry.

Swilling the amber liquid in the bell of the glass, I held it up to the light. Took another sip, then put the glass down on my desk.

"I met Rudy Carp today. He hired me to be part of Robert Solomon's defense team."

Harry stood up. Put the rest of the Scotch away and left the empty glass next to mine.

"In that case, I have to leave," said Harry.

"What? What's going on?"

He sighed, put his hands in his pants pockets and looked at the floor while he spoke.

"I guess you met him this morning. And you'd had no approach from Rudy Carp before that. No emails, or phone calls. Am I right?"

"Right. How did you know?"

"What did Rudy tell you about why you were being hired?"

"I kind of worked it out. I'm an expendable asset. I go after the cops. If it doesn't hit home with the jury, I get dropped by the defense team and they get to make like it never happened. I'm a buffer between Rudy and the jury. He gets to keep his reputation with the jurors if the play doesn't work out. It's not a great deal, but I want to help this guy, Bobby. I know he's a movie star, and all, but I like him. And I think he's innocent."

"I guess Rudy needed a story you'd buy. In a way, it's more convincing if you believe you're not getting a good deal. It explains why they hired you the day before jury selection."

It was my turn to get nervous. I sat up straight and gave Harry my full attention.

"Harry, stop messing around. Spit it out."

"Judge Collins called me Friday. Said she felt really strange. I wasn't surprised. For the past year she's been handling the trial prep for the Solomon case. There's already been a dozen evidential hearings, motions to dismiss, you name it. Two weeks ago she moved into a hotel so she could have space and peace to work. Rowena Collins, for all her faults, is a judge that doesn't mind hard work. Anyway, I thought it was stress. Case like that takes a toll."

Harry trailed off, lost in thought. I said nothing. He would tell me the rest when he'd gathered his thoughts.

"The hospital called me on Saturday morning. Rita had collapsed the night before, not long after we'd spoken. If it hadn't been for her regular room service delivery she might have died. A busboy found her on the floor. She was in respiratory failure. Thank God somebody found her when they did. Paramedics saved her life. She had some kind of cardiac episode and she's receiving intensive care. Critical, but stable. I saw her today. She's in bad shape.

"Apart from everything else, it put the Solomon trial in jeopardy. I didn't have anyone that could abandon their dockets for two weeks – so I stepped in. I'm the judge in the Solomon case."

CHAPTER TWELVE

Harry left my office pissed as all hell. He didn't like lawyers trying to game the system. The way Harry figured it, Rudy Carp was calling Harry's impartiality into question. There's no problem with lawyers and judges being friends. Judges don't drop their lawyer buddies soon as they get appointed to the bench. Lawyers and judges maintain friendships outside the courtroom, so do some prosecutors and defense attorneys. And when they find themselves in court together, they play by the rules. It's accepted. For one reason only. If they are on opposite sides, that relationship is stalled for the duration of the case. As long as I was part of Bobby Solomon's defense team, I couldn't drink or socialize with Harry. And that was what grated on him the most.

I took the laptop out of the briefcase, powered it up, and called Rudy Carp.

"Eddie, you couldn't have read the whole file already?" said Rudy.

"I haven't opened it yet. Just having a drink with my pal, Harry Ford."

Silence.

I waited for Rudy to say something. The only thing I heard was his breath on the line. Part of me wanted him to just admit it. Another part of me wanted him to stay silent, and squirm a little.

"Rudy, I should probably quit."

"No, no, no, no. Don't quit. Look, I had to hook you into the case somehow. And you're an excellent lawyer, Eddie. We wouldn't have you on the case if we didn't think you were good."

"How do I believe anything you say, now?"

"Look, what I told you is still true. We need somebody to go after the cops. You can do a great job working that angle. You've done it before. If you miss and hit the wall, we're still going to fire you to save face with the jury. If you happen to be best friends with the judge, well, maybe he won't be inclined to burn us for what you did. That wouldn't reflect too well on his pal, Eddie Flynn, now would it?"

It was smart. There are plenty of good lawyers in this town. Plenty with experience of roasting cops on the stand. Not many are best friends with Harry Ford.

"If you think Harry will give your client an easy ride because of me, you're mistaken."

"Don't worry, I'm not questioning the judge's character. He's not biased in our favor. I'm not saying that, but this strategy is risky. If the jury aren't buying it, Judge Ford won't let it reflect badly on our client, or you. That's all I'm saying. That doesn't make him biased, that makes him fair."

It was my turn to bite my tongue. I wanted to tell Rudy that I quit. That I would be sending the laptop right back with Holten. The laptop screen prompted me for a password. While I thought of what to say, I typed in "NotGuilty1" and the screen changed. An image of Bobby Solomon flashed up in front of me. Bobby and Ariella, in Christmas sweaters in their Brownstone, standing in front of a Christmas tree. The photo showed two young people who clearly did love each other. They held hands, and looked at one another. There was a promise in their gaze. A promise to each other. If I quit, I let Bobby down. For the wrong reasons.

"I don't like being used. You want me on the case, then the price just went up."

"I can see how this could make you angry, but we don't have an unlimited budget. Maybe we could sweeten the money a little, so there's no hard feelings. How about an extra twenty-five per cent?"

"How about a partnership at Carp Law? Junior partner. Full benefits. And I pick my cases. I don't need another bump of money to get me through the next six months. What I need is a steady job that doesn't put my head on the block."

"That's quite the ask," said Rudy.

"It's quite a case," I said.

He paused. I could hear him mumbling as he thought it over.

"How about a two-year contract as a senior associate? You bill your targets for two years, like every other senior associate, and we make you a junior partner. That's about the best I can do, Eddie," said Rudy.

"I'll take my original fee and the deal," I said. The fee would help, but I needed a job. Christine wanted me to have a regular gig that didn't get me or my family into trouble. That might go a long way to repairing our relationship, as well as providing a future.

"You got it," he said.

"Great, now what else haven't you told me about this case?"

"Nothing. I swear it. Read the file. And again, I'm sorry about the judge thing. It's not like I could've kept it a secret. You would've found out anyway, soon as you walked into court. Look, I think Bobby is innocent. I know it. I feel it. You know how rare that is for me? I would do anything to get this kid off. Read the file, and you'll see our case. Call me in the morning. I've got jury selection at nine."

He hung up.

I wondered then, exactly how far Rudy would be willing to go to save his client.

My fingers slid across the touchpad and brought up a selection of files on the home screen. No internet browser, no apps, nothing on this laptop apart from the files. There were five of them. Statements and Depositions. Photographic material. Forensics. Defense statements. Defense experts.

I grabbed a pencil off my desk, spun it around my fingers. It somehow allowed me to think better. It also kept my hands sharp. Before I was a lawyer, I'd worked all kinds of cons. Some required the ability to lift a wallet, a set of keys or a cell phone. My father always told me to keep my hands smart – which meant practice to maintain my reflexes and hand speed. So if I was thinking about something, it helped if I picked up a pen or a poker chip and ran it over my knuckles.

The first three files made up the prosecution case. The files marked "defense statements," and "defense experts" were made up of material generated by Carp Law. Most lawyers would go straight to the prosecution case, open up the statements and depositions and read every word. Each one is a story. An individual's recollections. Together they made up an overall narrative. This was the narrative the prosecution would try to feed to the jury.

The worst thing about narratives is that they're often unreliable.

My approach was a little different. The real story was in the photographs. Crime scene photos don't lie. They're not witnesses. They can't make a mistake, they can't hide the truth. And it made me imagine the prosecution's case. What kind of case would I build against Bobby Solomon if I were a prosecutor. In a murder trial it's not enough to know what your defense is going to be – you need to know what moves the DA is going to make, and plan for them.

The photos loaded on screen in a gallery view. Only the first one wasn't a photo. It was video. I hit play.

The screen turned black and for a moment I thought the video hadn't loaded properly. Then I saw that it was the security feed for a camera mounted outside somebody's front door. I could see the street below. A man in a hoodie and black jeans walked up the steps to the front door. Head down. No doubt his eyes were glued to the iPod screen he held in front of him. He flicked through some kind of list on the screen. A white cable led to earbuds. The man paused at the door, then when it opened he raised his head slightly. Enough for me to get a grainy view of a pale thin face and the beginnings of heavy, dark sunglasses. The man disappeared from view, presumably going inside.

The time stamp said 21:02.

Bobby Solomon on video getting home just after nine.

Switching off the video, I returned to the photographs. I could tell from the first image that somebody from the DA's office had attended the scene of the murders. The first batch of photos showed the front door. Smart.

It was an ordinary, thick, wood-paneled door. Painted dark green, recently. The photos had been taken that night, and the flash shone in the relatively fresh paint. A thick brass door knob sat in the center of the door. A close-up of the lock showed it to be in pristine condition. No chipping around the paint in this area. No damage to the lock. No damage to the door at all.

With two people lying butchered in the room upstairs, taking photos of a perfectly ordinary front door wouldn't be too high on the NYPD priority list. They want to catch a killer. Every minute they spend at the scene is designed to do just that. The DA's office has a different mindset. They want to make sure that when the killer is caught, they get convicted. Part of that process is anticipating a potential line of defense – that an intruder murdered Ariella Bloom and Carl Tozer – and cutting it off at the source.

No damage to the front door or lock.

I brought up the next set of photos. This is the beginning of the story. A series of shots taken of the hallway, living rooms, kitchen, the upstairs bathrooms, the spare bedrooms, every room in the house that didn't have two dead bodies in it.

The décor looked to be the same throughout the property. Modern. Minimalist. Everything in shades of white, gray, or beige. Only the odd splash of color here and there. A purple cushion on a taupe couch. A red, abstract canvas on the kitchen wall and an impressionist seascape in shades of muted blue hung on the living-room wall above a white fireplace. Everything looked impeccably clean and tidy. It looked like a house bought straight out of a catalog. There was no stamp on it. Nothing to say two young people lived there. Maybe they didn't get to spend too much time in the place given their professions.

Ten minutes of looking through the pictures cleared up a few questions. There was a back door. It was locked, with the key still in the deadbolt on the inside. On the outside of the back door was an ornamental metal grille. Padlocked. No signs of damage to either door.

The carpets were almost white. It looked like a fine covering of day-old snow on the floor. Soft. Fluffy. The kind of place where you take off your shoes at the door. The whole house was covered in this carpet. One drop of blood would be easy to spot. There were none.

The only photo that really stood out was the second-floor landing. A table was overturned and a broken vase lay on the floor. The table had sat beneath a large window, with ornate coving around it. People paid dearly for original features on a property like this. The next photo was the first of more than two dozen showing the murder scene. A violent death tells its own story. It's written on the victims. In their wounds. On their skin. Sometimes, in their eyes.

I'd never seen anything like this.

The NYPD crime scene photographer had taken the first shot standing at the foot of the bed. Ariella lay face-up on the left side of the bed, closest to the window facing the street. Carl lay beside her, on the right. The duvet was piled on the floor, beside Carl. Ariella wore pants, but nothing else. Her arms were by her sides, feet together. Mouth open. Eyes open. Her torso was red. A small pool of blood had formed in her belly button. I could see darker blotches dotted all over her chest. Stab wounds. The sheet beneath her was red too. Only spots of blood on her neck. No staining on her face, or her legs.

Carl lay on his right side, naked, facing Ariella. His legs were bent at the knee and his torso curled forward. From this angle his body lay almost in the shape of a swan. Far as I could see, there wasn't a single mark on him. No stab wounds. No bruising. He looked peaceful. As if he'd just curled up beside her and died. It wasn't until I saw a photo of his back that I saw the cause of death. The back of his head had been caved in. There was little blood, a dark red stain below his head, but from the shape of the wound a single blow had likely killed him. That probably accounted for his body position; legs curled up, in almost a fetal position, and head pointed down from the force of the blow.

Criminal defense attorneys, like cops, get used to looking at the horrific finality of life, the violence that we write on each other's bodies. It's human nature. If you do something often enough, it ceases to hold the same meaning, it ceases to have the same impact as it did the first time.

I had never gotten used to looking at violent death. I prayed I never would, because that part of me would die and never return. And I needed it. I welcomed that pain. A man and a woman had been ripped from this world – everything they had in life and everything that they would ever become had been taken from them. One word rolled around in my head. Innocent. Innocent. Innocent. They did nothing to deserve this.

Snap.

I looked at my hand and found I'd stopped twirling the pencil. I'd been gripping it so tightly I'd snapped it in two without realizing.

Whatever else my job entailed, I owed a duty to Ariella and Carl. Whoever had visited this hell upon them had to be punished. If that person was Bobby, then he had to be dealt with by the law. Somehow, looking at the victims, I became even more doubtful that Bobby was capable of such a thing.

Then I remembered. Deep down, we're all capable.

The causes of death, from what I'd seen, didn't fit exactly with what the media were reporting. The newspapers and TV were saying both victims were hacked to pieces in some kind of jealous, frenzied attack. That wasn't what I saw in the photos. And no stab wounds on Carl. Scrolling through a further set of photos led me to a close-up of a baseball bat on the bedroom floor. The business end of the bat looked as though it had been responsible for Carl's head injury.

Playing it through in my mind, what I'd seen didn't quite fit somehow. The killer had access to the house. He snuck in, or walked in with the keys, went up to the bedroom and found Ariella and Carl in bed. Carl would the first victim. It made sense to take out the biggest threat first. Delivering a wooden bat to the head with enough force to break the skull is going to make noise. A lot of noise. There would be no way to muffle that sound without lessening the impact damage of the blow itself. And yet Ariella had no defensive wounds. No cuts or bruises on her arms or hands. It appeared as though the first or second stab wound must've been fatal. Or at least severe enough to render her immobile.

Something was off about this scene.

Before I finished with the photo files, there were just two more collections. One had shots of Bobby Solomon. He was dressed in a red hooded top, white tee, and black track pants. The sleeves of the hooded sweatshirt had blood on them. His hands too. No blood anywhere else.

The last set of photos worried me. They were taken in the morgue. Carl Tozer lay naked on the steel table. I saw, for the first time, a thin purple bruise about three inches long across his throat.

Like he'd been hit with a thin metal rod, or something had been briefly strung around his throat and tugged hard. But that wasn't what worried me. The bruising didn't cause death, and may have been lividity; blood pooling in the fat around his neck as the heart stopped pumping.

No, it was the next set of images that worried me. The series of photos closed in on his mouth.

There was something under his tongue.

The photographer had switched to video to capture this last twist. I hit play. I watched a long set of metal tweezers entering Carl's mouth. When they came back out again they held something in their jaws that at first I didn't recognize. Whatever it was, it landed in a petri dish, and another set of tweezers worked on it. It looked like a note, folded in half with a small cone attached to it. The cone looked to be around the same size as the top of a pen. Both sets of tweezers worked on the note, unfolding it and the camera zoomed in.

This hadn't been in the papers. No way.

It wasn't a note. It was a bill. A one-dollar bill – folded many, many times. On the reverse side of a buck is the great seal of the United States. And in each corner of the bill is a figure "1" which sits behind the word "ONE". This representation sits on what looks like a spider's web. This bill had been folded in such a way that each corner looked like a pattern, or marking on a wing. Four wings spreading out from the central cone shape. Only the cone was the intricate fold of the center of the bill. It had been shaped to look like a thorax, and below, an abdomen. Spreading out from the thorax, on each side, was a forewing and a hindwing.

The killer had folded a one-dollar bill to look like a butterfly and put it in Carl Tozer's mouth.

CHAPTER THIRTEEN

After the aborted attempt for the briefcase, Kane circled the block. By the time he got back to his car his breathing had returned to normal. His hands no longer felt heavy. His pulse had ceased to throb in his fingertips. He threw his backpack on the passenger seat and waited.

Twenty minutes passed before he saw the man in the well-cut suit leaving Flynn's apartment. Kane watched him get into his convertible and drive away. The pulse returned to his fingers and he was suddenly very aware of the handgun in his jacket pocket. Just the guard, and Flynn. That guard would be watchful, now. Only at the last second, had Kane decided not to pull the gun on the men in the street. He'd waited too long before drawing the weapon. The guard had beaten him to it. Instead he'd drawn out his cell phone, and asked for directions. A good thing too, thought Kane. The guard would've shot him first.

The thought of that laptop, sitting in Flynn's apartment, made Kane grind his teeth. Kane looked at the building again. No telling what kind of security cameras were in place on the inside, or how many occupants there were. Maybe there was a doorman on a desk.

The engine coughed into life, struggling against the low temperature. Kane put the car in gear, slowly rolled out of West 46th Street.

Another time. When he was ready. Kane promised himself he would return.

For now, he had other business.

He headed east, toward the river. Rode 46th Street all the way to Second Avenue and then the FDR. The traffic was still heavy, and he made slow progress. Kane was not a native New Yorker. Not by any means. Even so, he barely looked at his satnav. Manhattan had been laid out on a grid. You land in Manhattan for the first time, spend five minutes with a map, and you knew your way around. From a map, the island looked like a circuit board. It only needed power to run. Kane thought that it wasn't the people, the inhabitants of Manhattan, who provided electricity needed to run that circuit-board city. It wasn't cars, either. Nor trains.

It was money.

Manhattan ran on green.

While stopped in traffic, he checked his reflection in the rear-view mirror. His nose had ballooned nicely. Perhaps too much. It made the rest of his face quite puffy. He made a mental note to ice his face later and bring the swelling down just a little. Plus, he would need to use more make-up. The bruising was beginning to show through the thin layer on his skin.

Anyone else would be in agony. Not Kane. He was special. That's what his mother told him.

He did not know his own body. There was a distance.

When he was eight years old, Kane discovered he was not like everyone else. A fall from an apple tree in the garden. A bad fall. He'd climbed high, and fell to the ground from the topmost branches of the tree. He did not cry as he lay on the grass. He never cried. After a moment, he got back up and was about to climb the tree again when he found that he couldn't hold on to a branch with his left hand. His wrist looked swollen. This was unusual and he went inside the kitchen to ask his mother why his wrist looked funny. By the time he'd made it to the house, his wrist had tripled in size and it looked as though someone had popped a table-tennis ball under his skin. Even to this day, Kane could remember the way his mother's face had twisted when she looked at his wrist. She dialed for an ambulance and eventually, sick of waiting, she wrapped two bags of frozen peas around his wrist, put Kane in the old car and drove him to the ER.

His mother had never driven so fast.

Kane recalled that drive precisely. The Stones were playing on the radio, his mother's face shone with tears. Panic drove her voice high and wild.

"It's okay, it's okay. Don't panic. We're gonna get you fixed right up. Does it hurt, honey?" she'd said.

"No," said Kane.

At the hospital the X-ray confirmed multiple fractures. The wrist required manipulation before a cast could be applied. The doctor had explained the urgency, and said they would do their best to relieve the pain of the procedure with gas and air. Little Joshua wouldn't inhale the strange-smelling stuff coming from the tube and ripped off his mask more than once.

During the procedure he did not cry out. He kept perfectly still and listened with dumb fascination to the muted rattle of his shattered bones as the doc pulled and pushed at his wrist. A nurse put a sticker on his T-shirt that said he was a brave patient. He told her he didn't need any medicine. He was fine.

Initially medical staff put it down to shock, but Kane's mother knew there was more to it. This was different. She pushed the hospital to test her son. To this day, he didn't know where she'd gotten the money to pay for the tests. At first the doctors thought there was something wrong with his brain. He didn't cry out when they pricked his skin with needles. He'd heard the word *"tumor"* but didn't know what it meant. Soon, they ruled out a growth on his brain. That made Kane's mother very happy, but still she worried and there were more tests to be done.

A year later Joshua Kane was diagnosed with a rare genetic condition; congenital analgesia. The pain receptors in his brain didn't function at all. Little Joshua had never felt pain, and never would. Sitting in the doctor's office, Kane recalled how his mother received the news with a mixture of happiness and fear. Happy that her son would never know physical pain, but nonetheless afraid. Kane could see his mother sitting in that chair in the doc's office, looking at him. She'd worn the same blue dress that she'd been wearing when he fell from the tree. The same fearful look lit a fire in her eyes.

And Kane had enjoyed every second of it.

He heard a car horn behind him, urging him forward, bringing his thoughts back to the present. An hour later Kane was in Brooklyn. He turned off the engine, got out of the car and texted his location to his contact.

Any calls to the NYPD and Kane and would get an early warning.

He made his way past rows of identical, middle-class, three-story suburban homes. The living space located on the first floor, above the garage. Fresh paint hiding the rust on the surrounding fences. He reached the house belonging to a man called Wally Cook.

Wally's face had appeared on the board in Carp Law as their number one pick for the jury more times than anyone else. He was a card-carrying liberal, donated profits from his Private Investigator business to the ACLU, and coached Little League at the weekends.

Kane couldn't rely on the prosecution objecting to Wally being on the jury, and it was too damn dangerous to leave him on the list. Plus, he was taking up a space that would allow Kane to fall into the defense picks.

A car and a van were parked in the driveway of Wally's house. Light shone in the first-floor window. A woman in her thirties with long brown hair was walking the floor with a baby in her arms. Wally approached them, kissed the woman and disappeared out of view. Kane unsheathed his filleting knife and made his way to the front door.

CHAPTER FOURTEEN

I waded through the rest of the files in the Solomon case in less than two hours. A lot of it I could skip through on a quick scan. Grounding statements from police officers confirming chain of custody, lengthy forensic reports, witness depositions. There were several key pieces of evidence.

The 911 emergency call from Bobby Solomon, made at 00:03. Not only did I have a transcript but an audio recording. Bobby sounded in a blind panic, choking on tears, rage, fear and his own colossal loss. It was all there in his voice.

Despatcher: 911 emergency, do you need fire, police or medical assistance?
Solomon: Help . . . Jesus . . . I'm at 275 West 88ᵗʰ Street. My wife . . . I think she's dead. Somebody . . . Oh God . . . somebody killed them.
Despatcher: I'm sending police officers and paramedics. Calm down sir, are you in any danger?
Solomon: I . . . I . . . don't know.
Despatcher: Are you in the property right now?
Solomon: Yeah, I . . . I . . . just found them. They're in the bedroom. They're dead.
(sounds of crying)
Despatcher: Sir? Sir? Take a deep breath, I need you tell me if you know of anyone else in the property right now.
(sounds of breaking glass and someone stumbling)
Solomon: I'm here. Ah, I haven't checked the house . . . Oh shit . . . please get the ambulance here right now. She's not breathing . . .
(Solomon drops phone)
Despatcher: Sir? Please pick up the phone. Sir? Sir?

*

Bobby told the police he'd been out drinking since that afternoon. He'd taken some pills too. Didn't remember where he'd been, but recalled visiting a few bars; he met a few people but didn't remember their names either. He took a cab outside of a nightclub and got home just before midnight. The light in the hall was out. Carl wasn't in the kitchen or living room. He went upstairs to find him. Saw Ariella's door open, and a lamp burning. He went in and found Ariella and Carl dead.

The call, Solomon's story, all seemed plausible at first. Bobby had a history of minor misdemeanors when he'd gone on a bender, and it wasn't unusual for him to have little or no memory of what he'd been up to while under the influence.

As alibis go, it was poor. But there was no reason to doubt Solomon's story.

Until I read the statement from Ken Eigerson. He lived at 277 West 88th Street. Ken is forty-three years old, and a hedge fund manager. Eigerson described getting home at nine p.m. that night, and saying "hi" to his famous next-door neighbor Bobby Solomon. He watched Bobby walk up the steps to his home. Eigerson knew the time, precisely, because his wife always works late on a Thursday night and the babysitter leaves at nine. Connie Brewkowski, the twenty-three-year-old au pair for the Eigersons confirmed she left their house when Eigerson returned home at nine.

I was thinking of ways to spin this. Some point of attack. And then I thought of the video. Security camera footage from outside the property. Date-stamped the night of the murder, and at nine p.m. it shows Solomon entering the property.

The camera is activated by a motion sensor. Nothing else is recorded until the cops showed up ten minutes after midnight.

No footage of Bobby coming home when he said he came home at midnight. Ariella and Carl are found dead by the NYPD when Bobby lets them in at ten after midnight.

The conclusion? Bobby Solomon was lying about what time he got home.

Forensics would seal Bobby's fate. Carl's blood on Bobby's baseball bat with Bobby's fingerprints on the bat. Ariella's blood on Bobby's clothes. And the cherry on top: the butterfly dollar bill in

Carl's mouth has Bobby's fingerprints and DNA on it. Bobby told the cops he'd never seen the butterfly bill before, and he certainly didn't fold it or put it in Carl's mouth.

Game over.

Rudy answered my call straight away.

"He's screwed," I said.

"I agree," said Rudy, "but you're not looking deep enough. NYPD forensics planted Bobby's DNA."

"What makes you so sure," I said.

"Because their tests showed up more than one DNA profile."

"Give me a sec," I said, and I opened up the forensics file. Sure enough, there was a report identifying the DNA profiles that had been successfully taken from the dollar. The DNA profiles were marked "A" and "B". The "A" profile was Bobby's DNA. Whereas the "B" profile matched an existing profile in the database for a man named Richard Pena.

"Hang on, Rudy. There's bound to be more than one DNA trace on any bill in circulation. I'm surprised they didn't find twenty DNA profiles on the bill. That doesn't mean NYPD planted Bobby's DNA."

"Yes it does. That profile match for Richard Pena proved DNA contamination at the lab," said Rudy.

"How?"

"We got some background discovery on Richard Pena. It's buried deep in the forensics. He was a convicted serial killer. Between 1998 and 1999 he murdered four women in North Carolina. The press called him The Chapel Hill Strangler. He got caught, convicted, and after his appeals went south, in double quick time, he was executed in 2001."

I didn't wait for Rudy to say any more. Instead I dragged up a picture of the dollar that had been taken after it was unfolded. First image that came up was the reverse of the bill. I noticed some small discoloration around the image of the American eagle, as if the bill had once been exposed to a pen, rattling around in a pocket. I didn't look too closely, I really wanted to see the other side of the dollar. I clicked again, this time I had what I was looking for. On the face of the bill, to the right of George Washington, was a series number. A new series number is only ever created on three occasions. The first is if a new design of the bill is being rolled out. The other reasons to run a new series are also linked to changes on the bills. Each bill has two signatures. One on either side of the picture of Washington. The first is the signature of the Treasurer of the United States, and the other is the signature of the Secretary of the Treasury. The signatures on the bill found in Carl's mouth were from Treasurer Rosa Gumataotoa Rios, and Secretary Jack Lew. The series number corresponded to the year Lew was appointed – 2013.

Rudy spelled it out for me.

"Richard Pena couldn't have touched that bill. At the time the bill was printed, Pena had been dead for twelve years, already."

"And no fingerprint for Pena, just DNA," I said.

"Right."

"If the only fingerprints on the note are from Bobby, and both Bobby and Pena's DNA are on the note . . . I'm thinking the forensic tech scrubbed the note before he planted Bobby's DNA and somehow he also planted Pena's at the same time, by mistake," I said.

"Now you're getting it. It's the only possible theory. DNA can be killed with exposure to household detergents. Easy to get rid of it. And how many hands had touched that bill since 2013? It's got to be in the hundreds, if not thousands. They messed up trying to frame Bobby. They wiped the bill, then messed up planting Bobby's DNA. Somehow Pena's got added in the lab. It's the only explanation. We've got them on this," said Rudy.

It made sense. Still, something troubled me. The butterfly was symbolic, in some way. It was important to someone. Probably the killer or the victim. And the police had exploited this piece of evidence. The NYPD had used it to frame Bobby, by planting his DNA on it, but they messed up.

"Pena's DNA would've been tested in another state. How did it get to the NYPD lab?"

"We don't know. But it did."

I listened to Rudy unload on the phone about police corruption, the media storm this evidence would create, and how this was the lynchpin of Bobby's defense. After thirty seconds I tuned out. In my mind, I was back at Carp Law. Sitting beside Bobby. Listening to him protest his innocence. In that moment, I wondered if I'd allowed myself to be convinced by Bobby. He was a talented actor. No doubt. Not all movie stars are great actors. Bobby was a craftsman, and he had the skills. Something else bothered me. In most cases, if a police force planted evidence against a suspect it was usually because they believed he was guilty. I couldn't see how anyone else could've gotten in and out of the house without being spotted on the motion-activated security camera. And there was the neighbor's testimony.

"Rudy, I bought Bobby's story. I can't lie to you or myself about that. I believed him when he told me he was innocent. I can't let anything else cloud that judgment. If it's alright with you I want to get started with my own investigator. We still don't have the knife used on Ariella. Tell me, what does Bobby say about the baseball bat used on Carl?"

"He said he kept the bat in the hallway. Sure, he had security but his old man always kept a bat beside the front door. Bobby has always done likewise. It's his bat, so that explains why his prints are all over it . . ."

"But not the blood. I need to look into this more," I said.

"Your fee's been wired to your account. If you want to blow some of that on investigation, be my guest. I'll be handling jury selection. Give me a call in the morning. And get some sleep," he said, and ended the call.

I scrolled through the contacts on my phone until I came to one labeled "Blow Me". I hit dial. I didn't check the time, the person I was calling was used to taking phone calls at all hours. Came with the job. The call connected. A female voice came on the line. Husky, a little Midwest twang in the accent.

"Eddie Flynn, con man at law. I've been wondering when you'd call me."

The voice belonged to a former FBI agent named Harper. She'd never told me her first name. Come to think of it, I couldn't be sure I'd ever asked for her first name. I'd met Harper a year ago, right before she'd quit the Bureau with her partner, Joe Washington. They'd set up a private security and investigations outfit in Manhattan and they were doing pretty good by all accounts. When we'd first met she'd slammed my head into the roof of my Mustang. A few months later we were chasing the same bad guy, and she'd saved not only my life, but the lives of her fellow agents. I could've looked into Bobby's case on my own, but I wanted Harper. She had good instincts. I trusted her judgment; if she thought Bobby was guilty I might think twice about things.

"Good to talk to you, too. Sorry I haven't been in touch, I've been waiting for the right case. I need an investigator. Know any good ones?"

"Blow me. Who's your client?"

I knew what was coming, before I'd even said it. I told her anyway.

"I'm on the defense team for Bobby Solomon. We're going to prove he was framed by the NYPD. You're going to help me."

She let out a burst of laughter and said, "That's a good one. Next you'll be telling me you're representing Charles Manson."

"I'm serious. A security guy from Carp Law will be at your apartment in the next hour with a laptop. He'll wait while you read the files. This is sensitive stuff. If any of this got out before the trial . . ."

Harper's laughter died in her throat.

"Eddie, come on. You serious?"

"I'm serious. Looks like we'll only have a day or two to get our heads around this thing. Read the file. Call me when you're done. We start in the morning at the murder scene. Unless you'd prefer me to take this someplace else?"

"I'll call when I'm done with the files. From what I've seen on TV, everything points to Solomon as the killer. You know that, right? This one looks like a loser."

"I've read all the newspapers too. Listened to all the legal experts on CNN. They think this trial is over before it starts. Maybe they're right. But I've talked to Bobby. So has Rudy Carp. We don't think he's a fit for these murders. All we've got to do is persuade twelve people that we're right."

CHAPTER FIFTEEN

With a flick of Kane's wrist, he'd reversed his grip on the knife. As he passed the van in the driveway he bent low and whipped the tip of the knife across the rear driver's side tire. The van lurched as the air hissed out of the rip in the tire wall. Kane pulled his cap way down, put the knife back in his pocket, walked up the few steps to the front door and rang the bell.

After a few moments, Wally answered the door. It was the first time Kane had gotten a good look at him. Up close, the man was probably in his late thirties. His hair was thinning around the temples and his face was flushed. Kane smelled wine on the man's breath, and the ruby staining above his top lip told him the man had just swallowed a large glass of red. Which explained the flush look to his otherwise hard face.

The man's face softened when he saw Kane. Whoever he might have been expecting, it wasn't anyone who matched Kane's current appearance.

Kane affected a southern accent. He often used it. Somehow, that southern drawl added credibility to whatever Kane said. It made people trust him.

"Sorry to bother you," said Kane. "I was passing by and I saw the tire on your van was just clean flat. Maybe you already knew that, but in case you didn't I just thought I'd do the neighborly thing."

Kane turned around. He'd been careful to shield his face by keeping his scarf high, and keeping his eyes low. It seemed to have done the trick.

"Oh . . . well, thank you," said Wally. "Ah, which tire did you say?"

"This one, I'll show you," said Kane.

Wally stepped out of the house, followed Kane to the rear of the van. He bent down on his haunches to get a look at the tire as

Kane stood beside him. There were no streetlights close by, and the light from the house didn't penetrate as far as the end of the drive.

"Jesus, something's ripped the goddamn shit out of this," said Wally.

He probed the hole with his fingers. It looked like a straight cut made by something hard and razor sharp. He was halfway to his feet when he said, "Hey, thanks for . . ." and froze. His knees were bent and his arms raised, palms open. He was staring at Kane's gun. Kane made sure Wally didn't miss this detail by pointing the weapon directly at his face.

When Kane spoke again, the warm southern honey had dissolved from his tongue as if it had never been there. Kane's voice became hard and flat.

"Don't speak. Don't move. When I tell you to, we're going to walk to my car. I'll ask you a few easy questions and if you answer them you get to go home. If you give me trouble, or you don't answer – then I'll have to ask your young wife a question."

Heavy breath misted in front of the barrel of the gun. Panicking, Wally's legs had begun to tremble and he couldn't take his eyes off Kane. He was looking at Kane's face, hidden in shadow. Kane imagined that the light which seemed to escape from his eyes was visible to the man in front of him and that's all he would be able to see – twin points of light in the darkness.

"Straighten up, let's go," said Kane. "Or do I have to ask your wife that question? It's a real simple one. Which would she be most upset about? Me shooting you in the face, or putting my knife in your baby's eye?"

The man straightened. His large Adam's apple bobbed up and down as he swallowed down his panic. Kane gestured for him to walk in front. Wally obliged.

"Turn right at the bottom of the drive, walk up the street and stand beside the passenger door of the station wagon. I'm five steps behind you. If you run, you die. So does the baby."

They walked in silence to the end of the street, Kane clutching the gun underneath his jacket. There was no one else on the street. Too damn cold and too damn late to be out walking. Wally turned right, and did as he was told. He stopped at the passenger door of Kane's car.

"What do you want from me?" said Wally, the fear raging through his chest like a drum.

Kane unlocked the vehicle and told Wally to get in slow. Both men slid into the car simultaneously, Kane now pointing the gun at Wally as he got into the driver's seat. Both men closed their doors. Wally stared straight ahead, shaking and puffing for air.

"Give me your cell phone," said Kane.

Wally's eyes moved down for a half a second. Kane spotted it. Wally had glanced at the gun Kane held in his left hand, low, across his belly, and pointed at Wally as he arched his back, so he could reach into his pants pocket.

"Slowly," said Kane.

Wally took a smartphone from his pocket, flicked his hand across the screen which lit up, but he was still shaking and he dropped the phone on the floor. He reached down. The station wagon's interior lights were off, so Kane could only see the light of the phone screen on the floor. The screen light was enough to let Kane see Wally's pant leg twitch. Kane stiffened and reached out but he was too late. Wally snapped bolt upright, and slammed a switchblade into the side of Kane's right leg. Kane grabbed Wally's wrist, even as Wally twisted the blade to start the blood flowing. But Kane's grip was too tight, he couldn't pull the knife free.

Kane smacked the barrel of the pistol off the top of Wally's head. Another blow, this time with the butt of the gun to the solar plexus. He let go the knife. Kane watched the man wheeze and struggle for breath. Most PIs carry some kind of back-up, and Kane had not thought to search Wally before putting him in the car. Kane placed the barrel of the gun to the side of Wally's head and looked down at the knife in his leg with a casual indifference.

"That's those pants ruined," said Kane.

"Wha – wha – what the hell is wrong with you man?" said Wally. He was holding the top of his head, pulling air into his chest in painful gulps and trying to make sense of the scene in front of him. Kane hadn't reacted to the knife in his leg. No grimace of pain. No scream. No grinding his teeth. Just total disinterest to a serious, painful wound.

"You're wondering why I'm not screaming? Give me your phone or I'll make you scream real loud," said Kane.

This time, he bent down real slow, retrieved the phone, and handed it over. Kane lowered the gun. Wally looked sideways at Kane, his hands up in front of his face, waiting for the pop from the pistol.

"Damn, I put a lot of effort into getting these pants to look right," said Kane. "Don't worry, I'm not going to shoot you," said Kane, tucking away the gun in his jacket. "But I'm going to have to keep your knife. Here, have mine."

Kane moved too fast for Wally to register. He still looked afraid, as if he was anticipating an attack. The hole in his skull from Kane's knife bubbled with blood. Kane turned over the engine, pushed Wally's head below the dash and took off. Kane switched on the headlights. When the dash lights went up they threw an orange glow on the chrome base of the blade that jutted from Kane's leg. He dared not remove the knife in case he bled out. He needed somewhere quiet to patch up and get rid of Wally's body.

Fifteen minutes later he'd found a commercial area. Transport yards, factories and garages. All closed up for the night, and some had been closed for years. Kane pulled into an open lot beside an abandoned factory and drove until he came to a wire fence at the back. No streetlights or security cameras. He got out of the car and switched the license plates. Normally he could do this in five minutes flat. Not this time. The blade in his thigh made it awkward to kneel, and he didn't have the strength in that leg. Kane wiped Wally's phone clean of any fingerprints, dropped it on the gravel lot. He pulled Wally's body out of the car, dumped him beside his phone. He had a jerry can of gas in the trunk. Dousing the body and the phone, he then lit the gas and watched for a few minutes. Looking around, there was no one and nothing to see until you hit the river. A body could lie there for a week or more, undiscovered. And when the cops did find it, it would take at least another week or so to ID it from dental records. More than enough time for Kane to have completed his work.

Would the cops even know that Wally had been due to undertake jury service? Maybe. When he didn't show tomorrow he would be put on a list to receive a subpoena to attend and explain why he didn't show up for jury duty. All that would take a few days at least, maybe more.

An hour later Kane pulled into his space at the parking garage opposite Carp Law. He waited for a few minutes for the motion-sensor lights to go out, throwing the floor into darkness. First he fetched a medic kit from the back seat and opened it. Using sharp scissors, he cut through his pants, exposing the blade buried hilt-deep in his thigh. Seeing a major injury on his body was always a moment of curiosity for Kane. He didn't feel a thing, but he knew there was probably deep muscle damage. When he'd changed the license plates, he'd limped, but he didn't know if this was simply because the knife was still in there. On the plus side, he knew there was no damage to any major arteries, or he would've bled out on the road back to Manhattan.

He knew he had to work fast. The engine was still ticking over. Kane killed the headlights and depressed the cigarette lighter on the dash.

Gauze and bandages at the ready, Kane pulled the knife. He stemmed the bleeding with the bandages. A steady flow of blood. He was glad. If there had been rhythmic jets of blood, in time with his heartbeat, he knew he would've had to get to a hospital. And that would raise questions.

The cigarette lighter popped.

For any normal person, what Kane did would have had them writhing, screaming, biting down on the agony before passing out. In Kane's case, all he had to do was concentrate and make sure he didn't lose his grip on the lighter as he plunged it deep into the wound. He held it there. When the bleeding stopped, Kane put the cigarette lighter back in its place and threaded a needle. He worked expertly. This wasn't the first time he'd stitched up his own skin. The sensation was the same. A pinched, tight feeling along the skin, but nothing uncomfortable. He bandaged up the wound with plenty of gauze and tape. He got out of the car, triggering the lights. Holding his jacket over his leg, Kane got into his second vehicle, stripped off the bloodied, ruined pants and put on a fresh pair of black jeans which he kept under the passenger seat along with a sweatshirt and a Knicks cap.

By the time Kane got back to the apartment he was tired. Undressing slowly, in front of the mirror, Kane examined his leg. There wasn't much blood. Hopefully, by tomorrow, the bleeding would have stopped.

He had a big day ahead of him.

TUESDAY

CHAPTER SIXTEEN

The Hot and Crusty bakery at the corner of West 88th Street and Broadway had good coffee and better pancakes. My car was still at the city auto pound, so I'd taken the subway early to beat the rush. That gave me some time for breakfast. I ate a stack of pancakes with crispy bacon on the side and put two cups of coffee away while I waited for Harper. Eight fifteen. And already there was a line of construction workers, office staff, and tourists waiting on their breakfast bagels.

I saw Holten before I saw Harper. He came in the front door, spotted me, and was halfway across the floor before Harper stepped out from behind him. It wasn't that Harper was small, it was more to do with Holten. You could stand him in front of a 1952 Buick and you wouldn't be able to see it. Harper was a little below average height, slim and fit, with her hair tied up in a ponytail. She wore jeans, lace-up boots and a leather jacket zipped up to the neck. Holten wore the same suit, and carried the same briefcase, chained to his wrist.

"I'm going on shift change at nine thirty. Yanni should be here by then. He'll look after the laptop till I come back on duty tonight," said Holten.

"Good morning to you, too," I said.

"Don't blame Holten, Eddie. He slept on my couch. You'd be grouchy too," said Harper.

"You mean he actually sleeps? I thought he just powered down and plugged himself into the socket to charge."

"Believe me," said Holten, "If Rudy Carp thought that was possible I would already have a power lead up my ass."

Holten had really warmed up. I guessed Harper was responsible. Both of them were ex-law enforcement. They had a lot in common.

Harper sat opposite me. Holten beside her. They both ordered bagels and I decided I hadn't quite had enough coffee.

"So you got permission from the DA for our little scouting mission?" said Harper.

"I did. Spoke to an assistant district attorney and he smoothed it over with the NYPD. There's been so much media interest the house has become some kind of weird shrine, for fans. The police commissioner had to authorize a special overtime roster just to keep a cop outside the front door twenty-four hours a day. Otherwise there'd be people all over the house, tearing it to pieces for souvenirs and taking pictures for the *Hollywood Reporter*. The cop on duty knows we're coming," I said.

Harper nodded, nudged Holten, who smiled back at her. I could tell Holten had the hots for Harper. He looked like a high school kid with that goofy smile.

"Told you it wouldn't be a problem getting inside. You should have more faith," said Harper. Holten held up his hands, acknowledging defeat.

I'd read the case papers. So had Harper. We were both experienced enough to know that no matter how many photographs we saw of the crime scene, there was nothing like being in that physical space. I needed a sense of the murder scene, the geography, the room layout. Plus I wanted to make sure Rudy and the cops hadn't missed anything.

"So what did you make of the case?" I said.

Instantly, Harper's face darkened. Her eyes shifted to the table and she cleared her throat.

"Let's put it this way, I'm not as convinced as you are. I think our client has too much explaining to do, and he hasn't done any of it yet," she said.

"You think he's lying about the murders?"

At that moment, their food arrived. We stayed quiet until the waitress was out of earshot. Then Harper said, "He's lying about something. Something important."

There was no conversation while they ate. Which didn't take long. Holten almost inhaled his bagel, and Harper ate like she was taking on fuel for a tough road ahead. Neither of them were tasting the food. I drank my coffee and waited.

Harper wiped her lips with a napkin and leaned back in her chair. There was something on her mind.

"I can't get the butterfly out of my mind," she said.

"I know, Bobby's fingerprint and the two sets of DNA. Rudy thinks the cops planted the DNA evidence. I think he might be right."

She nodded along with Holten and said, "Yeah, not sure how NYPD got Pena's DNA in the lab. That's a tough one. But I was more concerned about the butterfly itself. I tried to make one last night. Dollar origami is a *thing*, apparently. There are instructional videos on YouTube. I sat for forty-five minutes while I took a break from the files. I couldn't do it. Whoever did this took time to make that thing. And they did it before the murder. It's a cold-ass thing to do, messing with a dead body. Sends a statement."

"I'd considered that. I don't know how the DA will spin the significance of the butterfly, but I guess they'll say it shows Bobby didn't kill Carl and Ariella in a jealous rage. Like you said, it's a cold act. It shows intention, and premeditation," I said.

"It's a really weird thing to do. It's almost ritualistic. Like it's more to do with the killer than the victim. Maybe I'm reading too much into it, but I made a call to a buddy of mine in the Bureau at Behavioral Sciences. He's gonna check the database. FBI keeps a log on ritualistic murders. There's a team there that search for patterns of behavior. Maybe it's similar to someone else's MO," said Harper.

Holten counted out some bills, spreading them between his fingers. He had the laptop case in his lap, the long chain jingling as he moved the cash.

"Rudy already tried that. A whole team of us spent days chasing down blind alleys looking for a similar MO. The FBI wouldn't talk to us so we did our own research through news reports and PD contacts. We got nothing. Maybe you might get lucky with your pal," said Holten.

The waitress cleared the plates away and left the check.

"I'll get this," I said, laying down a stack of bills.

Harper and Holten both objected. Holten especially. Ex-cops were still in the habit of keeping out of the defense attorney's pockets. Except, it seemed, when they were on the payroll.

"I'll settle this," said Holten, handing back Harper's twenty, "Breakfast is on Carp Law. I'll chalk it up as expenses."

He gathered my pile of cash, threw down his own and gave me back my assortment of bills. The buck at the top of the pile of cash Holten left on the table drew my attention. The picture of Washington was face down. On the back of the bill was the great seal of the United States. A pyramid with an all-seeing eye at the top, and at the other end of the note, the eagle perched on a stars-and-stripes shield, olive branches in one claw, and arrows clutched in another. Right then, something was working at the back of my mind. Pure gut instinct that the bill in Carl's mouth was the key to the whole damn case.

The three of us walked around the corner and onto West 88th Street. It ran all the way to the river, but we didn't need to go that far. We passed a church, a couple hardware stores and a hotel. Then, on the other side of the street we saw the house. A three-story brownstone. Crime scene tape stood out bright against the door. In front of the house sat a cop in uniform who was taking five on the porch steps. The cop was smaller than Holten, but still a big guy with a shaved head and a thick neck. On the street were maybe a dozen people. They all wore black. Some had draped T-shirts, flowers and pictures of Ariella on the railings of the house. The group had fold-out chairs and raincoats. They were here for the day, probably every day. Candles were nestled at the foot of a tree opposite the house. A full-sized poster of Ariella had also been wrapped around the bark and tied around the tree with rope and tape.

As we walked up the steps, the cop got up, nodded and held his finger against his lips. His eyes darted over my shoulder, then he winked at me and he said, "Come on in, officers."

I nodded. The fans outside were mourning Ariella. I hadn't seen any T-shirts or posters of Bobby. If the cop let the crowd know we were representing Bobby things might get ugly. The cop pulled aside the crime scene tape and opened the front door a couple of feet, just enough for us to squeeze inside one by one. I could hear the rush of feet on the steps as the fans ran forward, hoping to catch a glimpse inside.

"Get back," said the cop. All of us made it inside and the cop closed the door behind him.

"Goddamn, those kids are crazy," he said. Harper approached the cop, her hand extended, "Hi, I'm Harper," she said, smiling. She'd been a fed for a long time. The kinship to law enforcement was still strong.

The cop put his hands in his coat pockets and said, "Back up, bitch. Don't nobody touch nothin'. Be out of here in a half-hour."

"Welcome to world of criminal defense, Harper," I said.

CHAPTER SEVENTEEN

Before he'd left the apartment that morning, Kane had thrown open the tarp covering the bathtub. He'd reached down and pulled the plug, turned on the shower. Within a minute, he was rinsing brittle, white bone. Careful to gather up the bones and teeth, Kane wrapped them in a towel and hammered them to dust. He then sprinkled the dust into the soap powder box and closed it. The bullet he put in his pocket. It would find its way into the river or into a storm drain shortly after Kane left. Job done. He showered, put on a fresh bandage to his leg wound, dressed, applied his make-up, checked the ice-pack had sufficiently reduced the swelling to his face, put on his coat and made his way onto the street.

Not long afterwards, Kane joined the line waiting to get through security outside the Center Street Criminal Courts Building. There were two lines. The people in Kane's line all held letters with a red banner at the top, warning them that they had to report for jury duty.

Both lines moved fast and it didn't take Kane long to get inside out of the cold. Despite the stab wound, he wasn't limping. No pain meant no natural alteration to his gait. He was searched, and had to put his jacket through the X-ray scanner. He didn't bring his bag with him that day. No weapons of any kind. Way too risky. After security Kane was directed to a bank of elevators and told to report to a court officer who would be waiting on his floor. Crowded elevators always made Kane uncomfortable. People stink. Aftershave, deodorant, cigarettes and body odor. Lowering his head, Kane buried his nose in his thick scarf.

He could feel the excitement in his gut, and he fought it down.

The elevator doors opened onto a pale, marble tiled corridor and Kane followed the crowd to a round-faced court officer standing at a reception desk. Kane waited his turn. He affected a look of mild bewilderment. Checking his summons, checking his ID. Looking around, tapping his fingers against his belt buckle. The court officer sent the woman ahead of Kane into a large antechamber to the right of the reception desk. A tingle of electricity started at the back of Kane's neck. Like somebody holding a hot bulb close to his skin. These delicious feelings of anxiety were a bonus for Kane. He loved the sensation.

"Summons and ID, sir," said the court officer. She wore bright red lipstick, some of which had smudged on her front teeth.

Kane handed over the ID and summons and looked over the officer's shoulder, toward the chamber behind her and to the right. She scanned the barcode on the summons, looked at the ID, glanced once at Kane, handed him back his ID and said, "Go on through and take a seat. The video presentation will be starting shortly. Next . . ."

Kane took the ID, put it back in his wallet. The ID wasn't his. The New York State driver's license belonged to the man who'd disappeared in his bathtub the day before. Kane suppressed the urge to pump his fist in the air. It wasn't always so easy to get past the ID check. Kane had chosen the mark well. Occasionally, even with the latex, dye job and make-up, Kane just couldn't get close enough to the mark's appearance. North Carolina had been one such occasion. The photo on the ID was over ten years old. Even the target himself didn't look anything like the photo in his own ID. The court officer had stared at Kane and the driver's license for a good two minutes, even called her supervisor before letting him through. Thankfully, New York was smiling on Kane today.

The antechamber looked tarnished. There were still nicotine stains on the ceiling from the time when prospective jurors could smoke while they awaited their fate. Kane joined another twenty or so potential jurors in the room. Each sat on a chair with a swivel half-desk attached to one arm of the seat. Another court officer approached him and handed him two pieces of paper. One was a questionnaire, the other was an information pamphlet – Jury Service FAQ.

Two seventy-five-inch TVs were mounted on the wall facing the desks. Kane completed the questionnaire, perhaps too quickly. He looked around and others were biting the top of their pens – thinking about their answers. The questionnaire had been designed to weed out jurors who knew any of the witnesses or major players in the trial ahead. It also asked generic questions designed to spot bias. None of the questions gave Kane any trouble – he was well-practiced in appearing neutral on paper.

No sooner had Kane put down his pen, than the TVs came to life. He sat up straight, put his hands in his lap and paid attention to the instructional video. It was a short, fifteen-minute film made by judges and lawyers to introduce jurors to the concept of a trial, let them know who would be in the courtroom and what roles they have, and of course to explain what justice expected of the typical New York juror. They had to keep an open mind, not talk about the case with anyone until its conclusion, and pay attention to the evidence. In return, each juror would be paid forty dollars per day, either by their employer or by the courts. If the trial lasted over thirty days, the courts, at their discretion, added an extra six bucks per diem. Lunch would be provided. The court would not reimburse traveling expenses or parking.

During pauses in the action, when the narrative stopped to change scenes, Kane glanced at the men and women sitting around him. A lot of them were more focused on their phones than the video. Some were paying attention. Some appeared to have drifted off to sleep. Kane looked back toward the screen, and that's when he saw him.

A man in a beige suit, standing under the alcove that led to this room. He was bald, and what little hair remained on each side of his head was slowly turning white. The man was overweight, but not obese. He carried an extra twenty or thirty pounds. No more. Spectacles hung at the end of his nose, almost as if they were about to slide off his face. The man kept his head down, pointed toward the screen on his smartphone. His fat thumb flicked over the screen. The light from the screen highlighted the man's double chin, and made him look like a villain from a fifties horror movie. It also allowed Kane to get a view of the man's dark, pitted eyes. They were a heavy brown, almost black. Small and pitiless. And those eyes were nowhere near the phone screen. Those eyes sought out each potential juror in turn. Lingering over them for four or maybe five seconds at most. An intense gaze. And then on to the next one.

Perhaps only Kane noticed the man. He'd seen him before. He knew his name. No one else in the room had spotted him. The man liked it that way. Kane knew it. He dressed in a boring suit. White shirt and pale tie. And none of his clothes looked to have been bought in recent years. That suit was ten years old at least. There was nothing distinguishing about his face either. This was a man you could sit down opposite on the subway, for an hour, and within ten seconds of leaving the subway car you would not be able to recall a single thing about him.

His name was Arnold Novoselic. Hired by Carp Law as their jury consultant for the Solomon trial. Night after night, for the past month, Kane had sat in the parking garage and watched Arnold moving faces around on a corkboard in the Carp Law offices. A whole team had been assembled to investigate every juror on the list. Photograph them. Probe their lives, their social media accounts, their bank accounts, their families, their beliefs. The man whose identity Kane had stolen had appeared on that board. And the face of the man he'd burned in a backlot last night.

In many ways, Arnold was the acid test for Kane. If anyone could spot that Kane had stolen the life of a man in the jury pool, it would be Arnold. He was watching the jurors – seeing which ones were taking this seriously and which were not.

All at once, Kane became hyper-aware that shortly Arnold's beady eyes would fall on him. The thought made him take a breath. He felt hot. Sweat was Kane's enemy. The make-up might run and slowly reveal the bruising around his eyes. While focusing on the screen, Kane absently took off his scarf and unbuttoned the collar of his shirt.

And then he felt it. Arnold's eyes were on him. He wanted to glance at him, to make sure, every nerve and instinct Kane possessed made him want to turn his head and stare back at Arnold. He didn't. He kept his neck and head firm and looked at the screen. His peripheral vision picked up Arnold. He couldn't be sure, but it looked like he'd put down the phone and was staring hard at him.

Kane shifted in his seat. He felt like he was caught in a police floodlight. Frozen. Exposed. Kane willed the video to end. Then he could look around. Then he could check what Arnold was doing. Every moment was agony.

Finally, the film ended and Kane looked at Arnold. He was staring to Kane's right. He'd moved on to someone else. Taking a peach-colored napkin from his shirt pocket, Kane dabbed at this forehead, gently. The perspiration wasn't as bad as he'd feared. Very little make-up came off on the napkin, and what had come off was roughly the same color as the paper. He'd thought ahead this time.

Kane heard a court officer making her way from the back of the room to the front. Her boots echoed on the parquet floor. She turned around and faced the group. Behind her, Kane saw another line of potential jurors waiting to come into the room.

The officer at the front of the room addressed the crowd.

"Ladies and gentlemen, thank you for your attention. If you'd like to put your questionnaires, with your juror number marked on the top of the page, into the blue box at the back of the room and follow my colleague Jim into the courtroom. Before you go, in case it hasn't been pointed out – this is the jury assembly room. If you are not selected to serve, please make your way back here and wait for a court officer. You are not free to leave if you have not been selected. Thank you."

Kane quickly gathered his things and walked fast to the back of the room. The closer he was to the top of the line, the better chance he'd have of getting a seat on the jury. He put his questionnaire into the box and stood in line behind a middle-aged woman with curly brown hair and a heavy green coat. She turned around and smiled at Kane.

"Exciting, isn't it," she said.

Kane nodded. This is it. He could plan, and work hard, even making mortal adjustments to the jury pool to increase his chances of being chosen by the defense, but it all came down to a bit of luck now. He'd been at this point before and failed. He reminded himself that he made his own luck, that he was smarter than everyone in that room.

The doors at the back of the room opened, and beyond Kane could see a corridor. That corridor led to the courtroom. Finally, after all this time.

His moment had arrived.

CHAPTER EIGHTEEN

There was ten feet of hard wooden flooring between the front door and the beginning of the white carpet that spread throughout the house. We all took time to wipe our feet on the welcome mat. The officer leaned up against the door and watched us. Before we came in I'd clocked the little black camera in a two o'clock position above the front door. I looked around the hallway, but couldn't see an alarm panel.

"Here," said Harper.

She hadn't found the panel, but she'd found where it used to be. Four screw holes in the wall, just to the right of the door. There was even a light snow of plaster dust sitting on the skirting board.

"Where's the security panel?" I said.

"It's been removed for examination, probably," said Harper. I made a note to ask Rudy about that when I saw him later.

The hallway was wide enough for three of us to walk abreast, even with Holten being one of those three. He had to hang back when we reached the table that leant against the left-hand wall. Holten went ahead on his own, Harper and I let him pass, then walked side by side past the table. It looked antique. Rosewood, maybe. A lamp stood, unlit, on the table beside a phone, an internet router and a stack of unopened mail. The staircase was on the right.

Holten hooked a left into what I guessed to be the kitchen. It looked bigger than what I'd imagined from the photos. Nothing untoward there. I glanced into the living room. The couches and chairs were torn up. Stuffing billowed out of the seats. There was one thing missing in the police files. And Bobby had been questioned about it extensively by the cops – they couldn't find the knife that had been used on Ariella.

The first floor contained a study and a room still full of boxes. A bathroom and two spare bedrooms. Nothing of significance. A large window on the landing gave me a good view of the back garden. It was small, walled in and overgrown. No ladders that I could see. In any event, the back door had been locked from the inside. No way anyone could've fled the scene that way.

The second floor housed the master bedroom. We went upstairs. Harper first.

One thing that was missing was the overturned table on the landing that sat beneath a window. I'd seen it in the crime scene photos along with a broken vase lying on the floor.

The master bedroom held all the secrets. Harper went in first. She stopped, pulled the top of her T-shirt out of the collar of her jacket and hooked it over her nose.

"It's dusty. Dust kills my sinuses," she said.

Again, I saw little furniture. A bedside table with a reading lamp. A dressing table. Both were white. The mirror on the dressing table was surrounded by forty-watt bulbs, the kind you'd see in a theatre dressing room. The bed had an antique, oval headboard. Wrought iron painted white, and twisted into patterns with decorative flowers painted red.

The mattress was still in place. A red and brown circular stain lay on one side of the bed from when Ariella bled out. No bloodstains that I could see on Carl's side. Harper stifled a sneeze. The place had lain empty for the best part of a year. While the house had a fusty kind of smell, there seemed to be a lot of dust in this room, and another smell. I thought it smelled like rust and bad cheese. The smell of old blood.

I closed my eyes and tried to ignore Harper. My mind filled with the images of the crime scene captured by the NYPD photographer. I thought about the bed covers lying on the floor, the bat in the corner, the way Ariella and Carl lay in the bed.

"Cops don't have the knife, do they?" said Harper.

I kept my eyes shut, said "No. They tested all the knives in the house. None had any trace of blood and they didn't quite match the wound pattern. They checked the garden. The attic. Tore the place apart at one stage. I imagine they even trawled the sewer.

No knife. It gives us a fighting chance. We can argue that whoever killed Ariella took the knife with them when they left."

I heard Harper step across the room. Floorboards creaking beneath the carpet. I opened my eyes, and stepped slowly around the bed. Not a drop of blood on that carpet. The only bloodstain on the floor was in the corner and came from the bat.

Harper pulled her T-shirt down, reached behind her back and fetched a bottle of water from the hip pocket of her jeans. She unscrewed the cap and took a drink. She must've breathed in with the water in her mouth, as a sudden sneeze and a cough shook her. Water spilled from between her fingers as she tried to cover her mouth.

"Shit, sorry," she said, and pulled her tee back up over her mouth.

"You okay? It's just water, don't worry," I said.

I came over and saw a small damp patch in the carpet, and some droplets on the bed. I knelt down and rubbed the carpet with a handkerchief, dried it up.

"I'm sorry, Eddie," she said.

"It's fine," I said. I was about to get up and wipe down the mattress when I stopped. There were fine droplets of water sitting on top of the mattress. They hadn't dried in. Harper put her palm on the mattress and quickly brushed away the droplets. I felt the mattress. It was bone dry.

We both looked at the bloodstain on the bed. Looked at each other.

"Son of a bitch," said Harper.

I nodded. She took her bottle of water from her pocket and dribbled at little on the mattress. The water lay there in fat pearls.

We waited.

Thirty seconds later the water was still there. Harper tapped at her phone, and I heard the digital sound effect of a camera shutter.

"We need a bed sheet," said Harper.

"I'm way ahead of you," I said, opening up the closet doors. Two of the built-in closets contained Ariella's clothes. A third closet held bunched-up linen sheets and bedclothes. I imagined that they had originally been folded neatly, but the cops had rifled through every inch of the place searching for the murder weapon that had been used on Ariella. I pulled out a sheet and laid it on top of the stain, then doubled it over. Harper lay down on it. I lay beside her. We looked at each other. Harper was smiling. I hadn't seen her since we wrapped on a case about a year ago. I'd spent many hours with her, working closely, talking, holding on for dear life in the passenger seat of her car while she drove.

In all that time it had never occurred to me how amazing her eyes looked.

"Arrh—hhh-hhh-mmm," said a voice. I sat up and saw Holten, standing in the doorway and clearing his throat.

"Did I interrupt your nap? Or something else?" he said.

Both of us rolled out of the bed. Harper tore the sheet off the bed, rolled it up and walked past me to put it back in the linen closet. Her cheeks were flushed, but the corners of her lips were still turned up in a smile.

"We were working on saving Bobby Solomon's ass. Looks like he could be innocent after all," said Harper.

Her phone rang. She took the call, stepped out onto the landing. While she talked on the phone, Holten and I exchanged a few uncomfortable looks. When Harper finished, she came back in and was about to say something when Holten beat her to it.

"I'm not tired, I think I'll call Yanni and tell him I can cover this shift. Just wanted to make sure we were still on for a drink later?" he said.

Harper took a step back, touched her hair but it was already neatly tucked back with a hair band.

"Sure," she said. "Guys, I just got a call from Joe Washington. He talked to a Bureau contact and we might have something, but we need to go now."

"Where?" said Holten.

"Federal Plaza. It's a long shot, but we might have a possible alternative suspect for the murders."

CHAPTER NINETEEN

Kane followed the line into a courtroom. The potential jurors emerged from a side door, and he immediately saw that the public gallery and benches were empty. The jurors would sit there. No public and no press for this part of the trial. Kane saw Rudy Carp sitting at the defendant's table beside Bobby Solomon. Arnold Novoselic sat at the corner of that table, beside Rudy. Solomon sat with a passive look on his face.

The prosecutor wore a smile. Kane had researched the man extensively. Art Pryor. He was taller than Kane anticipated, having watched him dish out a few press conferences in the last six months. A pale-blue, made-to-measure suit hung off wide shoulders. White shirt, yellow tie and a matching yellow handkerchief peered out of the breast pocket of his suit. Light brown hair, a tanned face, soft hands and a twinkle behind those green eyes made Pryor an interesting figure to behold. His movements were slow and graceful. This was the kind of man who kissed grandmothers on the cheek and dipped his light fingers into their purses just as cold lips touched their skin. He was an Alabama man. Born and bred. He primarily practiced in the south, and he always prosecuted. Even though he'd been pressured many times, he had never run for DA, or governor, or mayor. Pryor had no political ambitions. He liked the courtroom.

Kane thought that he had timed the point when he joined the line with perfection. The first twenty jurors sat in the front bench, and Kane started the line that filed into the second row. Being the first row sometimes made people look too keen. He'd learned that lawyers are suspicious of people who want to be jurors. Usually they want to serve their own agenda. Kane could not afford anyone to know he had a purpose.

He sat down and for the first time his eyes went to the front of the court. He did his best, but he found it hard to mask his surprise. The judge. The blond female judge who was due to hear the case was no longer sitting in the judge's chair. Instead, it was the man Kane had seen getting out of the green convertible at Eddie Flynn's offices, yesterday. For a moment, he froze. He didn't dare move in case the judge saw him. Kane didn't like surprises. This was intolerable. What if he recognized him? He thought about that exchange. Kane had used his own voice when he'd asked this man for directions. Not the voice he'd been practicing. Not the voice he was using now. And he'd done his best to hide his features beneath the ball cap.

The judge looked upon the jurors as they took their seats. His eyes fell upon Kane, and he stared back. Kane's heartbeat rocketed. Nothing registered with the judge, as far as Kane could see and he turned toward the lawyers. Kane gave himself a little shake, just to let the nerves settle.

He was so close now.

Two hours into jury selection and the judge was still working on the second row. Trouble was, he'd started at the opposite end of the row from Kane. How a jury found its way from the well of the court to the jury stand was largely up to the judge. Kane had seen it done a number of different ways. As long as there was some random factor involved, the judge escaped too much scrutiny. Some judges called out the juror ID numbers from the list, choosing them at random. Other judges found that potential jurors filed their way into court and sat down on the benches in a random order anyway, so to take a bench at a time into the jury box had a strong element of chance already built in. Judge Harry Ford, as he'd introduced himself, favored this method.

The judge had given a speech on the role of the jury and he'd explained how a criminal trial works. Kane had heard it all before, but never so clearly illustrated.

Then the culling began. First, it was the jurors. Half a dozen said they had vacations booked and paid for, they had sick relatives or hospital appointments and systemically they were given a pass.

Then the lawyers got their teeth in the panel.

One by one, jurors were questioned, accepted or dismissed by the defense and the prosecution. The defense had a finite number of challenges to a juror without having to show cause. They could do this twelve times. After that, they needed to show a reason why a juror could not serve. One woman had been dismissed by the defense without them even asking her a question. It seemed that a number of jurors met their fate this way, and the defense was down to its last challenge. The prosecutor had only dismissed one juror, by showing that the juror was a long-time fan of Bobby Solomon.

Kane let his fingernails dig into his skin. Not for the pain. There was none. It stopped him moving his hands, fidgeting. He didn't want to show his anxiety. Not now.

Ten jurors had been accepted by both sides. Only two spots left. There were four empty chairs on the jury stand. Two for jurors. Two for alternates. A man took his place on the witness stand for questioning. He'd given his name as Brian Dale. Married, but no kids. Manager in a Starbucks. Moved to New York with his wife six years ago from Savannah, Georgia. Rudy Carp didn't ask any questions. Arnold had already done his research on Brian and Rudy accepted him as a juror. Kane noticed that this was a first. No other juror had been accepted by the defense without question. They must really want Dale on the jury, thought Kane. He thought back to the photographs he'd taken of Brian. The man was closer in size to Kane's natural weight. Slim, muscular. Average height. Similar bone structure, especially the nose. It had come down to a choice for Kane between his current persona and Brian Dale.

"Does the prosecution have any questions," said Judge Ford.

"Just one or two, Your Honor," said Pryor, rising to his feet and buttoning his jacket. Kane loved hearing Pryor's voice. It sounded like honey being poured into a gun barrel.

"Now, Mr. Dale, I see that you have been blessed with the sacrament of marriage?"

"That's right. Sixteen years now," said Dale.

Kane watched Pryor stride toward the witness stand. The man had a swagger in his step, but it looked good on him. Not arrogant. A well-earned grace.

"Wonderful, there's nothing more important than the bond of husband and wife. What is your wife's name?"

A smile fought to show on Kane's face. He knew Pryor already had this information at his fingertips. This was a dance. Pryor was ready to waltz Dale right off the jury and Dale didn't even know it.

"Martha Mary Dale."

"A fine name if I may say so. Now, imagine you go home tonight to Martha Mary. You smell that delicious home-cooked meal as soon as you walk through the front door. Martha Mary has been working at that stove for hours. You wash up, sit down to dinner together and Martha Mary asks where you've been today. Imagine, if you will, that you didn't give Martha Mary an answer. Can you imagine that scenario, Mr. Dale?"

"I can, but I would always tell Martha Mary where I've been. We don't have secrets in our marriage."

"And can I be the first to commend you both. But imagine you didn't answer Martha Mary. Do you think Martha Mary would be suspicious about your silence?"

"Oh, yes, sir."

"What if Martha Mary then accused you of meeting another woman for an illicit liaison. If you didn't dispel her fears she would be entitled to think the worst of you, would she not?"

Kane noticed Dale nodding his head.

"She would be justified in thinking something bad happened, sure," said Dale.

"Of course she would. If a person is accused of committing some kind of heinous crime and they keep their mouth shut, and choose not to tell a jury that they're innocent – well don't you think that's suspicious?"

"I sure would, Mr. Pryor," said Dale.

Pryor's charm knew no bounds. He strode right up to the witness stand, slapped Dale on the shoulder and said, "Thank you for you service, Mr. Dale. Do give Martha Mary my best."

He swung around and spoke to the judge over his shoulder as he walked back to the prosecution table, "Your Honor, challenge Mr. Dale, with cause. He cannot render an impartial verdict."

"Granted," said the judge.

Kane thought Pryor was probably one of the best attorneys he'd seen. He'd just watched him bump a favorable juror to the defense by using their own tactics. The only thing that mattered when it came to jury selection was impartiality.

"Did I do something wrong?" said Dale, holding his hands wide. An embarrassed look in his face.

"Take a seat back in the waiting area, Mr. Dale. I'm sure a court officer will explain all to you," said the judge. "And just a reminder to remaining jurors who have reported for service. As I explained at the top – a defendant doesn't have to prove anything. If a defendant chooses not to testify, as they are entitled to do – you are not to imply anything from that decision."

One of the court officer's approached Dale, gently coaxed him out of the witness stand. Kane let out a small sigh. He'd almost decided to adopt Brian's identity for this job. Now, he felt nothing but relief that he'd decided against it. In the end, it was Martha Mary that became the deciding factor. She was almost six feet tall and weighed close to three hundred pounds, dwarfing Brian.

Kane knew he couldn't fit both of them in their bathtub.

"Next juror candidates, in order please," said the judge.

Kane stood and followed the court officer to the jury stand.

CHAPTER TWENTY

On the way to the FBI's New York field office at Federal Plaza, Harper filled us in on what her partner, Joe Washington, might have turned up. Holten drove, with Harper in the front passenger seat and me in the back. I leaned forward to catch Harper's story. Trying to persuade a jury that your client didn't commit murder is one thing. It's a hell of a lot easier if you can show your client didn't do it while pointing the finger at somebody else for the crime.

Harper set out the position for Holten. I just listened.

"I didn't leave the Bureau on the best of terms. My partner, Joe, did. He's more of a people person. So he called one of his old buddies and got him to run a search through ViCAP and NCIC. He got nothing. On a whim, Joe's pal suggested talking to BAU-2. See if anything rang a bell. Turns out there's an agent who might have something useful."

The FBI's Behavioral Analysis Unit 2 focused on serial murders of adults. This team knew more about serial killers than pretty much any law enforcement unit on the planet. The Violent Criminal Apprehension Program (ViCAP) and the National Crime Information Center (NCIC) ran federal databases hooking up law enforcement to unsolved crimes across the nation.

"Who is the agent?" I said.

"She's an analyst – Paige Delaney. Joe says she's working out of the New York field office this past month. She's been helping the locals with the Coney Island killer," said Harper.

"What's her connection to our case?" I said.

"Maybe none. Maybe something. The one thing I didn't like about the scene is how clean it was. If Solomon was the killer, he did a hell of a job his first time out. No DNA on the bodies, no defensive wounds on the victims, no scratches or cuts on him. He killed two people clean. Then he leaves a dollar bill with his fingerprint and DNA on it in Carl's mouth? I don't buy it. There's something off about that, but then again I don't really buy our client's story either."

"A lot of things in this case don't make a lot of sense – think about the murder weapons," I said. "Somehow, without leaving the house, Bobby hides the knife that killed Ariella, but leaves the bat that he used to kill Carl on the bedroom floor – with his finger-prints on it – and then calls the cops telling them he just found the bodies? Doesn't add up, does it? But the DA won't paint it that way. It's Bobby's bat. It's got his fingerprints on it already. They'll say he didn't want the crime scene to look too perfect. Otherwise it looks staged. And the butterfly is probably there to send the cops on a wild goose chase, or he's sending some kind of sick message. He messes up and leaves his DNA on it. A small mistake. Either way, they're gonna say Bobby planned it."

Burying the back of her skull in the headrest, Harper raised her eyes to the ceiling and thought it over.

"That's possible too, Eddie. Like I said, maybe the DA has the right man? Let's see what Paige has to say. I sent over a list of what could be signatures from the killer, and something on that list caught the FBI's eye, otherwise they wouldn't agree to meet."

Holten dropped us off at Federal Plaza, parked, and met us in the lobby of the Jacob K. Javits Building. He decided to wait. I took the laptop. Holten figured it was safe in here. After a thorough search, my shoes and the laptop passing through an X-ray scanner, Harper and I were allowed up to the twenty-third floor. I let Harper lead the way. She'd been stationed here for a couple of years, and she knew the lie of the land.

It didn't stop her getting filthy looks from a couple of agents in the reception area while we waited for her contact. And we waited. And waited. And after twenty minutes I was ready to leave Harper to it when a woman in faded gray jeans and a black sweater approached both of us. Paige Delaney looked to be in her early fifties, and aging well. She was in good physical shape and had allowed her hair to lighten with age. She wore glasses on a thin nose. Her mouth curled up at the outer edges of her lips giving her a welcoming appearance.

She shook hands with Harper. I got a look, the kind of look defense attorneys get used to, eventually. We followed her down a long, narrow corridor to a conference room. A laptop sat closed on the table. We sat down, Harper and I on one side, Delaney across the table in front of the laptop. She took off her glasses, placed them on the table.

"How's the PI life treating you?" said Delaney.

"It's good to be your own boss," replied Harper.

I kept quiet. This wasn't my world. Law enforcement has its own bond. I let Harper work her magic.

"Joe Washington sends his regards," said Harper.

"He was always very polite. I'm glad you're working with him. Joe is a good man. So, I guess you don't have much time, let's get to it. I took a look at your signatures," said Delaney. She opened the laptop, turned the screen toward the center of the table so both of them could read Harper's email.

"Most of these don't really qualify as signatures for search purposes," said Delaney, "We collate information on as many individual crime scene details as possible, but only what's distinct and relevant. If the killer used a particular weapon, or left a particular mark on the bodies, wrote a message or seemed to be following a narrative – all of that could be a signature. We identify victims of repeaters through their signatures. Sometimes signatures are deliberate: a killer playing out a fantasy of some kind. On other occasions, it's a subconscious act. If it shows a pattern, or gives some potential insight, we treat it as a potential signature which goes into ViCAP."

"Nothing showed up on ViCAP for our case," said Harper.

"The system isn't perfect. Not all law enforcement agencies use ViCAP. Some cops just aren't natural administrators. And of course, killers can change patterns. Mostly, the system relies on the officers inputting the data and checking on system alerts for new crimes. Plus, if the crime is solved, it doesn't go on the system at all. The system is designed to help police catch violent offenders, identify persons unknown and find missing persons. We don't post up details of the perps we caught and convicted straight away. That's the major weakness."

Harper leaned back, folded her arms. "How is that a weakness?" she said. "Surely closed homicide cases aren't relevant."

"The system makes no allowance for wrongful convictions," I said.

For the first time since we'd sat down, Delaney acknowledged my presence. She took a moment, then nodded.

"He's right. Research at the National Registry of Exonerations tells us that out of every twenty-five people who are convicted and given a death sentence in the United States, one of them is innocent. There are fifty to sixty murder convictions overturned every year. That's a lot of cases that aren't on our databases and aren't being tracked for signatures and that's not counting the innocent people who don't have a lawyer or can't overturn their convictions. The agent Joe talked to knows me. He thought something you sent through might be of interest. I don't know if it is yet, but I'm glad you came in. It's the last signature on your list – the dollar bill—"

She stopped short. I got the impression Delaney wanted to say more, but knew she couldn't. There was an intensity to both of these women. If Harper had a theory on a case, she'd run her legs into the ground to see where that theory led. She was quick thinking and had a physical energy that seemed to flow into everything she did. There was fire in Harper. Whereas it appeared that Delaney was more of a deep thinker. Someone who quietly ponders. Like a hard drive, buzzing to solve a problem.

Harper stayed quiet. I didn't speak. We were passively prompting Delaney for more. She didn't give us anything. I knew she would try and get as much information as she could without giving us anything. Harper knew it too. This was standard FBI practice.

"I need to see the dollar bill you mentioned," said Delaney.

"We only have photos," said Harper.

"Do you have them with you?" said Delaney.

Harper nodded, and to emphasize her position she placed both hands flat on the desk. Sat still. I tried to stay out of it. This was a game Harper knew how to play.

Nobody moved. Nobody spoke.

Eventually, Delaney shook her head and smiled.

"Can I see them? I can't help you otherwise," she said.

"Let's make a deal. We'll show you the photos. If they're relevant – you give us what you have. Everyone puts their cards on the table."

"I can't do that. I'm involved in a highly sensitive investigation and—"

I got up noisily, letting the chair legs scrape along the tiled floor. Harper moved an inch off her chair when Delaney put up a hand.

"Wait. I can tell you some of the details. Not all. But only if I think it's relevant. I don't know what case you're working, and if the dollar doesn't fit then I don't need to know. Please, sit down. Let me see the photos and if it's what I'm looking for I'll cut you in as much as I can."

I exchanged a glance with Harper. We both sat down. I opened up the case beside me took out the laptop and fired it up. I found the photos of the dollar bill butterfly, twisted the laptop around so we could all take a look.

Delaney took all of five seconds before she said, "No, doesn't look like this is related. Do you have any photos of the bill unfolded?" she said.

My heart sank a little. I could see Harper deflate in front of me. Her shoulders sagged and her chin dropped to the table.

I let out a sigh. For a second, I had a little hope that this might be something that would tell me Bobby Solomon was innocent.

"Sure," I said. I hit the trackpad, flicked over two screens and let Delaney take a look. Harper muttered, "Sorry, at least we've closed a dead end."

I nodded, then Delaney caught my attention. The skin around her eyes and forehead tightened. Her lips moved silently as she brought her eyes closer and closer to the screen. She reached over, leaned down behind the desk. She came back up with an artist's sketch pad. It looked old and worn. The pages had curled up at the edges. She flicked it open, found a page somewhere in the middle of the pad and eagerly looked back at the screen.

"I need to know everything about the case you're working. Right now," she said.

Harper said, "What? You've found something?"

She ignored Harper, drew a pencil from her bag and began marking the sketch pad. She was looking closely at the screen, then returning her attention to the pad and scribbling. She ignored Harper's question, and shot one back of her own.

"What's your working knowledge of serial killers?" said Delaney.

I felt a chill creep over my skin.

"Only what I've read in newspapers. Not much," I said.

"Usually white males, twenty-five to fifty, loners, socially inept, below average intelligence and often suffering from some form of psychotic illness," said Harper.

It fit with what little I knew about it. I rose up a little on my chair, and saw Delaney scribbling at an olive leaf on a sketch of the great seal of the United States in her pad. She raised her head again, and I saw her pencil hover over the clutch of arrows as her lips moved. She was counting. Her pencil dropped to the page and she started scribbling again.

"Almost everything you've just said is wrong," said Delaney. "In BAU we call them repeaters. They can be from any ethnic group. Any age, within reason. A lot of them are married with a big family. You could live next to one and never know it. The poor social skills and low intelligence are reasonable assumptions, but not always the case. Most evade capture for a long time due to their victim selection. Most victims of repeaters have never met their killer before. Even a dumb repeater can operate for years before the cops catch up to them. But then there's the one per cent. They have highly developed social skills, their IQ is off the scale and whatever it is in their heads that makes them kill can be successfully hidden from even their closest friends. We don't catch their kind too often. Best example would be Ted Bundy. And contrary to what you'll see on TV – these killers don't want to get caught. Ever. Some will go to extraordinary lengths to ensure they stay out of jail, including masking their kills. Others, while they still don't want to get caught, secretly want someone to acknowledge their work."

Delaney flipped the screen around. She'd zoomed in on the reverse of the bill, around the great seal. The discoloration I'd seen on the dollar, and ignored, now took up the whole screen. There were what looked to be three ink marks on the design of the seal.

One on an arrow. One on an olive leaf, and one on the star closest to the top of the cluster, on the left, above the eagle's head.

"What are we looking at?" I said.

Delaney twisted around her sketch pad and pushed it toward us. It was a drawing of the great seal, with some of the olive leaves, and arrowheads, and stars above the eagle shaded in with pencil.

I looked back at the screen. An olive leaf, an arrowhead and a star had been marked with red ink on the butterfly bill found in Carl's mouth.

"I've seen these markings on a dollar three times before. I marked them on this sketch," said Delaney. "One we found, folded up and placed between the toes of a dead mother-of-two. The other was placed on a bedside table of a cheap motel beside a murdered van salesman. The last one I saw was in the dead hand of a restaurant owner. I think this is a pattern: a signature from a one-per-cent-er. Whatever case you're looking at might be linked to one of the bogeymen of the behavioral analysis unit. I think he could be the most sophisticated serial killer in the Bureau's history. No one has seen him. All we have are markings on a bill so some analysts don't even think he exists, but the analysts who do, well, they call him Dollar Bill. So you two had better tell me everything about your case, right now."

CHAPTER TWENTY-ONE

Kane took the bible in his right hand and read the oath on the card as if he meant every word. The clerk took the bible from him, Kane stated his name like he was asked and then took a seat on the stand.

Carp and his jury consultant, Novoselic, huddled together and whispered. Eventually, after the judge cleared his throat, Carp got to his feet and asked a question. It didn't matter to Kane what question he was asked. He knew how to answer it for Carp. He knew what defense attorneys were looking for in a juror.

"To your knowledge, is there anything that would preclude you from serving on this jury?" said Carp.

It was a bullshit question. Kane knew it. He expected that Carp knew it too. They just wanted to see what he'd do.

Kane let his eyes wander to the side. He paused. Blinked a few times. Then he looked back at Carp and finally said, "No. Not that I can think of." The answer wasn't important. What was important was that Kane let the defense see him *think*. Kane knew that a juror who was considered a thinker would find favor with the defense and wouldn't necessarily upset the prosecution.

"Thank you. The defense accepts this juror," said Carp.

Pryor turned around in his seat, spoke to an assistant DA behind him. The conversation proved brief. Pryor stood and eyeballed Kane, who in turn listened to the resting noises from his fellow jurors. A jury was a living, breathing thing. Sure, they were all individuals. Yet put them together and they became a beast. A beast that Kane had to tame.

It had been three, maybe four seconds since Pryor stood up. To Kane, it felt like minutes. The room grew quiet. The rustling of papers ceased. The white noise that emanated from a crowd dimmed. Pryor examined Kane. Their eyes met for the briefest of moments. Not even half a second. And yet in that fragment of time something passed between them. It felt to Kane like both men came to an understanding.

"Your Honor," said Pryor, "the prosecution has no questions and we wish to reserve our position at this time."

The judge told Kane to take a seat in the jury stand. He stood, exited the witness stand and made his way back to the chairs reserved for the jury. He sat in the first row, almost at the end.

A further hour passed, with the defense and the prosecution jettisoning fifteen more potential jurors. Like he did with Kane, Pryor reserved his position on seven more jurors. Kane looked around the stand, and with the extra chairs, there were twenty jurors seated.

Pryor dismissed another juror who'd had a background as a child actor, and might have some loose connection to Bobby Solomon. Pryor didn't sit back down. Instead he looked at the full jury stand. He took his time, and examined all twenty of them. Then he picked up his notepad and approached the judge.

"Your Honor, the prosecution can thank Mrs. McKee, Mrs. Mackel, Mr. Wilson and Mr. O'Connor for their services. They are no longer required. The prosecution is content that we have a jury."

A man with salt-and-pepper hair stood up to the right of Kane, four seats along, and began to make his way out of the line of chairs. The man was able to skim past the knees of the other jurors, who were female and smaller, but Kane had to stand and move out of the row to let him past. The tall woman on Kane's left stood to the side to let Kane and the dismissed juror out from the front row.

"All jurors move as far to their right as possible. Budge up, folks," said Judge Ford.

The man brushed past Kane. When Kane turned back to the stand, he found the tall woman had taken his seat. She'd moved back into the line of chairs, before Kane, and moved to the right, along with the other jurors who were obeying the judge's orders. The woman glanced up at Kane and smiled politely as he sat down in the seat she had been warming for the past half-hour. Kane did not return her gesture. She was in her fifties with auburn hair and wore a pale-blue sweater. The last of the women that Pryor had dismissed from the jury left the row behind Kane.

"Ladies and gentlemen, you are our jury," said the Judge. "The first six of you in the back row, and the first six in the front row are jurors."

Kane looked around.

"Starting from your right, that is," said the judge. "The other four of you, the lady and two gentlemen in the back row, and the gentleman in the front row are our alternates."

The tall woman had taken more than just Kane's chair. She had taken his place on the jury. She looked pleased. Kane was now an alternate. He would watch the trial. He wouldn't get access to the jury room. He wouldn't get a vote on the jury. All because of the tall woman next to him.

Kane watched the clerk swear in the jury, assigning each of them a number. Kane was given the number thirteen. The other alternates behind him were fourteen, fifteen and sixteen.

The judge gave them a warning. Don't read newspapers. Don't watch the news. Purge all media commentary from your lives. Then the judge swore in the jury keeper, a court officer who would look after the jury – making sure they obeyed the rules.

The tall woman in the sweater, who had taken Kane's place, Juror twelve, tilted back her head and whispered to Kane, "It's fascinating, isn't it?"

Kane simply nodded.

She spoke in a New Jersey accent. Kane could smell that morning's cigarettes on her breath. It reminded him of his mother. Kane tried to focus on those memories. Anything to stop him thinking about his failure to get a seat on the jury. If he thought of all the preparation . . .

All blown away now. Like ash in the wind.

The judge spoke, breaking the rising anger inside Kane.

"Counselors, we had set aside two days for jury selection. We've got our jury early. I suggest we don't waste the court's time any further. This trial begins in the morning," said Judge Ford.

"We're ready, Your Honor. My client is eager to have his good name cleared, so that the police department can find the real killer," said Carp.

The judge's eyebrows shot up, as he threw Carp a look. Kane knew that Solomon's lawyers would take any chance they could get to tell the jury their client was innocent. Kane guessed that some jurors would start to believe that if they heard it often enough.

The court officer who acted as jury keeper led them out of the courtroom one by one, into a cold beige corridor. Kane lined up behind the woman in the sweater and stopped. A female court officer was going down the line, handing out forms and pamphlets to the jurors on how they could keep their bosses happy, and how they claimed their jury fee.

The woman in the blue sweater put her back to the wall, fixed Kane with a fake smile and held out a hand. Even though the smile was fake, Kane could sense the boundless, chintzy energy that radiated from her. She was the kind of woman who bakes cakes for the elderly and then tells the old person how grateful they should be and how much work went into the cake.

"I'm Brenda. Brenda Kowolski," she said.

Kane shook hands with her. Gave her his false name.

"This is my first time on jury duty. I'm really excited. I know we can't talk about the case, but I just wanted to tell someone how amazing it is to me to be able to pay something back to the city. You know what I mean? Jury duty is part of being a good citizen, I think."

He nodded.

The court officer gave a form and a pamphlet to Brenda, and then Kane.

"Any questions about the form speak to me. We don't pay for or validate parking. Be back here at eight thirty in the a.m., tomorrow, please. Have a nice day," said the officer.

Kane took the leaflet and the form and waved goodbye to Brenda as he walked away. It had been a long day for Kane. So much had gone right. And yet he hadn't made the jury. He thought about slicing his arms that night with one of his knives. Not to kill. To cut. To feel the strange, prickling sensation of the tip of the blade slicing through the top layer of his skin. No pain. Just the warmth from his own blood on his skin.

"Bye for now. I guess I'll see you tomorrow," said Brenda.

Kane stopped, swiveled back to Brenda. He put on a broad smile, winked and said, "Not if I see you first."

CHAPTER TWENTY-TWO

For a long time, neither Harper nor I knew what to say. If what Delaney had just said was correct, then Bobby Solomon was an innocent man. And Ariella and Carl were victims of a serial killer.

The press would love it.

My heartbeat quickened at the thought of it. We could subpoena Delaney and all her files. She could do her trick with the dollar, show the jury the pattern. She was an experienced, high-ranking FBI analyst. This was Bobby's ticket to walk. I wanted to call Carp right away, but something at the back of my mind held me firm in my seat. Not yet. Get more. I needed to cool it, but I was too damn excited. Harper couldn't keep the grin off her face. Her call had paid off. Big time.

"We can tell you everything," I said, "for a price. Our client goes on trial this week. We need to subpoena you and your files. We're gonna need you to testify in court to what you just told us," I said.

"I'm afraid that's impossible," said Delaney.

"What?" said Harper. She then thumped the flat of her hand on the table, making the laptop bounce.

At first I thought the fed was just holding out. She needed information from us. We needed her testimony. This was a negotiation. Then I realized it wasn't a negotiation. Delaney couldn't testify to what she'd told us. And there was no way we could get a court order to compel her testimony.

"It's a live investigation, isn't it?" I said. Delaney pursed her lips and nodded.

"You can't discuss it in open court, and we can't make you. You'd be broadcasting what you know, and what you don't know, straight to the killer," I said.

"Right. Now, I need to know what case you're working," said Delaney.

She hadn't really given us anything. No names. No real details. A few ink marks on dollar bills. It wasn't enough. I felt sure there was more to it. Something else linking these murders. It had to be more than a few spots of ink. Even if Delaney could testify, it would take more than that to convince a jury. As it stood, we had enough for a good headline – but no story.

"We can't reveal confidential client information," I said.

"Bullshit. If your case is linked to my investigation – then maybe I'm the best hope you've got of getting your client off. Withholding information from me isn't in your client's best interests."

"And what guarantee do we have that you'll help our client?" I said.

"None, but it's the only shot you've got."

"No, it's the only fresh lead *you've* got. I thought we had a deal. You need a name. We need three," I said.

Delaney threw her elbows on the desk, cupped her face with her hands and sighed.

"I can't let you have access to my case files, but I can leave this sketch on the desk for sixty seconds," she said.

I reached into my pocket, drew out a roll of bills, peeled off a one and started copying the marks on the sketch directly onto the dollar.

"I can't show you the files on Annie Hightower, Derek Cass, or . . . now what was the other one called?" she said, searching the ceiling with her eyes.

I got the picture.

"It wasn't Bobby Solomon? Was it?" I said.

Her head snapped forward, mouth open, staring straight at me. I thought I could see her lip quiver. For a moment, she forgot our little game. She was absorbing the name. The weight of it. The spotlight that surrounded it.

Finally, she closed her mouth, shook her head and said, "No, no, that wasn't it. Karen Harvey. That's the one. I can't show you anything from those files."

I finished copying the marks on the great seal onto my own dollar. Folded it, put it away. I then packed up the laptop. Harper and I got up, shook hands with Delaney. Harper first. It was a curt exchange. A formal handshake, brief and professional.

She led us out of the conference room and back down the corridor to reception, then Delaney turned and left. As we waited for the elevator, I studied the dollar I'd marked.

"What the hell is this about?" Harper said.

"I have no idea. If she's right, there's one sick individual out there. And they're playing some kind of game. We need to work on this. We have to find a way to call Delaney as a witness in Bobby's case," I said.

Harper shifted her weight, put a hand on one hip and fixed me with a confused look.

"You heard her. You even said it yourself – we can't force her to testify. It's an open case."

The elevator doors opened, we got in and Harper hit the button for the ground floor.

"There's one way we can force her to testify," I said.

"Blow me. There's not a chance. Go on, surprise me. I bet you a buck it won't work. Delaney will never testify about her case."

"Only reason she can't testify is because it's an open case. All we have to do is close it."

The car journey to Carp Law didn't take long, and no one spoke. Holten drove. Harper and I sat in the back seat, each of us poring over news articles on our phones.

Annie Hightower was found dead in November 2001 in the living room of her Springfield home. Her throat had been cut to the bone. Her kids were supposed to have had a weekend visit with their father, Omar Hightower. Instead, the kids were really with Omar's sister two blocks away from their mother's house. Omar told the court he'd recently come into money. He had a big football bet pay off. Close to a hundred grand. Even made the local paper. He'd spent some of it on drugs – smoked a bowl or twelve that afternoon, and his sister found the kids in Omar's kitchen playing with the microwave. The sister, Cheyenne, took the kids for the night to let Omar sleep it off. So Omar had no alibi for the night of the murder. He owed Annie close to a thousand dollars in child support and she had instructed a lawyer to get it back. The dollar bill found in between Annie's toes had Omar's fingerprints on it. I thought about the eagle on the great seal. The arrows and olive branches clutched in its talons. At the trial, Omar's defense attorney argued that his client had given Annie cash earlier in the week – and the killer had used one of those notes to frame Omar.

The jury didn't buy it.

A single paragraph article in 2008 confirmed Omar had been murdered in prison.

The case of Derek Cass seemed equally straightforward. Derek had been a family man. Wife. Three kids. Sold Transit vans out of his own lot in the heart of Wilmington. He would need to travel, on occasion, to meet clients and suppliers. Out on the road, Derek became Deelyla. In the summer of 2010 he got in trouble, as Deelyla, in a bar two miles outside of Newark. A part-time garage attendant named Pete Timson didn't take too kindly to finding out his hot date was really a man, and threatened to strangle Deelyla. He followed Deelyla back to her motel. Strangled her in the bed, and left a bill with his prints on it on the bedside table. Witnesses testified to the threat. Case closed.

"Karen Harvey doesn't quite fit," said Harper.

"I haven't gotten to her yet. How come?" I said.

Flicking her thumb across the screen to the beginning of the article, Harper said, "She's not the same as the others. Restaurant owner in Manchester, New Hampshire. Late fifties, divorced, successful. Died in what looks like a robbery in 1999. Shot in the stomach, then a double tap to the head, up close. The cash register had been damaged, but not opened. Only thing missing was half a dollar bill. When she was found she still held one half of the bill. The other half was found in the apartment of Roddy Rhodes. Bassist in a local band. Drug addict with a string of convictions for armed robbery. Local cops, acting on an anonymous tip, raided his apartment, found the torn bill and the murder weapon – a .45 Magnum. His fingerprints weren't on the bill, but Rhodes bought the rap anyway."

"He pleaded?"

"Murder two. He gets out in twenty-five years."

I thought about Bobby's fingerprint on the butterfly bill found in Carl's mouth.

Holten pulled up outside Carp Law. Harper and I got out and went inside. Holten would wait in the lobby. Rudy had left a message on my cell while we were still with the feds. He said jury selection was complete and the trial started tomorrow. The office was abuzz. Secretaries, lawyers, paralegals – everyone looked jazzed and busy.

In the conference room we found Rudy, Bobby and a man, sitting with his back to me, that I'd hoped never to see again. I'd last encountered him a few years ago when he caused me one or two problems with the FBI. I recognized him even from behind. I'd know that ugly, bald head anywhere. Arnold Novoselic. Jury consultancy was a dirty game. And Arnold was the dirtiest. I'd been involved in one of Arnold's games before.

"Hi, Arnold," I said.

He got up, turned around, and his jaw dropped when he saw me. He hadn't changed. Still fifty pounds heavier than was healthy for him. Still wearing drab suits. Still getting paid a fortune for cheating the justice game.

"You still lip-reading jurors?" I asked.

He didn't answer me. Instead he turned his anger on Rudy.

"I refuse to work with this man. He's a . . . a . . ."

"Crook? That's rich coming from you," I said.

"Stop it. Right now. Arnold, sit down. Please. Eddie, Arnold is our jury consultant for this trial. He is tried and tested and gets results. How he gets those results is not really my concern. Nor is it yours. Let Arnold do his job. You do your job, and we'll all get on like a house on fire. There's no room for arguments. Trial starts tomorrow," said Rudy.

Harry must've bumped the schedule. Good. I was looking forward to getting started. I shifted my focus from Arnold and I introduced Harper.

Rudy patted Bobby on the shoulder and offered him a bottle of water from a stack of them in the center of the table. He took it, cracked the bottle and drained it. He'd had just a taste of the court-room today. Even though I hadn't been there, I could tell this trial was becoming real for him. He looked nervous, shaken. Hunched over the desk, he clutched the empty bottle tight and twisted it.

I tore a single page off a notepad, made a short list of items I'd need.

"You clearer on the case now?" said Rudy.

Harper and I exchanged glances. I decided to go first.

"Harper will lay out what we've discovered. But yeah, things are a little clearer. There's still a lot of work to do. If it pays off we might win this. First, I need one of your paralegals to go do some shopping," I said, handing the list to Rudy.

He took it and I watched his eyebrows get closer together the more he read.

"There's a lot of weird stuff on here. A twelve-foot-wide plastic sheet? Corn syrup? What on earth is this, Eddie?" said Rudy.

"It's complicated. Plus, we think there might be a lead on an alternative suspect. Harper got us in to see an FBI analyst today. There is a single link between this case and an ongoing FBI investigation into a possible serial killer. We don't have enough yet. The link is small, and it's nowhere near reasonable doubt, but we're working on it. In the meantime, I need your help. I need you to subpoena a man named Gary Cheeseman. I'll give you his business address later. Put him on our list of witnesses and give it to the DA. And don't worry, I don't need to call him. I just need him in the public gallery."

I saw Harper racking her brains for the name. She came up short and said, "Who the hell is Gary Cheeseman?"

"Gary Cheeseman is the president of a company called Sweetlands Limited operating out of Illinois."

"And what is his connection with this case?" said Rudy.

"None. That's what makes it beautiful. Trust me, Gary Cheeseman is going to blow a big hole in the prosecution's case."

CHAPTER TWENTY-THREE

It was coming up on seven o'clock in the evening. The temperature had dropped and Kane's breath misted the air in front of his face, but he felt warm. He'd worked up a sweat after spending an hour washing down the Chevy Silverado in an abandoned garage. It hadn't taken him long to crowbar the lock, throw up the shutter, park the Chevy and then close up. Five minutes. Tops. The stab wound in his thigh felt tight.

A rusted oil drum sat in the corner. The previous owner had used it as a burn barrel. An aluminum vent sat above it. He siphoned some gas from the Chevy, poured it into the barrel, struck a match and let it fall.

Standing in front of the burning oil barrel, Kane took off his shirt and dropped it into the flames. He checked the pocket of his pants, drew out a single dollar, then stripped off the pants and put them in the barrel. For a second, he examined the bill before adding it to the flames. He had a fresh set of clothes in a bag in the back seat of the Chevy. Kane couldn't swear that it was real, but he thought he saw a green hue to the fire. Perhaps there was copper in the bottom of the barrel, or some chemical. It reminded him of Fitzgerald's Gatsby, staring at the green light across the dark waters. The American dream. Unobtainable, and receding before him with every crack of flame.

Kane knew this dream. His mother talked about it. She strove for it all her life, and failed. Just like he did before he realized the truth. The American dream wasn't money. It was freedom. True freedom.

He didn't like the tight feeling in his leg. He checked the dressing, loosened it a little, popped a double-dose of antibiotics and took his temperature with a digital thermometer. Ninety-eight point six. Perfect.

Kane knew a lot about pain for someone who had never experienced it. It had an important physiological function. A warning system. Signals from the brain to tell you that there is a problem. Headaches. Muscle injuries. Infection. If Kane didn't monitor his body closely, he could destroy it.

He heard his disposable cell vibrating. He picked up.

"Kids found the body you left in Brooklyn. Called it in. Don't worry, it'll take a while to identify," said the voice.

"Do I need to push the schedule forward?" asked Kane.

"They won't link the body to the jury summons immediately, maybe never. He was a private dick with a liberal agenda – there are plenty of better suspects and motives right now. All the same, the faster you can do this, the better. I see you were busy this afternoon too. Maybe you should calm things down."

"I'll bear that advice in mind," said Kane.

He heard the man sigh on the other end of the line.

"There's a state-wide APB on the Chevy. You clean the car? Change the plates?"

"Of course. Calm yourself. That car will never be traced. What have you heard about this afternoon's activities?"

"I know a guy in homicide in that precinct. He'll fill me in. I'll keep a watch on the wires. If they catch a lucky break I'll let you know."

"Make sure you do. If I learn you've been holding out on me . . . well, you know the consequences," said Kane.

CHAPTER TWENTY-FOUR

I needed a couple of hours' downtime. Just to let things work themselves out in my head. By the end of the meeting in Carp Law, I could tell everyone needed pretty much the same. They'd all listened. Rudy had heard every story under the sun, but he raised an eyebrow at this one. Eventually, we'd all agreed – we didn't have enough to point the finger at an unknown serial killer. Not nearly enough. But Rudy liked my other points and he'd sent a couple of paralegals out into Manhattan with the company credit card and my shopping list. Good enough. The only one who'd been silent during the meeting was Bobby. I couldn't read him. Most of the time, he just stared out the window at Times Square. I thought that maybe he was taking in the view as much as possible. Like a man who knew he wouldn't have a view like that from a prison cell for the next thirty or forty years.

The meeting broke up with arrangements to meet again in the morning, before court, to go through Rudy's opening statement to the jury.

I'd also promised Harper I would call her later, after her date with Holten.

At first she didn't want to acknowledge it was a date. Eventually, she nodded and said, "Yeah, it's a date. I know it's not exactly professional to meet people like this, but I figure what the hell? If Rudy Carp doesn't like it – he can blow me."

"You gotta stop saying *blow me*. Holten's gonna get the wrong idea," I said.

We laughed together for a few moments. It felt good. Soon as the elevator doors opened it felt like putting on a two-hundred-pound backpack. We were back on business.

"I'm going to call some friendlies in local law enforcement. Joe knows a lot of cops. I get on better with local PD than I do the feds so I'll hit the phones too. Sheriffs, deputies, detectives. Between them all they cover almost half of the United States. I want to send them details of the dollar bill – see if anything shakes loose," said Harper.

My cell phone rang. Christine.

"Hi, listen, I'm in the city. I had to come up and see a few old friends. By the time I get home I won't want to cook dinner. How about some Chinese food?" she said.

"Sure, I didn't know you were coming to Manhattan."

"I wasn't working today, so I decided to go see some people. I don't need to tell you my movements, Eddie."

"Sorry, that's not what I meant. I . . . look, dinner sounds great. I just thought I might get to see Amy tonight," I said.

"Well, you'll have to settle for me. The usual place? In an hour?"

I knew better than to argue. My time with Amy was very much dictated by Christine – and I didn't have it in me to fight about it. That only made things worse. No, I needed to make a good impression tonight. Finally, I had a way out of the life I'd been living. A steady job with Rudy. No risky cases. No psycho clients. No reason to worry that some lunatic would target my family to get to me. It was what Christine always wanted for us. What I had always wanted for us.

"Sure, see you there," I said.

I had time to go get my car. I didn't want to leave it any longer and I'd planned to take it that evening to make the drive to Riverhead for dinner with Amy and Christine.

I hailed a cab and rode north. Through rush hour. All the way to Pier 76. The Manhattan auto lot. I found the teller, showed him my ticket, paid the fine and he gave me my keys, a lot number and a map. When I finally found the Mustang, it had another McDonald's bag under the windshield wiper. I tore it off, threw it in the back seat and cursed Detective Granger.

Asshole.

A half-hour later I was in my car and headed for Chinatown. I parked up and jogged two blocks to Doyer Street. The Nom Wah Tea Parlor didn't look like much from the outside. It didn't get much better on the inside, either. Red vinyl booths, Formica tables.

A diner set-up, but the only difference was that you got chopsticks on a side plate instead of a knife and fork. It was nothing special, apart from the food. And the history. Chinatown had grown up around the place. It had been open since 1920 and they made dumplings and dim sum like nobody else in the city.

I was late, and Christine had already taken a booth and ordered some tea. She didn't smile when she saw me. Just waved her chopsticks and then turned her attention back to the dumplings and soy sauce. Because I'd ran part of the way, I was a little out of breath. My stomach felt tight, and I realized I was nervous. I wanted to tell her about the job at Carp Law, but didn't know how to do it. My mouth was dry, and I had the same feeling I'd had on our first date – fear. I knew when I first met her that she was special and I couldn't mess it up. Well, I'd done a pretty good job of messing things up so far. This was the last chance.

She'd cut her hair. The soft, dark brown hair that I'd known for so long was now cut in a bob. She looked different. A little more tanned than usual. I sat down opposite her and the waiter brought me a beer without me asking.

"I hear you're drinking again," said Christine.

"Hold up a second, I'm sorry I'm late. And I didn't order the beer. You did."

"Harry told me. Says you've got it under control. He figures a little drink every now and again, when he can watch you, is better than you pulling your fingernails out thinking that you'll never have a drink again," she said, casually, in between bites of pale dumpling.

I held up my hands in surrender.

"Hi, I'm real sorry I'm late. Can we start over?"

Christine took a mouthful of tea, sat back and wiped her lips with a napkin. Stared at me. Waved her hand and said, "I'm just a little cranky today. How are things?"

I told her about the Solomon case. At first she was pissed. Her eyebrows knitted together and her neck flushed. I knew all her little tells.

"I thought you were supposed to be winding down. Staying out of the spotlight. Cases like that bring attention. We all know the kind of attention you get is usually dangerous," she said.

It was a fair point. The exact reason that we weren't together. My job brought trouble. And my family was too important to me. If anything happened to them because of me, I don't know what I would do. There had been close scrapes before. And our daughter had suffered.

"This case isn't dangerous. And it's given me an opportunity. I'll tell you in a second, but look – you haven't told me how Amy's doing. I want to hear everything."

"She's great, Eddie. She passed that math test she was worried about. She's made a new friend in chess club. A boy, but they're just friends. For now. She's happy, and she seems to like Kevin . . ."

Kevin. Christine had gotten to know her boss very well. He'd helped her settle into Riverhead, introduced her to all the best people in town. He'd even done some handyman work on her apartment. I'd never met the guy, but I felt like doing some work on his face.

"Good. I'm glad. She still reading?"

"Every night. She's even read a couple of those dime detective novels you keep giving her."

I nodded. That felt good. I bet Kevin read books on legal procedure and the history of air conditioning. Amy and I always had the same taste in books.

I ate some food. Ignored the beer. I was buying time. Trying to work up the courage to talk about our relationship. We'd been apart for a long time. After a while, you stop talking about making things right – it's just too painful. But things were about to change in my life. This was my chance to make things right. A job like this was all we'd ever wanted. Stability, safety, and I get to go home every night for dinner without wondering who is going to kick in the front door.

I didn't know how to say it. The food made me feel sick and I could feel the sweat breaking out on my forehead.

"I got a job," I said, blurting it out. "In Carp Law. Regular litigation, some criminal work. Nothing dangerous. Nothing controversial. Nine-to-five and well paid. I'm out, Christine. Solomon is the last big case. I want you and Amy to come home. We can get our old place back in Queens . . ."

Her eyes began to water, and her lip trembled.

"Or we could, you know, get a new place. A fresh start. I can support you and Amy now. You wouldn't need to work. It could be like we always wanted. We could be a family again."

She wiped a tear from her cheek, threw her napkin at me.

"I waited for you. Through all the shit you went through. The drinking. Rehab. I waited. And then all those cases, Eddie. You made a choice. Your work put us in the firing line. And now you're done I'm supposed to come running?"

"It's not like that. People came to me. They needed help. I couldn't turn them away. What kind of man would I be if I let all those people go to prison? I couldn't live with myself if I let that happen. It's *not* a choice. There never was a choice. Not for me," I said.

"But I *do* have a choice. I didn't want this . . . this life. I don't want a husband who has to stay away from his family in case they get hurt. I tried, Eddie. I waited. I'm through waiting . . ."

"You don't have to wait. I told you, I got a job. It's safe. Things can go back to the way they were."

"There's no going back. I've thought about this. I wanted you to come up to the house and see Amy tonight, but I knew by this afternoon that I just had to tell you. I can't keep this hidden anymore. So I decided I'd come meet you here because I didn't want Amy to see this. I'm done, Eddie. I'm done waiting. Kevin and I have been seeing each other. He wants us to move in with him."

Right then, I wasn't sitting at a booth with Christine. I wasn't in the tea house. I wasn't even in Chinatown. At that moment, I saw exactly what I'd feared, what I'd dreamt about for months. My body lay at the foot of the Empire State Building. Christine stood on the Observatory, eighty-six floors up. She took her wedding ring from her purse and tossed it over the barrier. I lay on the sidewalk, and I knew it was coming. Faster and faster. A band of gold tumbling toward me. As it got closer, I could see it. I couldn't move. Couldn't breathe. All I could do is bury my fingernails between the paving flags and hold on.

And when it hit me in the chest, I woke up.

That pain felt real now. A gaping, hollow pain that took my breath away. And I'd seen it coming. Which made it worse.

"Don't—"

"Eddie, I've made up my mind. I'm sorry," she said. Her voice had gone cold.

"I'm sorry. I'm so, so sorry. Things are going to change. I'm going to change. This new job . . ." But the words died in my throat. I'd already lost her. Something woke inside me. All that pain I'd fought down with the booze. It came roaring back to life. And it made me fight.

"He doesn't love you like I do," I said.

Christine counted out some bills, put them on the table and her hand lingered on top of them for a moment. She was hesitating, but not over the check. I didn't dare say a word. I knew part of her still loved me. We'd shared too much. She blinked rapidly and shook her head. Christine got up, slid out of the booth and said, "Kevin loves me. I know that. He'll take care of Amy. And me. Don't call. Not for a while."

She made to leave, my hand snaked out. Fast. I took her wrist. She stopped. A dumb move. I let her go.

I listened to her heels on the floor as she left. That sound, growing ever more faint as she walked away. I looked at the beer on the table in front of me. A Miller. Cold. Golden. Bubbles of condensation sliding down the bottle. I wanted it. And another ten afterwards and then vodka, whiskey, everything I needed to numb the pain. I took the bottle in my hand and as I raised it to my lips I glanced at the money Christine had left on the table.

A gold ring sat on top of the stack of bills.

I put the bottle back on the table. Rubbed at my temples. It felt like there was a freight train running through each vein.

I got up, took the ring and put it in my pocket.

My feet took me to my car. I didn't look up the whole way to the parking lot. Not once. And when I got in and started the engine I had no memory of walking out of the restaurant. I felt sick. Like I'd swallowed a fully inflated balloon that I couldn't bring back up.

The drive to 46th Street seemed to have happened in a similar way. I turned into the street, without really knowing how I'd gotten there, or how long I'd been driving. I parked up outside my office and got out of the car. My keys rattled in my coat pocket as

I walked toward the steps leading to my office. Head down. My breath falling in sheets of cold mist toward my feet.

I didn't see Detective Granger until he shoved me backward.

I stumbled, but managed to stay on my feet. Car doors slammed. A lot of them. I looked around. Three meaty guys on my left. Two on my right. One of the guys on the right had a nightstick. Granger stepped backward, up the steps, keeping me in his sights. They'd been waiting for me. And despite only glancing at each of them, I made them as cops straight away, even before I'd seen the nightstick. The way they carried themselves. Their clothes. Levi's and wranglers. Boots. Shirts tucked into their jeans and loose jackets to hide their shoulder holsters.

I rolled my shoulders, shrugged off my heavy coat. It could've been the cold wind, or the fear flooding adrenaline through my system like a burst damn, but I started to tremble. I could feel my closed fist shaking.

Glass exploded behind me. Shards hit my back and I knew one of the guys was taking that stick to my car.

Granger's voice sounded almost warm. He'd waited forty-eight hours for this and he couldn't hide his satisfaction in his next three words.

"Not the face," he said.

Son of a bitch.

I didn't wait for it. It was happening. I could've run, but I knew I wouldn't have gotten far and they didn't want to kill me. But they might have if I'd taken off. A shot in the back. A suspect that wouldn't stop after they'd called out a warning.

Happened all the time. Welcome to New York.

The lead cop came from my right. Big guy. Short hair. Small, dark eyes. A thick mustache and no neck. Fists like a forty-dollar bag of quarters. He had three inches of height on me, and probably another four or five inches of reach. Easily the biggest of the bunch. A real hard ass.

He drew back his right fist, elbow jutting out behind his shoulder like he was about to put that thick arm to work on a suspect. His eyes grew even smaller as his face contorted into a snarl. Lips pulled back over clenched teeth. The others were standing back. Watching.

I saw him bend his knees. This shot was headed for my solar plexus. A massive blow, taking me out of the game. The rest of them would dance on my ribcage, my knees, and then my ankles. A half-hour later they'd all be downing cold beers and laughing about it. Patting Granger on the back. Reliving the moment they taught me a lesson I'd never forget.

Not tonight. No way.

I stepped back just as the big puss threw his punch. He may have been a massive guy, but he was also slow. In truth, that didn't matter. The muscle would do its job. You didn't need a lot of speed when there was that much weight behind a punch.

Lucky for me.

I'd worked speed bags six days a week in Hell's Kitchen for six years at the toughest Irish boxing gym in the neighborhood. Which pretty much meant it was the toughest boxing gym in New York.

I threw out my right. Blindingly fast. A snap punch as I moved back, out of range. The big guy didn't even see it. No hip movement, no weight behind it. I didn't need it. I had time to pick my spot and that was enough. The huge fist was an easy target. I knew where it was headed, how hard and how fast. I'd kept my fist vertical. Like I was going in for a fist bump. But I wasn't being friendly. My wrist was pointed down, slightly, so I had a straight line between my middle knuckle and elbow. A solid base of bone, perfectly angled to absorb the impact with zero damage.

All the damage was going in the opposite direction. That same middle knuckle of mine crunched into his fifth metacarpal: the knuckle of his little finger. And that made a God-awful sound. It was like the big guy had tried to punch me and caught his little finger on the corner of a brick wall. Every one of those cops heard the sound of bones breaking, the ligaments tearing, and the fractures multiplying all the way down the big guy's wrist. It sounded like a sledgehammer hitting a sack of peanuts.

The big guy brought his broken hand up to his face, protecting it, recoiling as the shock hit his body. Then I hit his body.

Stepping inside, I threw a left uppercut into his ribs as hard as I could. The punch hit deep and took him down into a ball on the sidewalk. I swung around, ready for the next guy.

Too late. I heard the *thunk* of the stick on the side of my head before I felt it. The pavement came up fast and I put out my hands to break my fall. A gold band danced in front of my eyes. Christine's ring had fallen out of my pocket. I heard the dull tinkle as it bounced along the pavement. I reached out, desperate to grab it. I was going to smack face down next to the ring. But I didn't land on the sidewalk. It turned hazy, swirled before my eyes and disappeared.

I was out cold before I hit the bricks.

CHAPTER TWENTY-FIVE

The light shining in my eyes hurt like a son-of-a-bitch. May as well have been stabbed in the head with an ice pick. The light went out and my vision swam. My legs felt cold, wet. My shirt too. I was lying on a couch. A figure loomed above me. That torch light hit my eyes again, and I closed them. Fingers prized them open. The light shone in each eye and I swore.

"You know, Eddie, I'm starting to think that a career in the law isn't quite working out for you," said Harry Ford.

Harry cut the light, stepped away. I was on the couch in my office.

"You've got a lump on the back of your head the size of an egg. I figure you've got at least one busted rib. Your pupils are reactive, and equal size. You haven't vomited. No blood in your nose or ears. You'll feel like you've been kicked in the head by a horse and you might have a mild concussion, but apart from that you're in the same shit condition you were in yesterday."

Harry had started out as a medic in Vietnam, aged sixteen. The fake ID he'd used to enlist said he was twenty-one. He soon rose up through the ranks, and he'd finished a distinguished military career only to start on a more rewarding career in the law. He was the only judge I knew who could strip and reassemble an M16 with a bottle of whiskey in his gut.

"How many fingers am I holding up?" said Harry, holding up three.

"Three," I said.

"What day is it?"

"Tuesday," I said.

"Who is the President of the United States?" asked Harry.

"Some asshole," I said.

"Correct."

I tried to sit up. The room spun. I laid my head back down and decided sitting up could wait.

"Where'd you find me?" I said.

"Just outside. A big black Escalade cut me off as I turned in. Damn thing took off like a getaway car. I parked and found you. I was going to call 911 but I checked you out and you seemed okay. You remember talking to me on the street?"

"No. What did I say?"

"You asked me to find this."

Harry held a gold wedding ring in his hand.

This time I managed to sit up. My side was killing me. Harry placed the ring on the table and fetched two coffee mugs. I saw a bottle of Scotch sitting on the table. Still in its brown paper sack.

"Thanks, Harry."

"Don't mention it. Christine called me. Told me what happened. You mind telling me how you ended up face down in the street. You get into a fight in a bar or something?" he said.

"It's complicated," I said.

"I'd be disappointed if it wasn't. Seriously, though. What the hell happened?"

"A bunch of cops jumped me. I pissed off a detective called Granger yesterday. He didn't take too kindly to it. He must've had a tip-off from the city pound that I'd picked up my car, gone to my office with a gang of cops and waited for me."

"I don't like what I'm hearing. You should talk to—"

"Who? A cop? I'll handle it," I said.

Harry broke the seal on the Scotch, poured each of us a drink. Every breath I took sent a flood of pain from my side into my already aching head. I took the large Scotch, put the mug back on the table empty. Harry filled me up. Another hit. He poured again.

"Take it easy," he said.

I lay back and closed my eyes. Let my brain cool. I knew I was running at my limit. My marriage had finally collapsed, my body was a close second. If I didn't get control of my head I was going to lose it. After a few minutes the pain in my skull eased. My side didn't. I figured Granger freaked out when I took a nightstick to the head and went down. They wanted to hurt me. Not kill me. One good kick in the ribs and Granger would've called it off. I didn't feel like it, but I knew I'd been lucky.

There was a photo of Amy and Christine in my wallet. I wanted to take it out and stare at it. Then rip my office to pieces.

Instead I drank more Scotch. I knew that I needed to start thinking about the case. I had to put Christine to the back of my mind. At least for now. Then, when I came up for air after the trial, it wouldn't be so fresh – so raw. I needed time. She needed time. She'd thought for a long moment before she put that ring on the stack of bills in the restaurant. Maybe, just maybe I could talk her around. Maybe there was still a chance of getting her back. I had to believe it. I did believe it. But I would have to wait until after the case was over. The case. Taking my time, I raised my head and opened my eyes.

"You shouldn't be here. The DA would have a fit if she knew where you were."

"Miriam Sullivan knows I'm here. I called her before I came over. We're not going to discuss the case and as you haven't officially appeared before the court yet, there's not an official problem. She's been through a divorce. She understands. Miriam is alright. And she won't let Art Pryor make a meal out of this either. But look, don't worry about that. You want to talk about Christine?" said Harry.

I didn't. I couldn't.

After a time I said, "Miriam parachuted Art Pryor in for this?"

"She did. You ever met him?"

"No. I only know his reputation."

With district attorneys' offices crammed to the ceiling with case-work, taking your top assistant district attorneys off their regular caseload and handing them a massive, complex case occasionally had catastrophic results. They couldn't handle their own files and devote the necessary time to the big case. So either the office hired more staff, or they struggled on and reconciled themselves to the fact that a lot of strong prosecutions might be lost because they didn't have the proper attention. And then, when an ADA pulled off a miracle and won a huge case – in a few years that same ADA would decide to run for office and take the DA's job.

The only safe bet was to bring in a lone ranger. Art Pryor was one of the best. He had a license to practice law in around twenty states. He only did murder trials. And he always prosecuted. And he always won. For the right price – Art came to town. A DA could leave all their other prosecutors to get on with the regular job – one or two would assist Art, then Art would get a conviction, put on his hat and leave town for the next big case without upsetting anyone's apple cart. He was good, too. Art practiced shotgun prosecution.

Most prosecutors in a murder case clog up the witness stand with every cop, profiler, forensic analyst and expert they can possibly think of. If a cop stopped his car at the murder scene to deliver donuts to his pals who hadn't had a break in four hours, you can bet your bottom dollar the DA would call him as a witness.

Art Pryor was the opposite. He ran a murder trial in Tennessee around ten years ago. The trial had been scheduled to last for six weeks. Art brought home a guilty verdict in four days. He only called essential witnesses, and never kept them waiting on the stand for too long. Many lawyers believed it to be a risky practice, and yet it always paid off for Pryor.

First time I heard about that case, it came from a young prosecutor who said he wanted to try and ape Pryor's style. He called him a revolutionary. I couldn't help but disabuse the guy of his lofty notions. See, Pryor got paid a set fee. Didn't matter if the trial lasted six months or six hours. Pryor's fee was the same. Why do six months' work when you get paid the same for winning in half the time.

Art Pryor was not a legal stylist. He was a businessman.

"I know Art has a reputation for sweet-hearting juries. It's that southern accent of his. New Yorkers love it. But don't be fooled. Art may play the wise country bumpkin – but he's devastating on his feet. I can't talk about the evidence in the case, but you should ask Rudy about Pryor bumping a juror today. It was a masterful display. Guy's a real pro," said Harry.

I took another drink. The pain was subsiding. Harry grabbed my empty glass, took it away.

"That's more than enough for tonight. Remember our deal: I say when you stop."

I nodded. Harry was right. I could handle a few drinks, but only in Harry's presence. Suddenly I wasn't thinking about the whiskey, my mind was on Pryor.

"Is he better than me?" I said.

"I guess we're going to find out," said Harry.

WEDNESDAY

CHAPTER TWENTY-SIX

Kane couldn't sleep.

The anticipation was too great. He'd finally given up on sleep sometime past four a.m. For two hours he exercised.

Five hundred push-ups.

A thousand sit-ups.

Twenty minutes of stretching.

He stood before the mirror. Sweat covered his head and chest. Taking his time, Kane examined his reflection. The extra weight he just had to put up with. No point in feeling bad about it. He was playing a part, after all. His biceps felt hard, strong. From the age of eighteen, Kane had hit the gym. Because of his condition, he didn't suffer the aches and pains that came with lifting weights. He ate right and worked out hard every day. Within a few years he had built a physique suitable for his purpose. Strong, lean, fit. The stretch marks over his chest had annoyed him at first; he was growing muscle faster than his skin could stretch. In time he came to love them. They served as reminders of his achievements.

Looking down at his chest, Kane rubbed at his latest scar. A half-inch cut, over his right pectoral muscle. The scar remained purple and raised. Another six months and the color would drain from it, like the others. The memory of the cut was still strong. It made him smile.

He opened the curtains and stared out at the night. Dawn threatened the sky. No one on the street below. The windows of the buildings opposite remained dark and silent. Leaning down, he flicked the catch and threw the window open. The freezing air hit his body like a cold wave from the Atlantic. Instantly the fatigue from the sleepless night left him. A shiver caught him. He didn't know if it was the icy breeze or the liberation of standing naked before the city. Kane let New York see him. His true form. No make-up. No wigs. Just him. Joshua Kane.

For a long time he'd fantasized about revealing himself to the world. His true self. He knew there had never been anyone like him before. He'd studied psychology, psychiatry and neurological dysfunctions. Kane didn't fit into a neat box of diagnoses. He didn't hear voices. He didn't have visions. There was no schizophrenia, no paranoia. No childhood abuse.

A psychopath, perhaps? Kane didn't feel for other people. There was no kinship, no empathy. For in Kane's mind, there was no need of such things. He didn't need to feel anything for anyone because he wasn't like anyone else. They were all beneath him. He was special.

He remembered his mother telling him that.

"You're special, Josh. You're different."

How right she had been, thought Kane.

He was one of a kind.

It hadn't always felt that way. The pride in that statement hadn't come easy. He didn't fit in. Not in school. If it wasn't for his gift for mimicry, and impersonations, he wouldn't have been able to cope in school. It was his Johnny Carson routine that earned him a date for his high school senior prom with a pretty, brown-haired girl called Jenny Muskie. She was cute, even with her braces. Jenny often had time off school because of tonsillitis. When she did return to school from a bout of sickness she was often still hoarse and earned the nickname "husky Muskie".

On the night of the prom, in his mother's car, wearing a rented tux, Kane had pulled up at Jenny's house and waited. He didn't go inside. He sat there for a long time with the engine running, fighting the urge to just drive away. Kane couldn't feel physical pain, but he knew all about worry, embarrassment, feeling shy and awkward. He knew those feelings all too well. Eventually he got out of the car, rang her doorbell. Her father, a large man smoking a cigarette, gave him a stern warning about looking after his daughter and then laughed and coughed when Jenny made Kane perform his Carson impression. Her dad was a big fan of *The Tonight Show*.

The car journey to the prom was mostly quiet. Kane didn't know what to say, and Jenny talked too fast, then shut up, and then talked again, nervously, before Kane even had time to process the first thing she'd said. Kane knew books. That was it. Jenny didn't read. And she hadn't read Kane's favorite book, *The Great Gatsby*. "What's a Gatsby?" she'd said.

Maybe out of embarrassment at the awkward silences, she asked him how he created his impersonations. He said he didn't know exactly – he just kind of studied people until he saw something, or heard something that he thought was the essence of that person. She didn't really get it, but Kane didn't mind. The only thing that mattered to him that night was that she was pretty and she was with *him*.

Kane walked into his senior prom, arm-in-arm with Jenny that night. Her in her blue dress, and Kane in his ill-fitting tuxedo. They got drinks, ate bad food, and separated after half an hour. Kane didn't dance, and he'd been worried about dancing with Jenny for weeks leading up to the big night. He hadn't had the chance to tell her that he couldn't dance, and didn't want to. He was just happy to talk to her.

It was another half-hour before Kane saw her again, kissing Rick Thompson on the dance floor. Jenny was Kane's girl. He wanted to march over there and pull Jenny away from Rick. But he couldn't. Instead, he drank sweet punch, sat on a plastic chair and watched Jenny all night. He watched her leave with Rick. Watched them get into his car. He drove behind them, keeping a respectable distance, until they reached a peak on Mulholland Drive and parked up at a beauty spot overlooking Los Angeles. He watched them make love in the back seat. It was then that Kane decided that he didn't want to see any more.

Kane closed the window to the night, and to his past. He returned to the bedroom and opened his make-up kit. He'd already laid out some clothes. The dead man whose life Kane had stolen didn't have much of a wardrobe, but such things didn't matter to Kane.

In a few hours it would begin. The trial he had dreamed of for most of his life. This one was special. The attention from the press was unbelievable. Beyond his wildest dreams. Everything that had come before had been mere practice. Everything had led him to this point.

He promised himself he would not fail.

CHAPTER TWENTY-SEVEN

For most of the night, Harry had tried and failed to get an ice-pack on my head. It was just too damn painful.

We talked for hours. Mostly about Christine. About me. It was the last thing I wanted to discuss – but we couldn't talk about the case.

Around two a.m. Harry called his clerk who arrived by cab and drove Harry home in the green convertible he'd parked outside my office. He was used to picking up the judge – and Harry made sure to pay back every favor. Harry and I would have sore heads come morning. For different reasons.

I woke up at five, still on the couch in my office. I got fresh ice from the mini-refrigerator beside my desk and held it against the lump on the back of my head. The swelling had gone down, and the pain woke me up as soon as the first ice cube touched my skull.

For a long time I lay on the couch and thought about my wife and daughter. It was all my fault. All of it. I'd screwed up my own life. I thought it might be better for Christine and Amy if I wasn't in their lives at all. Christine deserved better than me. So did Amy.

I reached for the whiskey bottle. Normally Harry takes it with him, but he must have forgotten it last night. I picked it up and unscrewed the cap. I hit pause before the whiskey hit the bottom of the mug. Put the cap back on the bottle with my glass still empty.

People were relying on me. Bobby Solomon. Harry. Rudy Carp. Harper too, in some ways. Even Ariella Bloom and Carl Tozer. I owed them most of all. Their deaths demanded a resolution, one way or another. If Solomon was guilty – he deserved to be punished. If he was innocent, the cops needed to find the real killer. Justice. Due Process.

It was bullshit. But it was the best bullshit we had.

I got up slow, made my way to the bathroom and filled the basin with cold water. I put my face beneath the surface, held it there until I felt my cheeks stinging.

That woke me up.

The phone rang. Caller display read, *"Blow me"*.

"Harper, you should be asleep. You got something?" I said.

"Who can sleep? I've been up all night. Joe pulled some strings. I've been reading the case files on the Dollar Bill murders."

"You got all three?"

"Yep. There's not much to them, really. The feds wouldn't release the files. For that we would've had to go through Delaney. So I went right to the source. The detective bureaus for Springfield, Wilmington and Manchester. Joe cooked up a story about running a training course on crime scene investigation. They're dead cases. Nobody is remotely worried about sharing the files."

"Anything leaping out?" I said.

"Nothing. No connections. Far as I can see, Annie Hightower, Derek Cass and Karen Harvey never met. There's extensive bios on each victim. There's nothing to connect the victims other than the dollar bills. And at the time, PD didn't think much of the dollars. But they kept them all. You know how cops work. They make a drug bust and find a suitcase full of cash – that case will probably be a little lighter by the time it's booked into evidence. But if it's a murder scene on Joe Public – nobody messes with a single dime. Everything is preserved. Perfectly."

I let out a sigh. I'd been hoping there would be something to connect them. I had no doubt that Delaney had already made some kind of connection between the victims. One that she couldn't tell us about. Delaney had a head start.

"In the cases of Cass and Hightower the perp's fingerprints were found on the bills. That's what sent them away. With Karen Harvey, the half dollar bill was found in Rhodes' apartment but his prints weren't on it. Any other prints or DNA on the bills?" I said.

"No DNA. There's a partial print on the bill in the Derek Cass murder. Multiple prints on the bill found between Annie Hightower's toes. None on the torn bill found in Roddy Rhodes's apartment linking him to Karen Harvey's robbery homicide. There's no record of matches with prints on the databases."

"Were those other prints tested, though?" I said.

"I would imagine so. Can't tell for sure."

"We need to be sure," I said.

I heard Harper's fingers tapping on a keyboard.

"I'll email the labs in each case. No harm in double-checking," she said.

"Any chance you could send the files to me?" I said.

"They're already waiting in your inbox."

Harper stayed on the line while I booted up my laptop. It didn't take long until I found the zip files and imported them.

"What's the link?" said Harper.

"I don't know. If it is a serial killer, like Delaney suspects, there may be no link other than the bills. What's it called? A signature?"

"Yeah, like a calling card. It's all linked to the killer's psychology. It's not like they're leaving a trail of breadcrumbs on purpose. The signature is part of who they are and why they kill," said Harper.

"I think there's something else. Has to be," I said. "No one would spot those bills without something else pointing toward it. The cases all have one thing in common – the bill led the cops to the killer. That's the thing. Maybe that's what Delaney spotted. If it is one man then they sure as hell don't want to be found. They're taking extreme measures to make sure someone else goes down for their crime. Why?"

Harper didn't hesitate. She knew already.

"What's the best way to get away with murder? Make sure the cops aren't looking for you. If the murder is solved it won't show up as a pattern. He's masking these crimes – taking extreme steps to ensure he's not discovered. Take a look at the files, I'm going to take a nap. I'll see you in court."

She hung up.

I brewed coffee and opened the files. By seven a.m. I'd read all three cases. The coffee was cold and my brain was on fire. I found my wallet, drew out the dollar bill I'd scribbled on in Delaney's office and examined the marks.

All my life I'd been used to handling money. Even conning people with it. Many a grafter could swap a hundred for a ten in the blink of an eye in front of a sleepy bartender in a nightclub. I'd seen it done. And I'd done it myself in another life.

I washed, shaved, dressed. Every second I thought about the Great Seal of the United States. The marks on the dollar. The arrow. The olive leaf. The star. Three marks per dollar. Three marks per murder.

And the fingerprint on the butterfly bill in Carl's mouth. How the hell did the cops get Richard Pena's DNA on the bill when he'd been dead long before the bill had even been printed?

I threw on my overcoat, drained the last of the bad coffee and headed out into the cold with my laptop in a bag. Soon as I opened the front door the chill hit my freshly shaved face like it was trying to rip off my skin. No way I was walking in this weather, but I couldn't take my car either. The windshield had a hole in it. Frost and snow had blown in on the passenger seat. I called a guy I know who used to run a chop-shop in the Bronx. He was obliging but expensive.

Leaving the key to my car on the top of the driver's side tire, I huddled into the folds of my coat and set off in search of a cab.

Five minutes later I was in a cab on my way to Center Street and the biggest trial the city had seen in years. My mind was a mess. I should've been thinking about the witnesses, the opening statements, Art Pryor's strategy . . .

Instead, I thought about the dollar bill.

Rudy had the trial covered. I was only playing a small part in this case. In a way, I was thankful. It took some of the pressure off.

The cab driver tried to start a conversation about the Knicks. I gave him one-word answers until he piped down.

The dollar.

I was close. There was something in those three murders that Delaney had found. When I thought about the bill in Bobby's case – I lost sight of something. Whatever was working away in the back of my mind, it wasn't Bobby or that butterfly.

I repeated the names of the victims I'd learned about yesterday. Derek Cass. Annie Hightower. Karen Harvey. There was something about those three that pulled a rope somewhere, deep inside. It felt like it was staring me in the face, but I couldn't see it.

Cass. Hightower. Harvey.

Cass died in Wilmington. Annie Hightower in Springfield. Karen Harvey was shot and robbed in Manchester.

We pulled up outside the court building. I paid the driver, tipped him.

It had just turned eight a.m. and already the masses were out in force. Two crowds of people. Both were waving signs, hollering and singing at each other. One crowd held up signs that read "Justice for Ari" while the others were holding posters supporting Bobby Solomon. The Solomon supporters looked to be in the minority. God knows what a jury would think, having to walk between these people. The crowds were getting bigger by the second, and NYPD officers were erecting barriers to keep both crowds apart.

I had to push past a line to get into the court building. Everyone wanted a spot in the courtroom for this trial. It was the hottest ticket in town. By the time I got through security and I'd pushed the button for the elevator, my mind had drifted back to Dollar Bill.

The stars.

I drew out a buck, stared at the seal as I rode up to the twenty-first floor. There were thirteen arrows clutched in the eagle's left claw. Thirteen olive leaves on the branches held in its right claw. Above it, a shield made of thirteen stars.

Stars. Shield. Derek Cass murdered in Wilmington. Annie Hightower murdered in Springfield. Karen Harvey gunned down in Manchester.

I flipped over the note and stared at George Washington, took out my cell phone and called Harper.

She picked up right away.

"I've got something. Where are you?"

"I'm on my way, I'll be there in ten minutes," she said.

"Pull over," I said.

"What?"

"Pull over. I need you to turn around and go see Delaney at Federal Plaza. Tell her you've found a link. And you have more information."

"Wait, just pulling over now," she said.

146

I heard the roar of Harper's Dodge Charger die down as she stopped the car.

"What've you got?" she said.

"The marks on the bills. It's a pattern. You got a buck on you?"

Harper must've had the phone on speaker. The sound of horns, air brakes and traffic played in the background. My elevator hit the twenty-first floor. I got out of the car and went right, toward the window in between elevator banks. I stared out at Manhattan through a window pane covered in dirt. It gave the city a muddy filter – like I was looking at an old photograph.

"Got one, what am I looking at?" she said.

"The Great Seal. There's thirteen olive leaves, thirteen arrows, and thirteen stars above the eagle. Why thirteen?"

"I don't know, off the top of my head. I never noticed before."

"You know this. You learned all about it in school. You just don't remember. Flip over the bill. Washington. First President of the United States. Before he was President he commanded troops in New York, defending the city against the British. He read out the Declaration of Independence to the army. When the Declaration of Independence was signed and Washington read it out, it had only been signed by thirteen states."

"Thirteen stars . . ." said Harper.

"It's a map. Cass was killed in Wilmington, Delaware. Hightower in Springfield, Massachusetts. Harvey in Manchester, New Hampshire. All were colonies whose representatives signed the declaration of independence. If we count Ariella Bloom and Carl Tozer, then that's New York. There may have been more murders. All along the eastern seaboard. Tell Delaney she needs to find out if anyone has been convicted of a murder due to some tie to a dollar bill. The dollar had to have been part of the evidence against them. She's probably done this, already, country-wide, but she can narrow the search. We're looking at the eight remaining states who signed the declaration – Pennsylvania, New Jersey, Georgia, Connecticut, Maryland, Virginia, Rhode Island, North Carolina . . ."

"Eddie, Richard Pena. The dead killer whose DNA was on the bill found in Tozer's mouth. He was convicted of killing those women in North Carolina. It could be a link," said Harper.

"You're right. It could be. We need to get on to that. Can you go talk to Delaney? She doesn't know about Pena."

"I'm on my way, but there's a couple things that don't add up yet. Why are there three marks on each bill? I can understand the stars – that's location. What are the other two for?"

"I don't know yet. Need to think about it. Maybe it's to do with the victims, somehow."

"There's something else we're not considering here. What if there are no other killings in those states? What if this guy is just getting started?"

"There's several years between some of these killings. I don't think he's been lying low. I think there are more victims we haven't found yet. And if Ariella Bloom and Carl Tozer were victims of this guy? Well, he's had a lot of practice. My guess is there are more out there. But I get it. This guy might still be playing his game. He could be targeting another victim right now."

"I know. But look, I don't want to waste too much time on Richard Pena. He had multiple victims. It doesn't fit like the others," said Harper.

"It might. In our case there were the same three marks on the bill and two victims."

I placed a dollar on the window sill, stared hard at it and read aloud the Latin phrase on the banner that fluttered across the eagle on the Great Seal.

E pluribus unum.

Out of many – one.

CHAPTER TWENTY-EIGHT

The jury room stank of old coffee, sweat, and fresh paint. Kane had sat quietly around the long table and listened. When he'd arrived, the jury keeper had told him to go on into the jury room. He didn't have to wait in the corridor on the hard plastic chairs like the other alternates. Judge's orders.

Kane sipped at a Styrofoam cup of tepid water and tried to tune in on the gossip. Already, certain cliques had developed among the other eleven jurors. Four women. Seven men. Three of the men were talking basketball. Trying to take their minds off the upcoming trial. You could see it though, the weight of their upcoming duty rested on their slumped shoulders.

The other four men barely spoke, they were listening to the women discuss juror twelve – Brenda Kowolski.

"I saw it on the news. It was her. It's so awful," said the short, blond lady called Anne. Kane had listened closely to all the jurors as they had been questioned during jury selection. Making mental notes. Occupations. Family. Children. Religious beliefs. The woman closest to Anne held her palm over her breast, tucked in her chin and let her mouth fall open. Rita.

"What happened to Brenda? She's the lady who was here yesterday, right? In the nice sweater?" said Rita.

"She's dead. A hit-and-run outside the library where she worked. It's so awful," said Anne. The other women shook their heads, stared at the grain on the old oak table. Kane had enjoyed listening to Arnold Novoselic talking about one of them – Betsy, in the mock trials. Arnold would be particularly happy that Rudy Carp had managed to seat her on the jury. The defense liked Betsy a lot.

Kane agreed. He liked Betsy too. She had long brown hair tied up in a ponytail. Kane wanted to stroke that hair.

The last of the four women – Cassandra – shook her head in amazement at the discussion of Brenda. Kane had watched Cassandra talking to Brenda yesterday, before he'd left. She was elegant and well-spoken.

"It's just so dangerous crossing the street these days. Poor Brenda," said Cassandra.

"I saw that on the news too," said Betsy. "I didn't know she was on the jury, My God. You know it said on the news the car backed up over her after the collision?"

"You know, you're not supposed to watch the news. Didn't you hear what the judge said yesterday?" said Spencer, one of the youngest of the jurors.

Anne started to flap. Her neck flushed red. Betsy waved Spencer away like he was an irritating fly.

"We just met her yesterday, and now she's dead. That's what's important here," said Betsy.

"No, what's important is that we do what the judge tells us. Like, people die every day. I don't mean to be bitchy about it, but like, so what? It's not like she was anyone's friend," said Spencer.

Kane rose from his seat, brought out his wallet, fished out a twenty and threw it down on the table.

"I spoke to Brenda yesterday. She seemed like a nice lady. Doesn't matter if we knew her or not. We were all in the same group. I don't know any of you, but I'd like to think if I died tomorrow somebody here might care. I say we put in some money and send a wreath. It's the least we can do," said Kane.

One by one, the jurors threw down cash. Some said, "Damn straight", or "Poor woman", or "Let's send a card too". All of them, except Spencer. He stood with his arms folded, his weight on one hip. Finally, after one of the male jurors stared at him hard enough, he rolled his eyes and put down a ten-dollar bill.

"Fine," he said.

A small victory. Kane knew that such gestures were vital. Subtle manoeuvers. Just one or two to start with. That would be all he needed to gain some standing. Kane gathered up the cash and asked Anne if she wouldn't mind picking something out.

She didn't mind at all. She beamed at Kane as she took the money. "That's so thoughtful of you. Thank you – everyone, I mean," she said, with just the right hint of emotion at the back of her throat. She swallowed and put the money in her purse.

The jurors felt better.

Kane sat down and thought about the sound made by Brenda's skull as it broke on the hood of his Chevy Silverado. The single drum-strike of something hard, and hollow, cracking on metal. And that crunch a microsecond earlier. Too close in time to be distinguishable. Yet it was there, in that cluster of sounds. Like a chord on a guitar, the echoes of her clavicle and cervical spine disintegrating. To Kane, it had sounded almost melodic. Like an orchestra unleashing a single blast of music before beginning their overture.

Kane sipped at his coffee, picked some fluff from his sweater and thought about the disappointingly silent bump from the pick-up on the second impact – when he'd reversed over her head.

Hey-ho, thought Kane.

The door at the rear of the jury room opened and the judge walked in. He wore black robes over a black suit.

Everyone fell quiet and gave their attention to the judge. Anne was really panicking – like she'd been caught breaking a rule she didn't really understand. Kane leaned over and patted her arm, gently.

Placing his large hands on the table, Judge Ford leaned over and spoke softly. As he did so, he let his gaze wander around the jury room. Occasionally letting it linger on certain jurors.

"Ladies and gentlemen, I have some distressing news. I felt I needed to tell you all this in private. Believe me, I'll be discussing this in a few moments with the lawyers in this case. That's important. However, I wanted you to hear it from me, first. I received a call this morning from the police commissioner. The police department have reason to believe that you're all in very real danger."

CARP LAW

Suite 421, Condé Nast Building, 4 Times Square, New York, NY.

Strictly Confidential,
Attorney Client Work Product

Juror Memo

The People -v- Robert Solomon
Manhattan Criminal Court

Anne Koppelmann

Age: 27

*Kindergarten teacher at Saint Ives. Single. No children.
Subscribes to the* New Yorker. *Plays the clarinet and piano.
Both parents deceased. Mother was a housewife, father worked
for the city. No financial issues. Social media interests – likes
include Black Lives Matter, Bernie Sanders, Democrats, etc.
Liberal. Loves* Real Time with Bill Maher.

Probability of Not Guilty vote: 64%

Arnold L. Novoselic

CHAPTER TWENTY-NINE

The elevator doors rolled open and a big ball of crazy spilled out.

First, a man in a green jacket came out of the elevator car backwards liked he'd been fired from a cannon. He hit the doors of the elevator opposite and an expensive-looking camera smashed by his side.

A phalanx of security guards dressed in black exited the elevator in one smooth movement. In the center of the flesh ball I could see the top of Bobby Solomon's head. Rudy beside him. The doors to the stairwell burst open beside me and a line of photographers trampled out like a platoon running into battle. Another elevator arrived and a mass of reporters and TV cameras erupted onto the scene. The corridor exploded in lens flare. Questions and microphones probed the circle of security, testing for weaknesses.

I ran for the courtroom and threw both doors wide. The security team picked up speed and pushed back against the advancing media.

Jesus, what a circus.

The security guards grabbed the men they were protecting and ran for the doors. I stepped aside just in time. If I'd stayed put I would've been crushed. A big security guy in a black bomber jacket spun around and closed the doors on the cameras.

I looked around. Apart from the clerk and court security officers, the courtroom was empty.

The circle broke. Some of the guards carried briefcases. Like the one Holten used to carry around the laptop. They made for the front of the court. I saw Bobby crouching down in the aisle, breathing hard. Rudy patted his back, told him it was okay.

I wandered over to Rudy, told him I needed a word. He hauled Bobby to his feet, adjusted Bobby's tie and smoothed down the jacket of his suit. Then he gave Bobby a pat on the arm and told him to sit down at the defense table. Rudy and I walked to the back of the room and I gave him my theory on Dollar Bill.

He nodded, politely at first. The more I talked, the less interested Rudy became. I could tell he was tense from the way he chewed his top lip. His hands wouldn't stay still. He was nervous. Anxious. First chair in a trial like this will do that to anyone.

"This FBI agent, Delaney, is she going to testify to any of this?" said Rudy.

"I doubt it. There might be a way around that. We're working on it."

He raised his chin, winked at me. Nodded and said, "Good. Now if you don't mind I have an opening statement to prepare. Oh, and one more thing," said Rudy. He beckoned me to come closer, lowered his voice to a whisper.

"We hired you to go after the cops in this case. We all know why, don't we? You're a soldier Eddie. And if you break through the police lies I'll carry you out of here on my shoulders. If you don't, well, we expect you to throw yourself on that grenade and protect the client. If that happens you'll disappear from this case like you were never here in the first place. Is that understood? I don't really want you wasting time and resources on leads that we just can't use. Just do the job you were hired to do. Okay? Sound reasonable?"

"I'm okay with that," I said, in a tone which told Rudy I was very far from being okay with it.

"Fine. Your shopping has arrived by the way. My paralegal has everything in an evidence storage room down the hall. They'll bring it in if and when it's required."

And with that, Rudy walked away and sat at the defense table beside Bobby. Rudy chatted to Bobby softly, trying to calm him down. I was fifty feet away, at least, but still I saw his back and shoulders trembling. Arnold Novoselic took up a corner seat at the defense table and sorted through some documents.

By the time I'd taken my seat at the defense table, I'd calmed down. No point in picking a fight with Rudy. Not now. I could always do it later. Sitting down put pressure on my chest. I popped some painkillers with water. It wasn't so bad if I stood up. For now, I had a lot of sitting to do. At least the pain from my broken rib took my mind off the headache.

The court officer opened the doors at the sound of a familiar holler. The man I recognized as Art Pryor made his way into court, flanked by a handful of prosecutors carrying heavy cardboard boxes. Pryor looked the part. Impeccable, blue, pin-striped suit. Tailored, of course. Crisp white shirt that almost shone, set off with a pink tie. Pryor liked pink ties, or so I'd heard. The handkerchief in his top pocket matched the tie. He had the walk too. It wasn't quite a swagger, but it was close.

He approached the defense table, greeted Rudy warmly. His teeth looked as though they were powered by the same electricity supply that had been hooked up to his shirt.

"Game time, Art. By the way, this is my second chair. Eddie Flynn."

I stood up, grateful for the respite it afforded my ribs, and held out my hand along with my best smile.

Pryor shook it. Said nothing. Stood back and flicked out his handkerchief in front of him, like a maître d' would before draping a napkin in your lap in a three-star Michelin restaurant. Pryor retained the smile as he carefully wiped his hands.

"Well, my, my – Mr. Flynn. We meet at last. I've heard a lot about you these past twenty-four hours," he said, in a southern accent straight out of a production of *A Streetcar Named Desire*.

Pryor had a twinkle in his eye. I could feel the hate radiating off his tanned skin. I'd met his kind before. Courtroom gladiators. Didn't matter about the case. It didn't matter that someone got hurt, or someone died. His kind treated a trial like it was sport. They wanted to win. And more than that, they wanted to crush their opponents. They got off on it. Made me feel sick. I could tell Pryor and I were not going to get along.

"Whatever good things you've heard about me probably aren't true. Whatever bad things you've heard are probably just the tip of the iceberg," I said.

He took a deep breath through his nose. Like he was inhaling the animosity in the air.

"I really hope you've brought your 'A' game, gentlemen. You'll need it," said Pryor. He walked backward to the prosecution table, keeping Bobby in his sights the whole way.

Before he got back to the prosecution table, a man in beige pants and a blue sports coat approached Pryor. The man wore a white shirt with a red tie, loose at the neck because of his open collar. Short fair hair, keen eyes and bad skin. Real bad. Angry red blotches escaped from his collar, clusters of blackheads on his cheeks and nose surrounded by white, flaky skin. And all of it highlighted by his pale skin tone. He had a press badge sticking out of the pocket of his coat and a shoulder bag.

"Who's the reporter talking to Pryor?" I said.

Rudy gave the man the once-over. Said, "Paul Benettio. He writes a celebrity rag column for the *New York Star*. Real piece of work, that guy. He hires PIs to dig up sex stories. He's a witness in this case. You read his statement?"

"I did, but I didn't know what he looked like. He doesn't say too much. It's mostly speculation that Bobby and Ariella weren't getting along," I said.

"Exactly, and he won't name his sources. Look at this," said Rudy.

He brought up Benettio's statement on the laptop, and pointed to the last paragraph.

"Journalistic privilege applies to my sources. I cannot name them, nor can I reveal further information at this time."

"Any follow-up on that?" I asked.

"No. Guy is a hack. No point in wasting resources on a loser like him," said Rudy.

I noticed Pryor and Benettio didn't shake hands. They leapt into full conversation, no smiles, no greetings of any kind, just an intense talk right off the bat. I couldn't hear what was being said. It appeared clear that these guys knew each other, and they'd spoken recently. At one point, both men stopped talking and looked my way.

Only they were looking past me, and directly at my client. I followed that line of vision to Bobby and immediately saw what had drawn their attention.

Bobby looked close to losing it. He flicked his hair back, tapped his fingers on the table. His legs were hammering up and down.

Bobby's chair tilted backward. I reached out to grab him, felt a shot of pain in my side which stopped me dead. The chair went over, and I saw Bobby's eyes roll back into his head before he hit the ground.

His body jackknifed. Foam spilled from the side of his mouth. His limbs flailed and shook. Arnold was the first man beside him on the floor. He tried to roll Bobby onto his side, and spoke calmly to him – calling his name.

"Paramedic!"

I don't know who shouted. Could've been Rudy. A crowd quickly formed around us. I knelt down, almost fainted myself with the pain. I held Bobby's head. Took out my wallet and jammed it into his mouth to stop him swallowing his tongue.

"Get a Goddamn paramedic in here now!"

This time I heard the shout from Rudy. People were crowding around. I saw the multiple flashes from a camera reflected on the tiled floor. Goddamn paparazzi. Benettio was there too, looking on with some satisfaction. A woman in a white shirt with red flashes on the shoulders broke through the crowd, shoving Benettio aside. She had a medical kit in one hand.

"Does he have epilepsy?" cried the medic, as she knelt down beside Bobby.

I looked up, saw Rudy. He froze.

"Does he have epilepsy? Is he taking any meds? Is he allergic to anything? Come on, I need to know," said the medic.

Rudy hesitated.

"Just tell her!" cried Arnold.

"He's epileptic. He's on clonazepam," said Rudy.

"Back up. Give us some room," I said.

The crowd cleared, and I saw Pryor across the courtroom, leaning back against the jury stand with his arms folded.

The asshole was still smiling. He looked around, making sure no one stood behind him in the jury stand and began typing a message into his cell phone.

CHAPTER THIRTY

Kane knew what was coming.

The judge spelled it out for the rest of the jury. Most couldn't take it all in.

"The police commissioner has informed me that he cannot rule out the possibility that Brenda Kowolski was deliberately targeted because she had been chosen to serve on this jury. In fact, there is evidence that this was no ordinary accident. As you may have seen on the news, the vehicle hit Brenda, and then reversed backward, over her body. Consequently, we are taking steps to ensure your safety," said the judge.

Spencer spoke first.

"I knew it. I . . . Jesusss. I mean, what kind of steps, man? Sir?"

Kane watched Judge Ford remain passive. He must've expected some kind of reaction, and he was sympathetic.

"When we break for lunch, each of you will be allowed to return home, and pack up some clothes. An officer will accompany each of you. When court finishes for the day you will all be taken to a hotel where you will remain under armed guard for the duration of this trial," said the judge.

Groans. Protests. Shock. Tears.

Kane let it all unfold in front of him.

The judge held firm, and said, "In a case like this, which has so much media attention, sequestering the jury was always a possibility. It's not a decision I've taken lightly, trust me. However, I do believe this is a necessary precaution. And I'm telling you all now in case you need to make calls to friends and family. Some of you might have to organize childcare for the evenings. I'll give you thirty minutes before we begin the trial."

A volley of protests and questions hit the judge, all from the male jurors, as he backed out of the room. Kane heard one question quite clearly. It came from the man in the pale-blue shirt and tie, Manuel.

"Sir? Sir? Where will we be staying?" he asked.

Kane moved forward in his seat, trying to zone out the background noise as much as possible.

"The court will be making those arrangements shortly," said the judge, right before he left the room.

Nodding, Kane felt the swell of excitement in his gut. He had anticipated this moment. In fact, he'd counted on it. The court were making the arrangements, but Kane knew exactly where the jury would be headed at five p.m.

And Kane had made arrangements of his own.

CARP LAW

Suite 421, Condé Nast Building, 4 Times Square, New York, NY.

Strictly Confidential, Attorney Client Work Product

Juror Memo

The People -v- Robert Solomon
Manhattan Criminal Court

Spencer Colbert

Age: 21

Barista at Starbucks, Union Square. DJs in various clubs in the Manhattan area on weekends. Single. Gay. High-school graduate. Democrat. Alternative lifestyle choices – regular marijuana user (no prior criminal record). Poor financials. Father deceased. Mother in poor health and resides in New Jersey. She is cared for by Spencer's sister, Penny.

Probability of Not Guilty vote: 88%

Arnold L. Novoselic

CHAPTER THIRTY-ONE

Rudy and I watched Bobby slowly come around in the medical bay. He was groggy at first. Didn't know where he was or what had happened. A medic gave him sips of water. Told him to lie down. Rudy stood in the corner, barking into his cell phone.

"He's not done. Not yet. Give me more time," he said.

I could only hear one side of the conversation. Didn't matter. I could tell it wasn't going well.

"So what if the press saw it? He's still an A-lister. Give me two weeks and I'll deliver . . ."

Whoever it was on the other end of the line had hung up. Rudy curled back his arm, ready to hurl his phone into the wall. He swore, let his arm drop to his side.

The medical bay consisted of a bed, a few drawers filled with painkillers and bandages and a defibrillator that sat in a case on the wall. Gently, Rudy asked the medic to give us a moment. Before she left she told us not to move Bobby for at least fifteen minutes and to let him come out of it slowly.

"I saw two reporters in the back of the courtroom. They weren't supposed to come in until everyone was set up and ready to go, but they must've snuck in. They saw the whole thing. Pictures too. It'll be front-page news tonight," said Rudy.

"I don't care anymore. I can still do a lot of roles," said Bobby.

"Hang on, I'm not following you. What has Bobby having an epileptic fit got to do with anything?" I said.

Rudy sighed, looked at the ground and said, "Nobody knew Bobby was an epileptic before today. Okay? You can't work on a three-hundred-million-dollar movie if you might suddenly take a fit and fall off a platform. The insurance premiums for Bobby alone would cost fifty million. The studio was launching Bobby as the new Bruce Willis. That's all gone now."

"There are bigger things to worry about than his career," I said, "Like going to jail for murder?"

"I know, but there's nothing we can do. Bobby, I'm sorry, the studio are releasing the movie this Friday, and they're pulling the firm off your case," said Rudy.

Bobby couldn't speak. He closed his eyes, lay back. Like a man about to fall off a steep cliff.

"They can't do that," I said.

"I tried, Eddie. The posters are up because of the trial. They don't need a long lead-up, and don't need to spend much more on advertising. The studio is getting all the free advertising it could ever want, all over the world. Bobby's deal is no good with the studio in the event his epilepsy becomes public knowledge. He knows that. He signed the contract. I had persuaded them to wait, let us get the trial over and secure an acquittal. They don't see the point anymore and they're through taking chances on a not-guilty verdict. They're getting the picture out while he's still innocent."

"We can't leave him," I said.

"It's done. It sticks in my throat, but the studio is the client here. I'll send word to the judge, Bobby. You'll get a continuance."

Bobby had heard everything. Movie star or not, he looked like a frightened kid to me. Head in his hands, his shoulder shook with tears.

As Rudy left the medical bay, he spoke to me over his shoulder. "Come on, Eddie, we're walking here."

I didn't move.

Rudy halted, walked back and laid it out straight.

"Eddie, the studio was backing this trial. They're our client. You come with me now, and you can start that job tomorrow. Great salary, easy work. Come on, you deserve it. We've got no choice."

"So that spiel you gave me about believing in Bobby – that was just a play to get me on board, wasn't it? You're going to walk out on this guy on the first day of a murder trial?"

"The trial hasn't started. I'll talk to the judge and he'll pull the trial until Bobby can get a new lawyer. Look, Eddie, I'm not a bad guy. I'm not walking out on Bobby. I'm following seventeen million dollars in legal fees, per year. I'm going with my client and so are you. Come on," he said.

If I turned my back on this, I would never get another chance. The job offer was the only shot I had at getting Christine back. Solid career. Easy life. No stress. No risk. No danger to the family. If I took the job at Carp Law I knew I stood a good chance of winning back my wife. Without it, she would never believe I had it in the first place. I'd be Eddie Flynn, the liar. Again.

I breathed out. A long, steady breath. Nodded.

I stepped into the corridor and followed Rudy to the elevators. He adjusted his tie, pushed the button to call the elevator. He saw me approach.

"Smart kid," said Rudy.

I stood in silence. Head bowed. The elevator doors opened. Rudy stepped inside. I didn't move.

The doors began to close and Rudy's hand shot out to grab them.

"Come on, Eddie. Time to go. The case is over," he said.

"No," I said. "The case is just getting started. Thanks for the job offer."

I was already around the corner and headed back to medical before I heard the doors shut. The medic had returned to the room, and I saw her trying to comfort Bobby. He saw me standing in the doorway. His face was soaking wet. He'd sweated through his shirt and the medic tried to get him to lie down, but he resisted.

"Can I come in?" I said.

He nodded. The medic stepped back. Hooking the sleeves of his shirt in his thumbs, Bobby wiped at his face. Sniffed. He looked pale. I could see him shivering. His voice sounded like dry branches cracking in a storm.

"I don't care about the studio. I just want this over with. I didn't kill Ari or Carl. I need people to believe that."

No two defendants react to a criminal trial in the same way. Some are wrecks from day one. Some don't give a shit one way or another – they've been inside before and they don't care about the prospect of doing serious time. Others, it hits them in stages. They'll be cocky at the start. Over-enthusiastic. Then as the trial gets closer, the more confident they become. But at the same time, the anxiety ramps up. The confidence is soon eroded by paralyzing fear. And when the machinery of justice finally starts turning those cogs on day one of the trial – they go to pieces.

Bobby fell into the latter category. Big time. Day one of a murder trial is sink or swim. Without doubt, Bobby was sinking.

"Looks like you need a lawyer," I said.

For a second, his eyes half closed. The tension left his shoulders, and they relaxed. The relief didn't last long.

"I can't pay as much as the studio," he said, and I saw his shoulders hunch up again. The panic returning to his face.

"Take it easy. Rudy paid me enough. I'm still on his dime. But you're my client. And I'll do everything I can to defend you. If you'll have me," I said.

He held out a hand. I took it.

"Thank you . . ."

"Don't thank me yet. We're still in the shit, here, Bobby."

Throwing back his head, Bobby let out a ripple of nervous laughter. It stopped abruptly, as reality kicked in again.

"I know, but at least I'm not in it alone," he said.

CHAPTER THIRTY-TWO

Juries have to get used to waiting. Most are not good at it. They get restless, angry and frustrated at time that they see as wasted. Kane had plenty of practice. He was a patient man. The old radiators began to rattle in the jury room, and the pipes squealed. It was cold outside and the heating system was struggling to keep it in check.

Kane remained still in his seat at the table. The rest of the jurors either sat restlessly, or helped themselves to coffee and made small talk. The women were still discussing Brenda. The men had started talking sports. Apart from Spencer, who wasn't a sports fan. He stared out the window as a fresh flurry of snow took to the air.

Spencer took out his wallet, fanned through the meager collection of bills. He turned to Kane, said, "Forty bucks a day. I ain't sending a guy to prison for the rest of his life for forty measly bucks a day," and then sucked his teeth.

Kane had seen Spencer's face on the defense team's panel of preferred jurors. Some jurors will always identify with law enforcement – with the authority figure. Some will always imagine themselves on trial. Spencer fell into the latter category. It wasn't difficult to see why the defense wanted him on the jury.

"When do you think we get paid?" asked Spencer.

Kane shook his head, but didn't speak.

Money. It always brought out the worst in people, thought Kane. He remembered a summer afternoon, long ago. Maybe a week after his tenth birthday. His mother stood at the kitchen sink with the sun in her hair. Washing dishes, listening to music. Her dress was so old it was almost transparent. She'd had a couple of drinks, like she always did in the afternoon. When she stepped away from the sink and twirled around, the sun shone through her dress. Her hair swung around, and soap suds flew off the dish brush, landing on Kane's nose. The floorboards in the old farmhouse moaned in the heat and in time to the music.

Kane remembered laughing. He thought, maybe that was the last time he'd been truly happy.

The man came later that same afternoon. Kane sat on the swing beneath that old tree that he'd fallen from a few years before. The sun low in the sky. The branch above him creaked as he swung his legs back and forth. And then he'd heard the sound of breaking glass. A scream. At first he thought it might have been the wind, or some strange sound from the ropes holding the swing, but he soon realized it had been neither. He ran toward the house, calling for his momma.

He found her on the kitchen floor. Blood on her face. A huge, black thing on top of her.

A man with dark brown hair. Dirty jeans, and a filthy shirt. He smelled the same as the pastor did on Sunday evenings. That strange, earthy, sweet smell. Momma had called it Bourbon. The man turned his head and locked his red eyes on Kane.

"So this is the boy," said the man.

"No, no, no I told you I didn't want you around here no more . . ." He slapped Kane's momma quiet.

"Go on outside for a while. I'll deal with you later," he said. Then turned back toward his mother and said, "He doesn't look anything like me. Good. Means we can keep our little arrangement. It's been a long time."

Kane's mother screamed and the boy rushed forward, until suddenly he found himself on the other side of the kitchen. The man had spun and back-handed Kane clean across the room. The crack of the man's callused hands on Kane's cheek was so loud, Kane's mother thought he might be dead. Kane had hit the back of his head against the far wall, and slumped down on the floor.

She screamed even louder.

A warm feeling spread over Kane's cheek. He got up from the floor, raised his hand and for the first time, he saw his own blood. The blow had split open his face. Where most boys would've been knocked out, or screaming in pain, or cowering in fear in the corner, Kane merely became angry. This man had hurt him. He was hurting his mother.

Quickly, Kane rushed toward the sink. He'd spotted the black handle of momma's big knife jutting from the wash basin. Momma had warned him, time and time again, that he wasn't allowed to touch the knife. And when Kane picked it up he hoped that his momma would forgive him for touching it.

The man looked up once, confused. He'd damn near taken the boy's head off, now the boy was standing in front of him. The man's look of confusion froze on his face. And then his left cheek drooped. His left eye, too. And the right eye turned white. Like a switch. But Kane knew the eyeball had just spun around, real quick.

Kane's mother scrambled up as the man toppled over on the floor. His mother held him, and rocked him and sang to him. All the while, Kane stared at the tip of the big knife protruding from the back of the man's head.

Kane fetched an old, rusted wheelbarrow and his mom rolled the body out of the house to the back field. He knew what she was going to do. He tried his best to stop her going too far into the field, but he knew it was pointless. She was headed over the big, moss-covered mound. Behind it, there was a hollow. If you buried a man there, no one would be able to see it until they were almost standing on the grave.

The wheelbarrow slipped out of her hands at the top of the mound, and the man's body spilled out when it hit the bottom of the hollow. The earth there was dark and soft. It yielded easily to the big shovel Kane had carried on his shoulder.

It didn't take long for Kane's mother to find the first set of bones. Little ones. The more she dug, the more she found. Animal bones. Buried in the shallow, wet earth. She said nothing to Kane and together, they buried him.

When they were done, Kane's mother was covered in soil and blood and she knelt down beside him. Took his soft, dirt-stained cheeks in her hands and said, "I won't tell about the animals. I knew it was you, all along. We'll keep all of this a secret. Just between you and me. I promise. Do you promise?"

Kane nodded, and neither of them spoke of it again until years later. At the age of fifteen he had learned the truth. She told Kane the man had been a cousin of hers. When Kane's grandfather had died, leaving her the old farmhouse, this cousin offered to help with money. He worked as a laborer, all over the county, and he always had cash for a willing woman. Kane's mother had been desperate. She had no food, and bills, and land she couldn't work. That money got her started. And she'd told Kane that she hated every minute she had spent with that man. And that Kane's father wasn't really a marine who got killed in a far-away place. It had been him, the one they'd buried together.

She told Kane she was sorry. She had needed the money.

Kane told her he had understood. And he did.

He didn't tell her the other part. The part he knew he was never supposed to tell anyone. That when he put that big knife through the man's face, he'd felt good.

Real good.

That feeling had been increasingly difficult to replicate as the years went by.

Kane blinked away the memory, and looked again at Spencer. He knew he had to deal with jurors like him. There was no persuading some people. No matter what happened in the courtroom, no matter how much he argued in the jury room Spencer was always going to vote one way. Same with the musician, Manuel. He was another defense favorite.

There was too much at stake for Kane. He couldn't take the chance that everything might fall apart in the jury room. He had to deal with his problem before it got that far.

And Kane knew exactly what to do with Spencer and Manuel.

CARP LAW

Suite 421, Condé Nast Building, 4 Times Square, New York, NY.

Strictly Confidential, Attorney Client Work Product

Juror Memo

The People -v- Robert Solomon Manhattan Criminal Court

Elizabeth (Betsy) Muller

Age: 35

Housewife. Five children under ten years of age. Husband is construction engineer. Karate instructor on weekends. Republican. Old parking ticket violations (not exclusionary to jury service). Finances tight. Refurbs furniture and sells on eBay. Social media – Facebook and Instagram – mainly martial arts and MMA related.

Probability of Not Guilty vote: 45%

Arnold L. Novoselic

CHAPTER THIRTY-THREE

I left Bobby in the medical bay and headed back to the courtroom. A clerk had called and told the medic Harry wanted to see me and the prosecutor in his chambers.

When I returned to the courtroom I found a single laptop sitting on the defense table. My own, with a zip file sitting ready to be opened: the case papers. At least I still had the files.

"Hey, mind if I stick around?" said a voice.

Arnold Novoselic took a seat at the table, and slammed a big paper file down next to my computer.

"I thought you'd be out the door with Carp," I said.

Pushing back his chair, Arnold faced me and said, "My fee has been paid in advance. I can walk anytime. But a jury consultant is only as good as his last case. You know that. I have to see this one through. Maybe I can help, I don't know. I've never walked out of a case before. I'm tempted with this one."

"I'm tempted to fire you, but it's not like I don't have an opening on the defense team. Plus, you were the first guy to help Bobby when he had his attack just now," I said.

"I have my moments of weakness," said Arnold. He opened up his file and handed me a document.

"This is our revised juror list. There are bios for each juror. I adjusted it this morning after we got the news," he said.

"What news?"

"Well, I had to add in the name of the alternate juror. See, one of the original jurors, Brenda Kowolski, got run over last night. She's dead. The cops are suspicious about it. I saw a lieutenant go and see the judge this morning."

"Shit."

"Tell me about it," said Arnold. "The clerk's looking for you. Pryor's already in there, waiting. Do your best to persuade the judge not to sequester."

"You trying to tell me how to do my job?" I said.

"No, but I don't trust you. And you don't like me. Let's start with honesty and go from there," he said.

I nodded, and let Arnold spread out his papers and files on the desk. Arnold and I didn't get along. Jury consultants were a necessary evil in big trials. They cost a fortune, and it was never clear how much they affected the outcome anyway.

However, Arnold was right about one thing. Sequestration of a jury was the worst thing that could happen in a trial and neither side wanted it. You take weeks, months, scoping out your ideal jurors. Usually, the defense looked for creative types. People who could show some imagination. The prosecution wanted drone bees. People who did what they were told for a living and didn't complain about it. And each side tried to fill the jury with their kind of people.

The defense wants thinkers.

The DA wants soldiers.

But what each side really wants is a juror who makes up their own damn mind by listening to the lawyers and witnesses. A jury is meant to be a collection of free minds, diverse and representative of the people of that area.

When a jury becomes closeted up, cut off from the outside world under sequestration – their minds change. They spend so much time together in a situation which isn't part of their normal lives. The jury comes together as a whole. They form a pack. Us against them. And the "them" is usually the judicial system which says they can't watch TV, or read a newspaper, or go home while the trial is running. The jury cease to be individuals and turn into a hive mind.

And that didn't suit either the defense or the DA, because no one ever knew which way a sequestered jury would go. Wherever they went, it would likely be fast. They're normally so bored, and fed up with the trial and the isolation that they give their verdict swiftly just to end the ordeal. Guilty or not guilty doesn't matter. Whatever is quickest to get the thing finished so they can go home.

The clerk signaled to me as she stood at the door leading to the back corridor. I walked up through the witness stand, past the judge's chair and followed her out of the courtroom and along a cold hallway to a room. Pryor leaned against the wall outside Harry's office. The clerk knocked on the door once, then let us both in.

Pryor said nothing until the door opened to Harry's chambers.

"How's your client?" he said.

"He'll be fine," I said.

"Come in and sit down," said Harry, before Pryor could speak again.

Judges' chambers were a reflection of their personality, but it was also a formal venue for proceedings so there was a limit on how much they were allowed to make it their own. Apart from a few pictures of Harry in uniform in Vietnam, and a framed, signed picture of him with Mick Jagger, there were no other personal items on display.

The clerk took a seat at a small desk in the corner. Pryor and I sat down in leather chairs in front of Harry's desk. We waited while Harry poured coffee for all of us, including the clerk. He sat down behind his desk and made room for his elbows by shifting some papers to the side. Harry leaned forward and took the coffee cup in both hands.

"Carp has left the building, that's our first problem. Eddie, I take it you need a continuance," he said.

"Maybe not," I said. "I've prepped for most of the police witnesses, and some of the experts. I was always going to handle those witnesses. As long as Mr. Pryor doesn't give me any surprises today I should be good to go. If we deal with police witnesses and experts up until Friday, that gives me time to prep for the civilian witnesses over the weekend."

"Speaking of witnesses, I've read both of your witness lists. Art, you've got thirty-five witnesses here. Eddie, twenty-seven. I take it you're bullshitting each other. I've read the trial bundle and I'd say, Art, you could prosecute this case on five, six witnesses at most. Eddie, I have no idea who half of the people are on your list. I appreciate Rudy drew up the list. But come on, seriously, who the hell is Gary Cheeseman?"

With trial witness lists – it was a game. You put everybody you could possibly think of on the list just in case you might need them. Plus, you put down some extra bodies just to mess with your opponents and get them to waste time chasing their tails.

"Look, Harry, I'm not going through my list and discussing the merits of each witness. If Art cuts back on his list, great. I will too. I know what you mean, look, we're grandstanding here with these lists. If we cut the bullshit we can get through this trial in a week and a half," I said.

"No. We're cutting the list and we're going to aim to finish this trial by Friday," said Harry.

"Friday? Well, that is ambitious," said Pryor.

We all took a moment. Drank coffee. Harry put down his cup and interlaced his fingers, elbows on the desk. He leaned his chin softly on the arch made by his hands and said, "I've sequestered the jury. It's within my judicial discretion to do so, and I don't want any arguments about it because I won't change my mind. I'm worried."

"Because of Ms. Kowolski? Surely that was just an unfortunate, tragic accident," said Pryor.

"I had NYPD in here this morning and they're pretty sure Ms. Kowolski was targeted. She was a librarian, she was well known in the community and well respected. No apparent motive. Other than the fact that she was sitting on this jury."

"That's a reach, in my opinion, Judge," said Pryor.

"In here, it's Harry. And maybe it is a reach. But if I don't sequester this jury and something happens to another juror . . ."

"Do what you think is right, Harry. Did the police say why they think *she* was targeted?" I said.

"No, but they're working on it. So, gentlemen, go check your witness lists. Cut it down. If you call a witness that I don't believe is essential, you'll get it in the neck from me. The longer this trial goes on, the more this jury is in the spotlight. Who are you calling first, Art?" said Harry.

"Lead detective. With opening statements, we'd do well to finish his testimony today," he said.

Harry nodded and said, "I heard your client had some kind of epileptic fit. Is he okay?"

"I think so. The sooner this trial is over, the better."

We left Harry's chambers together. The clerk stayed behind to prep the judge's files. We knew our way out and didn't need an escort.

"Just out of curiosity, who is Gary Cheeseman? My ADAs have been searching the internet, we just can't find any experts or anyone remotely connected to this crime with that name. Surprisingly, there's quite a few Gary Cheesemans in the US. I'd love to know why he just popped up on the list yesterday," said Pryor.

"I may not need to call him. That's all I can say for now."

"Well, I knew I'd get a good game from Rudy. Shame he's pulled out. I sure hope you don't disappoint."

I shook my head. Guys like Pryor sickened me. He was in this trial for the juice, and a check. Everyone eventually gets desensitized to dead bodies, tragedies, and the horrible things people did to one another. This was different. This wasn't cynicism, or anything close to it. It was just plain sick. Years ago, before I became a lawyer, I'd sworn that if I ever got used to looking at murder scenes without feeling anything for the victims – that was the time to quit.

"Look, I get it. You want to win. Fine. This isn't a pissing contest Pryor, two people are dead."

"And when this trial is over they'll still be dead," said Pryor.

I opened the door at the end of the corridor and stepped inside the courtroom. It was filled. Packed to the rafters with reporters, channel news anchors, and fans of Ariella Bloom and even a few of Bobby's fans. It was a Goddamn circus.

Pryor followed me into the courtroom, looked around at the full gallery and said, "You're wrong about one thing. This is a pissing contest. When it's all said and done, it comes down to who has the best lawyer. Your breeches are long enough for you to understand that, son. And come Friday, it's going to be me standing in front of those cameras, proclaiming justice for those victims. I haven't lost a case in twenty years. I'm not going to lose this one."

He beamed at the gallery with those pearly whites and stood in the well of the court, hands clasped above his head, already preparing for his victory. The crowd applauded. There were some whistles and hissing from Bobby's fans – but not many. Arnold had brought Bobby into court, and both of them sat patiently at the defense table. Bobby looked pale, and a fine sheen of sweat sat on his forehead. I took a seat next to him.

"Looks like everyone is against me," said Bobby.

"Don't worry about it," I said. "By the time we're done today, things will have turned around. Forget these people. The only people who matter in this court are the jury. As long as they're fair, we'll be okay."

"Speaking of the jury, have you read the up-to-date list?" said Arnold.

I unfolded the list he'd given to me and started reading. Time to get to know this jury. Twelve jurors. Twelve minds. Not the best jury I could've hoped for. Certainly not the worst. Three days to make them mine. My cell phone buzzed. Text message from Harper.

Meet me and Delaney at recess. We've found more victims.

CHAPTER THIRTY-FOUR

As Kane took his seat in the jury stand, he jostled for position with Rita. She moved along, let him take a seat. He was the last juror in the back row. Closest to the exit. Spencer sat in front of him, in a lowered seat, slightly to his right. If Kane looked directly at the witness stand in front of him, he could easily gaze over Spencer's shoulder.

Perfect.

The jury were given a trial bundle in a red lever-arch file together with some pens and a notebook. Judge Ford instructed the jury to place the bundles at their feet and that they would be directed to the relevant page by him or counsel, as and when required. They were free to take notes.

Most of the women, with the exception of Cassandra, held their notebooks open and pens at the ready. Spencer too. Only Manuel held his notebook on his lap and put his new pen between his teeth. The other men placed everything on the floor, spread their legs as wide as politely permissible, and folded their arms.

The voices of the people in the public seats rose to a clatter. There was excitement in the room. Courtroom junkies, true-crime novelists, journalists, and TV reporters all yakking to each other. Little details had been given out about the murder. Just the basics. It proved enough to set the dailies on fire. They had just enough information to run and rerun a story – but no real details. Kane already knew it had been dubbed "The Trial Of The Century" by the *Washington Post*. Most agreed. That is, until the next big celebrity murder trial came along. Until then, as far as New York and the rest of the country were concerned, this was big news. Nightly news.

The judge called for silence, and the noise from the crowd abated. Kane scanned the crowd – plenty of Ariella's family were in attendance. Kane glanced over toward the defense table. No Rudy Carp. Just Flynn, the defendant and Arnold Novoselic, the jury consultant.

Something was going on. Maybe Solomon had fired his other lawyers, and just hired Flynn. *That would be a bad mistake,* thought Kane.

The prosecution went first. Kane liked this part the most.

Pryor rose to his feet and placed himself in the center of the courtroom, facing the jury. Kane could smell his aftershave from way back. It was a strong odor, but not unpleasant. Before he spoke, Kane could see the prosecutor enjoying the silence. Every set of eyes in the room fell upon him.

With one step toward the jury, like a dancer moving with the first beat of the song, Pryor began his opening statement.

"Ladies and gentlemen of the jury, I've had the pleasure of speaking to some of you yesterday, during voir dire, but I thought I should introduce myself. My momma always told me that was polite. So, ladies and gentlemen, my name is Art Pryor. I want you to remember my name, because I'm here to make you three promises."

Kane sat up straight and noticed others on the jury did likewise. He watched Pryor hold up his index finger.

"One, I promise I will present facts to you which prove that Robert Solomon murdered Ariella Bloom and Carl Tozer in cold blood. I'm not going to *speculate*, I'm not going to *theorize*, I'm going to show you the *truth.*"

Pryor held up two fingers.

"Two, I promise to show you that Robert Solomon lied to the police about his movements on the night of the murders. He told police he got home around midnight. We will prove he lied about that crucial piece of evidence to hide his involvement in these murders."

Three fingers.

"Three, I promise to show you hard, forensic evidence which places Robert Solomon at the scene of the murder. I will show you his fingerprints and DNA on an object that was inserted into Carl Tozer's throat *after* he was murdered."

A shiver of pleasure rippled through Kane. Pryor was giving a mesmerizing performance. The best he'd ever seen. When Pryor eventually let his arm fall to his side, Kane resisted the urge to applaud. Pryor's voice was filled with empathy and compassion for the victims, and righteous anger when he mentioned Solomon's name.

"Ladies and gentlemen, I will keep my promises. My dear old momma would turn in her grave if I failed in that duty. This case is about sex, money and revenge. Robert Solomon found his wife in bed with their head of security, Carl Tozer. He knew they'd been having an affair and that the marriage was over. He caved in Carl Tozer's head with a baseball bat, and then took a knife and plunged it into his wife's body, *over* and *over* and *over* again. He folded a dollar bill, and placed it in Tozer's throat. Maybe he believed Tozer wanted Ariella's money? And he was not about to let that happen. If Ariella died, the defendant would inherit all of her money. All thirty-two million.

"I will show you he lied to the police. I will give you forensics which prove he is the killer. After that, it's over to you. You and only you have the power to give these victims the justice that they so richly deserve. You can't bring them back, but you can give them peace. You can find Robert Solomon guilty."

Pryor walked back to the prosecution table, and Kane watched him the whole way. He saw him remove his handkerchief and wipe his mouth. As if he was taking the anger from his lips. Most of the public gallery applauded. The judge silenced them.

Leaning forward, ever so slightly, Kane saw the notes that Spencer had written on his pad. He took a long look, noting the style, the size, and the key features of certain letters. When he returned his back to the upright seat, Kane looked around the jury stand. His fellow jurors were letting that wave of emotion sink in. Some nodded, probably without knowing it.

Damn, this guy was good, thought Kane.

CHAPTER THIRTY-FIVE

Harry had been right. Pryor was a real courtroom pro. I listened to his opening statement and watched the jury carefully.

When he'd finished, I looked at Bobby. He was shivering. He leaned over and said, "This is all lies. If Carl and Ari were sleeping together, I didn't know. I swear to God, Eddie. This is bullshit."

I nodded, told him to calm down. Arnold whispered, "Pryor's got the jury. You have to shake them out of it."

He was right. Pryor had used an old attorney's trick called the *mathematical truth*. It's all about the number three. Every word Pryor used had been carefully weighted, tested and rehearsed. And it all revolved around the number three.

Three really is the magic number. It holds some kind of important place in our minds and we see it all the time in our culture and daily lives. If you get a call from a wrong number once, well that's just life. If you get the same call from a wrong number again – that's coincidence. If you get a third call – you know something is going on. The number three equates to some form of truth or fact in our subconscious. It is somehow divine. Jesus rose on the third day. The Holy Trinity. Third time lucky. Three strikes and you're out.

Pryor made three promises. He said the word "guilty" three times. He said the word "three". He held up three fingers. The rhythms and cadences of his speech revolved around the number three.

I'm not going to speculate, *I'm not going to* theorize, *I'm going to show you the* truth . . . *this case is about* sex, money *and* revenge . . . *he plunged the knife into her body* over *and* over *and* over *again.*

Even the structure of Pryor's speech was built around that number.

First, he told the jury he was going to tell them three things. Second, he told them three things. Third, he told them what he'd just said.

He had every right to look pleased with himself. It was well rehearsed, well thought-out, psychologically manipulative and persuasive as all hell.

Before I stood to speak, I met Bobby's worried stare. I knew what he was thinking. He was wondering if he had the right lawyer. His life was on the line. People usually don't get second chances at a murder trial.

I didn't take it personally. If I was in Bobby's shoes, I'd probably feel the same way. I stood up, buttoned my suit jacket and stood just a few feet from the jury stand. Just close enough to be intimate.

While Pryor spoke with the force and command of a seasoned actor, I kept my voice at a level which the jury could hear, but it wouldn't hit the back of the room. As devastating as Pryor had been, he had revealed one weakness – vanity.

"My name is Eddie Flynn. I now represent the defendant, Robert Solomon. Unlike Mr. Pryor, I don't need you to remember my name. I'm not important. What I believe, doesn't matter. And I'm not going to make you any promises. I'm going to ask you to do one thing. I want each of you to keep the promise *you* made yesterday when you took the bible in your hand and you swore to deliver a true and faithful verdict in this case.

"You see, when you became a juror you took on a responsibility. You are responsible for every person in this courtroom, for every person in this state, for every person in this country. We have a justice system which says that it is better that a hundred guilty men go free, than one innocent man goes to prison. You are responsible for every innocent man and woman who is accused of a crime. You have to protect them."

I took a step forward. Two of the female jurors leaned toward me, and one man. My hands gripped the rail of the stand, and I bent low.

"Right now, the law of our country says Robert Solomon is innocent. The prosecution have to change your mind. They have to convince you beyond all reasonable doubt that he committed these murders. Keep that in your head. Are you sure that everything you hear from the prosecution is right? Is it true? Is that what really happened? Or could it have happened another way? *Could* it have been someone else who killed Ariella Bloom and Carl Tozer?

"The defense will show you that there is someone else who the prosecution have overlooked. Someone else who left their mark at the crime scene. Someone who the FBI have been chasing for years. Someone who has killed before, many times. Could it have been this killer? At the end of this trial, you'll have to ask yourselves that question. If the answer is *yes* then you send Robert Solomon home."

I held onto the rail, eyeballed each juror, then made my way back to the defense table. On the way, I couldn't resist glancing at Pryor.

His gaze spoke loud and clear – *Game on.*

For the first time today I saw something blossom behind Bobby's eyes. Something small, but significant.

Hope.

Arnold leaned over and gestured that I should do likewise.

"Good job. The jury ate that up. There was this one juror . . ." he said, but Pryor had gotten to his feet and Arnold saw him do it.

"It's nothing, doesn't matter," he said.

"The prosecution calls Detective Joseph Anderson," said Pryor.

He didn't want to leave the jury with my speech ringing in their ears. He needed to move fast – win them back and keep them. I'd read Anderson's statement. He was the lead detective.

A big guy in gray pants and a white shirt came forward. Six-foot-five. Short dark hair. He stepped into the witness stand and turned to face the room. Small, dark eyes. A thick mustache and no neck. He wore a cast on his right hand that went all the way to his elbow. The shirtsleeve rolled up to the top of the cast.

I didn't know it at the time, but I'd met Detective Anderson last night. He'd been one of the guys in Detective Mike Granger's crew. The one who'd tried to punch a hole in my chest and I'd T-boned his hand with a block-punch.

He'd already recognized me. I could see it in those little sharp eyes.

For the first time in three days, I relaxed a little. If Anderson was as dirty as Granger that meant there was a good chance they were taking the easy way out with this case. They'd probably cut corners, planted evidence, whatever it took to nail their perp.

This was going to be interesting.

CARP LAW

Suite 421, Condé Nast Building, 4 Times Square, New York, NY.

Strictly Confidential,
Attorney Client Work Product

Juror Memo

The People -v- Robert Solomon
Manhattan Criminal Court

Terry Andrews

Age: 49

Former basketball prospect. Suffered major ligament damage and retired from sport at 19. Restaurant owner – traditional deli and grill in the Bronx where he is also the grill chef. Divorced twice. Father of two. No contact with family. No voting history or political affiliations. Jazz fan. Poor financials, restaurant has been threatened with closure.

Probability of Not Guilty vote: 55%

Arnold L. Novoselic

CHAPTER THIRTY-SIX

"Detective Anderson, if you simply raise your left hand, that will suffice. I can see you can't hold the bible. The clerk will repeat the oath to you," said Judge Ford.

He watched the detective repeat the oath and take his seat in the witness stand. All the while, Kane thought back on the defense attorney's opening statement. He'd referred to another possible perpetrator. A killer. And the FBI were tracking him.

Kane thought back to a time long ago. His mother had lost the farm. They'd moved far away and changed their names. A new life, a new start. For a while, his mother had been happy. The cloak of a new identity had proved intoxicating. His mother had tried and failed at every job she'd managed to get – waitress, cleaner, bartender, store clerk. And the bills mounted up. Little brown envelopes were strewn all over their damp apartment. Until there was simply too many, and the landlord threw Kane and his mother onto the street.

They moved around a lot until she managed to hold down a job in a local factory, principally because it was a job no one else wanted. She cleaned the vats, after they'd been used for God knows what. Chemicals, was all she said to Kane, but she didn't know what kind. Day after day she came home a little paler, a little thinner, a little sicker. Until one day when she couldn't go to work. There was no health insurance, or any money for a doctor. Kane graduated high school with the highest grades the school had seen in years. Even though his education had been sporadic, there was no denying Kane's vast intellectual ability. He had a scholarship waiting for him at Brown University.

His mother died a week after his graduation. She died in bed in their little, grubby apartment. Same day she got a letter from the factory manager telling her she was fired. At the end, she could barely breathe, and every small movement was agony. That's when Kane knew he had to end it. She wasn't strong enough, but he knew how to be strong. There were various ways to end it: clamping shut her mouth and nose with his hand, holding a pillow on her face or maybe giving her an overdose of the cheap black-market morphine. Kane thought the morphine would work, but didn't know how much he would need to do the job. She could suffer with any of those methods. He needed something more efficient. Faster.

In the end, Kane settled on a method which he knew would be quick and reliable.

He fetched his axe.

Before he struck the single mercy blow to the head, Kane's mother saw what her son had become.

In her purse Kane found twenty dollars and forty-three cents. He went through the rest of her things and found what he thought was a scrapbook. Old photos of his mother when she was young. And newspaper clippings. Several of them. They all carried the same story and they were all around six years old. A man's body had been found buried on the outskirts of a farm. The police were looking for the former owner and her son. Seeing his name in the paper, his real name, gave Kane a rush like he'd never experienced. It was right there. In black and white.

Joshua Kane.

He kept the scrapbook. Stuffed it into a bag with some clothes.

Kane wasn't going to Brown. He'd known for some time that he couldn't. In a way, his mother's illness had been a blessing. She had been too sick to notice the smell coming from his room. He'd graduated on May 31st. His senior prom had been May 20th – the night his prom date, Jenny Muskie, had disappeared with another student named Rick Thompson. Cops put out a state-wide APB on Rick's car, but to no avail. The police had searched Kane's apartment the day after they went missing, apologized to his mother and found nothing. They'd spoken to Kane, three times after that, and he'd given the cops the same story each time. He'd gone to the senior prom with Jenny, or huskie Muskie as she was known in school, and soon after they arrived she took off with Rick. He hadn't seen them again.

No one had.

Kane put on his backpack, and returned to his room. He popped the can of gasoline he'd siphoned from the neighborhood cars and soaked his bed, the floors, his mother's room and the kitchen. But most of the gas he'd poured onto his bedroom floor. He didn't want the police to know about all of the things he'd done to Jenny's body. They would probably find it, when the floorboards broke in the heat.

Kane took one last look at the place, struck a pack of matches, threw them down and left.

He stole a car, and couldn't resist one last drive past the reservoir. If they ever drained the water they'd find Rick's car at the bottom. They'd find his body in the trunk, and his head jammed in between the dashboard and the accelerator.

That was the beginning. The push that he'd needed to go out into the world by himself. With purpose. His mother died chasing a dream of a better life. The dream that all poor Americans share – that if they work hard enough they can make it. She worked all those hours, in all those terrible places for what?

Forty-three dollars. His mother was all that he knew, and now she was gone.

Kane knew the dream his mother had chased was a lie. A lie that kept being perpetuated in the press and on TV. People who'd worked hard, or caught a lucky break and *made* it were held up as icons. Kane would make sure those people suffered for giving life to that dream, for adding fuel to that lie. Oh, how he would make them suffer.

Now, sitting in court, Kane remembered that feeling he'd had when he saw his name in the old clipping in his mother's scrapbook. He'd just felt it again when Flynn spoke. A killer who'd left his mark. A man the FBI have been chasing for years. A shiver of fear and pleasure washed over Kane. Like a cold, welcome hand reaching out and touching him on the shoulder.

I know your name. I know what you've done.

For a second, Kane was aware that the mask had slipped. His passive expression, open and neutral body language had changed as those thoughts flooded through his mind. He coughed, looked around. No one on the jury panel had noticed it. He looked at the defense attorney. Flynn didn't seem to have noticed either.

Something was wrong. Kane knew it. He felt it. This time, it wasn't the thrill that came with remembrance of his past labors, or even the gentle pleasure of nostalgia. This was something else.

Fear.

He suddenly felt naked. Exposed. As much as he desperately wanted to look around the courtroom, he did not dare to do so. Instead, he focused on Flynn, and let his peripheral vision do the work.

And there it was.

Kane confirmed it with a second's glance. Now there was no doubt.

The jury consultant, Arnold, was staring hard at Kane. He'd seen something. He'd seen his true face.

CHAPTER THIRTY-SEVEN

Anderson blazed through his fourteen years of experience as a New York homicide detective and cut to the chase.

"You see a lot in this job. After a while, you can read the murder from the crime scene. My experience told me this was personal."

My experience told me Anderson was full of shit. He had the guy he wanted for the crime, and he was gonna make everything else fit that case. If there was evidence that didn't sit with Solomon as the perp – the evidence got lost, or wasn't important.

"Detective Anderson, in what way was this *personal*?" asked Pryor.

"A young woman and her lover being murdered in their bed sounds pretty personal to me. Doesn't take a detective's badge to make you think the husband was a likely suspect. Yeah, we think we've got our man over there. The defendant, Robert Solomon."

Pryor took a moment, turned to look at Bobby, made sure the jury followed his gaze then returned to his direct examination.

"Detective, I'm going to post a photograph on the screen. It's an overhead shot of Ariella Bloom and Carl Tozer in the bedroom. It was taken by a forensic crime scene photographer and as I understand it these photos can be admitted without argument as exhibit one. I just want to warn the jury, and members of the public, this is a graphic image," said Pryor.

I'd already agreed we could skip calling the photographer. The photos didn't lie, so there was no reason to waste time calling him as a witness to formally prove the exhibit.

I wasn't looking at the screen beside the witness stand when Pryor loaded the picture. My attention was on Bobby. He'd closed his eyes, and pointed his head at the table. Gasps from the audience told me the photo was up. I heard Harry call for silence.

No camera phones were allowed in court. This photo wouldn't make it onto the daily news. It was far too graphic, anyway.

Bobby glanced at the screen, once, put his hands over his face.

Arnold shrugged, nodded at Bobby and then at the jury. I knew what he was trying to tell me. I'd had the same thought. It would be hard on Bobby, but it was in his interests.

"Bobby, I need you to look at the screen," I whispered.

"I can't. And I don't need to. I've had that image in my mind and I can't shake it," he said.

"You have to look. I know it's hard. That's why you have to do it. I know you don't want to look at what someone did your wife. I need the jury to see that in your eyes," I said.

He shook his head.

"Bobby, Eddie is giving you a choice," said Arnold. "Would you rather stare at the ceiling of a prison cell every night for the next thirty-five years or look at this photo? Do it now," he said.

I never thought I'd say it, but I was grateful Arnold was here.

Bobby sniffed, took a breath and did what he was told.

I didn't know if the jury saw it, but I did. Tears streaked his face, and his eyes spoke of loss, not guilt.

I nodded at Arnold, thanking him. He met my eyes with a sideways glance, nodded back.

"Detective Anderson, from this photograph, and the victim's injuries, could you tell the jury what you believe happened in this bedroom?" asked Pryor, plainly. As if he was asking Anderson if it was cold outside.

I didn't want to look at the photo either, but like Bobby I had no choice. I needed to follow Anderson's testimony.

Jesus, it was brutal.

Anderson and Pryor looked at the screen. The scene of two human beings destroyed in a torrent of violence, almost casually. They were business-like, as they discussed how these young people died.

"You'll notice first that Mr. Tozer's head is pointed down, and his legs curled up. According to the autopsy report, Mr. Tozer died from a massive head wound. His skull had been fractured, and there had been catastrophic injury to the brain. Even if he didn't die instantly, he would've been incapacitated from that blow. My reading is that Mr. Tozer would've been viewed as a threat to the murderer. Tozer was a trained security specialist. It makes sense to deal with him first. A single, forceful blow to the back of the head while he slept would cause such an injury and would account for the lack of defensive wounds," said Anderson.

"Have you been able to identify the weapon that was used on Mr. Tozer?" asked Pryor.

"Yes. I found a baseball bat in the corner of the room. It had blood on it consistent with it being used to strike someone. Subsequently, the lab confirmed the blood on the bat belonged to Mr. Tozer. It seems likely that this was the murder weapon. And before you ask, yes, the defendant's fingerprints were on the bat."

I felt sick watching Pryor break out a Hollywood smile at this answer. The jury didn't see it, they were too focused on Anderson.

Pryor took the bat, wrapped in a clear evidence bag, and held it above his head.

"This is the bat?" he asked.

"That's the one," said Anderson. The bat was logged into evidence, and Pryor gave it to the clerk.

"So, if as you say, Mr. Tozer was struck by this bat, what happened next?"

"Ariella Bloom was stabbed five times in the chest and abdomen area. One of the wounds penetrated the heart. She would've died very quickly."

At least Pryor had the good sense to pause and let the jury glance up at the photo of Ariella on the screen. He let everyone take a second to consider the way she died. Pryor knew an angry jury brought back guilty verdicts, nine times out of ten.

"The victims were examined by Sharon Morgan, the medical examiner, both at the scene and at the morgue. Were you informed of the outcome of those investigations?"

"Yes, the ME called me to attend when she'd found something in the back of Carl Tozer's mouth."

"What was it?"

"A dollar bill. It had been folded into the shape of a butterfly, then folded in half at the wings, and was placed inside Carl's mouth."

The ADA was Johnny-on-the-spot with the remote. He brought up a photograph of the bill on screen. The murmurs broke out amongst the crowd. This was all new to them. Nothing of this had been in the media before. The strange origami insect lay on a steel table. Shadows beneath its wings. I noticed some staining on the corners of the bill, maybe saliva or a tiny amount of blood.

Knowing that it had been in a dead man's mouth made it feel otherworldly. A macabre insect, beautiful and ominous, that only hatched within the dead.

"Was the butterfly examined, Detective?"

"It was, I had the NYPD forensic team do a full work-up. We found two sets of DNA on the bill. The first DNA profile came from another individual, but it's felt that this was unconnected to the crime. An anomaly. Unimportant. What was important was that the team found the defendant's fingerprints on the dollar. Thumb on the front of the bill, partial index finger on the reverse. In the same area as the thumbprint, the forensics team found DNA material. Touch DNA, from sweat and skin cells. The DNA matched the defendant."

That last sentence hit the room like a shockwave. People didn't talk, or exclaim out loud. It brought a deeper, total silence to the room. No one shuffled their feet, no one rustled their coats, or coughed or made any of the noises you'd expect from a large static crowd.

The silence broke with the sound of a woman crying into her hands. A family member, no doubt. Probably Ariella's mother. I didn't turn around. Some moments were best left private.

And Pryor played it perfectly. He stood still, and let the sound of a mother's grief echo through the minds of every person in the court. Looking around the room, most were stunned. Apart from one person. The reporter from the *New York Star*, Paul Benettio. He sat with his arms folded in the row directly behind the prosecution table. He didn't react to Anderson's testimony. My guess was he knew about it already. When the silence became uncomfortable, and he'd waited long enough, Pryor spoke again.

"Your Honor, we shall be calling the forensic officer who conducted those tests in due course."

Harry nodded, and Pryor got back to business.

"Detective, you spoke to the defendant at the scene, correct?"

"Yes. The defendant had blood on his sweatshirt, track pants, and his hands. He told me he'd gotten home around midnight, went upstairs and found his wife and chief of security dead in his bedroom. He then said he tried to revive Ariella, then he called 911."

Pryor swung around, pointed at one of the ADAs, who picked up a remote control and hit a button.

"We're just going to play the 911 call. I would like you to listen to this, please," said Pryor.

I'd heard it before. This was the first time for the jury. I thought the call supported Bobby's defense. He sounded like a man who'd just found his wife murdered. There was panic, disbelief, fear, grief – everything was there in that voice. I found the transcript on the laptop and read along to the recording.

Despatcher: 911 emergency, do you need fire, police or medical assistance?
Solomon: Help . . . Jesus . . . I'm at 275 West 88ᵗʰ Street. My wife . . . I think she's dead. Somebody . . . Oh God . . . somebody killed them.
Despatcher: I'm sending police officers and paramedics. Calm down, sir, are you in any danger?
Solomon: I . . . I . . . don't know.
Despatcher: Are you in the property right now?
Solomon: Yeah, in the bedroom, I . . . I . . . just found them. They're in the bedroom. They're dead.
(sounds of crying)
Despatcher: Sir? Sir? Take a deep breath, I need you tell me if you know of anyone else in the property right now.
(sounds of breaking glass and someone stumbling)
Solomon: I'm here. Ah, I haven't checked the house . . . Oh shit . . . please get the ambulance here right now. She's not breathing . . .
(Solomon drops phone)
Despatcher: Sir? Please pick up the phone. Sir? Sir?

"The call only lasts a matter of seconds. Detective, at the time you first attended the crime scene, had you heard this 911 call?" said Pryor.

I didn't like where this was headed.

"No, I had not," said Anderson.

I took Bobby's arm. "Bobby, when you made the 911 call, you fell, or something toppled over or got smashed. What was it?" I whispered.

"Uh, I'm trying to remember. I don't know for sure. Maybe I knocked something over on the bedside table. I wasn't paying attention," he said, his words trailing off as he felt himself in that moment again, in the room with the bodies.

I called up the crime scene photos on the laptop and started flicking through them, looking for the bedside table. In one shot, I could see most of the table. A picture lay smashed on the floor. He might have knocked it over and not noticed, in the circumstances. I had a bad feeling Pryor might have an alternative suggestion of where that sound came from.

"Detective Anderson, just tell the jury about photograph EZ17," said Pryor, as the ADA called it up on the screen.

It was a shot of the hallway on the second floor, with the upturned table and the smashed vase beneath the rear window. I had no idea where he was going with this line of questioning, but it seemed like he was winding up to deliver a knockout punch.

"Sure, when I got to the property I saw this table overturned on the landing. The vase had broken," said Anderson.

"Where is that table now?" said Pryor.

"It's at the crime lab. It had been disturbed, somehow, maybe before or after the murders. When I questioned the defendant in the precinct I asked him if he'd knocked over the table. He said he couldn't remember. He maintained that he had found the bodies, and that someone else had killed his wife and head of security. At that time in the investigation, the defendant was a suspect, but we weren't ruling out the possibility he was telling the truth. If he didn't knock over the table, maybe someone else did. We took it in for testing together with the shards from the vase."

"And what did you discover?" said Pryor.

I flicked through the inventory on the Solomon case file. There was no forensic report on the antique table. I was about to object when Anderson said, "Nothing. At first."

"Go on," said Pryor.

"Yesterday I visited the lab, and we looked at the table. See, the one piece of evidence we didn't have was the knife that was used to kill Ariella Bloom. An extensive search had been made of the house and the surrounding area. The table is old, an antique. I thought maybe there was a hidden drawer."

"And was there?" said Pryor.

"No. But I took a look at the prints again. We'd had some unusual results. The lab were looking for fingerprints, and there was nothing out of the ordinary there, but they also found an unusual pattern of markings on the table. I ordered further investigation on these marks and we just got the report this morning."

An ADA approached the defense table with a bound report. I took it. Opened it. Skim-read it.

It could've been worse. But not by much. I handed the report to Bobby. Last-minute, new evidence. I could rage and shout and prepare a motion to exclude it. But I knew there was no point. Harry would allow the evidence to be admitted.

Things had just gotten a lot more serious for Bobby.

The screen changed and we were looking at what appeared to be two sets of three parallel lines across part of the table. Like someone had just taken three brushes in their hand and smeared it across the table twice.

I wished it were brushes.

"What is this, Detective?"

"Tread marks," said Anderson. "The tread pattern matches a pair of Adidas sneakers that the defendant wore that night. It looks as though the defendant stood on the table and then it toppled, so his feet slid off of it."

Bobby said, "He's lying. I've never stood on top of that table." He said it loud enough to be heard, and Harry shot him a look that told him to shut the hell up.

Anderson continued, "So I visited the crime scene this morning. A little way away from the table is the hallway light. It's a suspended ceiling bulb with an ornate, colored glass lampshade in the shape of a bowl. I stood on a pair of step ladders and retrieved a knife that someone had placed in the lampshade."

Bobby's hands started to shake.

"And is this the knife?" said Pryor, signaling for another photo to be added to the screen.

I looked up and saw the same photo I'd just seen in the report. A switchblade. Black handle, with an ivory base. There was blood on it. And dust.

The only saving grace – no prints.

"Is this the knife that killed Ariella Bloom?" said Pryor.

Everyone in the courtroom knew the answer to that one. Bobby's chin dropped to his chest. That knife just cut the last strings holding Bobby's defense together.

CHAPTER THIRTY-EIGHT

Anderson confirmed the blood found on the knife matched the victim's blood type, and they were working up a DNA profile to confirm it. I whispered to Bobby to hold his head up. I didn't want him to look like he was beaten.

Not yet.

Pryor fired another question at the cop.

"Detective Anderson, it would be unusual for an intruder who uses a knife to stab someone to death, to hide that murder weapon in the victim's home?"

I stood up fast. Too fast. My side burst into a shockwave of pain, and I struggled to find the breath to speak.

"Objection, Your Honor, Mr. Pryor is testifying, not asking questions."

"Sustained," said Harry.

Slowly, I sat down. There wasn't much point in objecting. Pryor would rephrase the question – but Anderson was in no doubt about the answer he was supposed to give to the jury.

"Detective, in all your years on the force have you ever encountered a domestic stabbing scene where the perpetrator hid the offending weapon at the scene of the crime?" said Pryor.

"No, I've never seen that before. Not in my whole career. Normally, they take the knife with them. Either they keep it or dispose of it. There's no point in hiding it in the house. The only reason to hide it would be to create the impression for law enforcement that the murderer had left the property, and taken the weapon with them. Listening to that 911 call, it sounds like the defendant was standing on the table when he made the call. You can hear heavy, rapid footfalls. Like someone stumbling, and then something breaking. It sounds to me like the table went over with the defendant standing on it, and the vase broke."

"Thank you, Detective Anderson. Nothing further from me at this time. Now, I believe my colleague is about to complain about your police work and seek to have it excluded from this jury's consideration. In fact, I'm surprised he hasn't objected to the knife testimony already," said Pryor.

I whispered an instruction to Arnold. He left the courtroom. I stood and made my way toward Pryor. The pain was manageable if I took my time. Pryor leaned on the prosecution table, his left hand on his hip, looking mightily pleased with himself.

"We have no objections, Your Honor," I said, "In fact, this evidence assists the jury."

Harry looked at me like I'd gone mad. Pryor's cat-who-got-the-cream expression dropped faster than a mob informer in an elevator shaft.

A hush fell on the courtroom. I was in the zone. There was only Anderson and me. Nothing else mattered, no one else was watching. I blanked out the crowd, the prosecutor, the judge and the jury. Just him and me. I let the anticipation build. Anderson took a sip of water and waited.

I waited too. I didn't want to get into my cross until Arnold arrived back. He would be back any second, it wouldn't take long to move the equipment. From the store.

"Detective, I wanted to ask how your arm got broken," I said.

He had a jaw like a vise hanging off a workbench. And on either side of his face I saw those massive jaw muscles working, flexing, as he gritted his teeth real tight.

"I fell," he said.

"You fell?" I said.

Hesitation. His Adam's apple bobbed up and down in his throat.

"Yeah, slipped on the ice. After we're done here I'll tell you all about it," he replied, through dry lips. He took another sip of water. I'd seen a lot of witnesses go through anxiety on the stand. Some tremble, some give their answers much too fast, some give basic monosyllabic answers, some get a dry mouth.

I didn't expect him to tell the truth. And I didn't mention what really happened, but I wanted him to think that I might. Just to unnerve him. And in turn he'd threatened me.

The rear doors of the courtroom opened. Arnold returned, and he'd brought some of the court security staff with him. Around five of them. They formed an unlikely procession; carrying bags, boxes, and a heavy mattress between the two of them. I stopped asking questions and waited while the line made its way down the central aisle of the courtroom toward me. The procession of strange objects brought some mystified looks from the audience.

I heard Pryor scoring points with the crowd.

"Is there a marching band bringing up the rear of that procession?" he said.

Leaning over the prosecution table I said, "Yeah, there's a band. It's playing your funeral march."

Before Pryor and I got into it, I told Harry I needed to make a formal motion to allow a reconstruction during my cross-examination of Anderson. Harry sent out the jury and Pryor and I approached the bench.

"How scientific is this reconstruction?" asked Harry.

"I'm not a scientist, Judge, but we do have an expert witness and the rest is physics," I said.

"Your Honor, the prosecution has not been given any notice of this motion. We have no clue what Mr. Flynn is proposing and we move to have this motion denied. It's ambush."

"Motion granted," said Harry, "And before you get any ideas about stopping this trial to appeal my ruling you should think about one thing. I saw your little trick with the murder weapon. If Mr. Flynn had asked for time to deal with that evidence I would've granted it. My guess is you've had that in your back pocket for a while. You delay this trial and I might pass the time by deposing the analyst from the NYPD crime lab about when he really found those marks on that table."

Retreating, hands raised, Pryor said, "As your Honor pleases. I have no intention of delaying this trial."

Harry nodded, turned toward me and said, "I'm giving you a little leeway here. But from now on if either of you have evidence you want to admit – serve it on each other."

"Actually, there are some photographs I need to use. They were taken yesterday at the crime scene," I said.

"Serve them now," said Harry.

I took out my phone, brought up the photos Harper took in the bedroom yesterday morning and emailed them to the DA's office. I then took Pryor aside and showed him the photos on my phone. He didn't have a problem with me using them. Probably because he didn't know what was coming. If he had an inkling about what I was about to do, Pryor would've raised hell. I prayed it was a decision he would come to regret.

CARP LAW

Suite 421, Condé Nast Building, 4 Times Square, New York, NY.

Strictly Confidential,
Attorney Client Work Product

Juror Memo

The People -v- Robert Solomon
Manhattan Criminal Court

Rita Veste

Age: 33

Child Psychologist in private practice. Married. Spouse is Executive Chef at Maroni's. No children. Parents both retired and living in Florida. Democrat but did not vote in last election. No social media presence. Fine wine enthusiast. Never been called as expert witness. Financials sound.

Probability of Not Guilty vote: 65%

Arnold L. Novoselic

CHAPTER THIRTY-NINE

Pryor's direct examination of Detective Anderson enthralled Kane's fellow jurors. The detective gave the jurors their first taste of the evidence. He was the opening act. And all of the jurors seemed to be focused on the witness.

This certainly pleased Kane. For the testimony had proven to be a useful distraction. While Anderson testified, Kane took all the time he needed to examine Spencer's notes, which rested on his knee. None of the other jurors in the back row were tall enough to see over the shoulders of their fellow jurors in front. Except Kane. He'd made half a page of notes himself. Key words and phrases which formed an aide memoir of the testimony. He flicked over a page, and wrote a single word.

"Guilty."

He looked back at Spencer's notes. Then his own. Scribbled out the word "Guilty" heavily. Then he rewrote the word on a fresh sheet of paper. This time he made the "G" a little straighter and smaller, and put a longer tail on the letter "y". While he worked he was careful to lean over his notes, making sure no one on either side of him could see what he was writing. He was also careful to keep his pen raised, and not to touch this page with his bare hands.

For most of his life, Kane had been practicing at being other people. Sometimes these identities stuck around for a while, especially when Kane had taken the place of a real person. Sometimes the fake identities were used up and disposed of quickly after they had served their purpose. Of the identities that stayed around, Kane had a few fond favorites. And he'd soon learned, that in order to stay in his identity, he needed to be able to sign some documents – new driver's license, checks, money transfers, the usual. In his spare time, Kane would practice his identity's signature and learn how to forge it, perfectly. Over the years, he had become skilled. His pen control and hand-to-eye coordination became that of a fine artist.

Finally, satisfied with his penwork, Kane eased deeper into his seat, flicked the notepaper back to the first page of his notes and folded his arms.

Pryor finished his examination-in-chief, and Kane watched, transfixed as a line of people came through the back doors holding boxes and even a mattress. He saw Pryor arguing with Flynn.

"Your Honor, I would like to raise a motion to allow a formal demonstration during my cross-examination of this witness," said Flynn.

"Let's hear it, but before that we need the jury to be excused," said the judge.

The jurors on either side of Kane got up. He followed their lead, put his notebook in his pocket. The jury keeper led them out of the side door, back to the jury room. In a lot of cases juries were up and down and back and forth from the jury room ten or twelve times a day while the lawyers argued about the law. Kane was used to it.

The jury keeper stood outside the room, holding the door open for the jurors. As Kane approached her he said, "Sorry, is it okay if I use the bathroom?"

"Sure, down the hallway, second on the left," she said.

Kane thanked the officer, made his way down the hall. The bathroom was small, dark and smelled like most male bathrooms. One of the lights was out. Two urinals sat against white tiles. Kane made his way to the single cubicle, closed and locked the door.

He worked fast.

First he took out a pack of bubble gum from his pocket. It had already been opened and had one piece removed. He tipped the pack into his palm and the rest of the gum spilled out. Along with a small baggie around the same size as the individually wrapped pieces of gum. He removed the cellophane wrapping from the baggie and shook out a pair of impossibly thin, latex gloves. Quickly, he put them on. He removed the notebook from his pocket and tore off the page with the word "Guilty" written on it. Scrunching the paper in his hands, Kane made a small ball of paper, but was careful to keep at least the first three letters of the word in view. He put the balled-up note in his jacket, took off the gloves and put some pocket change inside of them, wrapped them in toilet paper, dropped them in the bowl and flushed.

The jury didn't have to wait too long. Ten minutes. Just enough time for Spencer to step out of line.

"Look, I know this doesn't look good for the defendant, but the case isn't over. And I don't trust that cop," said Spencer.

"Me either. And that slimy prosecutor had the knife all along. Just didn't want to give it to the defense," said Manuel.

"We don't know that. All I can say is it sure looks bad for Solomon right now," said Cassandra.

Kane had noticed Cassandra stealing the occasional glance at Spencer. He was young and slim and Cassandra had not yet worked up the courage to talk to him, but the attraction appeared obvious even to Kane.

"We have to keep an open mind. And we're not allowed to discuss the evidence until the trial is over," said Kane.

A few of the jurors nodded their approval.

Betsy said, "He's right. We can't discuss it."

"I'm just sayin' the same thing. We shouldn't trust this as Gospel just because it came from a cop. Open minds, people," said Spencer.

The jury took their seats and before Kane sat down, he took off his jacket and folded it. He draped the jacket over his right knee after he took his seat on the jury panel, right behind Spencer. The judge brought the trial back to life.

"Thank you, ladies and gentlemen. I have allowed Mr. Flynn some leeway in a practical demonstration. You should remember that the prosecution will have a right to elicit further testimony from this witness on any matter arising from the demonstration. Now, proceed Mr. Flynn," said the judge.

Kane let his jacket slide to the floor, ensuring it fell with the left sleeve facing toward him. He bent down to pick it up, careful to ensure the jurors on either side of him were focused on Eddie Flynn's opening question. Both Terry and Rita concentrated on the lawyer. As Kane gripped the jacket, he pushed the wad of paper from the right-hand pocket from the outside of the material. This meant the ball of paper was on the floor with his jacket on top. Kane lifted the jacket just an inch off the floor, in a sweeping motion. For the briefest of moments, he caught sight of the ball as it rolled into shadow beneath the bench in front of him.

He quickly checked the faces of the jurors on his left, and Rita on his right. None had seemed to notice.

As Flynn began his cross-examination, the tension between him and Anderson didn't escape Kane's notice. It happened when the cop talked about his broken wrist. The cop said it had happened because of a fall.

Kane wondered if Anderson had fallen, or if he'd taken a swing at the defense attorney and missed.

Flynn was in pain. He moved more slowly than when Kane had seen him yesterday. And he'd noticed the attorney fighting to hide a grimace every time he got up from his seat.

Kane thought that if he had to bet on it, Anderson and Flynn had had a fight of some sort the night before. The way the cop looked at Flynn had some weight behind hit. The hatred that rose from Anderson like steam was more than the passing disgust homicide cops usually felt for defense attorneys.

No, there was history there. Recent history.

Kane didn't mind cops. He had no hatred of them.

That's why he had chosen to work with one of them. They came in handy. He made a note to call his contact later. There was more work to be done.

CHAPTER FORTY

There are three basic elements to a good hustle. Doesn't matter if you're a con artist in Havana, London, or Beijing. You'll still go through these three stages. They might have different names, and may be used to different ends, but when it comes down to it these three processes lead to successful cons.

The magic number, again.

It just so happens there are three stages to a good cross-examination. It just so happens these stages are exactly the same as those used by two-bit hustlers and silk handkerchief con artists. The art of the con and the art of the cross were one and the same. And I knew how to use both.

Stage one. The convincer.

"Detective, from the photographs that we've seen, and the autopsy reports on the victims, and from your own investigations, these murders could have been committed by someone other than the defendant, correct?"

He didn't think about it at all. I knew he wouldn't. Once homicide cops get an idea in their head, it's damn near impossible to shake them out of it.

"No, incorrect. All of the evidence points toward the defendant as the murderer," he said, calmly.

"The defense does not accept that, but let's say for a moment that you're correct. That all of the evidence points toward the defendant as the killer. Is it possible that the real perpetrator of this crime simply wants you, and your colleagues, and the DA to believe that the *defendant* is guilty of this crime?"

"You mean somebody floated in and out of that property without being seen, and planted evidence against Bobby Solomon? No," he said, suppressing a laugh, "I'm sorry, that's just ridiculous."

"Could the murders have happened only in the way you described to the jury? The bat used on Carl Tozer, and then the knife used on Ariella Bloom as they both lay in bed?"

"That's the only scenario that fits the evidence," said Anderson.

I returned to my laptop, accessed the court video system with my password and loaded up two of the photographs Harper had taken yesterday morning. I looked at the screen, and saw Pryor had left up the picture of the murder scene. That was useful. I whispered instructions to Arnold on how to scroll through the images and transfer them to the court screen. He gave me the thumbs up, then got up and moved our equipment to the well of the court, the space on the tiled floor right in front of the judge, jury and witness.

I got up, winced at the increasing pain in my side and told myself I was due some more painkillers soon. I just had to hang on a little longer. For a moment, I looked at the boxes and the mattress, and the bag sitting on top of the mattress.

Stage two. The pay-off.

"Detective Anderson, the photo on the screen of the victims, is that exactly how you found them when you attended the scene?" I said.

He glanced at the photo again. Carl on his side, blood on the back of his head. Ariella on her back, blood on her stomach and chest and nowhere else.

"Yes, that's how we found them."

I'd read the medical examiner's report from the scene. It gave a detailed description of the positioning and injuries to the body. She'd arrived around one a.m. And had given the time of death to within three to four hours of her arrival.

I held out two fingers to Arnold, he changed the photo on the courtroom screen. A close-up of the product tag at the bottom of the mattress at the crime scene.

"Detective, the mattress on the floor here is a NemoSleep, product number 55612L. Can you confirm this is the identical product number to the mattress shown in the photograph with the victim's bloodstains on it?"

He looked at the photo, said, "It seems to be."

"The medical examiner records that Ariella's torso was positioned twelve inches from the left-hand side of the bed, and her head nine inches from the top of the bed, correct?"

"I believe so, I can't recall exactly without reading the report again," he said.

I paused while Pryor's ADA found a copy of the report and gave it to Anderson. I referred him to the relevant page from memory. It's a skill that's served me well in the law. I never forget.

"Yes, I'd say that's correct," he said.

He also confirmed Tozer's head was located at twenty-four inches from the top of the bed and eighteen inches from the right-hand side of the bed according to the medical examiner.

I picked up the bag from the mattress and laid out the items on the floor.

Tape measure. Magic marker. Shot glass. Corn syrup. Bottled water. Food dye. A bed sheet.

I opened the new bed sheet, spread it out on the mattress. I measured out the distances for the positioning of the victims recorded by the ME, and drew a circle around them on the sheet with the marker. I then raised a finger at Arnold – I needed the first photo on the screen.

The image on the courtroom screen changed. It showed a picture of the mattress taken yesterday. A heavy, wide bloodstain pattern on Ariella's side of the bed, and just a spot of staining on Tozer's side below his skull, around the same size as the bottom of a coffee cup.

"Detective, would you agree the marks that I've made on this bed correlate with the bloodstains in the photograph?"

He took his time, glancing between the screen and the mattress on the floor, then said, "More or less."

"You have the medical examiner's reports in front of you. She recorded Ariella Bloom's weight at one hundred and ten pounds and Carl Tozer's at two hundred and thirty-three pounds, isn't that right?"

He flicked over the pages, then said, "Yes."

"Detective, this isn't a math test, but Carl Tozer weighed more than twice as much as Ariella Bloom, wouldn't you say?"

He nodded. Shifted in his seat.

"You'll need to answer for the record," I said.

"Yes," he said, leaning forward into the microphone.

I opened the box, removed two kettlebells. Showed them to Anderson. He agreed one weighed twenty-five pounds, the other fifty pounds. I placed one in the circle on Ariella's side and one just below the spot on Tozer's side of the bed. I could tell before I went any further that this demonstration was going to work. I'd known that back in Bobby's bedroom when Harper and I had lain on the bed. The fifty-pound bell sat way lower on the mattress. It had sunk down with the weight. The twenty-five pound bell looked at least a couple of inches higher on the mattress.

"Detective, again, from the medical examiner's record, she noted that Ariella Bloom suffered significant blood loss. Almost a thousand ccs?"

He found the record, "Yes."

I opened the bottle of water, poured some out into my glass on the defense table, then trickled corn syrup into the water and two drops of food dye. I replaced the cap on the bottle and shook it up. Took off the cap and filled the shot glass.

"Detective, this shot glass, which you are free to examine, holds fifty ccs. Do you wish to examine it?" I said.

"I'll take your word for it," he said.

"The NYPD crime lab uses a mix of one part corn syrup to four parts water to replicate the consistency of blood. It's in their reconstruction handbook for blood spatter experts. Are you aware of this?"

"I wasn't, but again I don't disagree," he said. Anderson was careful not to concede points when he knew I had something up my sleeve. If he argued needlessly it might weaken his testimony. All NYPD cops had the same witness training. I'd cross-examined enough of them to know how they play it.

Slowly, I poured the shot glass over the kettlebell on Ariella's side of the bed. A pool formed around the base of the kettlebell then, the dark stain spread. It trickled across the bed and snaked around the kettlebell on Tozer's side. The ball of muscle in Anderson's jaw started working like a pump. I could hear the dull grind of his teeth ten feet away.

"Detective, you are free to get up and examine this mattress, if you wish, before you answer my question. I want you to look at the photograph of the mattress on screen and tell me what's wrong with that picture?"

Anderson looked at the screen, looked at the mattress. He was a poor actor. He rubbed at his temples then shook his head as he tried and failed to feign confusion.

"I don't see what you mean," he said.

I knew he was trying to make things difficult for me, but he'd given the wrong answer and opened the door for me to explain it all to *him*, and more importantly, to the *jury*.

The screen changed and Arnold brought up the photo of the victims taken at the scene. At least Arnold and I were on the same page. Before I opened my mouth, I saw Harry making notes. He was way ahead of me.

"Detective, there is no blood from Ariella Bloom on the body of Carl Tozer, is there?"

"No, I guess not," he said.

Pryor had listened to enough. He bounded out of this seat and stood beside me.

"Your Honor, the prosecution must object to this . . . this charade. Whether blood, or whatever it is on this mattress right here, flows downhill to another part of this mattress means nothing. The mattress in the defendant's home has not been tested. It is different. There is no evidence to say that what happens on this mattress would have happened, in principle, on the mattress at the crime scene."

Harry's eyebrows rose up on his head, and he tapped his pen on the desk.

"I've let this proceed, thus far, but Mr. Pryor raises a valid point, Mr. Flynn," said Harry.

Stage three. The moment when you realize you're a sucker.

I looked out over the crowd, who were all waiting anxiously on my answer. I saw a lot of things on the faces looking back at me. Some were dubious, some confused, but most were intrigued. For months they'd heard one story and one story alone – that Bobby Solomon had murdered his wife and chief of security. Now, maybe, they were hearing a different one.

Everyone loves a good story.

I found the face in the crowd that I'd been looking for.

"Mr. Cheeseman, would you stand up please?" I said.

A man around fifty years of age stood proud in the second row of the public seats. He had thick black hair, neatly combed, and a mustache that looked as if it was cared for like a much-loved family pet. A large man, in every department, in a midnight-blue suit, white shirt and emerald tie.

I turned back to Harry.

"Your Honor, this is Mr. Cheeseman. In 2003 he designed and patented the NemoSleep mattress. It's made with a latex and Kevlar-coated fabric that is one hundred per cent waterproof, guaranteed. This mattress has the same absorption rate as high carbon steel. It's also hypoallergenic, antibacterial, anti-fungal and used by the hotel industry worldwide. If it's required, Mr. Cheeseman can provide testimony now, out of sequence, if Mr. Pryor cares to cross-examine him."

Harry could barely keep the delight from his features as he stared at Mr. Cheeseman. What made it all the more satisfying was the look on Pryor's face. Surprise didn't quite cover it. He'd walked into a brick wall with "not guilty" written all over it.

"Ahm, Your Honor, I'm afraid I shall have to reserve my position on Mr. Cheeseman at this time," he said.

"I'm allowing this line of questioning to continue, for now," said Harry.

I had my foot back on Anderson's throat before Pryor had reached the prosecution table.

"Detective, as we have already established, there is no blood from Ariella Bloom on Mr. Tozer's body. Not one drop. If the victims were situated as you found them when they were murdered, there would be blood on Mr. Tozer. Do you accept that?"

"No, I believe the victims were murdered where they lay," said Anderson.

"Do you accept that liquid runs downhill?" I asked.

"I . . . of course I do," he said.

"It's simple physics, Detective. Carl Tozer was much heavier than Ariella Bloom. His weight caused the mattress to sag. Any blood escaping from Mrs. Bloom's body would trickle downhill, according to the laws of gravity, and would be found on Mr. Tozer, correct?"

He hesitated. His lips moved but no sound escaped from his throat.

"It's possible," he said.

I went in for the kill. The screen showed the photo Harper had taken of the staining on the mattress.

"If Tozer was on that bed when Mrs. Bloom was murdered, he would have blood on him. Detective, isn't it obvious, having seen the demonstration, that Carl Tozer was not in this bed when the other victim was murdered? The blood must have had time to dry and settle before Carl Tozer's weight was placed upon it?"

"It's possible," he said.

"You mean it's probable?"

He spoke through gritted teeth. "It's possible."

"And at the beginning of this cross-examination, you told the jury the murders could only have happened when both victims were in that bed, laying down together. The evidence now points somewhere else, doesn't it?" I said.

"Maybe. It doesn't change the fact that your client is the one who killed them," he said.

I was about to go at it with Anderson. There were a lot more questions about his investigation. Except the judge held up his hand and called for me to stop. A court officer was whispering to the judge. Harry got up and said, "Twenty-minute adjournment. I need to see both counsel in my chambers right this second."

He sounded pissed. The court officer and Harry exchanged words, Harry disappeared into the back corridor before the clerk yelled, "All rise."

I didn't know what was happening. Neither did Pryor.

But something was up. I saw the jury keeper collecting notebooks from the jurors. Shit. Last thing I needed was a fresh jury. I was just starting to win these people over.

Whatever had happened, Harry was real mad.

A noise caught my attention. Raised voices. I located the source of the commotion and took a step back. In all my years, I'd never seen anything like it.

A full-blown argument had erupted in the jury stand.

CARP LAW

Suite 421, Condé Nast Building, 4 Times Square, New York, NY.

Strictly Confidential, Attorney Client Work Product

Juror Memo

The People -v- Robert Solomon
Manhattan Criminal Court

Manuel Ortega

Age: 38

Pianist, flautist, guitarist. Main income is as a session musician. No bands currently. Divorced. One child, boy, aged eleven lives with the ex. Poor financials (aggressive creditors). No voting history. Moved to New York from Texas twenty years ago. Brother in prison. Social media posts show strong opinion against the prison system.

Probability of Not Guilty vote: 90%

Arnold L. Novoselic

FORTY-ONE

He'd waited for exactly the right moment.

Hard to judge. So many people around him. Sitting close to others had always been a particular source of discomfort for Kane. He had spent years being attuned to the finer details of the people he targeted: their tone of voice, speech patterns, body posture, habits, tics, the rhythm of their breath, their smell, even the way they folded their hands at rest.

When he sat amongst the other jurors, he was unable to just switch it off. This acute sense of others. At times it became overwhelming. At times, he was glad of it.

Like now.

He could sense it without even looking. Flynn had led the prosecutor into a hole. The tall, fat man in the second row. Cheeseman. Even the furniture seemed to turn toward him. It was a mesmerizing move.

Kane flicked out his right leg, then brought it smoothly over his left knee. He folded his hand over his crossed legs, and waited. He knew the ball of paper had been propelled forward, into the row in front. He'd felt his foot make contact. And heard only the briefest rustling of paper.

Spencer glanced to his left, looking for the source of the noise. Then right. He didn't see anything. He would've had to bend over to see the paper.

Kane could no longer see the wad of notepaper although he knew where it was, instinctively.

The juror to the right of Spencer, Betsy, put her palms down beside her, and adjusted her position on the seat, swinging her legs out, then tucking them underneath the bench by crossing her ankles.

She'd heard something. Kane heard it too. It had been louder this time. A crunch of paper. Betsy bent down to investigate, and came up with the wad of paper in her hand. She stayed motionless for a time, holding the paper in her hand and staring at it like it was a crystal ball.

The word, "Guilty" could clearly be seen on the paper. Rita was beside Kane. She'd watched Betsy pick something off the floor. Rita shuffled forward and placed a hand, delicately on Betsy's shoulder.

"Oh my God, does that say *guilty*," whispered Rita.

"Yeah, it does," said Betsy.

Both women craned their necks in Spencer's direction.

"What are you doing, Spencer?" said Betsy.

Spencer faced Betsy, momentarily perplexed.

"What is that?" he said.

The jury keeper heard their voices, and passed by Kane as she leaned down, ready to tell them to be silent. That's when she saw the wad of paper. Betsy swiveled it around so the jury officer could see what had been written upon it. The officer stood bolt upright. Told them to be quiet. Took the wad of paper and marched toward the judge.

Kane remained passive, and adopted a confused expression. Without the jury officer present, Betsy let it all out.

"You're a manipulative little bastard, you know that?" she said.

And the rest of the jury heard it.

CHAPTER FORTY-TWO

In the end it took all of the court security officers to calm the jury. Five of them. And they were still arguing as they were led out of the jury stand. In all the trials I'd done over the years, this was the first time the jury risked being in contempt of court.

Chris Pellosi, the pale-skinned web designer, pulled Spencer's sweater with one hand and pointed at Manuel Ortega with the other. Daniel Clay, the sci-fi fan, joined the elderly Bradley Summers and James Johnson, the translator, in shouting down the entire crowd. They'd lost the argument. Hollering at people to be quiet never worked.

Manuel, the musician, was in the face of big Terry Andrews. All the while, Betsy and Rita unleashed a torrent on Spencer Colbert.

Only one man kept out of the argument, sitting quietly with his head bowed – Alec Wynn. The court officers got the jury out of the room.

Even as the corridor door closed behind them, we could still hear the argument.

"Jesus, what is going on?" said Bobby.

I returned to my client, and sought to reassure him.

"I have no idea, but whatever it is, it might be good for you," I said.

"How? Good in what way?" he said.

"It's early days yet, but the jury look a little *divided* at the moment. That's a good sign. We hope it stays that way."

He seemed to understand. Bobby was looking better. The color had returned to his cheeks. It gave him a glow.

It was all worth it. I'd given up a lot to sit beside Bobby Solomon and represent him. Looking at him now, I knew I'd made the right choice.

"So we've got a chance? I mean, I've never laid eyes on that knife before today, Eddie. I promise you I've never even seen it before, never mind touched it," he said.

"Bobby, the bat that was in the bedroom. Rudy told me you would've normally kept that in the hallway, is that true?"

"Yeah, absolutely. I grew up on a farm and my dad didn't like guns. He kept a two-by-four beside the front door at all times. It's for protection, you know? He broke that wood over a debt collector's head once. He did a few months for that one. When he got out he went and bought himself a baseball bat. Kept that in the same place. Little alcove beside the door. Said it wouldn't break so easily. I've always done the same, no matter where I've lived or how much security I got. I never used it, though."

"Fair enough," I said. I had an idea about that bat in the hall and how it linked to the mysterious bruise across Carl Tozer's throat.

The clerk came rushing over. Harry wanted to see counsel right away. We followed the clerk to Harry's chambers, and this time Pryor kept his mouth shut. He must've been worried about the jury. Twelve people that don't all get along will not give him a unanimous guilty. He was fighting to win the jury back and he knew it.

Harry sat behind his desk. He'd taken his robes off and hung them up. He wore a white shirt and braces with black pants. A balled-up piece of paper sat on his desk and beside it a tall stack of notebooks.

We sat down in the plush chairs opposite Harry. The clerk sat down at her desk, and the stenographer came in too. She started typing as soon as Harry spoke. We were on the record for this conversation.

"Gentlemen," said Harry, "We've got ourselves a rogue juror."

"Goddamn it," said Pryor, slapping Harry's desk.

I rubbed my face, asked Harry for water. I took another dose of painkillers. I needed them, too. Now more than ever. Aside from the broken rib, my head had started to pound. My head had been fine for the most of the day, as long as I didn't touch the bump on the back of my skull. Now I could feel a full-blown headache coming on. And it had nothing to do with the bat that hit me last night.

Harry's words were like getting hit with a piano falling out of a crane sling.

A rogue juror.

Never had one before, but I'd heard lots of stories and read about them in the newspapers. A rogue juror is a juror with their own agenda. In most cases, they know the defendant. They're a distant family relative, or a friend. They have one goal in mind – to get on the jury and swing the trial in whatever direction suits their purpose.

"Who is it?" said Pryor.

Harry said, "Take a look at this, but don't pick it up. It has quite enough fingerprints on it already."

We both stood and examined the ball of paper on Harry's desk. Seeing that word, "*Guilty*" written on a piece of paper and passed around the jury, well, that sent another shockwave of pain through my skull.

"Are you going to pull the trial?" I said.

"I'm not sure yet. I've been through the notebooks that the court supplied to the jurors. I think I've got a match. Two notebooks are blank. The rest of them, well, the handwriting doesn't even get close to this. I'm no handwriting expert, but that looks remarkably similar to me," said Harry.

Harry gestured to an open notebook on his desk. The handwriting in the notebook didn't look similar to the handwriting on the balled-up note on the desk, it looked identical.

"Looks like a match to me, Judge," said Pryor.

"Me too," I said.

Harry asked the clerk to bring the juror to his chambers. We didn't have to wait long. The clerk brought Spencer Colbert inside, and asked him to take the extra chair at the edge of Harry's desk. I wouldn't necessarily mind losing this juror. On paper he looked like our kind of people. Creative, hipster, liberal who wore a lot of tight turtleneck sweaters and smoked weed. He should've been ideal.

He sat down uneasily, like a kid brought to the principal's office for fighting in the schoolyard.

"Mr. Colbert, we're on the record here. I want to know if you wrote that word on this piece of paper and left it as some kind of message for your fellow jurors?" said Harry.

"What? No, I had nothing to do with that."

"It sure looks like your handwriting," said Harry.

Colbert made an attempt to say something, then thought better of it. He shrugged, and then said, "I don't know anything about this note. It wasn't me, Judge."

"I've been around the block, sir. I've looked at the note and your notebook. This is your last chance, " said Harry.

The juror stared at the floor, he was about to say something then shook his head.

"Wait now, Mr. Colbert. Before you say anything, you should know I can go in and question each juror. Or you can save me some time. Cause if I have to waste more of my day talking to the other jurors you can bet that you'll have to spend the night in the Tombs next door while I make up my mind about what to do with you," said Harry.

He didn't need to say any more. The thought of spending an evening with twenty guys in a lock-up made an honest man out of Colbert.

"I didn't write the note. I don't think he's guilty anyway," he said, and immediately wished he hadn't said a word.

The judge swiveled around in his chair to face us, and said, "Mr. Colbert you are dismissed from this jury. You're not supposed to have made any kind of judgment yet. On that basis alone, you're gone. I have to say I don't believe you. I think you wrote that note. I think you wanted to persuade your fellow jurors that the defendant is guilty. In any event, I won't have you interfering with this trial any further. I haven't yet made up my mind about the note. I'm going to ask NYPD to look into it, and look into you. I hope you are telling the truth for your sake. If your fingerprints are on this, you'll hear from me again. Is that understood?"

Spencer nodded, and got the hell out of there before he made things worse.

"Jurors are just falling off the tree like overripe apples, Judge," said Pryor.

"Tell me about it. I should've appointed half a dozen alternates. I'll tell the jury to disregard the note. Either of you want to say anything else? I can tell each of you that I'm not entertaining any motions for a mistrial here."

Pryor and I shook our heads. No point in trying to get a mistrial on this. If Harry told the jury to disregard the note, legally there were no grounds for a mistrial. Nothing more I could do.

"Good," said Harry, "We'll bring in the second alternate juror. She's been here for the whole trial, and I don't see her having any problems. Now, let's get back to work," said Harry.

CARP LAW

Suite 421, Condé Nast Building, 4 Times Square, New York, NY.

Strictly Confidential,
Attorney Client Work Product

Juror Memo

The People -v- Robert Solomon
Manhattan Criminal Court

James Johnston

Age: 43

Moved to New York two years ago from DC. Parents deceased. One sibling, brother, who remains in DC. Translator (Arabic, French, Russian, German). Works from home for a translation service with private video-conferencing base. Sound financials. Volunteers to a number of community groups, mostly in an effort to meet people. No social life. Enjoys French cinema, non-fiction and cheese tasting. Non-voter.

Probability of Not Guilty vote: 50%

Arnold L. Novoselic

CHAPTER FORTY-THREE

Two court security officers stayed with the jury while they waited on their return to the courtroom. None of the jury spoke. Kane had some coffee and watched his fellow jurors. Most of them looked more and more pissed off.

When the jury were led back into court a new juror was waiting for them. Valerie Burlington was in her mid-forties, dressed in expensive black jeans and a black top. She wore a lot of jewelry, all of it gold and all of it real. The heavy chain around her wrist probably cost twenty grand on its own. Despite the expense, it made her look cheap. She sat away from Kane, at the opposite end of his bench.

The judge informed the jury that Spencer had gone, and he had appointed one of the alternates as a replacement. As promised, Harry instructed the jury to disregard the note, and he gave them a stern warning about discussing the case before they'd heard all of the testimony. He made it clear what the consequences would be.

With Spencer gone, the only other juror Kane had to worry about was Manuel.

But he would have to wait.

The voice of Bobby's lawyer broke Kane's concentration. He had underestimated this man – Eddie Flynn. He would not do so again.

CHAPTER FORTY-FOUR

Detective Anderson didn't look too pleased to see me again. Few witnesses were. I had lost my momentum, and Anderson had had time to think about what I might ask him. I'd lost the element of surprise.

"Detective, we've established that you accept these murders could have happened in a manner different to what you originally described to the jury. Let me suggest how. Take a look, again, at the autopsy report for Mr. Tozer," I said.

Anderson found the document in front of him and said, "I still believe both victims were murdered in that bed, Counselor. I don't know why there was no blood on Mr. Tozer, but that doesn't change a thing."

I ignored his statement for now. I had every intention of coming back to it.

"You'll see on the third page of the report, it mentions a line of bruising on Mr. Tozer's throat. It's a third of an inch wide, and three inches long. See that?"

"Yes."

"How do you suppose he got that bruise, given your scenario of the victims being murdered in the bed while they slept?"

He thought about it, turned a page on the report and looked at the diagram of the body, where the ME had made a body chart showing the injuries.

"I don't know. Maybe he got it before he got into bed? Perhaps it's nothing to do with the murder?" he said.

"It's certainly possible that it's nothing to do with the murder. Or it might be the most important thing. Take a look at these photographs, please," I said.

Arnold brought up the police photographs showing the rest of the house. The kitchen, the hallways, the living rooms. With the exception of the kitchen, all of the floors were covered in that snowy white carpet.

"If Mr. Tozer did not die in the bed, it's likely he was murdered elsewhere in the house. As you can see, there are no bloodstains anywhere, are there?" I said.

This time he was quick to answer.

"None whatsoever. The only blood we found that came from Mr. Tozer was in that bed," he said, somewhat triumphantly.

"Detective, if an intruder managed to gain entrance to the property and he placed a bag over Mr. Tozer's head, and pulled it from behind you could expect to find similar bruising on his throat, is that not so?"

Anderson put on the brakes. He hadn't seen this coming.

"Maybe, but Mr. Tozer didn't die from asphyxiation. He was beaten over the head with a bat."

"It seems so. Detective, do you know where the defendant normally kept that bat in the house?"

"Can't say I do," he said.

"In the hallway, by the front door," I said.

Anderson shrugged, shook his head. As if to say, *so what?*

"An intruder who'd managed to gain entry, say on false pretenses, could then place a bag over Mr. Tozer's head from behind, pull on it causing the bruising, then grab the defendant's bat and kill Mr. Tozer with a massive blow to the back of the head. That's possible, isn't it?"

The detective shook his head while I asked the question. He wasn't ready to concede this and he thought he had an answer for it. Pryor could've objected, but seemed happy to let Anderson try and swat the question away.

"No way. If he did that, then where's the bloodstain? A single drop of blood on that carpet would stand out. We wouldn't have missed blood on this carpet."

"But if the intruder had a bag over Mr. Tozer's head, maybe even a drawstring bag, then he could still deliver that blow anywhere in the house because the blood spatter from the impact would be sealed in the bag, wouldn't it?"

226

It made sense. It explained the bruising on his throat, and the lack of blood from Tozer on the carpet, and it explained why Ariella Bloom hadn't bled on Tozer in the bed. By the time Tozer had been hauled up the stairs and placed beside her body, her heart would've stopped pumping. Which meant no more bleeding. Any blood already there would stay compressed beneath her weight, and would have soaked into the sheet.

"I don't get it. If that happened, why kill Ariella Bloom and then put Tozer's body beside her in the bed?" asked Anderson.

It was a rookie mistake. Harry was about to tell Anderson not to ask counsel questions. Witnesses never asked questions – they only answered them. On this occasion, however, I was happy to answer it.

"Because if Tozer's body was found beside Ariella, it makes it look like someone found them in bed together and killed them. It provides a motive for Bobby Solomon and diverts all of the investigators' attention toward him, and away from the identity of the real killer, doesn't it?"

"That's *your* opinion," said Anderson.

"Let's move away from opinions, shall we? It's a plain fact that there were no defensive wounds, of any kind, found on Ms. Bloom's body, correct?"

"Yes. I guess she was still asleep when she was attacked," said Anderson.

"May I have exhibit eight, please?" I said, to the clerk.

The clerk reached down behind her, produced the baseball bat wrapped in a sealed, plastic evidence bag. I stepped over the mattress, swung the bat softly at the kettlebell on what would have been Tozer's side of the bed.

The dull *thunk* echoed around the room. I gave the bat back to the clerk.

"A maple-wood bat striking metal sure makes a hell of a sound. When that bat hit Carl Tozer's skull, there would've been a loud crack, wouldn't there?"

"There would have been some noise, I accept that."

"And Ms. Bloom, who you say was asleep just inches from the source of that sound, wouldn't have been woken by it?"

He breathed out through his nose. A long breath that got rid of his frustrations.

"I can't say," he said.

Time to move on, the table and the knife were important points in the case.

"How many times was the property searched for a possible murder weapon?" I said.

He thought about it, said, "Maybe a dozen times."

"And the knife was not found on any of those searches, was it?"

"No, like I said, I found it yesterday."

"It was a good hiding place, wasn't it?" I said.

He nodded, with a wry smile on his face. Said, "I suppose it was a good hiding place, but we found it in the end."

"The only reason the weapon was placed in that light fitting was because the killer didn't want it found, wouldn't you say?"

"Correct."

"So, let's say the defendant uses the table to stand on, and the knife, why then didn't he pick up the table and set it back in its original position?"

"I don't know," said Anderson.

"You only found the knife because the table was knocked over?"

"I suppose you could put it that way," he said.

"And it indicated to you that there may been some activity involving the murderer and that table, yes?"

"Yes."

"If the killer had put the table upright, you wouldn't have found the knife?"

"Probably not," said Anderson.

"There's almost seven minutes between that 911 call and the first police officer arriving on scene?"

"I believe so."

"Plenty of time to hide the fact that the killer had been at the table by simply turning it the right way up, wouldn't you say?"

"Again, it's possible."

"Let's say you're right, and the defendant was the murderer, trying to hide the knife. He doesn't want it to be found. He takes great pains to hide it in a place where no one would look for it. A light shade. And then he breaks a vase, and knocks over the table beneath the light. Are you telling me the defendant then left the table overturned and the smashed vase on the floor? Surely those items would lead the cops directly to the murder weapon, as you've already admitted. It doesn't make sense for the defendant to leave the table in that state if he was the killer, does it?"

"Killers make all kinds of mistakes. That's why we catch 'em."

I brought up the crime scene photo of the bedroom with the broken picture frame beside the bedside table.

"Detective, the sound of breaking glass on the 911 call, it could've been this picture frame being knocked off the bedside table by my client, couldn't it?"

"It's possible."

He was pleased with that answer. I was almost done with Anderson. I just needed to let the jury know we weren't ignoring the dollar found in Tozer's mouth.

"Detective, you didn't personally carry out any of those forensic tests on the dollar bill, did you?"

"No, no I didn't."

"That's okay. We can deal with that evidence with the forensic officer."

I thought about the night before, and decided I wanted to leave Anderson with a bad taste in his mouth. Rudy Carp's team had done their homework on Anderson, and I thought it would be rude to waste it.

"We only have your word that you found the murder weapon in that light fitting. How many times have you been investigated by internal affairs?"

Anderson's eyes narrowed, and he spat his answer at me.

"Twice. And I was cleared of any wrongdoing – twice."

I met Anderson's scowl and said, "When this case is over, it might be third time lucky."

Pryor objected. The jury was to disregard my last question.

"Thank you, Detective. Nothing further at this time," I said.

Pryor had no re-direct examination. As Anderson left the witness stand, he gave me a look like he wanted to kill me. I knew he was dirty. He was Mike Granger's buddy. His little party outside my office last night confirmed Anderson was as bad as they come in New York homicide. I'd made an enemy there. A real bad one.

It was getting close to one o'clock. I saw Harry looking at the time.

"Ladies and gentlemen, it's approaching the lunch hour. The jurors have some business to attend to over the lunch break. I propose we meet again at three o'clock. Court adjourned," said Harry.

When I returned to the defense table, Arnold gave me the rundown on the jury.

"They like you. Never thought I'd say that, but I can't deny it. I figure we've got four jurors on our side. Two of the women were nodding when you were talking about leaving the table overturned. And hitting the kettlebell with the bat went down well."

At this, Bobby leaned into the conversation and said, "Thanks. I'm glad I've got you on my side, guys."

"Let's not get too excited. There are still a lot more prosecution witnesses who can put you in serious trouble. And I have a feeling Pryor's got a few more surprises up his sleeve," I said.

As the courtroom began to empty, I saw a dozen men in suits lined up along the back of the court. Bobby still had a security detail. There were ready to take Bobby out of there safely, get him to a small room in the court building where he could eat a burrito and hold his secrets. I could almost see it weighing him down. The man had guilt on him. A truth he'd chosen to hide. No doubt connected to the night of the murders. *What are you holding back, Bobby?*

Before I could dwell on that, the crowd thinned and I saw two women pushing their way forward.

Harper and her FBI pal, Delaney. I didn't know what they'd found. It was hard to tell from the look on their faces. All I knew was that they'd found something big. They were pushing their way through the last of the audience, Harper made it to the defense table and said, "We need to talk, right now. You're not going to believe this."

CARP LAW

Suite 421, Condé Nast Building, 4 Times Square, New York, NY.

Strictly Confidential, Attorney Client Work Product

Juror Memo

The People -v- Robert Solomon Manhattan Criminal Court

Bradley Summers

Age: 64

Retired postal worker. Widower. Good financials with government pension. No debts. No assets. Estranged from both children (one lives in Australia and one in California). Plays chess in the park, occasionally. Democrat voter. No online presence. Reads the New York Times.

Probability of Not Guilty vote: 66%

Arnold L. Novoselic

CHAPTER FORTY-FIVE

Not for the first time, Kane was given a ride in a police cruiser. Together with his fellow jurors, he'd been led out of a side entrance to the court. Blue-and-white NYPD Crown Vics lined the sidewalk. They couldn't get the vehicles round front. Traffic management had to close half of Center Street because of the crowds outside the courthouse.

There was no talk from the cop who drove him to the apartment. Together, they took the elevator up three flights. The cop, Officer Locke, waited silently in the cramped hallway of the apartment while Kane went into the bedroom and packed a bag.

Pants, underwear, socks, two shirts and two pairs of pants in a bag. A special bag. Kane had it made for him in Vegas many years ago. It had been hand stitched, made from thick Italian leather and looked just as good as the day he'd picked it up from the shop. A razor, toothbrush and his pills also went into the bag. Antibiotics. He packed his digital thermometer, but not before checking his temperature, which was normal.

Kane felt around in the bag, running his hands along a seam on the inside. He found the thumb-shaped nick and pulled. A hidden sleeve lined with aluminum foil to throw off the metal detectors. The sleeve sat on the opposing side of a metal badge bearing the brand name of the manufacturer. Cops would assume their detectors were picking up the metal in the logo.

Kane fetched some essentials. The smaller items that made up a basic murder kit. These he placed in the hidden sleeve, zipped up the bag and joined the officer in the hall. Officer Locke flicked through one of the magazines that lay on the hall table.

"You fish?" said Locke.

"Yeah, when I get the chance," said Kane.

"Me and a couple of buddies go up to the Oswego river twice a year. Some good fishing up there."

"So I hear. When the season opens I'll be sure to check it out," said Kane.

They passed the ride back to Center Street by swapping fishing stories. Both men talked about the big one that got away. All fishing stories were the same. Locke led Kane back into the courthouse via the back entrance. The cop left. Kane was alone in the room. The first juror back. The trial shouldn't prove too difficult. He knew he had the measure of his fellow jurors. Kane's thoughts wandered beyond the trial. His next move had been planned for months. The trial had made him wonder whether he should change his plans.

Kane placed a dime on the table.

Heads – he stuck to his plan.

Tails – he made a new plan.

He tossed the coin.

Life and death spun in the air. Fate itself, decided purely by chance. Kane would be careful, no matter what way the coin landed. The uncertainty excited Kane. He could feel it low down in his stomach.

The coin bounced onto the table and became still.

Tails.

He put the dime away, and tucked into a sandwich. As he ate he thought of the man who would now live out his life, spared by the dime. He would never know the horror he had evaded. In fact, Rudy Carp would never even know he'd been in danger.

Of course, that meant someone else would have to pay that toll.

Picking up his bag, Kane left the room, went down the corridor, found the bathroom and made sure it was empty. He locked the stall, took his disposable cell from the hidden sleeve and made a call. It was answered almost immediately.

"Change of plan for Rhode Island," said Kane.

That coin of yours will get you into trouble one of these days. Let me guess, Carp gets a pass," said the voice.

"The coin chose wisely. Flynn will be on every newspaper and social media feed in America by morning. He's perfect. Now, can you get me what I need?" asked Kane.

"I thought you might go this way. Flynn was always going to steal the headlines. I think you'll be pleased. I left what you need in your car out by JFK," said the voice.

"You already have it?"

"I saw an opportunity. Took it. Flynn is asking too many questions, anyway. Anderson almost dropped the ball in court a couple of times. We have to protect him."

"Of course, that's what partners are for. I think Anderson will enjoy this," said Kane, "He hates Flynn."

"I know. I almost feel sorry for Flynn. He has no idea what's headed his way."

CHAPTER FORTY-SIX

The cramped consultation booth two floors down stank of cheap aftershave and body odor. Delaney didn't seem to mind. It proved more of a problem for Harper, who took a few minutes to adjust to the smell. She was sensitive about such things.

Both of them carried files and loose pages which they placed on the table in the consultation booth. Harper went first.

"Richard Pena's victims are linked to the Dollar Bill investigation," she said.

It was Pena's DNA on the dollar bill found in Carl Tozer's mouth. Along with the fingerprint and DNA for Bobby Solomon. Yet Pena had been dead for twelve years before the bill even got printed. Executed by the great state of North Carolina for quadruple homicide. The number of victims attributable to Pena made him stand out. Surely not all of them could have been linked to this killer.

"Were dollar bills found at the crime scenes?" I asked.

Neither of them answered immediately. Their eyes flicked toward each other asking who should be the one to tell me. In the end, Delaney opened a file and laid out some photographs.

Four photos. Four women. All of them white. All of them young. All of them dead. From the photos, they'd all been found on a lawn, or grassy area of some kind. They had been posed. Their limbs splayed out like they were performing jumping jacks. No, not jumping jacks. Star jumps.

Livid bruising stained their throats. There were no other signs of violence, yet it was difficult to tell just from the pictures. All of the girls were fully clothed. Hoodies, cardigans, T-shirts and jeans.

"They were all students at UNC in Chapel Hill. Their bodies were dumped on campus, probably from a van. The oldest girl was twenty-three," said Delaney.

A cracking sound interrupted my concentration. Without knowing it, I'd been holding the flimsy leg of the table and I'd damn near broken it in two.

I shook it off, tried to get past my rage and really look at the photos. At first, I didn't see it. Then, on one photo I saw something protruding from the blouse of one of the victims. A dollar, tucked inside her bra.

No sooner had I seen it, than Delaney whipped out another photo. This one was a collage of all four victims. Dollar bills slipped beneath the fabric of their bras.

"Shit," I said.

"Cops kept this out of the media. They found DNA on one of the dollars. At first they got no match for it on the database. Then the police and campus security carried out voluntary DNA testing of fourteen hundred males who lived or worked on campus. They got a hit on Richard Pena. He was a janitor, but he'd also briefly dated one of the victims. The last one, Jennifer Esposito. And yes, the dollars were marked," said Delaney.

She held up another four photographs. The great seal had been marked in the same places for each. Same arrowhead, same olive leaf, same star.

"The cops photographed the bills for evidential purposes. They didn't spot the markings, or if they did spot them, they didn't make much about it at the trial. The DNA and the strangling MO for all four victims proved to be their smoking gun," said Delaney.

"And Pena gave DNA voluntarily?" I asked.

"He didn't have much of a choice," said Harper. "The college pretty much made it compulsory for their staff. Maybe he thought there was no trace evidence left. The killer had been careful, after all. That DNA match was enough to convict him in record time. Before the murders, Chapel Hill was terrorized by a serial rapist on campus. They couldn't pin the rapes on Pena, but reading between the lines the cops figured Pena was the rapist and had just upped the ante. The town had been living in fear for months and they were

236

ready to put someone in the chair for this. Trial lasted two days. The jury deliberated for all of ten minutes. I guess you could say Pena didn't have much of a defense. He couldn't afford a lawyer and the public defender was asleep at the wheel, or didn't care. His appeals were declined fast and hard. The public wanted this guy dead and the state obliged."

That was fast. Justice took its sweet time about most things. Not in this case.

"Did Pena maintain his innocence?" I said.

"To his very last breath," said Harper.

"They all did," said Delaney.

I pushed the photos away and said, "What do you mean, *they all did*?"

Harper rose from the chair opposite me, and strode around the small space behind Delaney.

"We found more," said Delaney. "After you left I got approval to run fresh search bulletins. The dollar bill in the Solomon case gave me the ammo to go to my superiors. I ran alerts in all the sheriff and county police homicide bureaus in the thirteen states on the East Coast. The original states who signed the Declaration of Independence. I'm guessing you figured that out. Good. It took me a while. It was a theory with three victims, and not enough to go asking law enforcement to dig up closed cases with solid convictions. With Solomon, my director gave me the all-clear to run the alerts. I also got permission to post alerts to judges and clerks in each of the counties within those states. That was a first. We've never done that before. And it got results."

I pulled my chair closer to the table and watched Delaney pull documents out of her file. Four separate bundles held together with elastic bands. She placed them in front of me one by one. There were newspaper clippings, police reports, files for the DA.

"An arson attack on a black church in Georgia. Two people killed. A dollar bill found partially burned next to a can of gasoline. The dollar had been used to light the fire, then the arsonist stamped out the flames on the bill. Fingerprints on the gasoline sent away a white supremacist loser called Axcl who'd just won two million dollars in the state lottery."

She slapped the next one down.

"The Pennsylvania ripper. Three women torn to pieces in their own homes, partially cannibalized and mutilated post-mortem. All three were found inside of two weeks in the summer of 2003. Attacks occurred all over the state. Dollar bills found stuffed into their panties. Jonah Parks, a paranoid schizophrenic, confessed to the murders despite the protests from his new wife who gave him an alibi. It wasn't enough to save him from jail."

Another bundle. Another dead face staring at me. This time a man sitting behind the wheel of a rig.

"The Pitstop killer. Five men, all truck drivers. Picked up a hitchhiker in Connecticut and ended up dead. Shot in the head at close range and robbed. Dollar bill left on the dash. Cops thought it was a tip for the ride from the hiker. Fingerprint on the bill led cops to a drifter who'd just got re-housed after a distant relative died and left him a substantial inheritance. The man never got time to enjoy it."

Last one.

"Sixteen-year-old Sally Buckner. Maryland. Abducted, raped, murdered with a double-edged knife. Cops found the dollar bill in her hand when they pulled her body out from beneath her neighbor's porch. Eighty-one-year-old Alfred Gareck denied the killing. No DNA, but there was circumstantial evidence. She used to go to the store for him on Saturday mornings and he always paid her a couple of dollars for her trouble. Gareck's fingerprints on the bill. He died a week after his murder conviction," said Delaney.

She shook her head. Said, "The great seal had been marked up in the usual way on all the dollars. Arrowhead, leaf, star. We're still waiting to hear if we get any hits from New Jersey, South Carolina, Virginia and Rhode Island. Maybe he hasn't hit those states. Maybe he has and we just haven't found it yet."

None of us could speak. Harper put her back to the wall, stared at the floor. We all felt it. It was a black, evil thing in the room. Something that you don't allow yourself to think about. We'd all grown up afraid of something. The bogeyman, the monster in the closet, or the devil hiding under the bed. And your parents tell you it's just your imagination. There are no demons. No monsters.

But there are.

I'd done shitty things in my life. Hurt people. Killed people. I had no choice. Self-defense. Protecting my family. Protecting others. It's not easy killing a man, even in such circumstances. I knew from experience that Harper had pulled the trigger before. She'd put a man down. I couldn't say for sure if Delaney had ever hurt anyone, but she didn't need to have that experience to know what it felt like. It was a line that had to be crossed sometimes.

But it always left a scar.

Here was a man who'd murdered for pleasure. It was a game. Only this wasn't a man. This was one of the monsters.

I knew the question I wanted to ask, I just couldn't find the courage to let it out. My lips were dry. I wetted them, swallowed and said, "How many victims?"

Delaney knew the answer. So did Harper. Their knowledge weighed heavy on each of them. Harper closed her eyes and whispered the answer.

"Eighteen that we know of. Twenty if you count Ariella Bloom and Carl Tozer."

"And are we counting Ariella and Carl, Agent Delaney?" I asked.

"I think we are, but we're way behind on this. And it's still a live investigation. I'm sharing this with you because you brought it to me. I'm prepared to tell the court that the FBI are investigating the possible connection between the Bloom and Tozer murders and a known serial killer operating on the East Coast, but that's it. No other evidence or information. If Solomon is convicted of these murders it closes another door in my face. You know how hard it is to open a closed case? With a conviction in place? Try next to impossible."

The room fell silent again.

"Is there any connection between the victims? Surely there must be some way he's targeting these people. It can't be totally random," I said.

"We haven't found any connection yet," said Harper. "We're working on it. I figure I'm most useful to you by working this angle, Eddie. So far, no connections between the victims in each state. Different ages, different sex, different races, different backgrounds."

I nodded. She was right. But none of it was any use in helping Bobby at trial. Not really.

"There has to be a connection. The markings on the dollar? I mean, this is some kind of a dark mission this guy is on. He has a purpose. He has a plan. He's killed twenty people and the cops and the feds haven't even been looking for him. He's managed to lay the blame for each murder at someone else's door," I said.

That word, that strange red word – murder. Somehow that word felt like it got stuck on my tongue. My mind didn't want to let it go.

I took a moment to let things sink in. I was due back in court soon. I closed my eyes and let my mind wander. Somewhere in my subconscious, I had the answer.

It started slow. Like a low pulse in the room. Like the vibration from the heart of a violin. Tiny. Just from the pressure of the fingers on the strings right before the first note of the overture is struck. I could feel it. And then it was there, right in front of me.

"I need time to go over these cases. Hopefully, we might get something else from the other states. If we're going to use this stuff we have to get it organized and find the connection between the victims. And we have to serve this evidence on Pryor if you're willing to make a deal, Delaney? In the meantime I'll pull the case for today – ask Harry to give me a continuance till tomorrow. He's pretty much said I can take the continuance if I need it. And I do. We all do," I said.

As I spoke, my eyes wandered around the room with my thoughts. Then the maestro moved his hands. And the first note echoed around my mind.

"What kind of a deal are you talking about?" said Delaney.

"This is a one-time offer. No negotiation. Take it or leave it. You are going to be in court tomorrow. And I might need you to testify, but I don't think that'll be necessary. All I need is your agreement to share these files with the DA, and your word that if I need you – you'll tell the jury what you've told me."

She folded her arms, looked over her shoulder at Harper, then back to me.

"I already told you I can't. I can't compromise the investigation," she said.

"You won't be compromising anything. Come to court. Agree to testify so I can tell the DA you'll be a witness. But you won't have to testify. If you agree to this I swear you'll have your man in custody within twenty-four hours."

Delaney rocked back in her seat, surprised at such a bold claim.

"And how exactly are you going to deliver Dollar Bill?" she said.

"That's the best part. *I* won't be delivering him. If everything goes smoothly tomorrow, Dollar Bill is going to walk right into the arms of the FBI all by himself."

CARP LAW

Suite 421, Condé Nast Building, 4 Times Square, New York, NY.

Strictly Confidential, Attorney Client Work Product

Juror Memo

The People -v- Robert Solomon
Manhattan Criminal Court

Cassandra Deneuve

Age: 23

Changed her name two years ago. Previously known as Molly Freudenberger. Accepted to study Set Design at NYU, undergrad. Works at McDonald's. Financially sound due to parental support. Dropped out of two university courses in as many years. In a number of relationships. Large Instagram following. Likes cats. No voting history.

Probability of Not Guilty vote: 38%

Arnold L. Novoselic

CHAPTER FORTY-SEVEN

The new juror jangled and tinkled her way into court. She was already beginning to annoy Kane. She wore a charm bracelet on her left ankle which rattled with even the slightest of movements. The other jurors had noticed it too. Valerie Burlington, and her anklet, would soon become a razorblade on a chalkboard to even the most tolerant of the jurors.

Kane allowed himself to imagine what it would feel like to cut off her foot. He found himself staring at the veins just below her ankle, bulging through the fake tan like worms on a mud plain.

Valerie swung her foot, and ignored the tuts and whispers that fell around her ears.

Thankfully, the jury didn't have to wait long.

Kane felt disappointed when the judge adjourned the case until the morning. On the plus side, it gave him some more time to himself.

They filed back into the jury room, collected their bags and left the courthouse at the rear exit. A yellow city bus took them out of Manhattan. Two court officers went on the bus with the jury. They drove for almost an hour on the freeway, headed in the direction of JFK International. Only they weren't going to the airport. The one thing that's in plentiful supply around JFK is reasonably priced hotels. Many of them in the neighborhood of Jamaica; a middle-class slice of Queens. It was far too expensive to put up twelve jurors, and the alternates, in a Manhattan hotel.

The court office preferred three hotels. The Holiday Inn, the Garden Inn and if they were really stuck – Grady's Inn. Turns out they were stuck. Kane had made sure of it. A week before he'd used a number of prepaid credit cards to make various strategic bookings at both the Holiday Inn and the Garden Inn. Both hotels were busy, so he only had to make around a half dozen bookings in each hotel. All under different names. Some bookings made online, some by disposable cell phone. With each booking he'd specified a room and a floor either over the phone or via email with the hotel.

The result – neither the Holiday Inn nor the Garden Inn could offer fifteen rooms on the same floor to the court officer who'd tried to make the block booking. For security purposes, a guard had to be placed on the floor to monitor the jurors under sequestration. It wasn't possible to monitor two or three floors of a hotel. Court security didn't have the manpower. No, sir. One guard. One floor. Those were the rules.

That left the Grady Inn. One floor. One guard.

The bus pulled up at Grady's and Kane watched the disappointed looks on the faces of his fellow jurors when they laid eyes on their accommodation.

"When did they take down the *Bates Motel* sign?" said Betsy, to a ripple of nervous laughter from the jurors and the court officers.

The jury filed into the lobby. It looked more like a reception area for a funeral parlor. Dark oak paneling lined every wall, sucking away what little light penetrated the filth on the windows. Kane recognized the smell of stewed vegetables. The porter nodded at each of the jurors as they passed him in the entrance hall. He didn't take their bags. In fact, the guy looked a little loaded. Smelled that way too. Deer heads were mounted in a row behind the aging hotel receptionist. She was in her eighties and deaf. The court officer would have had an easier time talking to one of the deer.

Kane had made sure that while they waited in the lobby, he was standing next to Manuel. Kane nudged him. Manuel looked at Kane. Kane leaned over and whispered, "I know you think Solomon is innocent. We're on the same page. We can't let him go to jail for something he didn't do. We'll talk later, okay."

Kane nodded wisely. Manuel thought about this, then discreetly held up a thumb to say *okay*.

Fourteen keys were handed out. Real keys. Not swipe cards. It was that kind of place. The hotel had once been a grand house. Close to forty rooms were spread out over five floors. No elevator. The jurors followed the court officer to the fourth floor. Then they filed out past him to their rooms. Kane had been given room forty-one, on the right-hand side of the corridor. He fiddled with the key in the lock just long enough for another juror to reach the door behind him.

It was Valerie. He heard the jewelry cease its jingling behind him. He turned and said, "Valerie, I'm sorry, but I suffer from migraines. The sun will light up that room early in the morning and it sets off my headaches. Would it be possible for me to trade with you?" said Kane.

Valerie smiled, patted Kane on the arm and said, "Of course I don't mind, sweetpea. You take my room."

Kane took the key for room thirty-nine, smiled appreciatively and thanked Valerie. He opened the door to his new room, then closed it and locked it behind him. The room was small, but dirty. The large window overlooked the eaves of the floor below. To the left, it sloped down to a flat roof. The garden below was just visible.

Kane threw his bag on the bed, then lay down and slept.

Banging on his door woke him an hour later. He told the court officer he wasn't feeling well and wouldn't be coming for dinner. He would just get some sleep instead. No, he didn't need a doctor.

Kane managed to get back to sleep, and he woke up at one a.m. Bright. Alert. Rested.

He changed clothes, checked his temperature. After he popped more antibiotics, Kane packed his bag, put on his ski mask and climbed out of the window.

CARP LAW

Suite 421, Condé Nast Building, 4 Times Square, New York, NY.

Strictly Confidential, Attorney Client Work Product

Juror Memo

The People -v- Robert Solomon Manhattan Criminal Court

Alec Wynn

Age: 46

Air-conditioning engineer, currently out of work. Single. Republican. Financials look rocky, but not serious yet. Very little social contact. Loner. Outdoor-pursuits enthusiast — hunting, fishing, kayaking. Licensed firearm certificate for State of New York and Virginia. Owns three handguns; two in state. One held in Virginia. Licensed to hold bolt-action hunting rifle. Online interests include Brietbart News, Donald Trump, Republican Party, extreme pornography and various websites devoted to US military. Never served in the military.

Probability of Not Guilty vote: 20%

Arnold L. Novoselic

CHAPTER FORTY-EIGHT

Harry gave me a continuance in a heartbeat. Pryor didn't object. I had until the morning to get ready. When the courtroom cleared, it was just me, Arnold and Bobby. Holten, whose private security firm were contracted to Carp Law, said he would stay on and provide security for Bobby. I checked with Holten, and he'd already cleared it with Carp that Bobby could have his security detail at least until the weekend. After that, it was on his own dime. That was good of Rudy – at least Bobby would be safe before he got sent to jail for the rest of his life. There were five security guys in the hallway ready to escort Bobby home, along with Holten.

"Where are you staying?" I asked.

"Got a place in Midtown. Old house. It's quiet, nice neighborhood. The house even has an old panic room upstairs with a big steel door. I'll be safe there. Rudy rented it for me. He's paid for it until the end of the month. Say, do you still think we have a chance?" said Bobby. It had been a long day and it was beginning to show on him. I could've told Bobby the truth, but that wouldn't help him. I had a gut feeling that we might catch the real killer. I needed to be confident about it with Delaney, but deep down I doubted everything. This case was still riding on luck.

"I do think we have a chance. I'll know more tomorrow. I think Ariella and Carl were caught up in some kind of sick game. Their killer wanted to frame you. I don't know why just yet. Or exactly how he did it. I need you to go home and think. By tomorrow, you need to tell me where you were the night of the murders," I said.

"I already told you, I can't remember. Christ, I wish I knew," he said.

As he spoke, he looked at the floor.

He was lying. I knew it. Arnold saw it too.

"Bobby, you've got no choice in the matter. You have to tell me," I said.

Bobby shook his head, said, "I told you, I can't recall."

"Let's hope your memory improves by the morning. The jury will want to know where you were. If you can't tell them, you're in a lot of trouble," I said.

We walked Bobby to the hallway and the mass of security men who would take him home. Bobby promised to get some sleep, and take his meds. He left surrounded, headed into a frenzied crowd.

It was the first time I'd had a real chance to talk to Arnold. I brought him up to speed with the Dollar Bill theory. At first, he didn't believe it. The more details I gave him, the more he looked interested.

"You think this jury would buy that?" I said.

He rubbed his bald head, sighed and said, "It's worth a try. The key, now that the jury is sequestered, is figuring out the alpha."

"The alpha?"

"A sequestered jury very quickly slips into a pack mentality. The sequestration cuts them off from their normal lives and throws them all together in a stressful, heightened reality situation. It becomes 'us' and 'them'. The jury will bond. And a leader will emerge. Notice how I didn't say alpha *male*. Lot of the time it's a woman who leads the jury pack. Once you figure out who the alpha is, you just need to focus on them. If you win the alpha, the rest of the jury will follow their lead."

I nodded. It made sense. I was suddenly glad to have Arnold with me.

"Thanks, that's really useful," I said, with some sincerity. Arnold seemed to take it well. He was pleased to help.

"I know we haven't had the best of . . . well, you know . . . I'm sorry. I think you're doing a great job for Bobby," said Arnold, holding out a hand.

I took it. I don't hold grudges.

"Oh, there was something I meant to say to you earlier," said Arnold. "It's about one of the jurors, I saw him . . . well, this is going to sound a little weird . . ."

"Go on."

"It's hard to explain. Ahm, look, a few years ago I saw this movie on cable. Horror movie about socialites in New York. Maybe one was a lawyer, maybe one was a devil, I don't know. I don't remember that part. Anyway, I do remember one scene. A girl was changing in a store dressing room, and she smiled at the camera. Just for a second, her face changed. That grin turned into a . . . like, an evil snarl. She had sharp teeth and devil eyes. The other character, the main actress – her character couldn't be sure if she saw it or not, you know? Well, that's kinda how I feel. I saw this juror and he, well, his face changed. It was scary. Like a micro expression of . . . something. Something bad," he said.

Arnold was sweating, he had bags under his eyes that could hold ten pounds of potatoes. He looked gray, tired. And afraid.

"Who was it?" I said.

My cell phone buzzed. I took my phone out of my jacket and Arnold clocked it. I didn't recognize the number on the display.

"Can you give me a second?" I said.

"Look, forget it. I'm sorry. I don't even know what I'm saying. I've been working fifteen-hour days on this case for six months. It's been a long day. Take your call and I'll see you tomorrow."

"Go home. Get some rest, Arnold."

I watched him go. Stress causes all kinds of things. I wasn't sure, but it sounded like Arnold was hallucinating. Or maybe it was a trick of the light, or something.

I answered the call. It was a guy from the garage. My Mustang had a brand new windshield and it was ready to be picked up. The bill didn't sound too bad, and the mechanic had taken the opportunity to tune up the engine and change the oil. I thanked him, said I would come by soon as I could and pick it up.

I had a long night ahead of me. I needed to read the murder files for the new victims. And go over every piece of evidence for tomorrow. Delaney was setting up a crisis team in the New York field office and I had a breakfast meet-up with her and Harper at six a.m. It would be a while before I would have a chance to pick up my car.

A cab driver dropped me off at West 46th Street. There were no welcome parties this time. As I trudged up the stairs to my office I thought about calling Christine. When I got to the first landing I decided I would tell her that I wouldn't fight the divorce; I'd give her whatever she wanted. Whatever was best for her and Amy. By the time I got to the door of my office I'd decided to call and tell her I loved her. I loved her more than anything and when I was done with this case I would quit.

Instead, I turned off my cell phone. There was still a half bottle of whiskey on my desk. I poured a glass. Held it in my hand for a long time before I poured it down the sink and got to work.

I looked over the Solomon files first. Prepared my cross-examination. Then I turned to the murder files for Dollar Bill. I wasn't a trained psychologist. I wasn't a criminologist, or a criminal analyst, or a fed, or a cop. My skills in this area were limited.

But I knew two things.

I knew how to deceive. And there was a pattern here. A basic bait and switch. The victims were murdered. Different MOs in different states. The dollars were planted. And missed by the cops. I couldn't blame them for this. I'd seen the markings on the butterfly dollar and dismissed them just like the NYPD. We all did. All apart from Delaney. Once the evidence was planted it would lead to an innocent perp. And Dollar Bill would move to another state, another town, and start the whole thing over again.

The second thing I knew about was killing.

I'd grown up around guys who became killers. When I was a con artist, I'd dealt with trigger men on almost a daily basis. Some were in it for the money. Most were in it for the sport. I'd known men who took pleasure in killing. I could spot 'em a mile away. Only reason I was still breathing was that I made it my business to try and understand these guys so I would know how to stay off their radar and out of their sights.

When I next checked my watch it was four thirty a.m. Things were a lot clearer in my mind. I called Harper.

"You still awake?"

"I am now," she said. Her voice had a rough edge to it. She spoke slowly with a dry angry throat. "What do you need?"

"I've been over the files. There's no link between the victims."

"Didn't Delaney tell you that, like, yesterday?"

"She did. But she was looking at the wrong victims," I said.

I heard Harper groaning, and the rustle of bedclothes. I imagined her sitting upright, forcing herself awake.

"What do you mean, wrong victims?"

"Delaney looked at the murder victims. I don't think they were the real target. This killer is murdering people so that he can frame somebody for the crime. The men who were convicted of those crimes – they're the real target, I'm convinced of it."

"Same problem as the murder victims. Some of those men who were convicted never left the state."

"There's no geographic or social connection. I can't see these men ever having met. They never lived in the same places, they were in totally different social circles, different colleges, some didn't go to college. I got nothing. But I'm not the FBI. I can only go on what's in the files or what I can find on the internet. So far it's not much. I found a few articles online. Like Axel the arsonist. I found a piece on him winning the state lottery, and an article on Omar Hightower's football accumulator . . ."

"What?" asked Harper.

Saying something out loud sometimes made it real. At least for me.

"Harper, the real victims are the people who got framed. He chose them because their lives had just changed dramatically. Omar won that money, Axel won the lottery, the drifter who was convicted of the Pitstop killings just lucked out and got a big inheritance . . . all of that was in the local papers. I need you and Delaney to check on each convict and find out what happened. Something dramatic changed their lives. And the killer saw it. That's why he targeted them."

Harper was on the move. I heard her feet stomping around on a wooden floor. And I heard another voice on the line. Faint. In the background, "Who is that?"

She didn't answer at first. That hesitation was enough to make me feel like a total dick.

"Jeez, Harper. Sorry, I didn't know you had company. I'll hang up . . ." I said.

"It's okay. It's Holten. He doesn't mind," she said.

For a long time I didn't know what to say. Or how to feel. I found myself running my thumb over the wedding ring I still wore. Over the years I'd smoothed down the back of the ring. Worrying at the metal.

"Oh, okay, cool. I guess," I said, sounding like a sixth-grader.

"I'll check it out and call Delaney. Anything else?"

There wasn't. I apologized again. Disconnected the call. I buried my head in the desk, more out of embarrassment than fatigue.

As I lay there, my mind drifted back to the conversation I'd had with Arnold, earlier that afternoon. This was a finely balanced case, and I needed two things: Arnold with a clear head and a fair and impartial jury. No more rogue jurors.

Arnold's concern about one juror giving a strange look – it bothered me. Didn't matter how crazy it sounded. I needed to know more. Arnold was used to running big cases so he knew sleep was a relative concept in a murder trial. I called him. He picked up after a few rings.

"Hello?" said Arnold. I didn't detect any sleep in Arnold's voice. He sounded fully awake.

"I didn't wake you, did I?" I said.

"Can't sleep," he said.

"Look, sorry to call so early. I've been up all night working. I'm going to try and get a half-hour rest before I go meet the feds. But I can't go to sleep without knowing more about what you said earlier. About the juror? You thought you saw something."

"The juror?" said Arnold.

"The one you talked about. You know, their face . . . changed. You weren't sure what you saw, it was just a fleeting thing. It might be important. It might not. I just want to know who you were talking about."

"Oh, that," said Arnold. The penny had dropped. "Yeah, well, like you said, I'm not sure what I saw exactly. Their face did kinda change for a second."

"So who was it?"

He paused. I didn't know why, but I felt sure this was important.

"Alec Wynn," said Arnold.

Wynn was the gun nut. The guy who liked hunting, fishing, and Fox News. I wondered if Alec liked to hunt men as well as deer.

"Thanks, Arnold. Look, I know how hard you've been working. Get some rest and I'll see you sometime tomorrow."

He thanked me and I ended the call. I set my phone to wake me in thirty minutes. I could grab a power nap, then get ready and get to the FBI office at six.

I had a feeling today was going to be a long one.

THURSDAY

CHAPTER FORTY-NINE

By the time the sun rose on the other side of Grady's Inn, Kane had already showered and changed into a T-shirt. He lay in bed and allowed himself to drift off to sleep. The wound on his leg looked clean. It hadn't bled, despite his exertions during the night. After close inspection he'd reapplied the bandage. No signs of infection. Just to be on the safe side, he'd taken more antibiotics. Checked his temperature. All good.

He figured it would be an hour, maybe ninety minutes before the guard woke the jury for breakfast. His muscles relaxed. He took two deep breaths and allowed his mind to drift into that realm of half-sleep, where the subconscious takes control.

Kane felt satisfied with his night's work.

Soon the guard would knock on the doors. Then the banging would begin. And the shouting. And then – the screaming.

CARP LAW

Strictly Confidential, Attorney Client Work Product

Juror Memo

The People -v- Robert Solomon
Manhattan Criminal Court

Daniel Clay

Age: 49

Unemployed. On welfare. Single. No parents, no family. No friends. Financials couldn't be worse. Enjoys social media and reading sci-fi and fantasy novels. Doesn't read newspapers and avoids online news. Elvis fan. No criminal record. Interested in Scientology, but has not yet joined the church mainly due to poor finances.

Probability of Not Guilty vote: 25%

Arnold L. Novoselic

CHAPTER FIFTY

Say what you like about the Federal Bureau of Investigation. Their policies. Their secret political agendas. The corruption. The covert monitoring of every citizen in America. The mistakes. And the lives they took.

At six-oh-five a.m. on Thursday morning the FBI was alright by me. As long as they kept giving me coffee I was prepared to maintain a temporary truce.

Also in their favor was the speed at which they'd set up an incident room on the Dollar Bill murders. Delaney had enough evidence to force the directors to open the cash register. I'd been shown into a large windowless room. Well lit. Desks everywhere. A murder wall constructed on a long pane of glass that split the room down the middle. Pictures of the victims, their bios beneath, were grouped together with the men convicted of their murders. Arrows drawn in marker shot all over glass.

"We got one more," said Delaney, behind me.

She came forward and pinned up a picture of a girl with tight, black curly hair wearing a leather biker jacket. Pale skin. A cheerleader's smile. She was in her early twenties. The picture that went up beside her was of a tall, middle-aged man with a mustache. A mug shot.

"An English professor convicted of murdering a waitress in South Carolina," said Delaney.

"When?" I said.

"2014. The Professor had just sold his first novel to a big New York publishing house. They canceled the contract soon as he was arrested," said Delaney.

Across the room, on the back wall, was a timeline of the murders and the criminal trials that convicted the offenders. It began in 1998 with the first of the young women Pena was convicted of killing. It went all the way through to the most recent case, the professor in 2014.

"Sixteen years," I said, softly.

"Maybe," said Delaney. "We're still a few states short. New Jersey, Virginia and Rhode Island. Could be longer, but I guess not by much. This one has been busy."

I found it hard to focus on the photos of the victims. Each one of them had their lives ruthlessly, brutally ended. Men and women. They had parents, friends, some even had kids of their own. The devastation was too much to take in. I sat down at an empty desk. The room was already buzzing with feds. Just a glimpse of the pain that had been wrought by this man was too great to absorb – it was like a fire burning on the horizon. The faces of his victims seemed to smolder. I felt that if I went too close, or stared too hard at a face, that fire would engulf me and never let me go.

Delaney had the casual detachment of law enforcement. She looked upon the faces of the victims with a clinical eye.

"How do you do that?" I said.

"What?"

"You can look at all this. And it doesn't seem to get to you," I said.

"Oh, it gets to me. You better believe it," she said. "When I see the bodies, the sheer scale of this thing – it's the enormity of the suffering that can put you in the mental hospital if you let it. So I don't look. When I stare at a picture, I'm not looking at the victim – I'm looking for the killer. I'm trying to catch his scent, or spot a signature or discover a trail of some kind. You have to ignore the wreckage and look beyond it for the monster."

We fell silent for a time. I thought about all those people.

"So, has he told you how you're going to catch this sucker yet?" said Harper.

I hadn't noticed her arriving. She carried what looked like half a gallon of take-out coffee. The cup was weighing her down. She placed it on the table, took a seat beside me.

"Not yet," said Delaney.

In truth, I didn't know for sure that it would work. It was a long shot, but after spending a night thinking about Dollar Bill, I was pretty sure I had his number.

"It seems to me that the real targets are the men Dollar Bill has framed for the murders. The marks on the bills. Three of them. My guess is the arrow is for the victim. The olive branch to society is that the perp is caught and convicted. After Bill has framed them, of course. And the star. That's for the state. Has to be. But imagine you are this man."

Harper took a big sip of coffee, Delaney folded her arms and leaned back. I wasn't sure she was buying this.

"This guy has gone to extraordinary lengths to frame an innocent man for his killings. My guess is – that's got to feel good. You plan a murder, execute it and the cops aren't even looking for you. It's almost the perfect murder, isn't it? Now say you go to all that trouble of framing somebody, wouldn't you want to stick around and make sure the patsy goes down for your crime?"

Delaney reached for a pen, brought her chair close to the table and started making notes.

"What do you mean by sticking around?" said Harper.

"I think he watches the trials. It's more than a game for this asshole. It's a mission. Imagine the power of sitting in a courtroom and watching another man get convicted for your crime and the best part is *you* made it all happen. The plan is literally unfolding, perfectly, in front of you. I mean, this guy is really good at framing people. Every single person he has targeted he has managed to get convicted. I can't believe the defense lawyers couldn't win a single one of those cases. He got a conviction every time. That's got to make him feel powerful. A lot of killers put people in the ground because of power games. Why should this guy be any different?" I said.

The pen in Delaney's hand moved furiously across the page. She was nodding as she took notes.

"Have you met a lot of killers, Eddie?" said Delaney.

"I'll take the fifth amendment on that one," I said.

"TV coverage, photos of the trials in local papers, national papers, blogs. We can start looking for this guy," said Harper.

"And if I'm right that means he's going to be in court today to watch Bobby. You post a half dozen feds in the courtroom to watch the crowd. When I start cross-examining the DA's witnesses about Dollar Bill, we'll see what happens. With any luck we'll scare him. I want him to think we know a lot more about him than he's comfortable with. If he's smart, he'll get up and be on the next plane out of JFK. You've just got to catch him before he leaves the courtroom."

Delaney and Harper exchanged excited looks. It sounded like a plan. Delaney fished through a file and found what looked like a bound report of some kind.

"This is Dollar Bill's profile. We've been working it up overnight, so it's rough and I'll need to add to it. It's got his known whereabouts corresponding with the dates of the murders. And I'll update that to include the time periods covered by the subsequent criminal trials. I think you're right on the money about that, Eddie. And I got your message, Harper. There *is* a connection amongst those who were convicted of Bill's crimes. We were already on to it, but we couldn't confirm it until we looked at everyone again. Well, now we have."

She gave us copies of the profile, and we flicked forward through to a section of the report marked "victim selection".

There is no discernible physical, sexual or geographical commonality amongst the various groups of murder victims. It is likely that the victims were chosen for the connection, access to, or relationship with the person whom the unsub targeted for conviction for that specific murder or murder cluster. Those persons whom the unsub has potentially framed for his crimes share one common, unusual feature: in a time frame relative to the murders, the convicted persons had all undergone what could reasonably be described to be life-changing experiences. These include massive shifts in their financial or personal status (state lottery win, unexpected inheritance, restaurant franchise). The change in circumstances for that individual was always significant.

An examination of the markings on the dollar bills planted at the crime scenes, and subsequently used in the prosecutions, and the navigation of the states where the murders occurred reveals an important potential psychological insight and pathology.

The thirteen states symbolized by the thirteen stars on the one-dollar bill were the first states to sign the Declaration of

Independence. The declaration provides a legal foundation for the aspirational nature of American life.

The pattern is clear and the pathology is destruction of the aspirational nature of American life itself. It is likely, therefore, that the unsub or someone close to him failed to achieve some life goal. This is a pattern of revenge on a massive scale. The punishment for those who changed their lives is to have that new life destroyed by facing a murder charge. The unsub hates aspirational change. This is potentially symbolized by the folding of the dollar bill into a butterfly in the Bloom and Tozer murders.

I turned over to the last page and read the conclusion on the profile.

Sex: Male.

Age: Likely to be aged between thirty-eight and fifty years old.

Race: Unknown.

State origin: Unknown.

Physical Description: Given the physical force required to inflict the injuries sustained in some of the murders, unsub is likely to be strong and physically fit.

Psychology: Unsub is highly intelligent. Extremely organized. Socially adept. Manipulative. Narcissistic elements to his character. Sociopathy and psychopathy present, but the unsub remains a high-functioning individual who would have the intellectual capability to mask likely symptomology from the public, friends and family. The violence inflicted on the victims both ante, and in some cases, post mortem, implies a sadistic element to the murders. The framing of innocent men for his crimes could be a form of emotional sadism. High probability of psycho-sexual obsession with pain. Most likely a paraphilic disorder such as Sexual Sadism Disorder. Educated, probably to college level. High functioning knowledge of forensic procedures. The unsub, given his pathology, is someone who has probably failed in their chosen field, or had someone close to them fail to achieve their potential. To some extent, poverty is likely to have featured in unsub's life at one point. His mission is a twisted attack on American values and aspirations – most probably motivated by revenge.

*

"He thinks he's killing the American Dream," I said, out loud, without realizing.

I looked up from the profile and found both women staring at me.

"He must have researched his targets. Newspapers, local TV or something like that. You know, the good news story at the end of the nightly news. That's how he found them. I'll look for those," said Harper.

"I'll put you with two of my agents. They're calling local news outlets right now," said Delaney.

There was an energy in the room. Delaney knew she was closing in on this phantom. And yet, something about it bothered me. The theory looked good, but Bill had been relying on luck for a lot of this. He had to be. So far he had committed murder in eight states and gotten a man convicted in all eight instances. New York would make it nine. And there could've been more that Delaney hadn't yet uncovered.

I knew, more than most, anything can happen in a criminal trial. There were too many variables even in a case with strong forensics.

Had Bill just been lucky to get a conviction eight times out of eight?

"When you check with the local news outlets, make sure to get all of the images from the trials. There might be video, or photographs of crowds attending the trial. I think our man watched every moment of every trial. There's a chance a photographer just might have taken his picture," I said.

"It's a long shot, but we'll look into it," said Delaney, "Attending the hearings would fit with his psyche profile. A lot of killers revisit their crime scenes, or take trophies from their victims. It allows them to relive that moment of excitement over and over again. Of course, it's not the same thing as the murder. They don't get the same rush. But they get something out of it."

Harper stood and gathered her notes, anxious to get to work.

"Is this enough to get Solomon an acquittal?" she said.

"I don't know. Pryor's got a lot of strong evidence to put in front of the jury today. It would help if Bobby could remember where the hell he'd been on the night of the murders."

"He really doesn't know?" said Harper.

"He says he was drunk, and doesn't remember."

"Surely someone would've recognized him if he was out in a bar?" said Delaney.

"You'd think. But I saw the security video. He wore dark clothes, ball cap and a hoodie. A lot of celebrities get away with walking around in a city like New York if they cover up even . . ."

The words caught in my throat. Delaney had hit a nerve. Bobby should have been recognized. That was it.

"Delaney, do you have a list of FBI forensic techs in this building?" I said.

"I can get one. Why?"

"It's in both our interests if Bobby walks. I need your help," I said.

She was wary at first. Delaney folded her arms and stood.

"As long as it's nothing illegal, we might be able to lend a hand," she said.

"Ah, well, there might be a problem with that."

She looked at me. I smiled and said, "Technically it's only illegal if we get caught."

FIFTY-ONE

The court officer had been banging on the door for almost ten minutes. It was seven thirty. The smell of old vegetables in the corridor had been replaced with the odor of cooked eggs. Most of the jurors had already gone downstairs. Kane, the court officer, Betsy and Rita remained in the hallway and called out for the occupant to open the door.

"Goddamn it, where is that porter with the spare?" said the court officer. He hammered the door again, called out.

Right then the aging hotel porter wheezed his way around the corner and handed a key to the officer.

"You took your time," said the officer.

The porter shrugged.

"We're coming in," said Betsy.

Kane, like the others, was fully dressed. He'd showered, changed, and put on his make-up to hide the livid bruising on his face from the nasal fracture. Kane tried to stem his excitement while the officer put the key in the lock and opened the door.

"You awake? Court security," said the officer, as he stepped into the room. Kane gently nudged Betsy out of the way, and followed the officer inside.

The room looked immaculate. A gym bag lay on the bed. The sheets had been pulled back but the bed, on Kane's right, was empty. A light spilled out from the bathroom on the other side of the room and just beyond the bed. The officer made his way toward it, calling out.

"Oh my God!" cried Betsy.

The officer spun around. So did Kane. Betsy and Rita screamed. They were staring at the narrow space between the bed and the left-hand wall, closest to the door. The court officer pulled back the bed frame, moving it away from the wall. All of them stared at the corpse of Manuel Ortega. A bed sheet wrapped around his neck. He'd slumped down close to the floor. The other end of the sheet had been tied to the bedpost. It appeared as though he'd strangled himself.

Kane, keeping Betsy, Rita and the officer in his line of vision, stumbled backward, his hand covering his mouth. Quickly, while they stared in horror at Manuel's body and had their backs to Kane, he whipped the towel from his shoulders and covered the window lock. One quick turn and the window was secure from the inside. No prints, no DNA. Clean. He put the towel back over his shoulder, stepped forward.

It appeared to be suicide. The court officer was already on his radio, requesting NYPD assistance. Manuel's eyes were open and bulging out of his head. He stared at the beige carpet.

In the early hours of that same morning, Kane had rapped at Manuel's window. Shocked, at first, Manuel quietly let him in.

"What are you doing, man?" said Manuel, in a whisper.

"This is the only way we can talk in private. I'm so worried about this case. I think the cops framed Solomon. We have to make sure he gets off. I don't believe for a second he murdered those people."

"Me either. How do we do it?" said Manuel.

They discussed a strategy. How they could influence their fellow jurors. Ten minutes later Manuel went to the bathroom. Kane followed him, slipping on his gloves. He grabbed Manuel from behind, stuffing a rag into his mouth and holding it there. Kane's other arm snaked around Manuel's windpipe. It didn't take long to overpower him. It was quiet, quick and by the time Manuel had been strangled, Kane hadn't even broken a sweat. He moved the body to the space between the bed, tied one end of a sheet around the bedpost and the other around Manuel's throat. Cinched it tight.

Kane left the same way he'd come in. The only thing he couldn't do at that time was lock the window.

Now he had.

The court security officer in the hallway, the locked bedroom door, and now the locked window. That combination would lead the NYPD to chalk it up as suicide. There was no other way it could have happened.

"Everyone out," said the court officer.

Kane, Betsy and Rita left the room. They huddled in the hall and Kane put an arm on Rita as she wept. Betsy said, "I need to get out of here. This is so awful. What the hell is going on?"

He spoke softly to both women, suggested they go downstairs and get a stiff drink to calm their nerves. And so, with the sound of police sirens approaching Grady's Inn, Kane led both jurors, one on each arm, down the hall and the staircase toward the bar.

Now, Kane had cleaned the jury. Everyone else was open to Kane's persuasion. Robert Solomon's last chance of gaining an acquittal was Manuel. Now he was gone. At last, this was Kane's jury.

CARP LAW

Suite 421, Condé Nast Building, 4 Times Square, New York, NY.

Strictly Confidential, Attorney Client Work Product

Juror Memo

The People -v- Robert Solomon Manhattan Criminal Court

Christopher Pellosi

Age: 45

Web designer. Works from home. Single. Divorced. Heavy alcohol intake at weekends (all alcohol consumed at home). Poor social life. Both parents living in retirement home in Pennsylvania. Poor financials. Lost most of his money in bad investments prior to the crash. Interest in food and cooking. On mild meds for depression and anxiety.

Probability of Not Guilty vote: 32%

Arnold L. Novoselic

CHAPTER FIFTY-TWO

Before Pryor asked the first question of the day, I thought about all that had happened that morning.

After I'd left the FBI, I'd called Pryor, told him my investigator needed access to the Solomon property. He didn't object, but he sounded real pissed on the phone.

"Seems you're quite the celebrity," said Pryor.

"I've been working. Haven't watched the news," I said.

"You're the lead story on all channels. Your picture is on the front of the *New York Times*. How does it feel?" he said.

That's what was eating him. Pryor wanted the headlines.

"Like I said, I haven't seen it. You get my emails?"

Pryor confirmed he'd received my additional discovery. He thought I was clutching at straws trying to pin this murder on a serial killer.

Maybe he was right, but it was all I had.

We'd started the day in court with a visit to Harry's chambers. Another juror was dead. Manuel Ortega. NYPD confirmed it as suicide. His family had been informed. A few of the jurors had seen the body but they were okay. A victim protection officer had spoken to each of them and they were fit to continue to serve as jurors. Another alternate had been brought in. Rachel Coffee. Both Pryor and I were okay with her appointment. Harry said he wanted to get this trial finished before we lost any other jurors.

"This case is cursed," said Harry. "We need to finish this as soon as possible."

Bobby had a bad night. Hadn't slept at all. Holten and a bunch of security guards brought him to court, and Holten sat in the row behind us. He'd had an arm around Bobby for most of the morning.

Holding him up. Whispering words of encouragement. Telling Bobby that he had the best defense team on the planet.

I was grateful to Holten. Harper clearly liked the guy, and he'd been astute enough to know that whatever nerve Bobby had, had just about gotten him this far. He didn't have much left in the tank.

Bobby and I sat at the defense table, and I told him Arnold would be here later. Bobby glanced over his shoulder. Holten smiled at him, held up a fist and mouthed the words, *hold on.*

"It's okay, Bobby. We think we know who did this to Carl and Ariella. Today, I'll tell the jury. Just hang in there," I said.

Bobby nodded. He couldn't speak. I could see him swallowing down his fear. At least he'd taken his meds. And Holten had ensured a hot breakfast sandwich had been waiting for Bobby when he got into the SUV to bring him to court. He'd eaten some of it.

I poured Bobby some water. Made sure he was comfortable. Then I asked him the question. It was toxic, dangerous, but I didn't see that I had much choice.

"Bobby, I need to know where you were on the night of the murders. Are you ready to tell me the truth?"

He stared at me, trying to muster some indignation. It didn't work.

"I was drunk. I don't remember," he said.

"I don't believe you. That means the jury won't believe you," I said.

"That's my problem. I didn't kill anyone, Eddie, do you believe that?"

I nodded. But a sick feeling washed through my gut. I'd been wrong about clients before.

"If you don't tell me, I could walk away from this case. You know that, right?" I said.

He nodded. Said nothing. No one would be stupid enough to lose another lawyer in the middle of a murder trial. Yet Bobby didn't speak. I'd put as much pressure on him as I could. I didn't want him breaking down. At the same time, I still believed he wasn't a murderer. Whatever he was keeping to himself might have had more to do with personal guilt about the murders. If only he'd been at home, maybe Ariella and Carl would still be alive?

*

273

We all stood when Harry came into court. He called for the jury to be brought in, and I watched them carefully as they settled down into their seats. I was looking for two things. First was the alpha juror.

Out of the women, two stood out as potentially dominant. Rita Veste and Betsy Muller. Out of them, I thought Betsy would've been the most likely candidate. That morning, both women appeared solemn. I could tell they'd been crying. I could see it in their faces. Both women sat in defensive poses. Betsy hugged her arms around her body, and Rita folded her arms and crossed her legs.

Maybe they'd been the jurors who'd found Manuel's body.

I hadn't paid much attention to the men, but now I looked at each one closely.

The chef, Terry Andrews, was the tallest of the jurors. I didn't figure him for the alpha. He looked disinterested in the whole proceedings. Distracted even. A man concerned with his own business. Daniel Clay had something stuck in his teeth. He worked at it with his tongue and looked upon the proceedings with little interest.

James Johnson chatted to Chris Pellosi. The translator and web designer were strong characters and each of them would be contenders for the notional leader. The oldest juror at sixty-eight, Bradley Summers, bit his fingernails and stared at the ceiling. I took this as a good sign. He was thinking. Maybe not about the case, but at least he had a mind that was capable of rational analysis.

That brought me to the last male, Alec Wynn. The outdoorsman with a gun collection. The one Arnold had seen with a hateful expression that he'd attempted to hide. Wynn sat with his back straight. Hands on his lap. Attentive. Ready to do his duty.

I figured him for the alpha. I'd have to watch this guy closely.

Pryor had called medical examiner Sharon Morgan. A blond lady in a fitted, black suit. She was in her fifties, but had retained her youthful looks. More importantly, she was usually right on the money when it came to her testimony. She'd been at the crime scene, and she'd carried out the autopsies and found the dollar bill in Carl's mouth. Pryor took the jury through her credentials. Then the wounds, and the autopsies. The ME confirmed causes of death for each. Carl from a skull fracture and traumatic brain injury.

"And in relation to the female victim, were you able to establish a cause of death?" asked Pryor.

"Yes. The cluster of stab wounds to the chest area were the obvious source of trauma. I was able to establish the stab wound just below the left breast severed a major vein. The heart continued pumping and this created a vacuum. Air was sucked into the vein, traveled quickly to the heart and created a vapor lock which ceased blood flow causing major cardiac arrest. Death would have occurred in seconds," said Morgan.

"Does this explain why there were no defensive wounds on the victim?" said Pryor.

He was leading Morgan, but I didn't object. Pryor was trying to repair some of the damage I'd done yesterday in an attempt to prove both victims had been murdered in bed together.

I watched Wynn nodding. The prosecution were gaining points with Morgan. Pryor brought up a post-mortem photo of Ariella's chest. What looked like five gunshots to the untrained eye. Oval fissures in her chest.

"You've had time to examine the knife recovered from the defendant's home. What can you tell us about this knife and the wounds suffered by Ariella Bloom?"

"The wounds were inflicted by a single-bladed knife. Not double-edged. In this case, a flat edge to the bottom of the wound pattern indicated a single-edged weapon. The knife I examined is consistent with this wound pattern. A double-edged weapon would have created a diamond-like fissure. The knife is also consistent with wound depth."

Pryor sat down. I had three questions.

One would leave my theory of two separate attacks beyond question. The other questions would open the door for my closing speech – and Dollar Bill's involvement. When I'd been over the case yesterday, I'd seen more evidence that linked these murders to Bill. Now it was time to give some of that away.

The ME sat patiently awaiting my first question. She wouldn't allow herself to be drawn into theories. She was a pro when it came to testifying in court. I was relying on it.

"Doctor Morgan, you've already testified that there were five stab wounds to the victim's chest. These are spread out. As you can see from the photograph there is a single wound to the center of the chest between each breast, two parallel wounds below each breast, and a further two wounds below each stab wound on either side of the chest. The five stab wounds make up, perfectly, the five points of a star, is that correct?"

Morgan examined the photograph again.

"Yes," she said.

I changed the photograph on the screen to the unfolded dollar bill retrieved from Carl.

"You pulled the dollar bill from Carl Tozer's mouth. When you examined that bill, after photographing it, there were some markings on the great seal on the reverse of the bill. An arrow, an olive leaf and what else had been marked?"

She looked at the blown-up photo on screen.

"The star," she said.

Two female jurors, Betsy and Rita, seemed to lean forward. I would let it play on their imaginations for now.

"One more thing. The fatal wound to Carl Tozer's skull was due to blunt force trauma, as you've described. When that wound was inflicted, at the point of impact, it would have created a loud noise, isn't that right?"

"Almost certainly," said Morgan.

I returned to the defense table. I was looking for the photograph of the victims lying in the bed beside each other. I hadn't planned on another question, but something that had been working away in the back of my mind seemed to step forward. The photo filled my laptop screen. There it was. It would make no sense to the jury right now. In fact, it would confuse them. Pryor too. I decided it was worth the risk.

"One last thing, Doctor Morgan," I said, bringing up the photographs of the victims in bed on the court screen.

"You've testified that death would've been almost instant for both victims. Ariella Bloom has her hands by her sides, lying on her back. Carl Tozer is on his side, facing her, curled up, almost in the shape of a swan. Is it possible that the murderer may have posed these victims immediately after death?"

She looked at the photographs. "I think it's possible," she said.

"Looking at the victims here, Carl Tozer's body is the shape of a swan, or it could be the number two?"

"Yes."

"And Ariella, the number one?"

"Possibly," she said.

I'd known it. I just hadn't seen it until now. Dollar Bill had one more trial to complete. Ariella Bloom, Carl Tozer and Bobby Solomon would be his twelfth star. He'd lain out the bodies to look like the number twelve.

Twelve trials. Twelve innocent people. I had to stop this guy before there was a thirteenth.

I glanced toward the rear of the courtroom. Half a dozen FBI agents stood at the back. Delaney in the center. She shook her head. No one had tried to leave. Not yet. The doors of the courtroom opened and Harper came in with a small man in a gray suit. He spoke to Delaney. Harper came around the right side of the courtroom, then sat down at the defense table. She took a bundle of pages from her bag, placed them in front of me, and whispered, "You were right."

CHAPTER FIFTY-THREE

He kept a careful watch on his fellow juror's reactions. They bought the ME's evidence. Lapped it up. Only a few seemed interested in Flynn. Kane stiffened when Flynn talked about the dollar bill. The markings. He fought down his excitement, never letting it show in his face.

After all these years, was it possible that someone had stumbled upon his mission?

The position of the victims. Flynn knew. He'd seen Kane's hand in those deaths. In all the murders that Kane had committed, he'd resisted posing most of them. This one was special. Bobby was a star. Kane had reached the apex of his abilities, and he'd needed a challenge. Someone untouchable. A movie star.

If only she hadn't died so quickly, thought Kane.

The first stroke of the knife had woken her, and cut the light from her eyes a second later. His star. Kane's knife marked that star on her body. The kill needed something else, it had been over much too quickly, much too easily. She had looked peaceful, lying in the bed, arms by her sides. He had hauled the man upstairs. The bag over Carl's head, pulled taut around his neck, had formed a seal which meant no blood spatter in the house, just as Flynn had said. He had removed the bag after he placed Carl on the bed. Then, retrieved the bat from the hallway, placed the bat in the bag and smeared blood on it, and thrown the bat in the corner of the bedroom.

Twelve was an important landmark. He'd tucked Carl's legs beneath him, adjusted his position to take on the numeral 2. Of course, the thought had only occurred to him after he'd killed Ariella. He was so close to completing his mission. Part of Kane wanted someone to know. To understand. He saw Flynn looking at the woman at the back of the courtroom. And the other men standing around.

FBI.

Kane licked his lips.

Finally, the chase was on. But they had a long way to go to finding Kane. The feds were watching the crowd, not the jury.

Kane checked his watch. Took a deep breath to calm himself.

They would have discovered the body by now. The one he'd left for them last night after he'd paid a visit to Manuel.

It was starting again, for the last time.

CHAPTER FIFTY-FOUR

Pryor's next move was to nail Bobby to the DA's timeline, and expose him as a liar. He called the neighbor, Ken Eigerson. Ken was mid-forties, he wore a double-breasted suit that hid his gut, and a comb-over that failed to hide his bald head. One out of two ain't bad. Eigerson confirmed he worked on Wall Street, and he always made it home by nine p.m. on Thursdays. His wife taught Extreme Yoga on Thursday nights and he needed to get home as the babysitter, Connie, had to leave at nine to make her bus home.

"What did you see after you got out of your car?" said Pryor.

"I saw Robert Solomon. Plain as anything. I locked the car, and was walking toward my home when I heard footsteps on my left. I looked and he was there. I'd never spoken to him before. Seen him once or twice, you know, coming and going. I waved, said, 'Hi.' He waved back and that was it. I went home. The kids were asleep, and Connie, the sitter, left for the night."

"Are you sure it was him?" said Pryor.

"One hundred per cent. He's famous. I've seen him in a movie."

"And how is it you're sure it was nine p.m. when you got home," said Pryor.

"I left my desk at the office at eight thirty. Got my car, and when I parked I looked at the time on the dash. I'd been a little late the week before. Got home around ten after nine. Connie wasn't happy. She said she would miss her bus so I gave her fifty bucks for cab fare. You know how hard it is to get a good sitter? I made sure to be home on time. And I was. Right on the button."

"One last time, Mr. Eigerson. Because this sure is important. I want you to understand the gravity of what you're saying. The defendant says he got home at midnight. Either he's lying, or you're lying. If you're the least bit confused about anything, now's the time to tell this jury. So I'm going to ask you again. Are you sure you saw Robert Solomon go into his house at nine p.m. on the night of the murders?" said Pryor.

Eigerson turned toward the jury this time, looked straight at them and said, confidently, "I am sure. I saw him. It was nine p.m. I'd swear on my kids' lives."

"Your witness," said Pryor, pleased with himself. He turned away from the judge and the witness, and walked back to the prosecution table.

I got up fast, ignoring the barking pain in my side, grabbed Pryor by the arm before he got to his seat and said, "Wait there, Mr. Pryor, if you will." He tried to turn and look at the judge but I squeezed his arm. He stopped, gritted his teeth at me. Before he could raise an objection, or pull away, I pulled the trigger.

"Mr. Eigerson, you've been talking to Mr. Pryor for almost a half-hour. He stood around ten feet from you, and he was in your line of vision the whole time. Tell me, what color tie is Mr. Pryor wearing?" I said.

Pryor tutted. Still I didn't let him turn. He had his back to the witness stand.

"Red, I think," said Eigerson.

I let Pryor's arm go. He narrowed his eyes, and buttoned his jacket over his pink tie before he sat down at the prosecution table.

"Oh," said Eigerson. "I thought it was red. My mistake."

"Cheap. Real cheap," said Pryor.

I turned to the prosecutor and said, "I didn't ask how much the tie cost, but if you paid more than a buck fifty you were ripped off."

A ripple of laughter went through the room.

"Mr. Eigerson, you saw the man on your street for what? Two, maybe three seconds?"

"About that, yeah."

"How far away were you?"

"Twenty feet, maybe a little more," he said.

"So it could have been thirty feet?"

He thought about it.

"Maybe not as much as that. Maybe twenty-five, give or take."

"It was dark?"

"Yes," said Eigerson.

"The man you saw wore dark sunglasses and he had his hood pulled up. Isn't that right?"

"Yes, but it was him."

"It was him because he wore the same kind of clothes as Robert Solomon wears, and walked toward his house, isn't that right?"

"It was him," said Eigerson.

"So, from twenty-five feet away, in the dark, you saw a man with a hood pulled up over his head, wearing dark sunglasses. That's what you actually saw, wasn't it?"

"Yes. And it was . . ."

"It was a man who walked toward the house Robert Solomon lives in. That's why you thought it was the defendant. I'm right, aren't I?"

Eigerson said nothing. He was searching for the right answer.

"It could have been anyone, couldn't it? You didn't actually see much of his face?"

"I didn't see much of his face, but I know it was him," said Eigerson, defiantly.

As I asked my last question, I turned toward the jury.

"Was he wearing a tie?" I said.

The jury laughed. Everyone apart from Alec Wynn.

Eigerson didn't answer.

"No re-direct. The People call Todd Kinney," said Pryor.

Eigerson left the stand with his head bowed. Pryor didn't care. This was his style. Most prosecutors would've spent the entire morning with Eigerson. Not Pryor. He threw out witnesses like fastballs. And if the jury didn't like one witness, there would be another one straight after. It was a risky tactic. Quick volleys of testimony. On one hand, it kept things simple – made the trial move fast and ensured the jury stayed on its toes.

Kinney was a surprisingly young man. He wore a white shirt and tie, blue jeans and blue blazer, all of which looked to be at least two sizes too small. Even the tie didn't reach his waist. He was young. A hipster. Guy was wasted as a tech. He would've been great undercover.

Pryor was on his feet. His right foot tapping on the floor. I was getting to him. His shirt collar strained at his neck. I decided to increase the pressure.

On my way back to my table I stopped and whispered in Pryor's ear.

"Sorry about the tie. That was a cheap shot."

I heard Kinney approaching.

"It's not going to save your client. And if you ever touch me again I'll break your goddamn face," said Pryor, with a smile for the judge.

"I promise, I won't touch you again," I said, and backed away from Pryor, straight into the path of Kinney. He stumbled and I steadied him.

"Whoa, sorry about that," I said.

Kinney didn't reply. Just shook his head and made his way to the witness stand. I took my seat at the defense table and let Pryor do his thing. After Kinney had been sworn in, Pryor took him through his qualifications and experience as forensic tech and DNA profiler. It didn't take long and I let it play out. I was waiting for Pryor to get to the juice.

"You examined this dollar bill found in the mouth of Carl Tozer?" said Pryor, bringing up a picture of the butterfly fold.

"I did. It was preserved by the medical examiner. Initially, I tested for fingerprints. A good thumbprint had been retrieved and I swept the print surface area for DNA. I also took samples from the surface area around the print and over the remainder of the bill."

"What was the outcome of the fingerprint analysis?"

"A comparison fingerprint set had been retrieved from the defendant. The defendant's right thumbprint formed a full, twelve-point friction ridge match for the print taken from the dollar bill."

Pryor watched the jury as Kinney gave his answer. Some got it. Some didn't.

"What do you mean by full, twelve-point fingerprint match?" asked Pryor.

Kinney leaned into the question, but kept the science low-brow.

"Each human being on the planet carries a unique set of finger-prints. A fingerprint is the pattern made by the friction ridges on the surface of the skin. Our system tests these ridges, and reads them at twelve strategic points. It is generally accepted scientific fact that a twelve-point match means the prints are identical," said Kinney, slowly, keeping the jury in view as he spoke.

"Is it possible this print could've been a false identification?" asked Pryor. He was closing off my lines of attack, one by one.

"No. Impossible. I ran the tests myself. Plus, the DNA swabbed from the fingerprint area proved to be the defendant's DNA," said Kinney.

"How do you know that?"

"Again, I ran the tests personally. I obtained a swab of DNA from inside the defendant's cheek. This was tested and we were able to extract a full DNA profile. This profile was, to a mathematical probability of one billion, the same DNA profile extracted from the bill."

Kinney was a good scientist. He was just poor at explaining it to jurors.

"What do you mean by mathematical probability of one billion?"

"It means that the DNA on the bill matched the defendant, and if we tested a billion other people, we might get one other match for the DNA on the dollar."

"So, is it likely that the DNA on the dollar is the defendant's DNA?"

He didn't need time to think this one over, either. The answer sounded clear and unequivocal.

"I can say with a very high degree of certainty, that the DNA on the dollar belongs to the defendant."

"Thank you, please wait there. Mr. Flynn might have some questions," said Pryor.

I did have questions. A lot of them. Not many I could ask Kinney, though. I glanced over at Bobby. He looked like he'd been hit by a truck. Rudy had told him about this evidence, but hearing it in a courtroom in front of twelve people who are there to judge you is devastating. I poured him some more water. His hand shook as he brought the glass to his mouth. Bobby knew the power of Kinney's testimony. He was an actor, he felt the shift in the crowd. No two ways about it, Kinney's testimony hurt Bobby real bad. I'd been brought into this case to tear witnesses like Kinney apart. I knew, right from the start, we didn't have enough evidence to challenge this. The case all came down to this witness.

In a criminal trial, forensic evidence is God.

But I'm a defense attorney. I got the devil on my side. And he doesn't play fair.

I did my best to look confident as I strode toward the witness stand. I could feel the eyes of the jurors on me. From the corner of my eye, I saw Alec Wynn fold his arms. He was done. Didn't matter what I asked, he'd made up his mind.

"Officer Kinney, before you gave your testimony, you took an oath to tell the truth. Would you please pick up the Bible that's sitting next to you for a moment," I said.

I heard the squeak and bark from Pryor's chair as he pushed it back across the tiled floor. I imagined him folding his arms with that smug grin on his face. He knew the only line of attack on Kinney was his credibility. If I proved him to be a liar, I had a shot. Pryor would've prepared him for this.

Stick to the science – the results don't lie.

He took the bible in his right hand, and glanced over my shoulder at Pryor. Yep, Kinney had been prepped for this line of attack. He was ready. I knew he would be. I'd planned for it. I didn't ask him if he was being dishonest, I didn't remind him of his oath, or accuse him of lying. Instead, I prayed Kinney would tell the truth.

"Officer, please put the bible down," I said.

Kinney's eyebrows knotted together. Pryor's chair growled again, and I knew he was sitting up, pulling his chair close to the table so he could take notes. Pryor hadn't planned for this.

I picked up the bible, held it in front of my chest with both hands and turned toward the jury. They needed to see this.

"Officer, a number witnesses today have taken the oath on this bible. You held this bible when you gave your oath. Now I have it. Tell me, Officer, if you were to test this bible right now you'd probably find fingerprints and DNA from all of today's witnesses, correct?"

"Correct. There would be some fingerprints, maybe partials from the earlier witnesses if our prints hadn't wiped them out. We would get DNA from all of them. And you, Mr. Flynn," said Kinney.

"I agree. And DNA from the clerk, yesterday's witnesses, and anyone who'd touched this bible recently. There would be multiple DNA samples obtained from this book, correct?"

"Yes."

Kinney got an inkling of where I was headed. He was beginning to clam up, keeping his answers short and snappy.

"If you tested this bible and found only my DNA, then that would be unusual, wouldn't it?" I asked.

A handful of the jurors suddenly looked very interested. Rita Veste, the child psychologist, Betsy Muller the weekend karate instructor, Bradley Summers the sweet old-timer, and Terry Andrews the chef, they all concentrated closely on me and Kinney. They were listening. Alec Wynn kept his arms folded. He remained convinced by forensics. I had a handful of questions that might change his mind.

Kinney thought hard about his answer. Eventually he said, "Perhaps."

I went on full attack. There was no holding back, now.

"One of the reasons you may not find any other DNA on the bible, apart from mine, would be if someone cleaned the cover, isn't that right?"

"Yes."

I put the bible back down on the witness stand and focused on Kinney. It was time to fight.

"Officer, a dollar bill that's been in circulation in the United States for some years is likely to have hundreds, if not thousands of individual fingerprints and DNA profiles on it. Bank tellers, store clerks, ordinary citizens, basically anyone in the area who handles cash. Would you agree?"

"It's certainly possible, yes," he said.

"Come on, it's more probable than possible, isn't it?"

"Probably, then," he said, with just an ounce of irritation seeping into each syllable.

"The dollar bill in Carl Tozer's mouth had his DNA on it, the defendant's DNA and another profile, correct?"

"Yes."

"That third profile matched a man called Richard Pena who was executed in another State before this bill was even printed, correct?"

He'd been waiting for this.

"I'm satisfied that profile was an anomaly. It wasn't as strong a profile as the defendant's, and could have come from a close blood relative of Mr. Pena's. I checked our lab records, and as far as I can see Pena's DNA never left the state. It's never been in our lab so there's no possible means of contamination. The DNA must be a close blood relative."

"That's possible. Did you know Richard Pena was convicted of multiple murder, and each of his victims was found with a one-dollar bill tucked into the strap of her bra, with his DNA on one of the bills?"

I heard the jury murmuring, and slowly that noise spread out amongst the crowd. For now, I only wanted to plant that seed. I'd grow the tree later.

"No, I was not aware of that," said Kinney.

"Getting back to this case. We still don't know why there was no other DNA trace evidence on the bill found in Carl Tozer's mouth. We know Mr. Pena didn't handle it, we know it's been in circulation for years. The truth is someone scrubbed the DNA from the bill before the defendant touched it. That's the only explanation, isn't it?"

"I don't accept that."

"And the reason it was scrubbed was so that the defendant's DNA would be clear and recoverable from that dollar. In other words, someone placed it there because they wanted to frame Mr. Solomon for murder."

Kinney shook his head.

"That doesn't explain how the defendant's fingerprint got on the bill," said Kinney, smugly.

"I can help you with that. It's possible someone got him to touch the bill without him realizing the significance of that action. Then took it back from him and put it in Carl Tozer's mouth."

Kinney shook his head, scoffed at the idea. "That's never going to happen."

I turned to the jury, said, "Officer, please check your inside jacket pocket on the left side."

He blew a puff of air from his nose in surprise. Checked his pocket. Took a one-dollar bill from it and held it up with a look of total horror on his face.

287

"I didn't have a dollar in my jacket pocket this morning," he said.

"Of course you didn't, I put it there. Now your DNA is on it." I took a napkin from my pocket, reached out and plucked the bill from his hand with the napkin.

"It's easier than you thought, isn't it?" I said.

I walked back to my seat with Pryor's voice ringing in my ears. He was complaining to Harry, who sustained Pryor's objection.

Didn't matter. The jury had seen it. Some of them would be thinking about it and questioning the significance of the DNA evidence. If enough of them weren't sure, then we had a shot.

CHAPTER FIFTY-FIVE

Flynn took his seat and Todd Kinney stepped down from the witness stand. The judge called for a lunch break and Kane sure needed one. He thought his face would crack if he had to hold it in check for much longer. He filed out of the courtroom along with his fellow jurors. His jaw ached from clenching his teeth and he could taste blood in his mouth. Not much, just a sense of it. He'd swiped at his lips, and saw a faint trace of red. In his rage, he must have bitten the inside of his mouth. Of course, he hadn't felt it.

Kane wasn't given to hate in his most passionate moments. When he wielded a knife, or felt a throat closing beneath his fingers, the fear and the panic in his victim's faces only gave him pleasure. Hate was not a facet of his work.

It was all for pleasure.

Listening to Flynn, Kane began to feel that old familiar emotion. He'd hated many things: the lies that the media spread, the idea that people could better themselves, and most of all those who got lucky and were able to change their lives. Kane hadn't been so lucky. Neither had his mother. Hate was a part of it. Revenge, maybe. Mostly, he felt pity. Pity for the poor souls who thought money, or family, or opportunity, or even love could change anything. It was all a lie. To Kane, this was the great American lie.

Kane knew the truth. There was no dream. There was no change. There was only pain. He'd never felt its sting, but he knew it all the same. He'd seen it in too many faces.

The jurors sat around the long table in the jury room and the court officer came in with bags filled with sandwiches and drinks. Kane popped the tab on a Coke, watched one of the court officers counting out change and putting it with a receipt. He'd gone out and bought the jurors their lunch with cash from the court clerk's office. Kane had seen it done before. The officer swore, and said, "I'll be damned if I'm paying for the tip." The officer made a note on the receipt, folded a one-dollar bill and change and wrapped it in the receipt.

Kane's mind drifted back to a scene over a year ago. Laying down on the cold pavement, wearing filthy rags and a hat that he'd found in a dumpster. His homeless routine. It was effective because few New Yorkers took notice of the homeless. Walking past a person with dirt on their face, and no food, and no money, was part of everyday life in New York. Some spared their change. Some didn't. And it was the perfect way to watch a mark. Unlike the surveillance of the courthouse mail system, this stint as a nameless, homeless man had only taken a few days. And it was in a better neighborhood. Kane took up a spot on the corner of West 88th Street. Five hundred yards from Robert Solomon's home. On the third day, Solomon had walked past, wearing his iPod and headphones. Kane had tugged at his leg as he walked past.

"Spare a dollar, buddy?" said Kane.

Robert Solomon dove deep into his pocket, peeled off two one-dollar bills and handed them to Kane. Before he accepted them, he memorized the position of Solomon's fingers on the bills. The top bill would produce a nice juicy print on George Washington's face. Kane had raised his empty coffee cup, and the bills fell right in. He would clean the bills later with antibacterial spray, but careful to retain Solomon's print.

So simple. So easy. As Solomon walked away, Kane had put the lid back on his cup, stood and left.

That was the beginning of this particular job.

Kane took a bite of his sandwich, and watched the rest of the jury do the same. He checked his watch.

It would be soon, he was sure of it. He couldn't have accomplished all of this without help. It paid to have a friend, another dark one whom he'd allowed to drift to his cause. And he'd proved his worth.

Kane could not have come so far without his man on the inside.

CHAPTER FIFTY-SIX

"They're going to find me guilty, aren't they?" said Bobby.

"We're not beaten yet, Bobby. We still have a few surprises left," I said.

"You're innocent, Bobby. The jury will see that," said Holten.

Bobby sat in the consultation room with his food untouched in front of him. Holten had gone out and brought back some sandwiches. I couldn't eat either. Kinney had been a blow to Bobby's case. He wouldn't survive another one. Pryor had two witnesses left. The video tech who'd examined the motion-sensor security camera at Bobby's house, and the reporter Paul Benettio. Thanks to Harper, I had a good point against the video tech. The reporter didn't say much that worried me. He said Bobby and Ariella weren't getting along.

They were married. That doesn't mean he killed her.

I'd spoken to the agent that Harper had brought with her. The guy in the gray suit. He was a digital communications specialist working for the FBI and he was as sharp as that suit. Young, but damn qualified. Harper had introduced him as Angel Torres. He talked me through his findings from the visit to Bobby's house today. It wasn't a wrecking ball for the prosecution case, but it damn sure helped.

"And did the cop at the crime scene see you guys working?" I asked.

"No," said Harper. "He was a Knicks fan. So I kept him talking in the living room. He didn't much care what we did. He only cares about point-score average. Torres flashed his federal ID and the cop relaxed."

"It didn't take long, anyway. We were in and out in five minutes," said Torres.

"Good," I said.

Holten, Torres and Harper stood as they ate their sandwiches. Instead I popped some more painkillers and chugged them down with a soda.

Delaney came into the consultation room. She'd brought a bunch of files.

"How's it going with the jury?" said Delaney.

Bobby stared at me, waiting for a more positive answer.

"The DNA hurt us, but we knew it would. Maybe I was able to lessen the blow. We'll have to wait and see. Hang in there, Bobby. We're not done yet," I said.

"Have you told Eddie about the jurors, yet?" said Delaney.

"I was just about to," said Harper. "After Torres and I left Bobby's house, we went back to the federal building. I went through the stack of newspaper articles the agents had retrieved from the local papers' archives. I found two stories. The first is a little more interesting. Seems as though this lady was gunned down during an armed robbery. She was on the jury in Pena's trial."

She showed me the article on her phone.

The lady was in her early sixties, Roseanne Waughbasch. She worked in a second-hand store in Chapel Hill, North Carolina. Some hero had opened both barrels of a shotgun into her face. Nothing much was taken from the store, but the armed robbers took the contents of the cash register and the donation jar. The store owner believed they'd gotten away with close to a hundred dollars. The article focused on the loss of life, and the violence, over what? A hundred bucks and change.

"Can you tell what's wrong? Look at the picture," said Harper.

There was a photo of the street with the store closed. Crime scene tape across the door.

And I knew exactly what was wrong. Right next to the second-hand store was a seven-eleven. The neighbor on the other side was a liquor store. Beyond that, a small-town, local bank.

"This wasn't a robbery. It was a hit," I said.

"That's what I thought. Second-hand stores don't carry a lot of cash. They got nothing worth stealing and not much worth buying. If I was going to rob a store in that street I'd go for the seven-eleven.

The liquor store owner is likely to be armed, the bank would have heavy security but the seven-eleven would have very little. Maybe a baseball bat. No one who works as a clerk in a seven-eleven is likely to be a hero, either. Who would take that risk for that little money? And they carry plenty of cash. Much more than a second-hand store."

"What was the other story?" I said.

"I didn't bring the article with me. It was an ad in the *Wilmington Standard*. After Pete Timson was convicted of the Derek Haas murder, one of the jurors went missing. He didn't have family, but he had a job. He never showed up for work after the trial and his employer got worried about him. He contacted the police and even posted an ad. No one ever saw that guy after he walked out of the jury room."

The aching in my ribs started to subside. It was replaced by a hollow feeling in my chest, and a burning sensation in my throat. Delaney's theory about Dollar Bill had been right all along. Only we'd just seen the half of it. I slumped down a little on my chair, closed my eyes and rubbed at the lump on the back of my head. I needed a jolt of pain.

For the first time during this trial I felt afraid. Dollar Bill was far more sophisticated than we'd ever imagined.

"We've been looking in the wrong place," I said. "Everyone he put up for his crimes got convicted. Every single one. A trial can always go the other way. Even with forensics. How did he make sure he got his conviction? Planting the evidence wasn't enough for this guy. Dollar Bill wasn't watching these trials from the safety of the crowd. He was on the jury. It's like Harry said – we've got a rogue juror."

"What?" said Harper and Delaney, simultaneously.

Bobby and Holten exchanged open-mouthed looks.

"He somehow worked his way onto the jury. The juror in the Derek Haas murder – I think he didn't show up to work after the trial because he was already dead. Probably had been for a long time. At least since the week before the trial. He took his place. He ran Brenda Kowolski over in the street and, somehow, he strangled Manuel Ortega and shot the elderly juror in Pena's case. He got rid of them because they weren't going to vote his way."

"He kills the juror before jury selection and steals their identity. It's the only way it would work. That's why the juror disappeared after the trial," said Delaney, coldly. The realization spreading like a cold wind across her face.

"How did he know who was in the jury pool?" said Harper.

"He could've hacked the court server? Or the lawyer's offices? Or the DA's or gotten into the mail room somehow?" said Holten.

"This is crazy," said Harper.

"No, this is Bill," said Delaney "I already told you both. This one is highly intelligent. Maybe the smartest we've ever faced. We need to get the list of jurors from every one of those cases. We can check their IDs on the DMV, passport control, every damn database we've got. He would only be able to alter his appearance so much. We start with the juror who went missing after the Haas trial. We're going to get this guy. I'll testify, Eddie. I'll do everything necessary," said Delaney.

We talked strategy. This time we would watch the jury. But there was risk.

"Bobby, if this goes well we should be able to get a mistrial. That's what we're aiming for here. It means everything gets put on hold. Delaney can watch the jurors, track them until we can figure out which one is the killer. We must stop this trial. I can't let this get into the hands of the jury. Not if the killer is sitting there. But you have to know that I might not succeed. We have a theory. We don't have proof. If the judge refuses to grant a mistrial then there's the chance that Pryor could turn this around on us."

"What do you mean?" said Bobby.

"If we make the accusation that there's a serial killer sitting on the jury, and right now we don't know which one it is, then the entire jury will take it like we've accused them of this crime. They will all take it personally. That will mean they'll probably find you guilty. If we try this and it doesn't work, and we don't catch this guy, you could end up behind bars for the rest of your life."

I liked Bobby. For all the money and fame, he really hadn't changed much from the farm boy who'd left home with his father's savings in his pocket. Sure, he had his problems. We all do. But he didn't come to court in a Bentley. He didn't have twelve lackeys hanging off his shoulders telling him how great he was twenty-four hours a day. At an early age he discovered what he wanted to do with his life. He was lucky enough to be good at it, and he'd followed his dreams, fallen in love, and made the dream a reality. Now, he was a young man grieving for a lost love. No amount of money or fame could change any of that.

"This man killed Ariella and Carl. And all those other people. I want you to catch him. Do what you have to do. It doesn't matter about me. I know you're going to get him," said Bobby.

"There has to be another way," said Holten.

I didn't want to put Bobby at risk either. Right then, I couldn't think of another plan. I knew I was missing something. The DNA had bothered me from the start. How the hell did a dead man's DNA get onto a dollar bill?

It was impossible.

As soon as that thought flashed in my mind, I understood exactly how Pena's DNA had gotten onto the bill in Carl's mouth. I gave Delaney a short list of things to check out. Dollar Bill was plenty smart.

But nobody is perfect.

CHAPTER FIFTY-SEVEN

Interlacing his fingers over his stomach, Kane breathed out slowly and settled himself to watch Pryor take control of the case. The jury had talked during the lunch break. Whispers, here and there. If the jury had to vote now it would be a two-thirds, guilty vote. He guessed the rest were still undecided but most leaning toward guilty. Kane had faced worse situations in the jury room.

Pryor called his first witness of the afternoon. A tech called Williams who'd examined the motion-sensor security camera system installed at the Solomon property. The tech confirmed he'd taken the system away for examination and found a relevant video.

The court screen came to life with a black-and-white image of the street, looking out from above the front door of Solomon's home. In the bottom left-hand corner a time stamp displayed 21:01 as a hooded figure came into closer view. Kane couldn't make out the face. A glimpse of the man's chin came into view as the man raised his arm. He kept his arm raised.

"What is the figure in the video doing?" asked Pryor, pausing the footage.

"He may be putting his keys into the door. That's what it looks like in my opinion," said Williams.

The footage resumed. The hooded figure kept his head down, staring at the iPod. A white cable snaked from the device and disappeared into the hood: earbuds. The door opened and light spilled out. The figure stepped inside and the footage ended.

"How does this video security system work, Officer Williams?" said Pryor.

"It's motion-sensor activated. The camera turns on automatically when the motion sensor is triggered. I tested the sensor in the lab

296

and I can confirm it was fully functional, as you can see here. The sensor had a range of ten feet. Any movement within that field triggers the camera."

"The defendant, in this case, says that he got home around midnight. And that he did not meet his neighbor at nine p.m. What do you say to that proposition?"

"Not possible. The camera picks him up at nine-oh-one p.m. It looks like Bobby Solomon using his front door key to enter the property. I checked the system, and there are no videos after this one."

Pryor sat down, and Kane watched Flynn get to his feet. Before Flynn got started, Kane became distracted. He glanced to his left, toward the source of the disturbance. The courtroom doors were open and two NYPD detectives came in. One was Mike Anderson, still wearing his cast. The other, older man with gray, slicked back hair, Kane guessed to be Anderson's partner. Both men stood at the back of the court.

Kane diverted his gaze back to Flynn and thought about his knives. He imagined Flynn, tied up in a quiet place somewhere far away. Somewhere where he could let Flynn scream. He imagined himself, choosing a knife. Letting Flynn watch him choose it. Then the slow walk to the bound lawyer. Kane could make a cut last a lifetime. The slow insertion of steel into flesh was delicious.

He shook his head, trying to rid himself of the fantasy. His work here wasn't done yet. Not by a long way. Flynn strode over to Pryor, handed him a bound document. The prosecutor flicked through it. Even from the jury stand, Kane could hear the prosecutor clearly.

"How did you get this?" said Pryor.

"With the NYPD's permission. No one stopped him. And Torres is a federal agent. He had probable cause. No need for a warrant if there was no objection," said Flynn.

Kane listened for Pryor's reply, but didn't catch it. The two men approached the judge. He saw them argue. After a few minutes, Judge Ford said, "It's admissible. If there was no objection from NYPD, having granted access, then I'm allowing it."

CHAPTER FIFTY-EIGHT

I almost felt bad for the cop at Solomon's house. If he'd known the FBI were conducting an analysis he might have objected. And he might have arrested Harper and Torres. Thing is, he didn't notice. No objection. No problem. Harry let my report be admitted in evidence.

Man, I needed it.

Bobby needed it. If I couldn't get a mistrial I needed at least some of the jurors to vote our way.

I held on to a copy of the report. It felt like clinging to a life raft.

"Officer Williams, you can't see Robert Solomon's face in that video, can you?" I said.

"Not his full face. You can see part of his glasses, some of his mouth and chin. The hood is pulled up and it covers most of his face. But I can tell that it's him," said Williams.

When Pryor had finished his examination-in-chief, he'd rewound the video and paused it with a view of the hooded figure in the doorway.

"The person in that video is holding an electronic device. Can you tell what it is?" I asked.

"It looks like an iPod," said Williams.

"And just remind the jury what time this video is recorded at?"

"Just after nine p.m. on the night of the murders."

I used the screen control to bring up one of the crime scene photos. The view of the hallway. Staircase ahead, hall table on the left with the telephone, WiFi router and a vase resting on top of it. I gave the report Torres prepared to Williams and got to it.

"Officer, the report you have in front of you was prepared earlier today by Special Agent Torres of the FBI. It's a forensic examination

298

of the WiFi router you can see in this photograph. Did you examine the router?"

"No, I did not."

"Agent Torres was able to grab historic data from the router memory using an interface. You'll see the breakdown on page four. Take a look, please," I said.

Williams turned the pages, and started reading. I gave him thirty seconds. He finished reading and sat there with a blank look on his face.

"The defendant told police he got home around midnight. Look at the entry halfway down page four – the entry marked number eighteen. Please read it," I said.

"It says, *connection 00:03 Bobby's iPod*," said Williams.

"And look at the previous evening's entry at number seventeen."

"It reads, unconnected device – connection not authorized 21:02."

I grabbed the screen control and brought up the image of the hooded figure outside the front door.

"It's reasonable to assume, officer, that the device we can see in this still is the device that attempted to connect to the router in the defendant's home?"

"I can't say that for sure," he said.

"Of course you can't. But it would be a strange coincidence if it wasn't this device, isn't that fair?"

Williams swallowed, said, "That's fair."

"Because if someone had dressed up to look like Bobby Solomon to gain access to the house, they would know Bobby walks around with an iPod. It also gives them a good excuse to hide their face from the camera?"

"I don't know. Maybe," said Williams.

"Maybe, indeed. And if this person did gain access to the property, he could simply kill the power to the camera, couldn't he? That way the camera wouldn't pick up anyone else coming to the house," I said.

"He could do that, but I have no evidence that was the case," said Williams.

"Really?" I said.

He paused, thought about it. "Really," he replied.

"Okay, so, Officer Williams, I'd like you to show the jury the video of the police arriving and gaining access to the property through the front door."

Williams mouthed the word, shit.

"There is no video. The video of the defendant entering the property is the last recording on the device."

"But we know for a fact that the police attended the scene of the crime. The only way they wouldn't be on the video, and the only way my client wouldn't be on the video when he came home at midnight would be if someone turned off the camera earlier in the evening – correct?"

He shifted in his seat. Williams had scrambled for answers, and got himself tied in knots.

"That's possible. I mean, yes, that may have happened."

I could've pushed it further, but I was on shaky ground. For now, I wanted the jury to at least entertain the idea that this was someone else. Torres had given us that hope. Damn, I should've known to examine the router sooner.

Pryor did a quick re-direct.

"Officer, we have no information on the range of that router, do we?" said Pryor.

"Eh, no, no we don't. The router could've been picking up a device from a passing car," said Williams.

Good enough. Pryor adjusted his tie, and sat down.

"Just one point arising from that," I said, looking at Harry.

"One question, Mr. Flynn, that's all," said Harry.

I clicked play on the screen. We watched the forty-five-second video again. I stopped the playback and saw Williams had already realized what I was about to ask but he couldn't think of anything to say.

"Officer, just confirm for the record that the video gives us a view of the street, and there are no passing cars or pedestrians."

"Correct," said Williams, with a sigh.

I was done with this guy.

CHAPTER FIFTY-NINE

Shifting in his seat, Kane felt uncomfortable for the first time. He cursed himself, silently, for not thinking about the WiFi router. This lawyer was a curse. Kane was used to the ebb and flow of trial. He'd seen it before. Never like this. Flynn, out of all the defense lawyers he'd seen in action, was clearly the best. He wondered if Rudy Carp would have measured up to Flynn. Not that it mattered now.

Kane heard Pryor announce his final witness. The prosecutor moved at a brutal pace compared to others. It was effective. In one trial, many years ago, Kane had had to remind most of the jurors of the testimony they'd heard weeks ago. They'd forgotten most of the important pieces of evidence. No chance to do that with Pryor.

The reporter stepped up, took the bible and gave his oath. Kane wondered what the reporter would have to say. Very little. But then, Pryor was a player – perhaps not Flynn's equal, but close. One thing Kane had learned to rely upon was the underhanded methods of prosecutors.

He had a feeling that Pryor was about to play a card which he'd been keeping up his sleeve for the entire trial.

First of all, Pryor established Benettio's credentials. The reporter was well connected to Hollywood. He was an insider.

"What can you tell the jury about the relationship between the defendant and the second victim, Ariella Bloom?" said Pryor.

"They were recently married after meeting and falling in love on a movie set. Their marriage proved to be a powerful alliance. It was their union which allowed them to form a powerbase in Hollywood. You know the power of celebrity couples. Like Brad and Angelina. Soon after, they started their own reality TV show. And they were both cast as the leads in the recently released sci-fi epic. The studios were throwing money at them. They had it made, because they were married."

"And how was their personal relationship?"

"You know, in Hollywood there are always rumors. That's the nature of the beast. There are always those who cast doubt on a relationship. I'm one of them. In this case, I am going to break with journalistic privilege. I had a source. Right at the heart of their relationship. He told me the marriage was one of convenience. Sure, they got along. But they were more like brother and sister – on account of Robert Solomon's homosexuality."

CHAPTER SIXTY

I love America. I love New York. I love the people. But sometimes it depresses me. Not individuals, mostly the media. For all the news channels, newspapers, and digital news outlets, Americans are not served well by the media. The court was mostly filled with members of the media. And it was their gasps that were heard around the courtroom when Benettio said Robert was gay.

These reporters hadn't even blinked when Pryor had put up the pictures of Ariella's body, her wounds, her young life ripped apart and put on display in HD. But reveal someone famous had something other than a heterosexual lifestyle and they go crazy.

Bobby shook his head, and I whispered to him that it would be okay. He nodded, and said it was fine.

"Mr. Benettio, these are rather extraordinary claims. And they don't appear in your statement or deposition. Why not?" said Pryor.

"I wished to protect my source. Now that this trial is here, I feel compelled to reveal the truth," he said.

"And who is your source?"

"My source was Carl Tozer. He offered me a story on what really went on in their marriage. Ariella had always suspected it. She had even taken Carl into her bed. Ariella and Robert had separate lives. They were together for the cameras, but that's all. I believe that—"

"Objection, Your Honor," I said, but before Harry could shut him up, Benettio continued, even talking over the judge.

"It's my firm belief that Robert Solomon found out about Carl's contact with me and that's why he murdered him, and Ariella. Robert had lived a lie, and he couldn't face the truth. Coming out as a homosexual in Hollywood would have killed his career. He knew that. So he killed them instead!" said Benettio.

I objected again, citing speculation. Harry sustained it, and told the jury to disregard everything the witness had said. It was too late. Even as I spoke to Harry, Benettio had continued to talk. The jury heard it all. The damage had been done.

"Nothing further," said Pryor.

I knew if I started questioning Benettio he'd try and bring it up again. No point. The judge had told the jury to disregard him. There was no mileage in making the trial about Bobby's sexuality. I told Harry I had no questions.

"The prosecution rests," said Pryor.

Decision time. Pryor had already told me he didn't want to cross-examine the mattress guy, Gary Cheeseman. And Torres's report on the WiFi router was already in evidence, Pryor couldn't keep it out.

I only had two real witnesses. Delaney and Bobby.

"The defense calls Special Agent Paige Delaney," I said.

For over an hour, Delaney laid it out for jury. Dollar Bill, displayed in all his foul glory. We spent time talking through each case, each victim, the dollar bills and trace evidence leading to the innocent person who was to be framed for Dollar Bill's crimes, the markings on each bill, and the killer's psychology.

I kept one eye on the jury the whole time. Especially the men. They all listened, transfixed by Delaney's testimony. Daniel Clay, the unemployed sci-fi nut, lapped it up. He was the right age, but I didn't think he had it in him. Something about his eyes. He looked repulsed with each murder Delaney recounted. It wasn't him. Although his identity would be easy to steal.

The translator, James Johnson ticked a lot of boxes. He was the right age, and not many people would notice his disappearance for a few days. He worked from home. Again, though, he stared at Delaney with utter fascination. I could tell, from his body language and the way his lips moved, that he believed Delaney. And that scared him. No. It wasn't James.

Terry Andrews, the grill man, and Chris Pellosi, the web designer, were also possible candidates for Dollar Bill. Men whose identity could be plucked away for a short time. But Andrews was very tall.

And I thought the killer would've struggled to mimic such a tall man on so many occasions. Pellosi was a possible.

Sixty-eight-year-old, retired, Bradley Summers was the wrong age group. And looked to be popular amongst the other jurors. They seemed respectful to him, perhaps on account of his age.

That left Alec Wynn. Out-of-work college professor. Outdoorsman. A man who owned guns and kept himself to himself.

The man that Arnold had noticed. The man whose face had seemed to change.

Arnold hadn't made it to court, and I made a mental note to call him. I was flying by the seat of my pants, and in truth I was so used to trying cases on my own I hadn't immediately noticed he hadn't shown up. But I needed him here. I wanted his take on Wynn.

I stood in front of the jury, and asked Delaney my last question. We'd rehearsed it.

"Agent Delaney, how is it possible that Dollar Bill could ensure that the other men were convicted of his crimes? Surely a criminal trial can always go in a defendant's favor even with good evidence against them."

She wasn't looking at me. She was doing her final checks. There were agents at the back of the room. Harper was at the defense table, working and listening to the case. She had her laptop open and had been receiving articles all afternoon. Clippings and short videos from the trials of men who had been convicted of Dollar Bill's crimes. Harper must've heard my question. She closed her laptop, and stared at the jury.

Delaney gave me one look, and a nod, and then we both looked toward the jury as she spoke. Only I was focusing on one man. Alec Wynn. He sat with one hand on his lap, legs crossed, and stroked his chin. Listening intently to every word that fell from Delaney's lips.

This was it. We'd discussed it. Debated the pros and cons. And between us we'd decided there was nothing else for it.

"The FBI believe that the serial killer, Dollar Bill, infiltrated the juries who were trying those cases, and manipulated them to bring back guilty verdicts."

There must have been some kind of reaction from the crowd. Intakes of breath, involuntary outbursts of incredulity. Something. I was sure of it. If there was I didn't hear it. All I could hear was my heart hammering in my ears. My focus was total. I knew every inch of Wynn's face. I could see the rise and fall of his chest, his hands, even the slight swaying of his leg as he folded it over the other.

As Delaney delivered her answer, his expression changed. His eyes grew wider, lips parted.

I thought I would know. A statement like that is the equivalent of pulling off Dollar Bill's mask in a crowded room. It should have hit him like a two-by-four to the side of the head.

I wasn't sure.

Slowly, the world bled back into my consciousness. Sound, smells, taste, and the pain in my ribs all hit me at once, like I was just surfacing from deep water.

The rest of the jury had similar reactions. For some it was disbelief. Others it was shock and a very real fear in the realization that such a man could be walking around free as a bird.

Whoever Bill was, he'd played it super cool. He didn't give himself away. I took a long, last look at Alec Wynn.

I couldn't say for sure.

There was a follow-up question. A question that raised its head, inevitably, from Delaney's last answer. I could've asked her the question right then and there. I didn't. If I asked that question, it might look like I was playing for a mistrial. And it might look like I was pointing an accusatory finger at the jury. It might sound better coming from Pryor.

I let him do it.

"No further questions," I said.

Pryor had fired off his first salvo before I'd sat down. He was like a greyhound out of the gates.

"Special Agent Delaney, you are making the case that Ariella Bloom and Carl Tozer might have been victims of this serial killer, Dollar Bill, is that right?"

"Yes," said Delaney.

"And you've testified that Dollar Bill selects his victims, murders them, and then carefully plants evidence to frame an innocent person?"

"That's correct," said Delaney.

"But judging by the last question Mr. Flynn asked you, you believe he does much more than that. You believe he infiltrates the jury trying the innocent person for murder to ensure he is found guilty?"

"I believe so."

Pryor moved close to the jury, placed his hand on the rail of the jury stand. His positioning made it look as though he stood with the jury on this; that they were all on the same side.

"So, by implication, you believe this serial killer is in the room right now. And he's sitting on this jury, behind me?"

I held my breath.

"Before you answer that question, Special Agent Delaney," said Harry, "I'd like to see both counsel in my chambers right now."

CHAPTER SIXTY-ONE

No matter how many trials Kane had witnessed, there was always something new in every one of them. This one had a number of firsts.

In this trial, Kane felt like he was truly a part of it. Not simply as a juror, but as a participant. The FBI had finally caught up with him. The agent, Delaney, looked cunning. She had a sharpness around her eyes. Kane could sense a bristling intelligence that lay deep within her. A worthy opponent? Perhaps, he thought.

It was inevitable, thought Kane. After all these years, all those bodies, all those trials. Someone had to put it together eventually. He hadn't made it easy for them. Of course not. But Kane had harbored the fantasy that perhaps one day, long after he was dead, someone might be clever enough to piece it all together.

And, somehow, in doing so, that person would make a connection with Kane. They would see and appreciate his work like no one else had ever done before. His mission. His calling. Displayed to the world.

He hadn't expected it so soon. At least not until he had completed his masterpiece.

Another first came from the judge.

Before he'd ordered the lawyers into his private room, the judge had given an instruction to the jury keepers. Each juror was to be kept separate. Luckily, there were no trials ongoing in the adjacent courts, which freed up their offices, judge's chambers, clerks' rooms and the courtrooms themselves. More than enough room to keep the jurors separated. The jury keeper had called for additional court officers, to assist in escorting the jurors to their separate rooms.

Kane had never seen anything like it. The judge didn't want the jury to implode, to begin to doubt one another, to begin to suspect that one of their number might, just might, be a killer.

It took some time for the court officers to assemble, then they each took one juror from the court. The officer who accompanied Kane was a young man with fair hair and pale skin who couldn't have been older than twenty-five. He escorted Kane out of the courtroom, down the hall and into a small office off the main hallway. Kane sat in an office chair in front of a dead computer screen. The officer closed the door.

Another first. In hindsight, it had to happen sometime. Nevertheless, it came as a surprise to Kane.

He wanted to run. The FBI were closing in. His mask was slipping. Kane looked around the small office. Two desks, both facing a wall with a calendar pinned up. Neither desk could be said to be tidy. Staplers, Post-it notes and pens were scattered around the keyboards, and stacks of files were perched on the edge of the desks or on the floor beside them. Kane took his head in his hands.

He could wait it out. The case was close to going to the jury.

He could knock on the door, and ask the officer to come inside. It would only take a minute to close the door and break the officer's neck. The officer's uniform would be a tight fit, but he figured he could get away with it if he changed quickly and walked straight out of the door and down the hallway. He'd have to keep his head low, or turn his face to the wall when he saw a camera.

He hated not knowing what to do. No matter what choice he made, he knew he might regret it in time. Either sitting in a jail cell for the rest of his life, kicking himself that he didn't run, or far away from New York, sitting in a café dreaming of what could have happened if he'd just hung on a little longer.

He made a decision, got up and knocked on the door. The officer opened it and peered inside. He had a boy's face.

"Say, could I get a glass of water?" said Kane.

"Sure," said the officer.

He began to close the door, but Kane took it in one hand and said, "Wait, just leave it open a little please. I get claustrophobic in places like this."

The guard nodded, and left. Kane sat down, breathing hard now. His blood felt hot beneath his skin. The rush of anticipation for what was to come. He could see it all clearly in his mind. The officer would place the water on the desk, Kane would grab his wrist with one hand, twist, and fire his extended fingers into the officer's throat. What happened next would be a matter of logistics. If the officer went down, Kane would get on top, flip him over onto his front, grab his chin, kneel on his back and pull up sharply. If the officer managed to stay on his feet, Kane needed to shoot behind him, get his gun away before wrapping his arms around the officer's neck and pushing forward, then snapping back and to the left.

He could almost hear the sound of his vertebrae cracking.

The officer returned to the room carrying a plastic cup of water.

"Just put it down on the desk, please. Thank you," said Kane.

The officer's boots made his approach easy to track. Kane stared straight ahead, and watched the officer place the water on the desk in the reflection from the computer screen.

Kane's hand shot out and grabbed the officer's wrist.

CHAPTER SIXTY-TWO

"What in God's name is going on out there?" said Harry.

He hadn't even got to his desk yet. All three of us stood in his chambers. Harry was pissed, but he was also concerned. Pryor waded in with both feet before I could say anything. He'd fired himself up into a ball of righteous indignation. Or what passed for righteousness from a career prosecutor.

"The defense are scrambling, Your Honor, that's what's going on. They know the evidence in this case is solid and they can't shake it. So they're playing for a mistrial. You know it. I know it. They're not going to get one throwing wild accusations at a jury without any proof whatsoever, no sir."

"If we had proof we'd come to you, Harry," I said. "Look, the FBI don't go around testifying for the defense in murder trials on a simple hunch. You know that. If Agent Delaney is right, and the killer is on the jury then letting this trial proceed any further is an egregious injustice to my client. I don't want to point fingers at a jury who holds Solomon's fate in their hands, but there's been too much going on in this trial already. Two jurors are dead and one has been kicked for potential jury tampering. You need to see the bigger picture here."

"And what's that? A rogue juror who is actually the real killer in this case? That's incredible," said Harry.

"It's possible," I said.

"It's ridiculous," said Pryor.

"Enough!" cried Harry. He turned away from us, went to his desk and brought out a bottle of ten-year-old and three glasses.

"Not for me, Judge," said Pryor.

The bottle hovered over a glass and Harry fixed his eyes on the prosecutor. Nothing was said. Harry just stared at the guy. The silence grew uncomfortable and Harry's face retained a stoic impression of disapproval.

"Just a small one, then," said Pryor.

Harry poured three glasses. Handed one to me and Pryor. We put the shots of Scotch away. All of us. Pryor coughed and his face flushed. He wasn't used to good liquor.

"When I was a young defense attorney I remember being in these very chambers, with old Judge Fuller. He was a character. Kept a .45 in his desk drawer. He used to say no attorney should give a closing speech in a murder trial unless they've had at least three fingers of Scotch," said Harry.

I put my empty glass on Harry's desk. He'd made his decision.

"I have concerns about this case, about this jury too. I don't have to tell either of you what a difficult decision this is for me. Ultimately, I have to follow the evidence. There is suspicion about one juror on this panel. I'm not in a position to evaluate that suspicion. There is no evidence before this court to convince me that the jury has been compromised. I have to tell you, Mr. Pryor, I'm not happy about this. But I have to follow the law. I'm sorry, Eddie. I'm overruling your question, Mr. Pryor. Do you have any other questions for Agent Delaney?"

"No, I don't."

"Does the defense wish to call any further witnesses?" asked Harry.

"No, we're not calling the defendant," I said.

I never call my client to testify. If it gets to the stage where you're relying on your client to protest their innocence – you've already lost. The case is won during the prosecution evidence. Or lost. I didn't rate Bobby's chances with the jury. Letting Pryor tear him to pieces over his whereabouts would only lessen his odds.

His only chance was a great closing speech. Clarence Darrow, one of the finest trial attorneys who ever opened a bottle of Scotch, won most of his cases in his closing speech. It's the last thing the jury hears before they go into their private room and decide the client's fate. Darrow saved more than one life with the power of his words.

Sometimes, that's all a defense attorney has – their voice. Trouble is, it's the same voice that ordered one for the road: the same voice that broke up their marriage: it's the same voice that messed up everything. But now it has to save a life.

Words never weigh so much as when they're spoken for somebody else. I felt the weight now, sitting on my chest. If the verdict came back guilty, that weight would never shift.

"We can finish this case today, but I'd like one thing."

"What's that?" Harry said.

"I want you to give Delaney the name of the cop who has the notebooks that you took off the jury."

CHAPTER SIXTY-THREE

"You okay?" said the young, boyish court officer.

Kane tightened his grip, momentarily. The fingers on his other hand extended, stiffened. They formed a blade of flesh, sinew and bone. Ready to be thrust into the officer's throat.

He hesitated.

Just a few more hours.

He released his grip on the officer's wrist and said, "Sorry, you startled me. Thanks for the water."

Kane drained the plastic cup, watched the officer leave and close the door. He breathed out and stared at the black screen of the computer monitor in front of him. His thoughts drifted to Gatsby – reaching out his hands to the unquiet, black waters, toward the dim green light far, far away. If he gave up now, if he failed to complete his work then others would waste their lives searching for the green light, dreaming away their lives in the hope of something better.

There was no hope. Kane's dreams had always been dark. Full of monsters and boys digging in the earth for bones.

He didn't have long to wait. The court officer brought Kane back to the courtroom where he joined the rest of the jury. The judge told them the defense had rested. It was close to five o'clock, but both attorneys felt they could deliver their final speeches before six. The jury could go back to their accommodation, think about the case and then return in the morning to consider their verdict.

The pace of this trial thrilled Kane. He was glad he'd let the officer live. He didn't have to run. Not yet. Not until this was over.

As Pryor got up from his seat to address the jury, a stillness fell on the room. Kane could feel it. The prosecutor broke the silence with a vow.

"I promise you, each and every one of you, that the decision you make in this case will become part of your lives. I know it will. You have to make the right decision. Get it wrong, and it will become a needle that works its way through your veins a little more every day. Until it reaches your heart. You hold a man's life in your hands. The defense will tell you that. Mr. Flynn will probably remind you of that a lot. But in reality you hold much more. You hold in your hands the fate of every citizen in this city. We rely on the law to protect us. To punish those who would take our lives. We diminish our very natures if we do not honor that responsibility. We forget the victims, if we do not do our duty. And let's be clear about this – your duty in this case, if you've listened carefully to all of the evidence, is to find the defendant guilty."

CHAPTER SIXTY-FOUR

I watched Bobby shrink before my eyes. With every word that Pryor spoke, Bobby seemed to get smaller, frailer, as if the life inside of him was evaporating further with each minute that passed.

Pryor reminded the jury of the key points. Bobby hadn't told anyone where he was on the night of the murders. His fingerprints were on the baseball bat. He lied about what time he came home. His fingerprint and DNA were on the dollar bill found in Carl's mouth. He had motive, opportunity, he had Ariella's blood on him, and the knife used to kill her never left the house. And the theory about another killer? It was a defense trick. Nothing more.

By the time Pryor took his seat, sweat had broken out on his face. He'd given it his all for a full thirty minutes.

My turn.

I reminded the jury that the WiFi router in the Solomon house registered the presence of an unknown device at precisely the same time the person who was dressed like Bobby arrived at the property. I reminded them whoever got inside the property at that time must have turned off the motion sensor on the security camera. Some of the jurors, particularly Rita and Betsy, seemed to be following my logic.

Wynn sat with his arms folded throughout.

The murders couldn't have happened in the way the prosecution described. Carl was most likely taken from behind by a bag over the head, followed by the bat that Bobby kept in the hall. This was why Ariella had still been asleep when the killer stole into her bedroom. And the dollar bill, scrubbed of DNA, save for Bobby and a dead man.

"Members of the jury, Mr. Pryor reminded you of your duty. Let me clarify his remarks. Your only duty is to yourselves. The only question you have to ask yourself is: are you sure Robert Solomon murdered

Ariella Bloom and Carl Tozer? Are you *sure*? I say that Mr. Eigerson was not sure that he saw the defendant that night. I say we can't be sure that the bill found in Carl Tozer's mouth had not been interfered with in some way by forensics. But what I say doesn't matter a damn. It's what you know that matters. You know, in your heart, you can't be sure Robert killed those people. Now all you have to do is say it."

The next few minutes in my life passed in a blur. I seemed to be talking to the jury one minute, and the next I'm packing my bag and saying goodbye to Bobby. He was leaving for the night with Holten and his security crew. We would get our verdict in the morning, maybe. The jury were led out, and the courtroom began to empty. Harry had leaned over the bench, talking with the clerk of the court. There were only a few stragglers left in the courtroom. Delaney and Harper were waiting for me. They seemed to sense that I needed a little time to let my thoughts settle. I'd given everything in the final speech. My brain was mush.

I slung my laptop bag over my shoulder, and pushed open the gate that separated the public seating area from the rest of the court. Delaney and Harper ahead of me. I felt tired. Sore. Done. Yet I knew a night's work lay ahead. There was still a chance we might catch a break in the Dollar Bill case. I had a bad feeling that this was Bobby's only chance.

Something moved on my left. Fast. Low. I only caught sight of it in my peripheral vision. Someone had been kneeling down in the row of seats to my left. I turned to see what was happening, but not fast enough.

A fist cracked into my jaw. I heard Delaney shout out. Harper too. I was already going down. The floor came up fast. I put out my hands and managed to stop my head from breaking open, but the impact of my ribs on the tiled floor caused me to cry out. I couldn't breathe. Through the waves of pain, I had a dim sense of what was going on around me. Harper got thrown to the floor ahead of me. She landed on her back. I heard footsteps behind me; Harry running to see what the hell was going on.

I felt a strong grip on both of my wrists, then my arms were folded behind me. Instantly, I knew what was happening. I'd been arrested enough times before to know how cops operate. No sooner had the thought occurred, than I felt the cold sting of cuffs wrapping around my left wrist, then the right. My arms were pinned behind me. Hands underneath my arms hauled me backward and up onto my feet. I tried to speak but my jaw barked out a protest. It had almost dislocated with the first strike.

I managed to crane my neck back and to my left.

Detective Granger. And behind him I saw Anderson.

"Eddie Flynn, you're under arrest. You have the right to remain silent . . ." said Granger. He continued to mirandize me as he pushed me forward. Ahead, waiting at the courtroom doors was a uniformed cop with his hands on his gun belt.

"You can't do this," shouted Harry. "Stop right there, right now."

"We can do this. We are doing this," said Anderson.

Harper got up, and Delaney held her back.

"I'm a federal agent, what the hell are you doing? What's the charge?" said Delaney.

"This isn't a federal matter. You got no jurisdiction here. We're taking this man to Rhode Island PD for questioning," said Granger.

I couldn't breathe. The pain came in waves now. Each one crushing my lungs. I looked up and saw the cop waiting at the end of the aisle wore a slightly different uniform. Rhode Island PD. Anderson and Granger had a liaison officer with them. They were making the arrest and taking me out of state.

"Wha – what's – charge?" I managed to say. If I asked, they had to tell me. I had a right to know. The sheer effort to get those words out of me almost shut my lights down. Granger tugged on my arms, sending fresh hell into my ribs. I could feel my feet growing heavy. I was almost out when I heard Anderson's answer.

"You're under arrest for the murder of Arnold Novoselic," he said.

Jesus. Arnold. Until a couple of days ago I wouldn't have been sad to hear that Arnold had bought the big ticket. Now, I felt differently. I'd just spoken to him early this morning. The shock of hearing about his death almost dulled the fact that I was being arrested.

"Why would Eddie murder his own jury consultant?" said Delaney. She was following me and shouting questions at Anderson.

"Maybe you should ask Flynn," said Anderson. "Ask him why he didn't wear any gloves when he stuffed thirteen one-dollar bills down Novoselic's throat."

CHAPTER SIXTY-FIVE

The bus pulled out of the lot at the back of the court. The jurors were silent. Each of them weighing the final arguments in the case. Most just seemed glad that it was nearly over. Kane looked out of the window as the bus passed the courthouse just in time to see Flynn being brought out by the police and bundled into a plain Sedan.

Kane allowed himself a smile. The benefit of friendship.

He'd gotten from Jamaica, New York, to Arnold's apartment in Rhode Island in record time. Initially, the jury consultant didn't want to let him in. Kane had promised him a revelation. Inside information on a rogue juror, sitting on the jury right then. It was too much for Arnold to resist. Kane had entered the luxury apartment, asked for water, and strangled Arnold from behind then laid him out on the kitchen floor. He'd taken the dollar bills in a baggie that he'd retrieved from the glove box of a drop car he had hidden in a long-term parking garage at JFK. He had to work quickly, and he used a spoon to wedge some of the bills deep into Arnold's throat. However, Kane had made sure to leave one bill protruding from Arnold's mouth. The bill he'd marked with a red pen – coloring in all the stars, the arrows and the olive leaves on the Great Seal. The final bill.

The bill that carried Eddie Flynn's fingerprints and DNA.

The one that would put Eddie Flynn behind bars, just when his legal career was about to enter the stratosphere. Flynn was all over the news, and the papers. The hottest lawyer in New York City. Kane had seen it coming.

Eddie Flynn's American Dream was over.

CHAPTER SIXTY-SIX

Granger took the cuffs off, told me to turn around, then cuffed my hands to the front. It was a small act of mercy. Sitting in a police car with my hands cuffed behind my back would've put more pressure on my ribs. I would've passed out before we'd gone two blocks. He pushed my head down and forced me into the back seat of an unmarked police car. A detective's car from the pool. It smelled of stale food and the seats were ripped.

The thought of Arnold, murdered, choked on money, made my skin crawl. Dollar Bill had set me up. Just like he'd set up all the others.

It took everything I had to calm myself down. I had to ignore the pain and think.

The driver's door opened and Granger got in. The Rhode Island cop entered the vehicle on my side and sat in front of me in the passenger seat. I felt the car dip and Anderson got in beside me on the left. He still wore that cast. I looked into his face and saw something that frightened me.

Anderson was sweating. Trembling too. Granger pulled into traffic and set off. I couldn't keep my eyes off Anderson. I'd gone hard at him in court. I'd busted up his hand pretty good, too. He should've been gloating right now. Staring me down, enjoying the victory. Granger and Anderson should've been cracking jokes and pissing on my defense. Scaring me. Telling me it was all over – that I'd spend the rest of my life in jail.

Instead, the air inside the car felt thick with atmosphere. It reminded me of the times I'd spent in the back of vans, or sitting in cars, waiting to start a con job.

"Thanks for letting us pick this guy up," said Granger. He started the engine and pulled into traffic.

"No problem. Evening, Mr. Flynn, my name's Officer Valasquez," said the Rhode Island cop, before turning his attention back to Granger. "Glad your precinct put me in touch with you, and it saves any hassle on jurisdiction. I could tell you guys had a hard-on for Flynn as soon as we spoke."

"Oh yeah. We've got a history," said Granger. He looked in the mirror, and instead of a satisfied, smug look I saw something else. Excitement. If I sat up straight I could still see Granger's eyes in the rear-view mirror. His gaze darted around, frantically. He was checking the road, the sidewalk, glancing back at Anderson, and making sure he kept an eye on the Rhode Island cop, Valasquez.

I knew something was going down. The only thing I didn't know was whether Valasquez was in on it. I guessed not.

As we drove along Center Street, I leaned back, felt my phone in my jacket pocket. No one had searched me. I figured between the three of them, bearing in mind their ages, and the way they held themselves, they probably had fifty years on the job between them.

It would be unusual for one cop, ten years in, to forget to search a suspect. It made me nervous. Granger made a couple of turns, and we headed north. That didn't help my anxiety. They were supposed to be taking me to Rhode Island. Fastest way was south, straight onto the FDR, hug the river until the freeway stretches onto I-95. No homicide cop in New York would go any other way. They knew the city better than most.

"Where are we going?" I said, slowly dropping my hands to the bottom of my jacket and sliding both arms to the right, over my jacket, toward the door handle.

"Shut the hell up," said Granger.

"Blow me," I said.

"Do what he says, shut your Goddamn mouth," said Anderson. I didn't.

"If we're going to Rhode Island why aren't we using FDR Drive?" I asked.

The cop in front of me in the passenger seat turned and stared at Granger.

"Much as it hurts me to say it, the lawyer has a point," said Valasquez, and checked his watch.

"Too much traffic. It'll be jammed up to hell at this time," said Granger.

The last rays of daylight were fast disappearing. Every car we passed had lit up its headlights. The squad car remained dark as Granger hooked a left. Now we were headed west. A series of quick right and left turns kept us headed in that direction.

I looked out of the window and said, "West 13th Street and 9th Avenue? What are we doing in the Meatpacking District?"

"Shortcut," said Granger.

The car turned left into a side street. Steam billowed up from the sewers, illuminated by the streetlights it looked like hell lay beneath Manhattan.

"I gotta make a quick stop," said Granger.

This was it. Granger wasn't making a stop. And I wasn't going to make it to Rhode Island.

Anderson leaned toward me. He was fishing something out of his jacket with his left hand. Because of the cast on his right arm, Anderson was basically one-handed. He tilted back toward the driver's side of the car and I saw something shiny in his left hand. He threw it at my feet, then dived back into his jacket with the same hand. A glance was all I had time for. It was all I needed. Between my feet lay a small pistol.

"Gun," cried Anderson. His arm came up with his weapon drawn. He was going to kill me and claim self-defense. That's why I wasn't searched before they put me in the car. All of these thoughts flashed through my mind as I dove toward Anderson. My head cracked against his nose, I reached out and caught his left arm with both of my hands. The handcuffs bit into my wrists as I forced his left arm down.

He was struggling, wildly. I threw myself off the seat and managed to catch the back of Granger's head with my elbow. He fell to the side and his foot stretched out, flattening the accelerator. The car lurched forward and I was thrown back into my seat.

So much pain. The adrenaline let me fight through it.

Anderson had dropped his gun too. He was leaning forward trying to reach it. It must have fallen underneath Granger's seat. I could see his arm stretching out for it. The car shuddered and I saw sparks outside Anderson's window. We must've been sliding into a parked car.

Anderson sat up and pointed his gun at me.

Then his head shot into the roof of the car. The gun went off and glass sprayed over my face. He'd shot out my window. I was thrown around and landed on my back, on the back seat. I sat up and saw Valasquez holding his head. He hadn't worn a seat belt. A lamp post was now buried in the front of the squad car.

Before Anderson could take another shot, I drew my knees up to my chest, pinned my arms against the door behind my head and threw both soles of my feet at Anderson's face. The effort started with my back, and I used my arms, my chest muscles, my abdominals and my legs. My body unfolded like a bow that had just let an arrow fly. I'd kicked as hard as I could, and I'd missed. I hit him in the body. The force of the impact sent Anderson bursting through the passenger door, out onto the street.

That last kick took everything I had left. I tried to sit up, but the pain was too great. I flopped back down and tried to scream it all away. I needed to move. I had to get the hell out of this car, but I couldn't even sit up. My breath came in ragged gasps, each one a blaze of agony.

"You're gonna die, you son of a bitch," said Granger. I looked up, saw him step out of the driver's door. The door itself had burst open in the impact, half throwing him out of the car. I heard his feet crunch on the glass that lay on the street. I could only see him through the side windows of the car, but I saw him draw his weapon from a shoulder holster. He stepped over Anderson, cried, "He's armed," as he fired a shot.

I covered my head.

I didn't feel the bullet strike. No shockwave of pain. I only felt the spray of something warm hit my face.

Valasquez was holding his shoulder, crying out.

Granger had shot him. I heard Granger's gun kicking again as Valasquez's head ripped open.

"You just killed a cop. This is what happens when you threaten one of us with internal affairs. You mess with us, you catch a bullet," he said. Then, I saw Granger's face. He'd ducked down onto his knees. He held the gun in a two-handed grip. The sight pointed at my head. Anderson lay on the sidewalk beneath him, I could just see his arm raised in the air behind Granger.

I wanted to cry out. To scream. No sound came. If I had, I wouldn't have heard it anyway. All I could hear was the blood thumping in my ears like the ocean. My heartbeat was a soundwave in my head.

The anger came fast when I thought of my daughter. This man was robbing her of a father. A shit father, but a father nonetheless. I put one hand beneath me on the leather seat, gritted my teeth and put everything I had left into sitting up. The small pistol Anderson had thrown in the footwell was just inches away from my fingertips. It may as well have been at the other end of a football field.

My hand slipped and I collapsed. I tilted my head toward Granger.

The son of a bitch had a smile on his face. He straightened his arm, lined up the shot, and then disappeared in a storm of sparks, shearing metal and sound.

I shook my head. Shut my eyes. Opened them. I was looking at the flank of a car. A blue one. The car backed up, at speed. I heard the familiar growl from a V8. The car left my line of sight. The door behind me opened, and I saw Harper's face above me. Her eyes were wide and she was out of breath. In one hand she held her phone. My name was lit up on her screen. I'd hit the voice command button on my cell, and said the name I'd listed for Harper.

"You owe me a new car," she said, her eyes wet. Gently, she placed a hand on my chest.

"Blow me," I said.

I heard Harry's voice, and he appeared beside Harper.

"I said is he okay?" said Harry.

I heard sirens in the distance, getting closer.

"I'm okay, Harry."

"Thank God. Remind me never to get into a car with Harper again. I think I'm going to have a heart attack," he said.

"Delaney said she'd call Rhode Island PD. Dollar Bill set you up. We can get all this straightened out," said Harper.

I knew Delaney would be persuasive.

"Anderson and Granger, are they . . . ?"

"They're not going to make it," said Harper.

I nodded, closed my eyes, tasted the blood in my mouth and swallowed it down. This was going to be a long night.

FRIDAY

CHAPTER SIXTY-SEVEN

Two seventeen a.m.

Kane lay in bed and stared at the ceiling. Too much excitement to even contemplate sleep. He'd never brought two missions so close together. The risk was great, but with the end of his dream in sight, Kane had decided to take the chance. Throughout his life, he had felt a certain invulnerability.

He was special. Just like his momma always told him.

Somewhere on the landing there must have been an old clock. Kane heard it ticking, faintly. In a dark, silent room, in the middle of the night, all such sounds became artificially amplified. He turned his head, checked the digital clock on the bedside table.

Two nineteen a.m.

He sighed. No point in even trying to sleep. He flung back the covers, swung his feet to the floor. The wound in his leg was healing nicely. He'd changed the bandage before going to bed. No pus, no smell, no angry swelling around the cut.

He stretched his back, let his finger reach for the ceiling and yawned.

That's when he heard it. Kane froze. The clock still ticked away somewhere in the hallway, but now he heard something else.

Movement. Feet on the stairs. Lots of them. Kane got up, silently. Put on his underwear, pants and his socks.

When he was tying his laces he heard the floorboards creak. Once. Twice. Three times. The second or third row of floorboards in the hallway had a loose board. He'd noticed it yesterday.

No time to even grab a shirt, he tucked his knife into his pants pocket and crept toward the door. He put his ear to the wood, held his breath and listened. Someone was in the hallway. Slowly, Kane stood and put his eye to the peephole in the door.

Outside his room were four men in full SWAT gear. Black, Kevlar armor. Jackets, gloves, helmets with cams on the side and each of them cradled an assault rifle. Kane slid away from the door, put his back to the wall beside it and struggled to control his breathing. They'd found him. After all these years, they'd finally done it. In one way, Kane felt a certain sense of pride. The FBI had finally recognized what he was doing. He hoped that at least one of them would see his method, and understand his work.

The digital clock on the nightstand read two twenty-three a.m.

He took a deep breath, blew it out and started running when he heard the sound of wood splintering as the door crashed open and the SWAT team yelled out to get on the floor.

CHAPTER SIXTY-EIGHT

I checked my watch.

Two o'clock in the morning.

I was freezing my ass off in the back of an FBI command vehicle, which was little more than a van with a steel floor and a bank of computer screens on one side.

I sat on the opposite side, blowing steam off a cup of coffee. My hands were wrapped around the cup for warmth. I'd had nothing enter my body for fifteen hours apart from coffee and morphine. Both were good, but the morphine was a little ahead at this moment. I felt punchy, but the pain had subsided. The evening hadn't been as bad as I'd feared. Four hours in a police precinct and I'd been released. If I hadn't had a New York Supreme Court judge, an ex-FBI private detective and one of the Bureau's chief analysts backing my side of the story I wouldn't have set foot outside a cell for two days. In the end, Harper had settled it. Not only had she taken my call, but she'd recorded it.

Within an hour internal affairs had joined the investigation, and they had a file on Anderson and Granger a foot long. It took them no time to access Anderson and Granger's cell phone records, voicemails, text messages and WhatsApp messages. It was all there. They were paranoid that, faced with a life sentence for murdering Arnold, I'd try to sell the DA Anderson and Granger for a reduced sentence. In the world of corrupt cops, the mob, and just about any organized crime operation, nothing will get you killed faster than an arrest.

I'd seen it before.

The plan was to kill me, then Anderson would pick up the small pistol and put two in the back of the Valasquez's head. They'd blame the out-of-town cop for not searching me. It was all there in their messages and voicemails. They hadn't had time to ditch the burner cell phones they'd been using.

Anderson and Granger had taken their chance once they heard Rhode Island PD had forensics on me. I wondered if Dollar Bill had anticipated Anderson and Granger trying to kill me. It didn't fit with his MO. He wanted a messy, public trial. He wouldn't have wanted me to take a bullet in the back of a cop car.

Preliminary forensics came back after three hours and confirmed Valasquez had been shot by someone outside the car, using Granger's weapon. Granger tested positive to GSR. I didn't.

I would have to come back and make a full deposition to internal affairs – so they could ride through the rest of the homicide department like a tornado, but for now they were content to let me go after I'd seen the medic and he'd given me some pain relief.

By the time I'd made it out, Harper and I both had a string of missed calls from Delaney. Harper called her back, and we headed straight over to Federal Plaza. She asked if Harry would come too. The FBI had made progress, they were going to need a federal search warrant and they needed Harry's help to get it.

That was some hours ago. Now I was freezing my ass off in the back of a van parked on the single-lane road that led to Grady's Inn. The back doors were opened and Harry stepped inside followed by June, the court stenographer. She was a lady in her fifties, wearing a pearl blouse, heavy skirt and a thick woolen coat. She'd brought her stenotype machine in a portable bag and, judging by her expression, she was carrying around a big bag of resentment for being hauled out of her bed to come here at two in the morning.

"Pryor's here. I saw him pull in," said Harry.

I nodded, took a sip of coffee. Harry produced a hip flask and enjoyed a deep drink. We all have our ways of staying warm. June took a seat beside Harry, opened up her bag and placed her machine on her lap.

Pryor climbed into the van, followed by Delaney. We sat on the pull-down seats on one side. It was a big van and there was plenty of room for another four or five people as long as you remembered to duck your head once you were inside. Delaney sat in a swivel chair that faced the monitors. She draped an earpiece and mic over her head and said, "Fox Team, standby for orders."

"Mind telling me exactly what I'm doing here?" said Pryor.

"Are we on the record, June?" said Harry.

She pursed her lips, but the ferocity with which she hit the keys on her stenotype machine answered Harry's question all the same.

"Mr. Pryor we're on the record in the People v Solomon. I wanted you here because I'm about to authorize law enforcement to take action in relation to a juror on this case. Now, legally, under sequestration rules the jury is in my care and under my sole authority until they deliver a verdict. Since we don't have a verdict yet, if any law enforcement official or government body wishes to speak to a juror they require my authorization. I wanted you and Mr. Flynn here so you can raise any objections, and to witness this intervention if it takes place. We're at this location at the request of the FBI and for the safety of the jurors. This is a fluid situation and the FBI can't spare the time to travel into the courthouse. This operation has to be authorized on site. Clear?"

"No, what's going on?" said Pryor.

"It's Dollar Bill, he's really on the jury," I said.

A loud thump echoed around the van from Pryor's head slamming into the roof of the van. He was a born lawyer – and lawyers make their arguments on their feet. He sat back down, rubbing the top of his skull.

"This is all smoke and mirrors. By authorizing this interference with the jury you are giving credence to the defendant's whole argument. You're basically saying the defense are correct. Judge, you can't do this," said Pryor.

"I can, Mr. Pryor. Are you calling for a mistrial?" said Harry.

That shut him up. He knew he had a strong case. He had to weigh up whether this tipped the balance in my favor.

"I'll reserve my position on a mistrial until the morning, Your Honor, if that pleases the court?" said Pryor, carefully.

"Fine. Now, based on information relayed to me by Special Agent Paige Delaney, I'm authorizing the arrest of the juror known as Alec Wynn," said Harry. "We have reason to believe that Alec is the serial murderer dubbed Dollar Bill, whose modus operandi is to frame innocent men for his crimes by planting dollar bills at the crime scene connecting these men to the perpetrator's crimes. Dollar Bill will then murder and steal the identity of a potential juror in the trial of that innocent man for Bill's crimes in order to ensure a conviction. The compelling evidence presented to me by Agent Delaney this evening is as follows . . ."

I knew the evidence already. Delaney had been through it with me and Harper at Federal Plaza. It all stacked up.

Harry continued, for the record. "I authorized a forensic examination of each of the jurors' notebooks which I retained in my possession following an order recusing juror Spencer Colbert. The FBI have taken possession of the notebooks with my permission and, according to the affidavit of Agent Delaney, the first notebook subjected to examination was that of juror Alec Wynn. The agent confirms that this notebook was selected for examination based on probable cause evidence supplied by defense attorney Eddie Flynn."

Pryor leveled his gaze at me, then back to Harry. He was seething.

"For the record, Mr. Flynn, what evidence did you provide to Agent Delaney?"

"I relayed the content of a telephone call I'd had with Arnold Novoselic, a jury consultant retained by the defense. He'd seen suspicious activity from this juror . . ."

"Objection," said Pryor. "Suspicious activity?"

"He'd noticed this juror's appearance changing. His facial expressions. Arnold was an expert in body language amongst other things and he found this behavior extraordinary enough to inform me," I said.

"That's it? You're going to authorize the arrest of a juror on hearsay testimony about a facial expression?" said Pryor. He was getting his punches in early. If this operation went south, Pryor wanted his objections on the record.

"No," said Delaney. "The fingerprint evidence obtained from the notebook of Alec Wynn is compelling. The fingerprints from the notebook match a suspect on the National Database named Joshua Kane. The details on this individual are scarce. No place of birth, no DOB, no current address. We do know he is wanted in relation to a triple homicide and arson. We have no further details on those crimes other than they originate in Virginia. We've asked for that file to be sent to us and we are awaiting receipt from Williamsburg PD. That request was made two hours ago and we've expedited the request a number of times. We expect the file and a picture of Kane soon."

Harry nodded.

"On the basis of the fingerprint identification and the possible link to the Dollar Bill case I am authorizing the arrest of juror Alec Wynn. Counsel, any representations?" said Harry.

"None," I said.

"I want my objection noted. This action strikes at the heart of due process," said Pryor.

"Noted. Agent Delaney, you may proceed," said Harry.

"Fox Team, we are go," said Delaney, swiveling around in her chair to face the monitors.

There were five screens spread across half the length of the van. Four were helmet cams belonging to a small SWAT team. The other screen was Delaney's email. She refreshed her email screen every few seconds. The more information she had on Kane, the better. The view from the four helmet cams bobbed up and down. We could hear their boots on the ground and as they rounded a turn, Grady's Inn came into view. An old place. Real old. It looked like a hotel that tourists went to when they wanted to die.

The first of the SWAT guys flashed his ID at a concierge who looked as though he was even older than the hotel. They spoke softly to the night porter at reception, checked the room number for Alec Wynn and told him not to make any calls. Slowly they crept up the stairs. I watched one of the cams of the agents in the middle of the pack. I could see an agent in front of him, and he flashed his badge and beckoned to the court officer who guarded the hallway. They whispered to the guard to get behind them, that they had a warrant from the judge to arrest Alec Wynn. The court officer confirmed the room number, and slowly the SWAT team advanced.

They halted outside the door. Switched on flashlights that must have sat beneath the muzzles of their assault rifles.

The SWAT leader counted down from three.

The clock on their helmet cams read two twenty-three a.m.

Three.

Two.

Ping. An email marked *urgent* hit Delaney's account.

One.

The door burst open and the flashlights caught Wynn standing at the foot of his bed, wide-eyed and bare-chested. Instinctively, he raised his hands.

"Federal agents! Down, down on the floor now!"

He knelt down, his hands shaking and spread his arms out on the floor. Within seconds he had been searched and cuffed.

"I've had enough of this," said Pryor. He got up, folded his coat over his chest and got out of the van. He slammed the door shut. I turned my attention back to the bank of monitors. One of the SWAT team guys hauled Wynn to his feet, and the other looked at him. We had the full view on the camera.

"Jesus Christ, please don't h-hurt me. I haven't done anything," said Wynn. His face was covered in tears and snot, and his whole body shook with fear.

The SWAT who was facing Wynn backed up, and we saw him raise his hand to his face. He swore softly just as we saw what he was looking at.

A dark patch spread over Wynn's crotch, and it grew as it spread down one leg. Wynn had lost control of his bodily functions. He was quivering with panic, barely able to speak.

Delaney swore, checked her email. It was from Williamsburg PD. It was a precis of their file on Joshua Kane. Harry and I got up off our seats and leaned over Delaney's shoulder. Kane was wanted in connection with the murder and rape of a high school student named Jennifer Muskie, and another high school student named Rick Thompson. Both of them were last seen the night of their high school prom. The third victim was Raquel Kane. Kane's mother. Police suspected he'd abducted, raped and murdered Jennifer and stashed her body in his mother's apartment. His mother had been murdered and the whole apartment set alight.

The file continued that Rick Thompson's body had been found in the reservoir, along with his car.

There was a black-and-white mugshot of Kane – it had been poorly scanned and it was hard to make out the finer details of his features, but he didn't look like Wynn.

I looked back at the monitor again. Wynn had completely broken down. He was crying and begging for mercy. It wasn't an act. Joshua Kane must've had steel-plated balls to pull off those crimes and maneuver himself onto those juries. Wynn didn't look like he could find his balls with either hand.

"Shit," I said. I took out my phone and found my call log. Flicked through until I found the entry for my call to Arnold last night. I'd made the call at four thirty a.m. It hadn't been a long call. I figured now that Arnold was at home, in his apartment in Rhode Island. Even with a consistent disregard for the speed limits, and allowing for little or no traffic, it would've taken Kane just around two and a quarter hours to drive from Rhode Island back to JFK.

"Delaney, ask the SWAT guy to check with the court officer – what time did he wake the jurors for breakfast yesterday?" I said.

She relayed the request, and one of the SWAT guys went into the hall and we saw him talk to the jury keeper.

"I'd say we woke them around six forty-five, seven a.m. at the latest," he said.

He couldn't have murdered Arnold after my call, driven back, hidden a car, made it back to Grady's and snuck into his room all in that time.

"We've got the wrong man," I said.

Delaney said nothing. She was still reading the email on Kane. Harry started rubbing his head, and he took another tot of whiskey from his hip flask.

"Arnold told me on the phone last night it was Wynn he'd seen masking his true expression. But, thinking it through now, when I made that call I figure Arnold was already dead. I wasn't talking to Arnold on the phone. I was talking to Kane," I said.

"Kane?" said Delaney.

"Thinking about it now, he wouldn't have had time to get back to the hotel from Rhode Island. It's not possible unless he'd already murdered Arnold. Dollar Bill steered us away from him, toward Wynn," I said.

"Jesus," said Delaney. She picked up her cell, made a call. Whoever was on the other end picked up.

"The notebook we had tested. It had Alec Wynn's name on it. I want you to check every notebook and tell me if there's another notebook with his name on it," said Delaney.

While we waited, she continued to flick through the pages of the original file that Williamsburg PD had scanned and emailed to Delaney.

I saw her twitch. She'd found something.

"It's definitely not Wynn," she said, staring at the screen. A voice came on the other end of the line, confirming there were two jurors notebooks with the name Alec Wynn marked on them. Kane had put Wynn's name on his notebook.

I moved closer, to check what Delaney was looking at.

Jennifer Muskie and Raquel Kane were both murdered in 1969. In that moment, I knew who Joshua Kane really was. So did Delaney. She had to act fast, push down her disbelief and work in the moment.

Delaney barked orders at the SWAT team, directing them away from Wynn and to a different target.

My cell phone pinged. It was Harper, she was on her way here and she'd found a picture of Dollar Bill in the old newspaper clippings. She followed up her text with the name of a juror.

It was the same juror I was thinking of.

That son of a bitch.

CHAPTER SIXTY-NINE

While the SWAT team were taking down the door of the room next to Kane, he'd quickly opened the window and crawled out onto the roof. No time to scramble over the tiles to the lower roof, with the trestle at one end of the gable.

Every second was precious now. Kane slid down the roof, trailing his arms behind him. He wore no shirt, and he could feel the tiles scraping his skin. There was no pain, merely the sensation of his back being grated on tile. Kane let his legs slide off one end of the roof, then his torso. He grabbed guttering with both hands, arresting his fall, and letting him guide his drop into a snow bank. Twelve feet into snow.

Kane rolled out of the snow at the back of the hotel and darted into the trees away from the lights he could see up ahead. Red, white and blue, flashing lights. A security team straight ahead at the entrance to the private lane which led to Grady's Inn. Kane didn't hesitate, he started running just to the left of the lights. He was breathing hard, his breath a fog in the cold night air. Even though he was naked from the waist up, Kane felt no pain. He didn't feel cold or heat like a normal person. Those senses were muted, but the chill air still made him shiver.

At the edge of the trees he saw headlights from a vehicle leaving the Inn. A white Aston Martin. Kane stepped into the road and waved his arms in the air. The car stopped and Art Pryor got out of the driver's door.

"Mr. Summers?" said Pryor. "Are you alright? What are you doing out here in this weather? You'll catch your death at this age."

Kane held his arms over his chest, shivering.

"Y-y-your coat, please," said Kane.

Pryor threw off his cashmere overcoat and draped it around Kane's shoulders.

"I heard gunshots, shouting, I got scared and ran," said Kane.

"Get in and I'll take you somewhere safe," said Pryor.

Feeding his arms through the sleeves of the coat, Kane walked around the car to the passenger side and got in. Pryor sat in the driver's seat, closed the door and when he turned to look at the juror he'd known as sixty-three-year-old Bradley Summers, he stared in horror at the man's chest. Kane had allowed the coat to drift open, letting Pryor see his work.

"My God," said Pryor.

Few men had seen Kane's chest and Pryor got to look upon its full glory in the interior lights of a vehicle. Kane's chest was a mass of white scar tissue. Intricate lines of ridged scars that formed the Great Seal. An eagle clutching arrows and olive branches. Its claws spread over both sides of Kane's belly. The shield, and stars above the eagle's head, grouped together over his sternum.

"Take us out of here. There's a Holiday Inn a mile away. Park there and I won't hurt you," said Kane, removing the knife from his pants pocket and placing it in his lap.

Pryor revved the engine, his foot too heavy on the accelerator, as he stared at the knife – Kane told him to calm down. They pulled out and drove for a few minutes, until they reached the Holiday Inn. All the while Pryor was panting, pleading for his life.

They parked in a dark corner of the deserted back lot. The Holiday Inn was a thousand yards away.

"I need your clothes and your car. I'll let you have your wallet. It's a short walk to the Holiday Inn across the lot. If you refuse, I'll have to take it by force."

He didn't need to ask him twice. He stripped to his underwear, tossing the clothes in the back of the car, as Kane had instructed.

"Now get out of the car," said Kane.

Pryor opened the door and Kane could see the temperature hit him straight away. He stood, in his shoes and socks holding himself against the cold in the dark, empty parking lot.

"My wallet," said Pryor.

Kane climbed into the driver's seat, closed the door, rolled down the window and dropped the wallet onto the asphalt.

Pryor came closer, bent down to pick up his wallet. As he stood up he came face to face with Kane, staring out at Pryor.

He froze. His legs quivered, shook, then Kane drew his knife from Pryor's left eye socket and let his body fall.

Quickly, Kane dressed in Pryor's clothes. They were too big, but it didn't matter much. Within a few minutes, Kane was headed toward Manhattan in the Aston Martin. He couldn't allow the FBI to interfere with his pattern. He had a man to kill.

And nothing could stop him.

CHAPTER SEVENTY

SWAT found the room that had been occupied by Bradley Summers empty. The window had been left open. The SWAT leader had climbed out onto the roof, looked around and noticed footprints in the snow, leading away from a snow bank that had been disturbed. Just to be sure, Delaney ordered a bricks and mortar search of the hotel and grounds. It took a half-hour, and by the time the feds had finished they were satisfied that they'd pissed off every resident of the hotel, and that the footprints had led to the road leaving the Inn and there was no sign Dollar Bill had doubled back.

Joshua Kane was in the wind.

The speed at which the FBI worked was fascinating and frightening. Within minutes of the completed search, all law enforcement agencies were notified of the alert. Harper arrived. She'd found two photographs in newspaper clippings. What looked like the same man, in his late fifties, was captured in both. One leaving a courthouse, the other entering the courthouse. The man was in the background of the shot on both occasions. Different hair color, different clothes, but the facial features were roughly the same. With the exception of the broken nose that Summers had, it was the same man. Delaney and I sat in the command vehicle and studied the pictures. Harry was still trying to get Pryor to answer his cell phone. Bobby was headed for a mistrial. No doubt about it.

"Where would he run to?" said Delaney, studying the pictures.

"Maybe back to Bradley Summers' apartment?" said Harper.

"I've got an agent headed there now, but it's a long shot. This guy didn't survive undetected for so long by making rookie mistakes."

"It's incredible that he's gotten away with this. I mean, he's been doing this for decades," replied Harper.

It galled me that law enforcement had let it happen. Maybe that was the way of things. Nearly every homicide department in every city, in every state, was overworked. They followed the evidence all the way. They didn't have time to question it too much. In a way, it wasn't their fault. They'd been manipulated by a highly intelligent, cold-blooded killer and they simply didn't have time to consider alternatives. All the same, Dollar Bill probably had his fair share of luck to get this far. So many victims. All in aid of some kind of seriously screwed-up vision of his own.

I thought about everything I knew about Kane. The murders. The trials. The victims. The pattern and the Great Seal.

No way this guy was going to let it all fall apart. He wanted to complete his mission.

"Harper, call Holten. Right now. This crazy asshole is driven and meticulous. He's going to try to end this on his terms. I think Kane's going after Bobby," I said.

Three minutes later I was in the passenger seat of Harper's rental car, my hands spread out on the dash while Harper followed the SWAT van and weaved in and out of traffic, riding the wake of the sirens.

"Try Holten's cell again," I said.

Harper used the voice command for her cell phone, which rattled around in a well on the dash. I saw the screen light up, reflected on the windshield, and the dial tone echoed through the car's Bluetooth system.

No answer.

"I'll try Bobby again," I said.

I called him. His cell must have been switched off. At least Holten's was ringing. All we needed was for him to pick up the damn phone.

"The cops must be on their way by now, anyway," said Harper.

Before we left, Delaney had put an urgent call in to NYPD to attend at Bobby's property and check he was okay. They would be there any minute. She'd also called for a field agent from Federal Plaza to get over there and make sure the place was locked down.

From Jamaica to Midtown Manhattan usually took close to an hour in a car. We crossed the Queens Midtown Expressway in just under ten minutes, and that familiar skyline loomed ahead; the United Nations Building lit up like a postcard just beyond the Midtown tunnel.

Harper's cell buzzed. It was Delaney.

"NYPD just called. They talked to Solomon's security. It's all quiet. I've asked PD to send the squad car away and I've told my agent to pull back. We're going to blaze the sirens through the tunnel then we're going to go silent. I'll be switching to an unmarked car and sweeping the area. Kane hasn't made it to Solomon's house yet, and if he's there and watching the property, I don't want to spook him."

"Agreed," said Harper, "but there's no harm in Eddie and me paying a visit, is there?"

"Let me sweep it first. Then I'll let you know. By the way, I just heard from forensics on the DNA profile we took from the Wynn notebook with Kane's fingerprints on it. The DNA processing isn't complete, and won't be for another ten hours, but early results are a fit for Richard Pena, our dead man whose DNA was on the bill in Tozer's mouth. Once the profile is complete we'll know for sure. I'll need you to update me on where you've got to with Pena's profile, Harper. There's a link somewhere to Kane," said Delaney.

We lost all phone signals as soon as we entered the tunnel. It didn't matter. I wouldn't have been able to take my hands off the dash anyway, not the way Harper drove; hugging the tail of the SWAT vehicle at seventy-five miles an hour with cars and a wall within inches of us on either side. I wanted to ask Harper about Pena's DNA, and what she'd discovered, but I was too scared about crashing into the wall if I distracted her.

Once out of the tunnel, the panic was over. We pulled in on 38th street, one block away from Bobby's rental and waited. This part of Midtown was a pretty quiet area. The residents were mostly dentists and doctors. The cars that lined the sidewalk were either high-end SUVs or sports cars for the dentists going through their mid-life crises.

"Did you get anywhere on the Pena DNA?" I said.

"I did. Richard Pena was identified as the Chapel Hill killer from his DNA profile. His DNA matched a profile on a dollar bill. Fourteen hundred men in the area volunteered their DNA. Pena was one of them. The cop in Chapel Hill said that because so many men came forward they couldn't cope with collecting the DNA swabs. They had to train up campus security officers to take swabs from the college faculty, staff and students. A security officer named Russell McPartland testified that he took the swab from Pena, sealed it and gave it to the police. I got a cop from Chapel Hill PD wading through the university's personnel files as we speak."

"How do you get cops to do all this for you?" I said.

She flashed a smile, said, "I can be persuasive."

I didn't doubt it. I figured Russell McPartland for another alias of Joshua Kane. He couldn't commit all those murders so cleanly every single time. Sooner or later he was going to leave behind DNA. My guess was he got a job at campus security under an assumed name. Job like that would give him unfettered access to a trusting, female student body. When there was a killer on the loose, vulnerable young women would be more likely to trust a campus security officer if he approached them, or offered to escort them home. But then, he'd messed up. Kane must have left his own DNA on one of the dollars found with a victim. He would've known it as soon as the Police Department called for DNA samples from the males in the area. Only Kane had used this to his advantage. He'd taken a swab from Pena, the janitor. Easy as rubbing a cotton bud around the inside of Pena's cheek, and sealing it in a tube. But Kane must have substituted Pena's sample for his own. So that Kane's sample was incorrectly logged as Pena's. The Pena DNA profile was actually Kane's. Pena couldn't afford a defense attorney – and no one would represent the Chapel Hill strangler pro bono. No public defender's office in those days was going to blow its budget on retesting DNA.

That's why the sample on the dollar in Tozer's mouth came back as Pena's. It couldn't have been Pena who'd touched the bill because he was already dead. It was Kane's DNA all along – which he'd had labeled, at source as Pena's.

Pretty smart.

I figured all campus security officers would have photo ID logged in their personnel files. I was waiting on Harper's contact pulling up a picture of Kane on the ID for Russell McPartland.

There was no other explanation.

Harper's cell phone rang and she picked up. Delaney's voice played on the car stereo.

"We've swept the street and a five-block radius. No sign of Kane. There's a few people wandering around, but nothing out the ordinary. People on their way home from nightclubs and bars, couple of junkies in blankets at the end of the block, there's even a guy parked outside O'Brien's pub sleeping off a bellyful in the passenger seat of his Aston Martin. We're watching now, but there's no sign of Kane. Not yet."

"Is it okay if I go see Bobby?" I said.

"Sure, but don't be too long," said Delaney, and hung up.

"You go. I'll drop you off and park up on the street," said Harper.

We drove around to 39th street, Bobby's house was halfway along. I thought about Bobby and how he would react to what I had to say. I was pretty sure I could get the case against him kicked out of court in the morning if the feds caught Bill tonight. So much had happened. Arnold was dead and I hadn't even had time to process it. Somehow, Kane had set me up for Arnold's murder with another dollar.

"Stop the car," I said.

"What?" said Harper.

"Stop right now. I need you to call the cop in Chapel Hill. Kane hasn't just been riding his luck all these years," I said.

Harper called the cop. We waited. He answered and said he'd just found the file on the campus security guard named McPartland. He was going to email it to Harper in the morning, but she persuaded him to take pictures of the file on his phone and send them via SMS. The cop had come through. I called Delaney, laid it all out for her.

At last, all of the pieces fitted together. We talked it over for ten minutes, then Harper let me out of the car outside Bobby's house. It was a nondescript Brownstone. Perfect neighborhood for hiding from a media storm.

I walked up the steps and knocked on Bobby's front door. The cold scraped at my cheeks, and I blew into my hands. Holten answered the door, and I could feel the heat pouring out of the house.

He was still in his black suit pants, and tie. He'd lost the jacket. I felt reassured to see he still wore his sidearm. A Glock in a pancake holster, slung onto his belt.

"You okay?" he said.

"I feel like shit. Is Bobby alright?"

"Come in, he's upstairs. Any news?"

I stepped inside, past Holten and was immediately grateful when he closed the door behind me. I didn't have my overcoat with me, and the short walk from the car to the door had sent me shivering. Thankfully, the morphine was still doing its job, otherwise I'd be crippled with the pain from my busted ribs.

The hallway was dark, but light spilled into the corners from the living room. I heard a basketball game on the TV. I stepped aside, let Holten pass me.

"Go on up and see him. He's on the second floor. I recorded the game. Just catching up. Might as well. I don't feel so exposed with the feds parked outside. I can kind of relax a little, you know?" said Holten.

I nodded, "Sure. It's been a tough few days. I think things have finally swung in Bobby's favor. Hopefully this will be over soon."

Holten had already turned away and was headed back into the living room. I saw him flop down onto a big couch in front of a massive flatscreen as he said, "Did you get the guy? Dollar Bill?"

"Maybe," I said. "I think we have enough to get a mistrial at least. If we catch him, I think we'll get an acquittal."

I saw Holten crack open a bottle of beer and hold it out to me. "You want one? You look like you could use it," he said.

He was right. I could use it. And twenty more alongside of it.

"No thanks," I said.

I went upstairs, found the first floor, followed the landing to the staircase leading up and called out to Bobby.

No answer. When I got to the top of the flight of stairs, I felt cold again. The lights were off, and I figured Bobby might be in bed. An icy breeze brushed my cheek. The window looking out onto the street was open. I walked over to it, silently. Peered out. The window was open maybe a foot or so, and it led out onto the fire escape. I stuck my head out, looked around. No one above me or below me on the fire escape.

I ducked back inside and a hand clamped over my mouth, forcing my head back. For a second, I didn't move. My breath had already left my body. My instinct was to grab the wrist, back into my attacker and pivot around, trapping his wrist behind his back.

That's when I felt something sharp at my back. The tip of a knife.

I brought my eyes down to the window. There, reflected in the glass, was juror Bradley Summers. He stood behind me, but I could see his face. He was staring at the reflection too, meeting my gaze. I could still hear the distant voices of the commentators on TV downstairs.

I didn't dare move. If I did, there would be no doubt of the outcome. Kane would push that blade through my back.

My phone was still in my jacket. If I could reach it, I might be able to voice call Harper, like I did in the back of the police car just hours ago.

All these thoughts floated through my mind in a second. And then I realized Kane had probably had the exact same thoughts. He was studying me in the glass, checking my reaction. His head moved closer, and I could feel his breath in my ear as he hissed at me.

"Don't move. Don't even think about moving or calling for help. You're going to die tonight, Flynn. The only question is how slow, and whether I kill that pretty investigator of yours. If you want it to be quick and painless, I can oblige. You just have to do as I say."

CHAPTER SEVENTY-ONE

Kane could feel Flynn's heartbeat. With his left hand pressed tightly over Flynn's mouth, his forearm was also pressing into the neck. There it was again. That rush. That glorious pulse – alive and beating that familiar drum of fear and adrenaline.

"I'm going to take my hand away. You're going to do exactly what I say. Do not shout out. Do not say a thing. One word, one whisper, and I'll kill you. Then I'll kill her, the investigator. Only this time I'll do it slow. I'll peel her skin till she begs me to die. If you understand, nod your head," said Kane.

Flynn nodded, once.

Kane relaxed his grip, took his hand away from Flynn's mouth. The lawyer took a huge breath. The panic was almost suffocating.

"With one hand, I want you to take out your phone and drop it on the floor," said Kane.

Flynn reached into his jacket pocket, took out a cell phone and let it fall. It bounced twice on the thick, carpeted floor, with little or no sound.

Kane took a step back and said, "The door on your right. Open it and go inside."

Flynn turned, opened the door and stepped into a dark bedroom. The curtains weren't drawn, so a little of the streetlight still managed to illuminate the room in a dim, yellow glow. A bed sat on the right. Straight ahead was a heavy, cast-iron door.

It was shut. A security camera with a red dot above it sat just above the door. It was pointed downwards, to pick up the area immediately outside the security door.

Kane stepped toward the door, and waited at the threshold of the bedroom.

"Solomon managed to get to the panic room before I could get to him. I need you to persuade him to come out. He's watching you on the camera. Tell him I've gone. Tell him the police are here and he's safe. Get him out of there now, please," said Kane.

The lawyer didn't move. Kane saw him studying the table next to the door. There was a lamp on it, and a phone. The phone cable led down the back of the table to a socket in the wall for the landline. Beside the panic room door, a cable cover ran to the same socket. The cover had been ripped off the wall, and the cable that ran to the landline had been cut. This was an old panic room, probably built before the telephone connection was installed. There was no way to drill through the concrete for a connection, the wire had to be run out of the room to the socket. Kane was still thankful for that. He'd managed to cut the wire before Solomon could make the call from the phone inside the panic room.

"You're wasting time," said Kane. "Tell him it's safe. Get him out."

The lawyer stepped forward and stood in front of the door.

"Tell him," said Kane.

Raising his head, Flynn looked toward the camera and said, "Bobby, it's me, Eddie."

Kane reversed his grip on the knife, stepped slowly into the room, careful to stay out of the view of the camera.

"Bobby, listen to me very carefully. You're safe. You're totally safe. Now, there's something I need you to do . . ." said Flynn.

A long tongue snaked from Kane's mouth and ran around his lips. He could feel his heart beat quickening, aching for the kill.

"Bobby, no matter what happens, don't open this door," said Flynn.

Fool, thought Kane.

He would get to Solomon. Maybe not tonight. But soon. Right now, the lawyer had to pay. He gripped the ceramic blade, felt the first wave of heat from his blood rush. He watched the lawyer grab his tie, and hold it over his mouth and nose.

That's when the window on his left shattered, and the room filled with tear gas.

CHAPTER SEVENTY-TWO

Soon as the first canister exploded in the corner of the bedroom, I heard glass breaking all around me. Two federal agents in SWAT gear and gas masks burst through the bedroom window. I heard glass breaking in the hallway, and saw another SWAT team member land on his feet behind Kane. The agent closest to me handed me a mask and I managed to drop to my knees and crawl into a corner before I slipped it on. My eyes were stinging by the time I'd tied the Velcro strap at the back of my head.

I heard the agents announce themselves and shout out a warning to Kane to drop the knife and get on the floor. I couldn't see them. With the window in the bedroom and the hallway smashed open, and the winter wind outside, the room had quickly become a cloud of impenetrable white smoke. The windows were sucking the cloud outside, but for those first few moments I couldn't see a thing.

A ripple of automatic fire. The sound of empty shell cases tinkling as they spilled onto the floor. Then nothing. I heard a groan, and the sound of something heavy falling on the floor. Then the firing really started. Two heavy bursts of deafening gunfire. I saw the muzzle flash in the smoke, but couldn't detect the direction of fire.

A figure moved quickly through the smoke. I could see the outline only. The figure bent low in the corner of the room, stood up, and then I heard the sound of glass breaking, and saw an arc of smoke from the window. Footsteps on the staircase. Heavy. Fast.

The smoke cleared some more. I stood up, and almost tripped over the body of an agent on the floor. The one who'd handed me the gas mask. His throat had been ripped open. And his weapon was missing. Beyond him, a second agent lay face down. Then, in the hallway, I saw Kane standing over the body of the last agent to break through the windows onto the second floor. He was lying on the carpet, twitching. Kane emptied the rest of the magazine into his body. The agent lay still. Kane dropped the weapon, picked up his knife and came for me.

His eyes were red and streaming tears, but he didn't seem to mind. I saw a dark patch on his shirt, over his belly. He'd been hit before he'd managed to kill the first agent and take his weapon.

Again, it didn't seem to have fazed him or slowed him down. Not one bit.

What the hell was this guy?

There was ten feet between me and Kane. The footsteps on the stairs grew louder. I backed up until my legs hit the steel door of the panic room. Kane strode forward, a smile on his face.

I drew Holten's Glock from my coat pocket and shot Kane square in the chest. I'd swiped the weapon when Holten had his back to me, closing the front door. The shot threw Kane back a few steps, but miraculously he stayed on his feet. He looked down, saw the massive impact wound. His head came up and his mouth opened. Blood spouted from his lips and he started toward me again.

Another shot took him in the shoulder. This time he didn't even stop.

Eight feet from me. The knife still in his Goddamn hand.

I pulled the trigger again and again and again. Missing, hitting him in the stomach and the chest and still the bastard kept coming.

Five feet. Footsteps in the hallway now.

I aimed low and fired twice. Missed the first time. Second shot blew out Kane's knee and he dropped. He started crawling, wheezing blood.

Three feet and he lashed out with the knife, the blade bit into my thigh. Kane's eyes changed in that last moment. They softened, relaxed. Almost as if some burden had been lifted as he stared up at the barrel of the Glock.

I pulled the trigger one last time and blew the back of his head off.

My knees gave out as the pain ripped through me. There was a long slash right across my thigh, and I could feel the blood soaking my pants. My mind drifted. The room tilted. I must have slumped onto the floor. I saw Holten's gun in front of me. I must've dropped it. I looked up and saw Holten standing over me, panting. He bent down, picked up his gun.

Staring up at him, I saw the decision on his face. He ejected the magazine, looked at it. There was at least a couple of rounds left. I couldn't breathe with that damn mask on. I tore it off.

"Tuesday, in the Diner. We met for breakfast before we went to the crime scene," I said.

Holten knelt down, stared at Kane's body.

"Never thought I would see the day," said Holten.

He shook his head in disbelief at Kane's corpse.

"There was no one like him. He couldn't be hurt. Didn't feel pain. I thought he wasn't human," said Holten.

"The Diner. You took the cash I'd counted out to pay the check, then gave it back to me and said you'd pay. You took one of the dollars, gave it to Kane. You helped him set me up. You helped him all along," I said.

He stood up, turned toward me and a smile broke free on his face.

It was a twisted, evil thing – that smile. I'd seen the photo that the Chapel Hill cop sent to Harper. Holten hadn't changed a bit. I wanted him to know his cover had been blown, that there was no more hiding behind a false name. My voice was breaking, the pain was too much. Somehow, I said, "You switched Richard Pena's DNA swab for Kane's in Chapel Hill. Isn't that right, Officer Russell McPartland?"

He slid the mag home, chambered a round and pointed the gun at my head.

I gritted my teeth. Met his eyes.

His body began to jerk and the broken glass that still clung to the window frame turned a violent shade of red before Holten's body fell out through the window.

Delaney and Harper stood side by side in the hallway. They lowered their guns. I heard Delaney call for a paramedic and the room fell dark again. I tried opening my eyes, but found that I couldn't. My head felt heavy and I was covered in sweat. I felt my back sliding down the door, and I couldn't get my feet underneath me to stop myself. I was going under, fast.

Before I drifted off I felt a hand on my cheek. I couldn't make out what was being said. Someone was banging on a metal door. Bobby, asking if it was safe to come out. I tried to tell him it was okay. I tried to tell him that he wasn't going to court in the morning, that the case against him was over, but I couldn't find the words.

CHAPTER SEVENTY-THREE

In the eight weeks that had passed since the 39th-street shootout, the full picture of Dollar Bill's crimes had emerged. I was too weak to meet Delaney, but she'd called Harry and told him. I was staying in Harry's apartment while I healed, and he'd told me the full story.

Kane had been a prolific killer, and his DNA was found at three further crime scenes. A man called Wally Cook had gone missing the week of the trial. Kane's DNA was found on the slashed tire of Cook's car, parked in his driveway. Cook's body had been burned, but was subsequently identified by dental records. He had been on the jury list for the Solomon trial. Also, Pryor had been found dead at the wheel of his Aston Martin parked right on Bobby's street.

Kane had left Grady's Inn, met Pryor, taken his clothes, killed him, put an overcoat on him and a hat over his face to cover the hole in his eye socket.

Although it could never be conclusively proven, Kane was also believed to have murdered the jurors Manuel Ortega and Brenda Kowolski.

Delaney also got more information on Holten, whose real name was Russell McPartland. He'd been dishonorably discharged from the army after a string of allegations of sexual harassment. None of which were proven, but it gave the command enough impetus to get McPartland kicked out for a series of minor infractions, most of which his fellow officers had engineered. McPartland got a job as a security officer at UNC Chapel Hill, not long before a series of brutal rapes started happening on campus. For all intents and purposes, he was a cop and the young women trusted him when they saw him coming for them. When the first victim of the Chapel Hill Strangler was found, it was believed that the rapist had upped the ante, but the FBI now thought differently. Delaney was convinced Kane sought out McPartland, and threatened to expose him unless he helped Kane hide his crimes.

The two worked well together. McPartland had a security background, contacts who were cops. All the resources Kane needed. And of course, he knew the right people when it came to altering IDs. Kane hadn't been merely lucky for all those years – he'd had help.

Then the exonerations started to happen. Some were posthumous, most were not. Men who were convicted of Dollar Bill's crimes were released and started the long road to obtain damages for wrongful convictions. No matter what they got – it wouldn't give them their lives back.

I lay on Harry's couch, watching reruns of *Cagney and Lacey*. Bobby had been calling me every day, wanting to thank me for saving his life. Again, Harry was kind enough to talk to him for me. And I'd watched Bobby's interview on CNN. He talked about the ordeal of being on trial for a crime he didn't commit. He talked about his epilepsy, and how he'd hidden it from the industry. And he talked about his sexuality. He told the reporter he'd been with another man on the night Ariella and Carl had been murdered. Another actor. Another world-famous man, living a lie. How that still haunted him, and how he'd hidden that shame from everyone – even his lawyers.

America forgave Bobby, even if Hollywood wouldn't. I heard the front door open, and Harry came in with a bottle-shaped brown bag.

He put the bag on the coffee table along with a stack of mail, fetched two glasses and poured each of us a drink.

"What are you watching?" he said.

"*Cagney and Lacey*," I said.

"I always liked that show," said Harry.

He sipped at his bourbon, put down the glass and said, "Bobby Solomon wants to hire you."

"What for?"

"He's working on a pilot for Netflix, about a con artist who becomes a lawyer," he said, smiling.

"That'll never work," I said.

Harry saw me staring at the mail. He picked it up, and took it away.

"Are there papers in there for me?" I said.

He didn't answer. I'd seen a brown envelope, large, familiar.

"Give it to me, Harry," I said.

He sighed, selected the brown envelope from the stack of mail and brought back to me.

"You don't need to do this now," he said.

I opened the envelope, drew out the papers and sat up. My leg was still painful as hell, but I was healing. Doc said in a few weeks I could get rid of the walking stick. I only felt a dull ache now. The papers in front of me on the coffee table hurt a lot more. I picked up a pen from the stack Harry kept in a pot on the table, flicked over a few pages and signed my divorce and custody papers.

I drained my glass, feeling the first hit of alcohol in a long time. Harry filled up the glass again.

"I can talk to Christine," he said.

"Don't," I said. "It's better for them. The further they are away from me, the safer they are. That's just the way it is. When I was in Bobby's house in Midtown, and Kane threatened me and Harper, I was almost glad. If I'd been with Christine and Amy, he would've threatened their lives, or worse. It's better if they are far away from me."

"Bobby paid you well. You could bow out of this game, Eddie. Go do something else."

"What else could I do? I'm not in the best shape to go back into the con game."

"I didn't mean that. You know, take up some other career. Something legal."

The commercials came on, and the first was a trailer for a documentary on Bobby Solomon and Ariella Bloom. The media were milking Bobby for everything while he was still hot.

Following that trailer, I saw another ad for an interview with Rudy Carp. Rudy had been on every talk show and news channel, claiming victory for the Solomon case. I didn't care. I let him have it. No point in fighting for glory with a lawyer like Rudy. I didn't do the case for the publicity. That was the last thing I needed.

"I think I'll stick around as a defense attorney for a while yet," I said.

"Why? Look at all this has cost you, Eddie. Why do it?"

I wasn't even looking at Harry, but I could sense he already knew the answer.

"Because I can. Because I have to. Because there will always be the Art Pryors, and Rudy Carps of this business. Somebody's gotta do the right thing."

"It doesn't always have to be you," said Harry.

"What if everyone said that? What if nobody stood up for anyone because they expected the other guy to do it? Somebody has to be standing on the other side of the line. And if I fall, somebody will have to come along and take my place. All I have to do is keep standing for as long as I can."

"You're not doing much standing lately. Harper wants to see you."

I let the silence build.

I gathered up the papers Christine's lawyer had prepared, put them back in the envelope. My mind went back to that bedroom, in Midtown. I pulled off my wedding ring, dropped it inside the envelope. It was better for them if I didn't have a family. They were too good for me. And I loved them far too much.

I kept Christine's wedding ring in my wallet. Right then, I didn't know what to do with it. I would go through with the divorce and agree to everything Christine wanted, of course. It was for the best. For them.

I drained the glass, poured another and lay back down on the couch.

"So what are you going to do?" said Harry.

I took out my phone, thought about calling Christine. I wanted to call her, but I had no clue what to say to her. On the other hand, I knew I had a lot to say to Harper, but I thought that perhaps those things were better left unsaid.

I stared at the phone for a long time before I selected a contact and hit dial.

ACKNOWLEDGMENTS

My thanks, as ever, to Euan Thorneycroft and the whole team at AM Heath. An author couldn't wish for a better agent. Francesca Pathak and Bethan Jones at Orion have bashed this novel into shape with considerable aplomb – my thanks to them, and the whole Orion team, especially Jon Wood, for believing in this book.

My podcast partner Luca Veste – for keeping me sane, keeping me laughing and for reading this one. To all my friends and colleagues. My thanks to all the booksellers and readers who support me.

Special thanks to my wife Tracy, who is first reader, first opinion, first everything. Because she is the best.

Eddie Flynn has 48 hours to save his daughter . . .

'A gripping, twisty thriller' Ian Rankin

'*The Defence* is everything a great thriller should be' Mark Billingham

It's been over a year since Eddie vowed never to set foot in a courtroom again. But now he doesn't have a choice. Olek Volchek, the infamous head of the Russian mafia in New York, has strapped a bomb to Eddie's back and kidnapped his ten-year-old daughter, Amy. Eddie only has forty-eight hours to defend Volchek in an impossible murder trial – and win – if he wants to save his daughter.

Under the scrutiny of the media and the FBI, Eddie must use his razor-sharp wit and every trick in the con-artist book to defend his 'client' and ensure Amy's safety. With the timer on his back ticking away, can Eddie convince the jury of the impossible?

Out now in paperback and ebook.

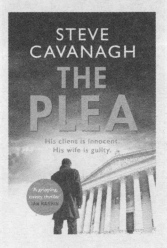

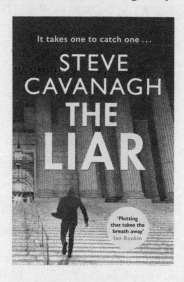